THE BEST IN

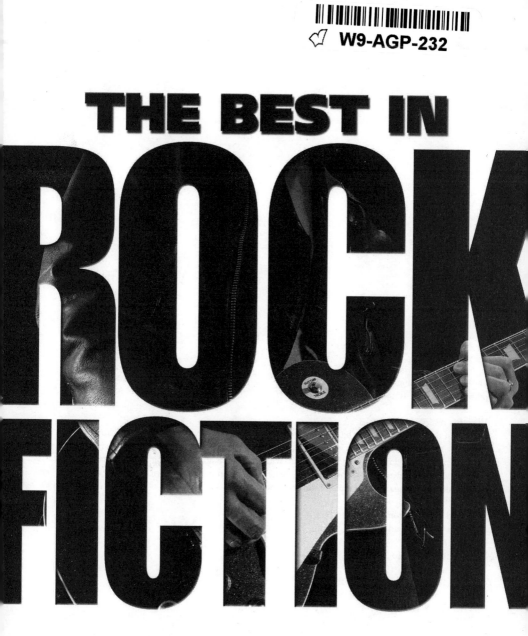

ROCK FICTION

HAL•LEONARD®

The Best in Rock Fiction
Copyright © 2005 June Skinner Sawyers, editor.

Published by Hal Leonard Corporation
7777 Bluemound Road
P.O. Box 13819
Milwaukee, WI 53213

Trade Book Division Editorial Offices
151 West 46th Street, 8th Floor
New York, NY 10036

Library of Congress Cataloging-in-Publication Data

The best in rock fiction / June Skinner Sawyers, editor.
     p. cm.
  ISBN 0-634-08028-8
  1. Rock musicians—Fiction. 2. Short stories, American. 3. Short stories, English. 4. Rock
music—Fiction. 5. Musical fiction. I. Sawyers, June Skinner, 1957-
PS648.R63B47 2004
813'.0108357—dc22
                                        2004014452
Printed in the United States of America
First Edition
Visit Hal Leonard online at **www.halleonard.com**

Contents

Preface
June Skinner Sawyers

Rock fiction has not received the proper respect it deserves, which is unfortunate given the caliber of writers who have captured its fleeting essence on the written page. I am thinking here of writers with a rock and roll sensibility, writers such as Sherman Alexie, T. C. Boyle, Don DeLillo, Roddy Doyle, Nick Hornby, Stephen King, Jonathan Lethem, Rick Moody, and Tom Perrotta, among others. In 2003, novelist Madison Smartt Bell has gone one step further by actually recording, along with poet and songwriter Wyn Cooper (who incidentally also wrote Sheryl Crow's hit song, "All I Wanna Do") *Forty Words for Fear*, a brooding record that recalls the quirky intelligence of a Leonard Cohen or a James McMurtry.

In the preface to his bleakly existential novel *Garden State*, Rick Moody talks about a New Jersey band called the Feelies and the effect their music had on his writing. He is touched by their humanity and awed by the doleful beauty of songs that seem to speak directly to his experience. "Music, see," he writes, "exerted a considerable influence on what I was doing. Music taught me a lot of whatever I know about prose, about the way prose should sound."

I wanted to capture the way rock sounds on the page, its unpredictability, the possibility that anything could happen. Perhaps because rock promises so much, it has been a challenge for writers to create characters that ring true. Given their larger-than-life images, an accurate approximation of the rock star is difficult to portray in fiction. And so naturally our best writers have turned to such iconic figures as Elvis Presley, Bob Dylan, Jim Morrison, Janis Joplin, Mick Jagger, and Bruce Springsteen for inspiration, figures famous as much for their elusive mystery as for their majestic luster. But the stories here also address more ordinary concerns and more everyday people.

No less than John Lennon is credited with writing the first work of fiction by a rock and roller. *In His Own Write* (1964), a quirky collection of stories, poems, and drawings, gave rock a level of respectability that many at that time thought was not possible. Since then, of course, others musicians have followed suit, including

Leonard Cohen, the late Richard Fariña, Ray Davies, Graham Parker, Pete Townshend, Richard Hell, Nick Cave, Steve Earle, and, most recently, Elvis Costello and Billy Corgan.

This collection is intended to showcase some of the finest rock fiction that has been published since the music first entered our collective consciousness. Because of length and budgetary restraints, it can only feature a sampling of the literature of course, but I do believe it gives an indication of the richness and variety of the writing that this literary genre has produced.

The Best in Rock Fiction is the first title in a series that will include the forthcoming *The Best in Blues Fiction* and *The Best in Jazz Fiction*. Each title will feature an annotated further reading list and filmography and will be introduced by a noted music or literary critic. This initial volume is introduced by Anthony DeCurtis, executive editor of *Tracks* magazine and contributing editor at *Rolling Stone*.

I wish to thank John Cerullo at Hal Leonard for making the series possible. I would also like to offer words of appreciation to Michael Messina and Belinda Yong, also at Hal Leonard. Eric Alterman offered invaluable suggestions and for that I remain grateful. As always, Theresa Albini was my companion along the way.

Introduction
Anthony DeCurtis

Rock stars—they're the very definition of characters who are larger than life and stranger than fiction. And, of course, that's the exact problem they present to fiction writers. Creating a convincing portrait of an environment as routinely garish and extreme as the world of rock and roll is not so much a challenge as an impossibility. There's just about no way to do it straight. Rock journalism succeeds because it relies on the reader's assumption that whatever is being described— however ludicrous or operatic—actually happened. Once you admit the possibility that the author might be making the descriptions up, though, everything sounds fake.

A much-admired band of earnest indie darlings snorting up a small mountain of cocaine? A socially conscious rocker launching unprovoked into a vicious diatribe about the triviality of the AIDS crisis? A wide-eyed fifteen-year-old girl, accompanied to a hotel lobby by a sweethearted high school boyfriend, instantly transforming into a seductive sexual predator at the sight of the band headlining at the local arena? In fiction, such events would be either clichés or obviously melodramatic contrivances designed to meet or defeat reader expectations and advance a hackneyed plot. Who could bother to make up crap like that? Certainly not me—but then again, I don't have to. Those events, and hundreds more just like them, are real; I was there, and I witnessed them. They just happened to happen. In journalism, they're gripping insider set pieces. In fiction, they're a joke.

Only the greatest writers can take up the strange challenge of making convincing fiction of unreal events. In the spectacular opening passage of his 1973 novel, *Great Jones Street*, Don DeLillo finds a language that defines the problem fiction writers confront in dealing with rock and roll at its most excessive. Bucky Wunderlick, DeLillo writes of his rock star hero, occupies "extreme regions, monstrous and vulval, damp with memories of violation. . . . Fame, this special kind, feeds itself on outrage, on what the counselors of lesser men would consider bad publicity—hysteria in limousines, knife fights in the audience, bizarre litigation, treachery, pandemonium and drugs."

To explore those "extreme regions," DeLillo creates a character who has opted out of the madness of life in his band. Wunderlick's strategic retreat to a relatively anonymous life in a hovel on Great Jones Street in lower Manhattan gives the author just enough detachment to examine the violent impulses and desperate longings that rock channels for both performers and audience. This is chaos recollected in a kind of stunned tranquility, an approach taken by a number of other writers in this collection as well. The rock stars in these stories are never at the peak of their success. They're either yearning for fame or yearning to escape it; they're on this side or that of the blast furnace heat of celebrity. The lurid details recede in those circumstances, and the contours of their lives assume vivid shape. Stardom becomes an unnerving metaphor for self-realization, and its pursuit, attainment, and loss embody all the hopes, illusions, and disappointments that the forging of an identity inevitably entails.

Tom Piazza's story, "Burn Me Up," finds Billy Sundown—"one of the original Wild Men of Rock and Roll"—long past the height of his fame. He has peaked, disappeared, and been rediscovered, but the same fire that made him one of rock's visceral originators will not allow him to find any version of peace or acceptance. Recognition has come, but the crown of elder statesmanship sits very uncomfortably on his head. Every slight, real or imagined, in the present or from decades earlier, still stings. Every insult nettles, and nothing can make things right. Meanwhile, the members of Coyote Springs, the spirited Native American band in Sherman Alexie's *Reservation Blues*, are rummaging to come up with enough change for candy bars and struggling to keep their dream of a recording contract alive. And in a splendid passage from his 1987 novel, *The Commitments*, Roddy Doyle describes the fateful first meeting between the leader of a young, aspiring Dublin R&B band and the veteran trumpet player whose long experience as a sideman for the pantheon—"Wilson Pickett, Jackie Wilson, Sam an' Dave, Eddie Floyd, Booker T. and the MGs of course, Joe Tex," he intones, reciting his resume as if it were a litany of saints—offers a galvanizing link to the primal soul sonic force.

Speaking of the pantheon, the gods of rock and roll exert a huge influence on the lives of artists and fans, and not always for the better. Inevitably, the King proves an irresistible subject—and target. An excerpt from Mark Childress's 1990 novel *Tender* evokes the moment when a young truck driver entered the Sun Studios in Memphis to make a vanity record as a birthday gift for his mother, catching the perceptive eye and ear of the woman operating the tape for the historic session. In T. Corraghessan Boyle's "All Shook Up," a timid young man's obsession with the explosive audacity of Elvis Presley's breakthrough in the 50s leads him to a pathetic life as an Elvis imitator (his show is called "Young Elvis, the Boy Who Dared to Rock") and leads also to his wife's affair with a more rational, if no less emotionally dislocated, neighbor. And then there's the redoubtable Murray Jay Siskind in Don DeLillo's classic *White Noise*, who hopes to found—with a prescience neither he nor the author could possibly have realized—a department of Elvis Studies at the university where he is teaching.

Perhaps the most enigmatic figure in the history of rock and roll, Bob Dylan emerges in a selection from Brian Morton's 1991 novel, *The Dylanist*, less as a person than a sensibility. "You don't believe in causes," one character tells another. "You just believe in feelings." That scene transports the famous shout of "Judas!" that interrupted one of Dylan's 1966 concerts directly into the emotional lives of people living in the wake of the singer's vexing elusiveness. Just as the cause-oriented folk movement of the '60s regarded Dylan as a traitor for abandoning protest songs for the knotty, internally driven parables of his later work, a social activist in this novel views the singer as validating an approach to life that requires no sense of commitment, either personal or political. It is a vision of Dylan as the essential post-modernist, a detached poet who allows meanings to swirl without ever settling into conviction.

Along similar lines, the Dylan figure who haunts Scott Spencer's 1998 novel, *The Rich Man's Table*, is himself a Dylanist, a character who has fled responsibility to maintain his freedom regardless of the cost to others. Billy Rothschild searches vainly for a connection with his famous father, who refuses to acknowledge him. Rothschild battles not only with his own conflicted feelings, but with those of his mother, who refuses to renounce her affection for the man who abandoned her and her son. In both Morton and Spencer's work, Dylan embodies the notion of the artistic master bound by nothing but his own desires and his own genius. He is a man as coolly focused as he is gifted, as absent as he is sought after, and as awful as he is awe-inspiring.

The Fab Four, for their part, make a cameo appearance in Robert Hemenway's "The Girl Who Sang with the Beatles," a story in which, somewhat like Dylan in *The Dylanist*, they become emblematic of the siren call of popular music as a retreat from the complexities and compromises of real life. In the florid hothouse imagination of Cynthia, one of the story's main characters, the world of the Beatles shimmers with glamour, joy, and expressiveness. Her fantasy life flourishes while passion drains from her marriage and home life. "It's more real than here," she says of her fictional sojourns with the Beatles, and anyone who has ever drifted, however briefly, into the comforting exhilaration of such delusions knows precisely what she means.

But even the realization of a rock and fantasy may not deliver on its promise. In Lewis Shiner's "Jeff Beck," the protagonist is dumbfounded to discover that his mystically acquired ability to play just as exquisitely as the guitar hero he most admires brings his life to ruin. "Why wasn't he happy?" he is left to wonder.

The irony is that such dreams of deliverance are not all that far removed from the wild idealism that rock and roll seems so naturally to encourage. Ideals may die hard, but they certainly can die; their survival relies on a tireless effort to preserve them against the relentless assaults of cynics, who often come in the deceptive guise of realists. Dave Raymond, a thirty-one-year-old guitarist in a wedding band in Tom Perrotta's novel *The Wishbones*, is forced to ponder the wisdom of his own wedding plans when his wife-to-be makes it clear that she would like him to quit the group. Is acceding to her wishes a form of maturity or the first step of what will be a long, slow psychic death?

Rob Fleming, the hero of Nick Hornby's *High Fidelity*, faces a similar conflict. He's the owner of Championship Vinyl, a resolutely hip record store that reflects both his unfailing good taste and the narrow sliver of humanity ("young men, always young men, with John Lennon specs and leather jackets") to whom that taste appeals. His hilarious penchant for lists ("OK, guys, best five pop songs about death") and elaborate filing systems for his thousands of albums (most recently arranged in "the order I bought them") display a fondness for order that his personal life, in perpetual sad disarray, denies him. "Well, I'd like my life to be like a Bruce Springsteen song," he says, recalling the similar yearning for transport of Cynthia in "The Girl Who Sang with the Beatles." Is his love of music the sort of passion that makes life worth living, or a pitiable holdover from the dead-end emotional purism of adolescence?

In Bill Flanagan's novel *A&R*, thirty-year-old Jim Cantone seeks to preserve some semblance of his integrity—and his small-town New England sense of propriety—as he negotiates the bruising, big-time, big-stakes world of the New York record business. Is his love of music, which brought him his opportunities in the first place, an advantage or a handicap in his search for the next big thing? The section of *A&R* excerpted here finds Cantone analyzing the semiotics of music-biz codes of dress and deportment. Is it okay to dye your hair? Whiten your teeth? Do only devils wear Prada? Do changes on the outside portend—or, more scarily, follow—less noticeable, but more deadly, changes on the inside?

While ideals may die, myths never seem to. Particularly when an artist dies young and tragically, it's all too easy for sentimental speculations about what might have been to harden into theories about recordings that existed but that now no longer can be found. As every music lover knows, there's always the glinting image of that holy grail, that better version of even the best song that no one ever quite captured on tape, or even if they did, that now has vanished, perhaps forever.

And maybe that's a metaphor for the nature of music itself, for the evanescent experience of listening to it, and for its edgy relationship with the written word. Words are long-standing symbols of permanence. Words are bonds—to give someone your word is to swear an oath. Music ultimately is ephemeral, evaporating into your unreliable memory once you've heard it. "It's here, and then it's gone," as Mick Jagger sings in "No Expectations." In taking music as their inspiration, writers seek to capture some of that immediacy, that spirit of the moment, and hold it still for their readers' pleasure. *The Best in Rock Fiction* achieves that. Like the most resonant songs, once you've read these tales, you won't be able to shake them out of your mind. Nor will you want to.

The Best
——In——
Rock Fiction

Sherman Alexie

The spirit of Robert Johnson lives on in this darkly humorous novel when the legendary bluesman passes on his guitar to Thomas-Builds-the-Fire, the resident storyteller of the Spokane Indian reservation in Washington State. Somewhat of a misfit himself, Thomas decides to form an all-Indian Catholic rock band called Coyote Springs. Reservation Blues, *Alexie's first novel, follows the raucous adventures of the dysfunctional rock band as they wind their way from the reservation to Seattle to New York City. And when two A&R representatives from the aptly named Cavalry Records show up at the reservation in a black limousine, they set in motion a destructive series of events. Alexie's Native-American characters are fully realized human beings— warts and all (you will find no stereotypically noble Indians here). In addition to his fiction, Alexie is a poet, songwriter, filmmaker, and stand-up comic. His other works include the novel* Indian Killer *(1996) and several short story collections,* The Lone Ranger and Tonto Fist Fight in Heaven *(1993),* The Toughest Indian in the World *(2000), and* Ten Little Indians *(2003). His poetry collections include* First Indian on the Moon *(1993),* Old Shirts & New Skins *(1993),* I Would Steal Horses *(1993),* Water Flowing Home *(1995),* The Summer of Black Widows *(1996), and* The Man Who Loves Salmon *(1998), and two screenplays,* Smoke Signals *(1998) and* The Business of Fancydancing *(2003). In 1995, Alexie and singer-songwriter Jim Boyd recorded an accompanying soundtrack (Thunderwolf Productions). They co-wrote the songs; Boyd provided the vocals, and played the guitar, bass, keyboards, and flute while Alexie read several of the songs.* Reservation Blues *is about many things—alcoholism and its devastating effects, cultural identity, survival, tradition.*

From
Reservation Blues

Chess wondered which member of Coyote Springs most closely resembled the Cowardly Lion as they pulled into the Emerald City, Seattle. The drive from Indian John Rest Area to downtown Seattle took six hours, because the blue van refused to go more than forty miles per hour.

"This van don't want to go to Seattle, enit?" Junior asked.

"Van might be the only smart one," Chess said.

The van drove into downtown and found a Super 8 Motel, right next to the Pink Elephant Car Wash. Coyote Springs all strained their necks to look at everything: the Space Needle, the Olympic and Cascade mountains, the ocean. None of them had ever visited Seattle before, so the sheer number of people frightened them. Especially the number of white people.

"Jeez," Victor said, "no wonder the Indians lost. Look at all these whites."

Thomas parked the van at the motel, and the band climbed out.

"How many rooms should we get, Chess?" Thomas asked.

"How much money we got?"

"Not much."

"Shit," Victor said, "shouldn't those guys at the Backboard be paying for all of this anyway?"

"Yeah, they probably should," Chess said, forced to agree with Victor for the very first time.

Coyote Springs walked into the lobby and surprised the desk clerk. Up to that point, how many desk clerks had seen a group of long-haired Indians carrying guitar cases? That clerk was a white guy in his twenties, a part-time business student at the University of Washington.

"Can I help you?" the clerk asked.

"Yeah," Thomas said. "We need a couple rooms."

"And how will you be paying for your rooms?"

"With money," Victor said. "What did you think? Seashells?"

"He means cash or credit," Chess said.

"Cash, then," Victor said. "What Indian has a goddamn credit card?"

"Okay," the clerk said. "And how long do you plan on staying with us?"

"Three nights," Thomas said. "But listen, I need to use your phone and call the Backboard club. They'll be paying for our rooms."

"The Backboard?" the clerk asked. "Are you guys in a band?"

"Damn right," Victor said. "What do you think we have in these cases? Machine guns? Bows and arrows?"

"What's your name?" the clerk asked, already learning to ignore Victor.

"Coyote Springs," Thomas said.

"Coyote Springs? I haven't heard of you. Got any CDs out?"

"Not yet," Victor said. "That's why we're in Seattle. We're here to take over the whole goddamn city."

"Oh," the clerk said. "Well, here's the phone. Which one of you is the lead singer?"

"I am," said Thomas, and the clerk handed the phone to him.

As Thomas dialed the number, the rest of Coyote Springs wandered around the lobby. Junior and Chess sat on couches and watched a huge television set in one corner. Victor bought a Pepsi from a vending machine. Chess watched him. She knew that kind of stuff tickled Victor. He looked like a little kid, counted out his quarters for pop and hoped he had enough change for a Snickers bar. He just stared at all the selections like the machines offered white women and beer.

"Hey, Victor," Chess shouted. "That's a vending machine, you savage. It works on electricity."

"Hello," Thomas said into the phone. "This is Thomas Builds-the-Fire. Lead singer of Coyote Springs. Yeah. Coyote Springs. We're here for the gig tomorrow night. Yeah, that's right. We're the Indian band."

Thomas smiled at Chess to let her know everything was cool.

"Yeah, we're over at the Super 8 Motel by that Pink Elephant Car Wash. We got a couple rooms, and the clerk wondered how you were going to pay for it."

Thomas lost his smile. Chess looked around the room for it.

"I don't understand. You mean we have to pay for it ourselves? But you invited us."

Thomas listened carefully to the voice at the other end.

"Okay, okay. I see. Well, thanks. What time should we be there tomorrow?"

Thomas hung up the phone and walked over to the rest of the band.

"What's wrong?" Chess asked.

"They said we're supposed to pay for it," Thomas said.

"No fucking way," Victor said.

"What's happening?" Junior asked.

"I guess it's a contest tomorrow," Thomas said. "A lot of bands are going to be there. The winner gets a thousand dollars. The losers don't get nothing. I guess I didn't understand the invitation too well."

"What are you talking about?" Coyote Springs asked.

"It's a Battle of the Bands tomorrow. We have to play the best to get the money. Otherwise, we don't get nothing."

"Jeez," Junior said. "How many bands are there going to be?"

"Twenty or so."

"Shit," Victor said. "Let's forget that shit. Let's go home. We don't need this. We're Coyote Springs."

"We don't have enough money to get home," Thomas said.

"Fuck," Victor said. "Well, let's get the goddamn rooms ourselves and kick some ass at that contest tomorrow night."

"We don't have enough money to get the rooms and eat, too."

"Thomas," Chess said, "how much money do we have?"

"Enough to eat on. But we can't afford the rooms."

"Looks like Checkers was right in staying home," Chess sat and missed her sister.

"What are we going to do?" Junior asked.

"We can sleep in the van," Thomas said, feigning confidence. "Then we go and win that contest tomorrow. A thousand bucks. We go home in style, enit?"

Coyote Springs had no other options. Thomas started the van without a word, pulled out of the motel parking lot, and searched for a supermarket. He found a Foodmart and went inside. The rest of

Coyote Springs waited for Thomas. He came out with a case of Pepsi, a loaf of bread, and a package of bologna. Silently, Coyote Springs built simple sandwiches and ate them.

Coyote Springs spent most of their time in Thomas's house over the next few weeks. They ventured out for food but were mostly greeted with hateful stares and silence. They didn't go to church. Only a few people showed any support. Fights broke out between the supporters and enemies of Coyote Springs. After a while, the Trading Post refused to let Coyote Springs in the door because there had been so many fights. The Tribal Council even held an emergency meeting to discuss the situation.

"I move we excommunicate them from the Tribe," Dave WalksAlong said. "They are creating an aura of violence in our community."

The Tribe narrowly voted to keep Coyote Springs but deadlocked on the vote to kick Chess and Checkers off the reservation.

"They're not even Spokanes," WalksAlong argued. The Council was trying to break the tie when Lester FallsApart staggered into the meeting, cast to his vote to keep Chess and Checkers, and passed out.

"Shit," Junior said as he ate another mouthful of commodity peanut butter, the only source of protein in reservation diets. Victor strummed his guitar a little; his fingers had long since calloused over. He barely felt the burning. Thomas snuck out of the house to make frantic calls at the pay phone outside the Trading Post. Chess and Checkers sat beside each other on the couch, holding hands. The television didn't work.

Coyote Springs might have sat there in Thomas's house for years, silent and still, until their shadows could have been used to tell the time. But that Cadillac rolled onto the reservation and changed everything. All the Spokanes saw it but just assumed it was the FBI, CIA, or Jehovah's Witnesses. That Cadillac pulled up in front of the Trading Post. The rear window rolled down.

"Hey, you," a voice called out from the Cadillac.

"Me?" the-man-who-was-probably-Lakota asked.

"Yeah, you. Do you know where we can find Coyote Springs?"

"Sure, you go down to the dirt road over there, turn left, follow that for a little while, then go right. Then left at Old Bessie's house. You'll recognize her house by the smell of her fry bread. Third best on the reservation. Then, right again."

"Wait, wait," the voice said. "Why don't you just get in here and show us the way?"

"That's a nice car. But I can't fit in there," the-man-who-was-probably-Lakota said. "I'll just run. Follow me."

"Okay, but this ain't our car anyway. We rented it and this goofy driver, too."

The-man-who-was-probably-Lakota shrugged his shoulders and ran down the road with the Cadillac in close pursuit.

"Can't we go any faster?" the voice yelled from the Cadillac.

"Sure," the-man-who-was-probably-Lakota said and picked up the pace. He ran past a few other cars, which forced the Cadillac to make daring passes. They reached Old Bessie's house and then made a right.

"Damn, that fry bread does smell good, doesn't it?" one white man in the car said to another.

Thomas's house sat in a little depression beside the road.

"That's where you'll find Coyote Springs," the-man-who-was-probably-Lakota said. He leaned down to look inside the car.

"You sure, Chief?" the voice asked.

"I'm sure. Did you know the end of the world is near?"

"We've been there and back, Chief."

The-man-who-was-probably-Lakota saw two pasty white men sitting in the back sea. They looked small inside the car, but the smell of cigar smoke and whiskey was huge. The driver was some skinny white guy in a cheap suit. Curious, the-man-who-was-probably-Lakota watched for a while, then ran back toward the Trading Post. He had work to do.

The driver stayed in the Cadillac, but the two other white men climbed out of the back of the Cadillac. Both were short and stocky, dark-haired, with moustaches that threatened to take over their faces. Those short white men walked to the front door and knocked. They knocked again. Thomas opened the door wide.

"Hello," the white men said. "We're Phil Sheridan and George Wright from Cavalry Records in New York City. We've come to talk to you about a recording contract."

Madison Smartt Bell

"I had this dream in which Kurt Cobain taught me how to play his song 'Lithium' on guitar, and that started the whole thing," Madison Smartt Bell told a writer from the New York Times Magazine *in August 2003. Borrowing the name from Nirvana's seminal recording, Bell wrote the short story "Never Mind" —which originally appeared in the anthology* It's Only Rock and Roll, *edited by Janice Eidus and John Kastan (1998)—and then adapted into the first chapter of* Anything Goes. *In the novel, Bell tells the story of Jesse, a bass player in a bar band called Anything Goes. During the course of a year, we follow Jesse's life on the road, and all the complex personal relationships that are part of the adventure. Bell is also the author of* The Stone that the Builder Refused *(2004),* Master of the Crossroads *(2000),* Ten Indians *(1996),* All Souls' Rising *(1995),* Save Me, Joe Louis *(1993),* Doctor Sleep *(1991),* Soldier's Joy *(1989),* The Year of Silence *(1987),* Straight Cut *(1986),* Waiting for the End of the World *(1985), and* The Washington Square Ensemble *(1983). In 1999, Bell was appointed Director of the Kratz Center for Creative Writing at Goucher College. In 2003, with poet Wyn Cooper, he released his first rock album,* Forty Words for Fear *(Gaff Music)—the novel features the lyrics to six original songs co-authored with Cooper.*

From
Anything Goes

The place was on a strip toward the edge of town, a few miles out the four-lane highway. The name of it was something like Rebel's Roost but Perry called it the Black Cat. We played roadhouses like that one all up and down the East Coast, following the weather, and Perry called all of them the Black Cat, it was one of his notions. He said you didn't have to remember the name as long as you knew how to find the place. The original Black Cat was down in South Carolina, a cinder-block biker joint without any windows, but this one in Ocean City was a big old wooden barn. A poster for Anything Goes was peeling off the door, with a way-back promo picture from when Melissa was still singing with the band. Anything Goes was Perry's name for us—he said it would put people in mind to party. *Ought to call it Anything Don't Go,* Chris would bitch when his mood was sour, *Anything Goes if Perry Says It Does.*

Inside there were a few people at the pool tables in the front bar area and maybe twenty more in the big back room where the stage was. The place felt empty (it would hold a hundred or so), and you could smell the old smoke and stale beer. Later on when it filled up you wouldn't notice that smell anymore, it would be people, sweat, perfume, fresh cigarettes. I saw right off, walking to the stage, that Chris's guitars were set up there, the Strat and Les Paul too, which was a big relief because there'd been no sign of his car out front. There was more parking, though, around the back.

I climbed on the stage after Allston and plugged in my bass and switched on the amp, then slapped it around a little just to show I knew how. Perry was fussing around with the P.A. I put the bass on a stand and slung on the Les Paul, but goddamn it was heavy, so I sat down on a stool to shed the weight. They were playing a Clapton album of old blues stuff, and I followed a little bit of his lead, leaving Chris's amp turned low. The fretboard felt nice and natural to me—it was no-frets like the one I had before I sold it when I switched to bass.

Allston was sitting at his drum set—he gave everything a sort of pat and tightened the spring on his snare. The Clapton tape had run out, so I turned up a little and hit the low E hard, letting it throb till the snare talked back to it from behind me. Then E, G-flat, D-flat, A, and louder, C, D, hold on B and back to the top except Cobain, the dead guy, was shaking his head—*uh-uh, it turns around on D before it repeats*—and that was it, you could hear it in the lyrics too because even they were sort of mismatched with the chords, slip-sliding around on top of the progression. I stood up, not noticing the guitar weight so much anymore. In the verse it was all power chords, you only had to hold down the major triads, vamp it just a little. I had the rhythm now, damping a little with the heel of my hand, but the tone needed a little sand in it or something. Chris had this effects thing on the floor that looked like he might have pried it off the dashboard of an intergalactic spaceship, and I kicked the foot switches till I found something that sounded like the flanger. A little shimmer, a little crunch, a now that was more like it. . . . Cobain, the dead guy, would be nodding his head except in reality he didn't have a head since he blown it off with that shotgun. Then in the chorus you want to open it up and play more of the full chord without damping, and all of a sudden Allston was backing me on the drums and we didn't sound half bad, I thought *I like it I'm not gonna—*

Perry swung around from the mixing board and killed my amp.

"The hell you think you're doing?" he snarled. "Nobody wants to hear that Seattle crap."

So he was still in his tricky mood, I could tell. But all right, we didn't play Nirvana, we didn't play punk and we didn't play grunge, we definitely didn't play any originals and we also (praise the Lord!) didn't play Top 40. We did play Chicago blues standards, and white boy blues like Clapton and Allmans and Stevie Ray Vaughan, plus rock warhorses from Hendrix and the Stones and Neil Young, or we might even take it a little bit country too if that's what people seemed to want. Which was in fact the way I liked it—I never was a Nirvana fancier, it was just this one odd thing.

I unslung the Les Paul, but Perry was going, "I didn't *say* put it down."

I looked at him.

"He ain't here, Jesse," Perry told me. "So guess what?"

"Don't tell me that," I said, and I went on and set the guitar on the stand.

"Hey," Perry said, "Wasn't my idea to play fruit-basket turnover."

My hand was twinging me already. I jumped off the stage and headed for the front bar, taking a long look at everybody. Some more people had been coming in, mostly guys so far but none of them was Chris. Mike poured me a double shot of bourbon and I sat there nursing it and looking at my hand—it didn't seem to be shaking at least, though I could feel butterflies in my stomach. The pain wasn't *there* there, but I could just feel it waiting. When I did use to be on guitar it would get so bad sometimes I couldn't even pick up a coffee cup with my left hand, much less hold down a bar chord. Tendonitis, the doctor said, from repetitive motion. I could rest it and soak and eat aspirins on it. But what really helped was playing bass instead, which meant it had to be partly a head thing because I had to work my hand harder on bass anyway, because of the longer reaches. The good thing about bass was I could hang back with Allston and keep my head down and be *the quiet one*, nobody paying me much mind—except tonight it wasn't gonna be that way.

"Jesse," Perry was calling me over the mike. Ten minutes or so had gone by somehow, and I saw I had drank up my whiskey. I got a beer to have on the stand, and I went back to the other room.

"'One Way Out,'" Perry told me when I got up on the stage. He had my bass strapped on him already. Our usual lineup was Perry on an acoustic/electric Gibson, singing and strumming or Travis-picking while Chris did the major guitar work. But Perry could play passable bass and sing over it if he had to, and it was do-what-you-have-to time.

I flipped the Les Paul to the front pickup and stomped the floor controller for clean. The basic riff was simple enough—Perry would usually play it himself on the L-5. *Bap Bap Badda da DOT dot da dada dada.* . . . I went through it a few times for an intro, long enough to start turning people toward the stage. Next should have been Chris coming in on the Strat with slide but this wasn't available so Allston just landed hard on the drums and then Perry stepped up to the mike for the first verse. . . . He had a decent voice, Perry, sounded something like Greg Allman, on a good day. Then the verse was done and I didn't quite know what to do next being that I was out there all by myself, so I just kept on with the riff over the I chord, vamped the IV, riff over I, vamp the V and back. Perry was giving me a look that said *That's pretty lame* which it was, and me shooting one back that wanted to say *Yeah, but this is supposed to be a two-guitar project* and quite a few other things as well.

I hit the turnaround, so Perry had to start singing. At the end of the second verse I thought I'd better try the solo, since Perry looked like he was fixing to kick me or something if I didn't. I could of handled it if there'd been the other guitar to keep the riff going behind it or better yet, me doing that while Chris took the lead, but it was too thin with one guitar, plus I was trying to come back and quote the basic riff fairly often so people would remember what it was they were supposed to be listening to. Two things at once was too many for me, and I got lost, couldn't hear the progression, dropped out the bottom on the wrong note and then I couldn't hit the riff again, just could not play it. I had a handful of broken matchsticks where my fingers had been, and there was sweat breaking out all over my body. I thought the weight of the Les Paul was going to bring me right down. I had stopped playing, just stopped cold, and Perry wouldn't even look at me. He was having to sing the third verse over just bass and cymbals while I stood there frozen, wondering if I was going to puke or pass out first. I was thinking I should have borrowed Cobain's shotgun instead of his song. Then my ears started working again and I realized it didn't sound bad that way, kind of cool actually. My hands came back and I started throwing in some fills. At the end of the verse Perry mouthed something at me and I knew he meant to try and pull it out by doing the first verse one more time, so we did that, and Allston smashed it out and we were done.

I looked over the room and what do you know? The people in front were stamping and hooting and the usual turkey was hollering "'Whipping Post!'" (which we probably would get around to sooner or later). Everybody that was listening was already drunk and the people that weren't drunk weren't really listening. Same as every other Black

Cat from Key West to Alaska.

Meanwhile, Perry was leaning across and kind of bellering in my ear. "Why? Why does he have to do this to me?"

This was a question that might have a long answer—wasn't the first time Chris had dusted off that way. Always after Perry had come down a little hard on his case. If he really wanted to leave us screwed and tattooed, he would have taken his guitars along with him when he cut out, but what he wanted to prove instead was that we needed him. Which was a fact. He'd come back once he made this point, usually by the second or third set but sometimes not till the next night. The catch this time was it was the last night of this entire trip. Sometimes we stopped out at the Black Cats of Virginia on the way down, but tomorrow we were just headed straight home.

"You maybe were ragging on him too hard," I told Perry. "Could be it makes him think you don't love him."

"Jesus Christ on a cracker," Perry said. "Ain't enough I carry the son of a bitch?" His voice went down to the preaching register, gloomy and dour like he'd just had to shoulder the whole entire burden of God. "Ain't enough I carry him—he wants me to love him too."

Then Perry appeared to think this was funny because he all of a sudden bust out laughing.

"What the hell," Perry said. "Let's try and make'm happy."

So we played "Sweet Home Alabama." This went over well enough that the usual turkey started hollering for "Free Bird." We did "Cajun Moon," and the turkey hollered for "Cocaine," which made him a smarter turkey than I'd have suspected. But Perry seemed like he really wanted to mess with the guy, take it out on him more or less, so we did "After Midnight"—not Clapton-style but the J.J. way, which is right and true but also a little narcotized for the first set at a Black Cat on a Saturday night. People were drifting when we got done with that one, and the turkey didn't holler for anything at all.

Then we did "Wicked Game," to throw a curve—the girls seemed to like that one. There were more of them there by this time; the place was filling up. Almost an even-steven mix of blue-collar and college types, with the turkey and his friends sort of on the fence in between, over-the-hill underemployed frat boys with their livers starting to go bad. Chris Isaak didn't seem to say anything to that sector, so we did "Sympathy for the Devil," "Jumping Jack Flash." This started up some dancing. The turkey hollered for "Brown Sugar" but we did "Midnight Rampler," which seemed to put Perry in a straight blues mood, so we did "Gypsy Woman," "I'm a Man," "Red House," "Statesboro Blues." The turkey hollered for "Whipping Post" again, naturally, after "Statesboro."

"'Blue Sky,'" Perry said to me off-mike, and threw a wink.

"Duane's dead," I told him. "I ain't trying that one with just one guitar." I had been holding my own up to then, was even beginning to somewhat enjoy myself, so I felt like I had a right to refuse one.

Perry shrugged. "'Cinnamon Girl.'"

When we got done with that, the turkey hollered for "Down by the River," of course, but Perry called "Tonight's the Night." Actually what he did first was yell for tequila, then stood there waiting till it came—a water glass about half-full of something that looked like old fry oil. Perry killed half of it and showed it to Allston, who of course shook his head. Perry passed the glass to me.

"Just do it," he said. I took a sniff. I didn't know what he had in mind but we'd been up there an hour or so, so what the. . . . *Aaargh.* Never wished for a lemon so bad.

"Tonight's the niiiight," Perry sang, and hit the signature bass line. For a second I thought I was playing it myself—the tequila had smashed between my eyes like a bullet and I almost forgot I had the guitar. Then I recovered, partly, and hit the foot controller for max distortion. Perry was singing over the slow bass walkdown. *Tonight's the ni-i-i-i-ight—waaaarrgghhh-aauuwmpp*—that last part was me. By now I was feeling no pain whatsoever, but luckily this song only has about one and a half chords in it so I could get away with almost anything. By the end I was doing knee bends behind the amp and turning the Les Paul belly-up to scoop huge bowlfuls of black feedback and dump them out over the crowd while Perry muttered and groaned the words and I wondered how much of this it would take to french-fry the P.A. altogether. . . . was thinking I better pull back a little when I came up halfway out of a crouch and *there she was.* The stage was only about a foot high so we were almost nose to nose. She was dressed different, cigarette jeans and a loose white shirt, hair pulled back tight instead of swinging like the night before. It was her. Her look was clear and unintelligible (I don't know what mine would have said to her either) but still I could see well enough that whatever had happened between us hadn't harmed her, which was, I guess, what I'd been hoping to learn somehow all day. She wasn't skulking under some rock. She was out and showing her face, and looked proud of it.

I wanted to play something just for her, something to show I got that message, but Perry was going to take us on break, I knew, once this one ended. I straightened up, holding my feedback crescendo still, while Perry stared at me wondering when I'd ever let it drop. They had opened the second bar in the band room and I saw Chris was standing there with of course Big Blondie. I felt relieved, a little disappointed too. This would be my last one. "Brown-Eyed Girl"—Perry wouldn't sing it; "Beautiful Brown Eyes"—too country for tonight; "Brown Eyes Blue"—not without Meredith. Then I found it, or my hand did; I could just swing over on the same note into A minor. I was already playing the hook and Perry was giving me the hairy eyeball, but he was stuck, he had to sing it now or else look stupid.

Didn't matter it wasn't my voice singing, I was talking with the guitar, my fingers humming on the strings and my eyes connected straight to hers. I took the middle solo close to the sound barrier as it would go, hand running deep into the cutout. I saw the sound wave lifting her wings, billowing the white cloth of her shirt, like she was standing in a wind tunnel or a cyclone. *Like a hurricane.* . . . Perry was belting it out. She twirled, a maple seed in a windstorm, and I lost her in the crowd. I held that last note hanging in the air like a sheet of hammered foil, till Allston shattered it with a cymbal smash and the shreds came glittering down on everything like snow.

"We'll be back," Perry was saying. The Les Paul was on the stand and I was down, pushing through the people toward the back bar. A couple of strangers said stuff to me—my ears were ringing and I couldn't hear, but they were smiling. A bartender stuck on a Little Feat tape, which sounded thin and far away. I had a cigarette stuck in my mouth and was feeling for a match, but at the bar Chris snapped his lighter and waved me over for a drink, which I was more than ready for. The girl was gone, but it didn't matter.

T. Coraghessan Boyle

T. Coraghessan Boyle is the author of more than a dozen books, including the novels Water Music *(1982),* World's End *(1987),* The Road to Wellville *(1993),* Riven Rock *(1998),* Drop City *(2003), and, most recently,* The Inner Circle *(2004). Boyle has made no secret of his love for rock. He once told an NPR reporter, "I think every writer of my generation and down is only writing because we can't have our own rock bands." Actually, in the 1980s, Boyle sang lead with a group called the Ventilators and even today his literary style owes much to rock and roll rhythms. "Somehow," he said, "the sense of rhythm has infected my work. Anyone who hears me read aloud will understand the importance to me of rhythm." One of Boyle's best known short stories, "Greasy Lake," was inspired by Bruce Springsteen's song "Spirit in the Night" while in* Drop City, *Van Morrison's "Mystic Eyes" accentuates the conflict between a hippie commune in Alaska and the locals who want nothing to do with them. "All Shook Up," about the ill-fated love affair between a bored high school counselor and the wife of an Elvis impersonator, is from* Greasy Lake & Other Stories *(1985).*

"All Shook Up"

About a week after the FOR RENT sign disappeared from the window of the place next door, a van the color of cough syrup swung off the blacktop road and into the driveway. The color didn't do much for me, nor the oversize tires with the raised white letters, but the side panel was a real eye-catcher. It featured a life-size portrait of a man with high-piled hair and a guitar, beneath which appeared the legend: *Young Elvis, The Boy Who Dared To Rock.* When the van pulled in I was sitting in the kitchen, rereading the newspaper and blowing into my eighth cup of coffee. I was on vacation. My wife was on vacation too. Only she was in Mill Valley, California, with a guy named Fred, and I was in Shrub Oak, New York.

The door of the van eased open and a kid about nineteen stepped out. He was wearing a black leather jacket with the collar turned up, even though it must have been ninety, and his hair was a glistening, blue-black construction of grease and hair spray that rose from the crown of his head like a bird's nest perched atop a cliff. The girl got out on the far side and then ducked round the van to stand gaping at the paint-blistered Cape Cod as if it were Graceland itself. She was small-boned and tentative, her big black-rimmed eyes like puncture wounds. In her arms, as slack and yielding as a bag of oranges, was a baby. It couldn't have been more than six months old.

I fished three beers out of the refrigerator, slapped through the screen door, and crossed the lawn to where they stood huddled in the driveway, looking lost. "Welcome to the neighborhood," I said, proffering the beers.

The kid was wearing black ankle boots. He ground the toe of the right one into the pavement as if stubbing out a cigarette, then glanced up and said, "I don't drink."

"How about you?" I said, grinning at the girl.

"Sure, thanks," she said, reaching out a slim, veiny hand bright with lacquered nails. She gave the kid a glance, then took the beer, saluted me with a wink, and raised it to her lips. The baby never stirred.

I felt awkward with the two open bottles, so I gingerly set one down on the grass, then straightened up and took a hit from the other. "Patrick," I said, extending my free hand.

The kid took my hand and nodded, a bright wet spit curl swaying loose over his forehead. "Joey Greco," he said. "Glad to meet you, This here is Cindy."

There was something peculiar about his voice—tone and accent both. For one thing, it was surprisingly deep, as if he were throwing his voice or doing an impersonation. Then too, I couldn't quite place the accent. I gave Cindy a big welcoming smile and turned back to him. "You from down South?" I said.

The toe began to grind again and the hint of a smile tugged at the corner of his mouth, but he suppressed it. When he looked up at me his eyes were alive. "No," he said. "Not really."

A jay flew screaming out of the maple in back of the house, wheeled overhead, and disappeared in the hedge. I took another sip of beer. My face was beginning to ache from grinning so much and I could feel the sweat leaching out of my armpit and into my last clean T-shirt.

"No," he said again, and his voice was pitched a shade higher. "I'm from Brooklyn."

Two days later I was out back in the hammock, reading a thriller about a double agent who turns triple agent for a while, is discovered, pursued, captured, and finally persuaded under torture to become a quadruple agent, at which point his wife leaves him and his children change their surname. I was also drinking my way through a bottle of Chivas Regal Fred had given my wife for Christmas, and contemplatively rubbing tanning butter into my navel. The doorbell took me by surprise. I sat up, plucked a leaf from the maple for a bookmark, and padded round the house in bare feet and paint-stained cutoffs.

Cindy was standing at the front door, her back to me, peering through the screen. At first I didn't recognize her: she looked waifish, lost, a Girl Scout peddling cookies in a strange neighborhood. Just as I was about to say something, she pushed the doorbell again. "Hello," she called, cupping her hands and leaning into the screen.

The chimes tinnily reproduced the first seven notes of

"Camptown Races," an effect my wife had found endearing; I made a mental note to disconnect them first thing in the morning. "Anybody home?" Cindy called.

"Hello," I said, and watched her jump. "Looking for me?"

"Oh," she gasped, swinging round with a laugh. "Hi." She was wearing a halter top and gym shorts, her hair was pinned up, and her perfect little toes looked freshly painted. "Patrick, right?" she said.

"That's right," I said. "And you're Cindy."

She nodded, and gave me the sort of look you get from a haberdasher when you go in to buy a suit. "Nice tan."

I glanced down at my feet, rubbed a slick hand across my chest. "I'm on vacation."

"That's great," she said. "From what?"

"I work up at the high school? I'm in Guidance."

"Oh, wow," she said, "that's really great." She stepped down off the porch. "I really mean it—that's something." And then: "Aren't you kind of young to be a guidance counselor?"

"I'm twenty-nine."

"You're kidding, right? You don't look it. Really. I would've thought you were twenty-five, maybe, or something." She patted her hair tentatively, once around, as it to make sure it was all still there. "Anyway, what I came over to ask is you'd like to come to dinner over at our place tonight."

I was half drunk, the thriller wasn't all that thrilling, and I hadn't been out of the yard in four days. "What time?" I said.

"About six."

There was a silence, during which the birds could be heard cursing one another in the trees. Down the block someone fired up a rotary mower. "Well, listen, I got to go put the meat up," she said, turning to leave. But then she swung round with an afterthought. "I forgot to ask: are you married?"

She must have seen the hesitation on my face.

"Because if you are, I mean, we want to invite her too." She stood there watching me. Her eyes were gray, and there was a violet clock in the right one. The hands pointed to three-thirty.

"Yes," I said finally, "I am." There was the sound of a stinging ricochet and a heartfelt guttural curse as the unseen mower hit a stone. "But my wife's away. On vacation."

I'd been in the house only once before, nearly eight years back. The McCareys had lived there then, and Judy and I had just graduated from the state teachers' college. We'd been married two weeks, the world had been freshly created from out of the void, and we were moving into our new house. I was standing in the driveway, unloading boxes of wedding loot from the trunk of the car, when Henry McCarey ambled across the lawn to introduce himself. He must have been around seventy-five. His pale, bald brow swept up and back from his eyes like a helmet, square and imposing, but the flesh had fallen in on itself from the cheekbones down, giving his face a mismatched look. He wore wire-rim glasses. "If you've got a minute there," he said, "we'd like to show you and your wife something." I looked up. Henry's wife, Irma, stood framed in the doorway behind him. Her hair was pulled back in a bun and she wore a print dress that fell to the tops of her white sweat socks.

I called Judy. She smiled, I smiled, Henry smiled; Irma, smiling, held the door for us, and we found ourselves in the dark, cluttered living room with its excess furniture, its framed photographs of eras gone by, and its bric-a-brac. Irma asked us if we'd like a cup of tea. "Over here," Henry said, gesturing from the far corner of the room.

We edged forward, smiling but ill at ease. We were twenty-two, besotted with passion and confidence, and these people made our grandparents look young. I didn't know what to say to them, didn't know how to act: I wanted to get back to the car and the boxes piled on the lawn.

Henry was standing before a glass case that stood atop a mound of doilies on a rickety-looking corner table. He fumbled behind it for a moment, and then a little white Christmas bulb flickered on inside the case. I saw a silver trowellike thing with an inscription on it and a rippled, petrified chunk of something that looked as if it might once have been organic. It was a moment before I realized it was a piece of wedding cake.

"It's from our golden anniversary," Henry said, "six years ago. And that there is the cake knife—can you read what it says?"

I felt numb, felt as if I'd been poking around in the dirt and unearthed the traces of a forgotten civilization. I stole a look at Judy. She was transfixed, her face drawn up as if she were about to cry: she was so beautiful, so rapt, so moved by the moment and its auguries, that I began to feel choked up myself. She took my hand.

"It says 'Henry and Irma, 1926–1976, Semper Fidelis.' That last bit, that's Latin," Henry added, and then he translated for us. Things were different now.

I rapped at the flimsy aluminum storm door and Joey bobbed into view through the dark mesh of the screen. He was wearing a tight black sports coat with the collar turned up, a pink shirt, and black pants with jagged pink lightning bolts ascending the outer seam. At first he didn't seem to recognize me, and for an instant standing there in my cutoffs and T-shirt with half a bottle of Chivas in my hand, I felt more like an interloper than an honored guest—she *had* said tonight, hadn't she?—but then he was ducking his head in greeting and swinging back the door to admit me.

"Glad you could make it," he said without enthusiasm.

"Yeah, me too," I breathed, wondering if I was making a mistake.

I followed him into the living room, where spavined boxes and green plastic trash bags stuffed with underwear and sweaters gave testimony to an ongoing adventure in moving. The place was as close and dark as I'd remembered, but where before there'd been doilies, bric-a-brac, and end tables with carved feet, now there was a plaid sofa, an exercycle, and a dirty off-white beanbag lounger. Gone was the shrine to marital fidelity, replaced by a Fender amp, a microphone stand, and an acoustic guitar with capo and pickup. (Henry was gone too, dead of emphysema, and Irma was in a nursing home on the other side of town.) There was a stereo with great black monolithic speakers, and the walls were hung with posters of Elvis. I looked at Joey. He was posed beside a sneering young Elvis, rocking back and forth on the heels of his boots. "Pretty slick," I said, indicating his get-up.

"Oh, this?" he said, as if surprised I'd noticed. "I've been rehearsing—trying on outfits, you know."

I'd figured he was some sort of Elvis impersonator, judging from the van, the clothes, and the achieved accent, but aside from the hair I couldn't really see much resemblance between him and the King. "You, uh—you do an Elvis act?"

He looked at me as if I'd just asked if the thing above our heads was the ceiling. Finally he just said, "Yeah."

It was then that Cindy emerged from the kitchen. She was wearing a white peasant dress and sandals, and she was holding a glass of wine in one hand and a zucchini the size of a souvenir baseball bat in the other. "Patrick," she said, crossing the room to brush my cheek with a kiss. I embraced her ritualistically—you might have thought we'd known each other for a decade—and held her a moment while Joey and Elvis looked on. When she stepped back, I caught a whiff of perfume and alcohol. "You like zucchini?" she said.

"Uh-huh, sure." I was wondering what to do with my hands. Suddenly I remembered the bottle and held it up like a turkey I'd shot in the woods. "I brought you this."

Cindy made a gracious noise or two, I shrugged in deprecation— "It's only half full," I said—and Joey ground his toe into the carpet. I might have been imagining it, but he seemed agitated, worked up over something.

"How long till dinner?" he said, a reedy, adolescent whine snaking through the Nashville basso.

Cindy's eyes were unsteady. She drained her wine in a gulp and held out the glass for me to refill. With Scotch. "I don't know," she said, watching the glass. "Half an hour."

"Because I think I want to work on a couple numbers, you know?"

She gave him a look. I didn't know either of them well enough to know what it meant. That look could have said, "Go screw yourself," or, "I'm just wild about you and Elvis"—I couldn't tell.

"No problem," she said finally, sipping at her drink, the zucchini tucked under her arm. "Patrick was going to help me in the kitchen, anyway—right, Patrick?"

"Sure," I said.

At dinner, Joey cut into his braciola, lifted a forkful of tomatoes, peppers, and zucchini to his lips, and talked about Elvis. "He was the most photographed man in the history of the world. He had sixty-two cars and over a hundred guitars." Fork, knife, meat, vegetable. "He was the greatest there ever was."

I didn't know about that. By the time I gave up pellet guns and minibikes and began listening to rock and roll, it was the Doors, Stones, and Hendrix, and Elvis was already degenerating into a caricature of himself. I remembered him as a bloated old has-been in a white jumpsuit, crooning corny ballads and slobbering on middle-aged women. Besides, between the Chivas and the bottle of red Cindy had opened for dinner, I was pretty far gone. "Hmph," was about all I could manage.

For forty-five minutes, while I'd sat on a cracked vinyl barstool at the kitchen counter, helping slice vegetables and trading stories with Cindy, I'd heard Joey's rendition of half a dozen Elvis classics. He was in the living room, thundering; I was in the kitchen, drinking. Every once in a while he'd give the guitar a rest or step back from the microphone, and I would hear the real Elvis moaning faintly in the background: *Don't be cruel/To a heart that's true* or *You ain't nothin' but a hound dog.*

"He's pretty good," I said to Cindy after a particularly thunderous rendition of "Jailhouse Rock." I was making conversation.

She shrugged. "Yeah, I guess so," she said. The baby lay in a portable cradle by the window, giving off subtle emanations of feces and urine. It was asleep, I supposed. If it weren't for the smell, I would have guessed it was dead. "You know, we had to get married," she said.

I made a gesture of dismissal, tried for a surprised expression. Of course they'd had to get married. I'd seen a hundred girls just like her—they passed through the guidance office like flocks of unfledged birds flying in the wrong direction, north in the winter, south in the summer. Slumped over, bony, eyes sunk into their heads, and made up like showgirls or whores, they slouched in the easy chair in my office and told me their stories. They thought they were hip and depraved, thought they were nihilists and libertines, thought they'd invented sex.

Two years later they were housewives with preschoolers and station wagons. Two years after that they were divorced.

"First time I heard Elvis, first time I remember, anyway," Joey was saying now, "was in December of '68 when he did that TV concert—the Singer Special? It blew me away. I just couldn't believe it."

"Sixty-eight?" I echoed. "What were you, four?"

Cindy giggled. I turned to look at her, a sloppy grin on my face. I was drunk.

Joey didn't bat an eye. "I was seven," he said. And then: "That was the day I stopped being a kid." He'd tucked a napkin under his collar to protect his pink shirt, and strands of hair hung loose over his forehead. "Next day my mom picked up a copy of *Elvis's Greatest Hits, Volume One*, and a week later she got me my first guitar. I've been at it ever since."

Joey was looking hard at me. He was trying to impress me; that much was clear. That's why he'd worn the suit, dabbled his lids with green eye shadow, greased his hair, and hammered out his repertoire from the next room so I couldn't help but catch every lick. Somehow, though, I wasn't impressed. Whether it was the booze, my indifference to Elvis, or the fear and loathing that had gripped me since Judy's defection, I couldn't say. All I knew was that I didn't give a shit. For Elvis, for Joey, for Fred, Judy, Little Richard, or Leonard Bernstein. For anybody. I sipped my wine in silence.

"My agent's trying to book me into the Catskills—some of the resorts and all, you know? He says my act's really hot." Joey patted his napkin, raised a glass of milk to his lips, and took a quick swallow. "I'll be auditioning up there at Brown's in about a week. Meanwhile, Friday night I got this warm-up gig—no big deal, just some dump out in the sticks. It's over in Brewster—you ever heard of it?"

"The sticks, or Brewster?" I said.

"No, really, why not drop by?"

Cindy was watching me. Earlier, over the chopping board, she'd given me the rundown on this and other matters. She was twenty, Joey was twenty-one. Her father owned a contracting company in Putnam Valley and had set them up with the house. She'd met Joey in

Brooklyn the summer before, when she was staying with her cousin. He was in a band then. Now he did Elvis. Nothing but. He'd had gigs in the City and out on the Island, but he wasn't making anything and he refused to take a day job: nobody but hacks did that. So they'd come to the hinterlands, where her father could see they didn't starve to death and Cindy could work as a secretary in his office. They were hoping the Brewster thing would catch on—nobody was doing much with Elvis up here.

I chewed, swallowed, washed it down with a swig of wine. "Sounds good," I said. "I'll be there."

Later, after Joey had gone to bed, Cindy and I sat side by side on the plaid sofa and listened to a tape of *Swan Lake* I'd gone next door to fetch ("Something soft," she'd said. "Have you got something soft?"). We were drinking coffee, and a sweet yellowish cordial she'd dug out of one of the boxes of kitchen things. We'd been talking. I'd told her about Judy. And Fred. Told her I'd been feeling pretty rotten and that I was glad she'd moved in. "Really," I said, "I mean it. And I really appreciate you inviting me over too."

She was right beside me, her arms bare in the peasant dress, legs folded under her yoga-style. "No problem," she said, looking me in the eye.

I glanced away and saw Elvis. Crouching, dipping, leering, humping the microphone, and spraying musk over the first three rows, Elvis in full rut. "So how do you feel about all this"—and I waved my arm to take in the posters, the guitar and amp, the undefined space above us where Joey lay sleeping—"I mean, living with the King?" I laughed and held my cupped hand under her chin. "Go ahead, dear—speak right into the mike."

She surprised me then. Her expression was dead serious, no time for levity. Slowly, deliberately, she set down the coffee cup and leaned forward to swing round so that she was kneeling beside me on the couch; then she kicked her leg out as if mounting a horse and brought her knee softly down between my legs until I could feel the pressure lighting up my groin. From the stereo, I could hear the swan maidens bursting into flight. "It's like being married to a clone," she whispered.

When I got home, the phone was ringing. I slammed through the front door, stumbled over something in the dark, and took the stairs to the bedroom two at a time. "Yeah?" I said breathlessly as I snatched up the receiver.

"Pat?"

It was Judy. Before I could react, her voice was coming at me, soft and passionate, syllables kneading me like fingers. "Pat, listen," she said. "I want to explain something—"

I hung up.

The club was called Delvecchio's, and it sat amid an expanse of black-top like a cruise ship on a flat, dark sea. It was a big place, with two separate stages, a disco, three bars, and a game room. I recognized it instantly: teen nirvana. Neon pulsed, raked Chevys rumbled out front, guys in Hawaiian shirts and girls in spike heels stood outside the door, smoking joints and cigarettes and examining one another with frozen eyes. The parking lot was already beginning to fill when Cindy and I pulled in around nine.

"Big on the sixteen-year-old crowd tonight," I said. "Want me to gun the engine?"

Cindy was wearing a sleeveless blouse, pedal pushers, and heels. She'd made herself up to look like a cover girl for *Slash* magazine, and she smelled like a candy store. "Come on, Pat," she said in a hoarse whisper. "Don't be that way."

"What way?" I said, but I knew what she meant. We were out to have a good time, to hear Joey on his big night, and there was no reason to kill it with cynicism.

Joey had gone on ahead in the van to set up his equipment and do a sound check. Earlier, he'd made a special trip over to my place to ask if I'd mind taking Cindy to the club. He stood just inside the door, working the toe of his patent-leather boot and gazing beyond me to the wreckage wrought by Judy's absence: the cardboard containers of takeout Chinese stacked atop the TV, the beer bottles and Devil Dog wrappers on the coffee table, the clothes scattered about like the leavings of a river in flood. I looked him in the eye, wondering just how much he knew of the passionate groping Cindy and I had engaged in while he was getting his beauty rest the other night, wondering if he had even the faintest notion that I felt evil and betrayed and wanted his wife because I had wounds to salve and because she was there, wanted her like forbidden fruit, wanted her like I'd wanted half the knocked-up, washed-out, defiant little twits that paraded through my office each year. He held my gaze until I looked away. "Sure," I murmured, playing Tristan to his Mark. "Be happy to."

And so, come eight o'clock, I'd showered and shaved, slicked back my hair, turned up the collar of my favorite gigolo shirt, and strolled across the lawn to pick her up. The baby (her name was Gladys, after Elvis's mother) was left in the care of one of the legions of pubescent girls I knew from school, Cindy emerged from the bedroom on brisk heels to peck my cheek with a kiss, and we strolled back across the lawn to my car.

There was an awkward silence. Though we'd talked two or three times since the night of the *braciola* and the couch, neither of us had referred to it. We'd done some pretty heavy petting and fondling, we'd got the feel of each other's dentition and a taste of abandon. I was the one who backed off. I had a vision of Joey standing in the doorway in his pajamas, head bowed under the weight of his pompadour. "What about Joey," I whispered, and we both swiveled our heads to gaze up at the flat, unrevealing surface of the ceiling. Then I got up and went home to bed.

Now, as we reached the car and I swung back the door for her, I found something to say. "I can't believe it"—I laughed, hearty, jocular, all my teeth showing—"but I feel like I'm out on a date or something."

Cindy just cocked her head and gave me a little smirk. "You are," she said.

They'd booked Joey into the Troubadour Room, a place that seated sixty or seventy and had the atmosphere of a small club. Comedians played there once in a while, and the occasional folk singer or balladeer—acts that might be expected to draw a slightly older, more contemplative crowd. Most of the action, obviously, centered on the rock bands that played the main stage, or the pounding fantasia of the disco. We didn't exactly have to fight for a seat.

Cindy ordered a Black Russian. I stuck with Scotch. We talked about Elvis, Joey, rock and roll. We talked about Gladys and how precocious she was and how her baby raptures alternated with baby traumas. We talked about the watercolors Cindy had done in high school and how she'd like to get back to them. We talked about Judy. About Fred. About guidance counseling. We were on our third drink—or maybe it was the fourth—when the stage lights went up and the emcee announced Joey.

"Excited?" I said.

She shrugged, scanning the stage a moment as the drummer, bass player, and guitarist took their places. Then she found my hand under the table and gave it a squeeze.

At that moment Joey whirled out of the wings and pounced on the mike as if it were alive. He was dressed in a mustard-colored suit spangled with gold glitter, a sheeny gold tie, and white patent-leather loafers. For a moment he just stood there, trying his best to radiate the kind of outlaw sensuality that was Elvis's signature, but managing instead to look merely awkward, like a kid dressed up for a costume party. Still, he knew the moves. Suddenly his right fist shot up over his head and the musicians froze; he gave up his best sneer, then the fist came crashing down across the face of his guitar, the band lurched into "Heartbreak Hotel," and Joey threw back his head and let loose.

Nothing happened.

The band rumbled on confusedly for a bar or two, then cut out as Joey stood there tapping at the microphone and looking foolish.

"AC/DC!" someone shouted from the darkness to my left.

"Def Leppard!"

The emcee, a balding character in a flowered shirt, scurried out onstage and crouched over the pedestal of the antiquated mike Joey had insisted on for authenticity. Someone shouted an obscenity, and Joey turned his back. There were more calls for heavy-metal bands, quips and laughter. The other band members—older guys with beards and expressionless faces—looked about as concerned as sleepwalkers.

I stole a look at Cindy; she was biting her lip.

Finally the mike came to life, the emcee vanished, and Joey breathed "Testing, testing," through the PA system. "Ah'm sorry 'bout the de-lay, folks," he murmured in his deepest, backwoodsiest basso, "but we're 'bout ready to give it another shot. A-one, two, three!" he shouted, and "Heartbreak Hotel," take two, thumped lamely through the speakers:

> Well, since my baby left me,
> I found a new place to dwell,
> It's down at the end of Lonely Street,
> That's Heartbreak Hotel.

Something was wrong, that much was clear from the start. It wasn't just that he was bad, that he looked nervous and maybe a bit effeminate and out of control, or that he forgot the words to the third verse and went flat on the choruses, or that the half-assed pickup band couldn't have played together if they'd rehearsed eight hours a day since Elvis was laid in his grave—no, it went deeper than that. The key to the whole thing was in creating an illusion—Joey had to convince his audience, for even an instant, that the real flesh-and-blood Elvis, the boy who dared to rock, stood before them. Unfortunately, he just couldn't cut it. Musically or visually. No matter if you stopped your ears and squinted till the lights blurred, this awkward, greasy-haired kid in the green eye shadow didn't come close, not even for a second. And the audience let him know it.

Hoots and catcalls drowned out the last chord of "Heartbreak Hotel," as Joey segued into one of those trembly, heavy-breathing ballads that were the bane of the King's middle years. I don't remember the tune or the lyrics—but it was soppy and out of key. Joey was sweating now, and the hair hung down in his eyes. He leaned into the microphone, picked a woman out of the audience, and attempted a seductive leer that wound up looking more like indigestion than passion. Midway through the song a female voice shouted "Faggot!" from the back of the room, and two guys in fraternity jackets begun to howl like hound dogs in heat.

Joey faltered, missed his entrance after the guitar break, and had to stand there strumming over nothing for a whole verse and chorus till it came round again. People were openly derisive now, and the fraternity guys, encouraged, began to intersperse their howls with yips and yodels. Joey bowed his head, as if in defeat, and let the guitar dangle loose as the band closed out the number. He picked up the tempo a bit on the next one—"Teddy Bear," I think it was—but he never got anywhere with the audience. I watched Cindy out of the corner of my eye. Her face was white. She sat through the first four numbers wordlessly, then leaned across the table and took hold of my arm. "Take me home," she said.

We sat in the driveway awhile, listening to the radio. It was warm, and with the windows rolled down we could hear the crickets and whatnot going at it in the bushes. Cindy hadn't said much on the way back— the scene at the club had been pretty devastating—and I'd tried to distract her with a line of happy chatter. Now she reached forward and snapped off the radio. "He really stinks, doesn't he?" she said.

I wasn't biting. I wanted her, yes, but I wasn't about to run anybody down to get her. "I don't know," I said. "I mean, with that band Elvis himself would've stunk."

She considered this a moment, then fished around in her purse for a cigarette, lit it, and expelled the smoke with a sigh. The sigh seemed to say: "Okay, and what now?" We both knew that the babysitter was hunkered down obliviously in front of the TV next door and that Joey still had another set to get through. We had hours. If we wanted them.

The light from her place fell across the lawn and caught in her hair; her face was in shadow. "You want to go inside a minute?" I said, remembering the way she'd moved against me on the couch. "Have a drink or something?"

When she said "Sure," I felt my knees go weak. This was it: counselor, counsel thyself. I followed her into the house and led her up the dark stairs to the bedroom. We didn't bother with the drink. Or lights. She felt good, and a little strange: she wasn't Judy.

I got us a drink afterward, and then another. Then I brought the bottle to bed with me and we made love again—a slow, easeful, rhythmic love, the crickets keeping time from beyond the windows. I was ecstatic. I was drunk. I was in love. We moved together and I was tonguing her ear and serenading her in a passionate whisper, mimicking Elvis, mimicking Joey. "Well-a-bless-a my soul, what's-a wrong with me," I murmured, "I'm itchin' like a ma-han on a fuzzy tree. . . . oh-oh-oh, oh, oh yeah." She laughed, and then she got serious. We shared a cigarette and a shot of sticky liqueur afterward; then I must have drifted off.

I don't know what time it was when I heard the van pull in next door. Downstairs the door slammed and I went to the window to watch Cindy's dark form hurrying across the lawn. Then I saw Joey standing in the doorway, the babysitter behind him. There was a curse, a shout, the sound of a blow, and then Joey and the babysitter were in the van, the brake lights flashed, and they were gone.

I felt bad. I felt like a dog, a sinner, a homewrecker, and a Lothario. I felt like Fred must have felt. Naked, in the dark, I poured myself another drink and watched Cindy's house for movement. There was none. A minute later I was asleep.

I woke early. My throat was dry and my head throbbed. I slipped into a pair of running shorts I found in the clutter on the floor, brushed my teeth, rinsed my face, and contemplated the toilet for a long while, trying to gauge whether or not I was going to vomit.

Half a dozen aspirin and three glasses of water later, I stepped gingerly down the stairs. I was thinking poached eggs and dry toast—and maybe, if I could take it, half a cup of coffee—when I drifted into the living room and saw her huddled there on the couch. Her eyes were red, her makeup smeared, and she was wearing the same clothes she'd had on the night before. Beside her, wrapped in a pink blanket the size of a bath towel, was the baby.

"Cindy?"

She shoved the hair back from her face and narrowed her eyes, studying me. "I didn't know where else to go," she murmured.

"You mean, he—?"

I should have held her, I guess, should have probed deep in my counselor's lexicon for words of comfort and assurance, but I couldn't. Conflicting thoughts were running through my head, acid rose in my throat, and the baby, conscious for the first time since I'd laid eyes on it, was fixing me with a steady, unblinking gaze of accusation. This wasn't what I'd wanted, not at all.

"Listen," I said, "can I get you anything—a cup of coffee or some cereal or something? Milk for the baby?"

She shook her head and began to make small sounds of grief and anguish. She bit her lip and averted her face.

I felt like a criminal. "God," I said, "I'm sorry. I didn't—" I started for her, hoping she'd raise her tear-stained face to me, tell me it wasn't my fault, rise bravely from the couch, and trudge off across the lawn and out of my life.

At that moment there was a knock at the door. We both froze. It came again, louder, booming, the sound of rage and impatience. I crossed the room, swung open the door, and found Joey on the doorstep. He was pale, and his hair was in disarray. When the door pulled back, his eyes locked on mine with a look of hatred and contempt. I made no move to open the storm door that separated us.

"You want her?" he said, and he ground the toe of his boot into the welcome mat like a ram pawing the earth before it charges.

I had six inches and forty pounds on him; I could have shoved through the door and drowned my guilt in blood. But it wasn't Joey I wanted to hurt, it was Fred. Or, no, down deep, at the root of it all, it was Judy I wanted to hurt. I glanced into his eyes through the flimsy mesh of the screen and then looked away.

"'Cause you can have her," he went on, dropping the Nashville twang and reverting to pure Brooklynese. "She's a whore. I don't need no whore. Shit," he spat, looking beyond me to where she sat huddled on the couch with the baby, "Elvis went through a hundred just like her. A thousand."

Cindy was staring at the floor. I had nothing to say.

"Fuck you both," he said finally, then turned and marched across the lawn. I watched him slam into the van, fire up the engine, and back out of the driveway. Then the boy who dared to rock was gone.

I looked at Cindy. Her knees were drawn up under her chin and she was crying softly. I knew I should comfort her, tell her it would be all right and that everything would work out fine. But I didn't. This was no pregnant fifteen-year-old who hated her mother or a kid who skipped cheerleading practice to smoke pot and hang out at the video arcade—this wasn't a problem that would walk out of my office and go home by itself. No, the problem was at my doorstep, here on my couch: I was involved—I was responsible—and I wanted no part of it.

"Patrick," she stammered finally. "I-I don't know what to say. I mean"—and here she was on the verge of tears again—"I feel as if . . . . as if—"

I didn't get to hear how she felt. Not then, anyway. Because at that moment the phone began to ring. From upstairs, in the bedroom. Cindy paused in mid-phrase; I froze. The phone rang twice, three times. We looked at each other. On the fourth ring I turned and bounded up the stairs.

"Hello?"

"Pat, listen to me." It was Judy. She sounded breathless, as if she'd been running. "Now don't hang up. Please."

The blood was beating in my head. The receiver weighed six tons. I struggled to hold it to my ear.

"I made a mistake," she said. "I know it. Fred's a jerk. I left him three days ago in some winery in St. Helena." There was a pause. "I'm down in Monterey now and I'm lonely. I miss you."

I held my breath.

"Pat?"

"Yeah?"

"I'm coming home, okay?"

I thought of Joey, of Cindy downstairs with her baby. I glanced out the window at the place next door, vacant once again, and thought of Henry and Irma and the progress of the years. And then I felt something give way, as if a spell had been broken.

"Okay," I said.

Mark Childress

In Tender *(1990), Mark Childress follows the meteoric rise of man-child Leroy Kirby, from humble roots in Mississippi to unimaginable wealth and fame. The fictional Leroy, born in a shotgun shack in a dirt-poor town, is the youngest of identical twins; his brother, Jessie, is stillborn. Sound familiar? Actually, Childress's reinvention of the Elvis myth and his recreation of the early days of rock and roll is done with great sympathy and understanding as he tries to imagine what happens when dreams turn into nightmares. Childress is also the author of* A World Made of Fire *(1984),* V for Victor *(1988),* Crazy in Alabama *(1993), and* Gone for Good *(1999). The following excerpt finds Leroy in the studio for the first time, as he records a ballad for his beloved mother.*

From
Tender

Leroy carried the Sound Star with him in the cab of the Crown Electric truck. Often he had an hour to kill between runs, and he'd park the truck in some quiet alley where no one could hear him practicing.

His job was delivering switches and condensers and rolls of wire to electricians all over town. It was a fine way to make forty-one fifty a week—on his own, cruising Memphis all day, searching out addresses in the industrial parts of town. He had wanted to be a truck driver since he was a little boy. So what if it was just an old Ford pick-'em-up and he never got to stray very far beyond the city limits? He was breathing real air, not cooped up in some stupid school. He had plenty of time with the Sound Star.

This was a slow, hot afternoon, growing hotter. The sun whitened the sky. Nobody worried much about electricity in such heat. Leroy sat in the Ford behind Crump Stadium, under great shady oak trees, drinking his third Coca-Cola of the day. The bugs sang a hymn to the heat. He sang along, strumming the chords to "My Happiness."

Some days his voice sounded tinny or hollow. Some days it would break. Today, for some reason, he sounded better than ever. *Evening shadows make me blue. . . .*

Thwang, thwangg! That was it! Enough! He knew that song backward and upside down.

There would come a day when he would quit practicing and go ahead and do the thing.

Why was he so shy about it? Did he think his fantasies of stardom might wither and die the minute he stood up to real microphone? Was he afraid someone would laugh or say the wrong thing?

He had been restless since the morning of Miss Waverly. The world offered a host of tantalizing secrets; he was ready to start finding them out. For the moment he was happy enough to drive the Crown truck. But he always knew he was driving toward a brighter light, just over the horizon.

His voice sounded good today.

At this moment he was parked within ten blocks of the Mid-South Recording Service. This was fate.

He drained the Coke, rubbed his thumb on the mouth of the bottle.

He had money in his pocket, an hour before his next run.

He scratched off in the parking lot gravel. His work shirt was dirty, his hair all over the place—but then he wasn't auditioning for Cecil B. De Mille. He was paying these people to make a record, something they did every day.

He parked across Union Street from the studio.

No excuses. Go to it. Do it. You can.

You are Amazing New Leroy.

Holding the old trusty Sound Star by its neck, he got out of the truck. He wished his mother were here to hold his hand.

He carried the Sound Star across the street, put his hand on the doorknob, pushed in.

It was just as hot inside. A large electric fan turned its face side to side, moving the hot air around. Leroy had expected a big room with recording equipment and photos of singing stars on the walls. This looked like an insurance office—two desks piled with papers, filing cabinets standing open. But also there were reels of recording tape with their tongues hanging out and four guitars propped on a sofa. This must be the place.

"Anybody home?"

The studio must be past the large curtained windows. That door was closed. A hand-lettered sign said SHHHH. A red light glowed on the wall. Leroy sat down to wait.

He peered at the papers on the desk—mostly invoices and bills, but there was one letter with a large official-looking seal that looked interesting, even from a distance.

He inched closer. A quartet called The Rhythmaires had been requested by the governor of Tennessee for a performance at his Labor Day picnic, and since Mr. Dan Tobias held an exclusive contract with the group, it was necessary that his permission—

The door swung in. "Oh! You startled me," said the woman behind it, who was carrying a box of rolled-up electrical cords. "How long have you been here?"

Leroy moved away from the desk. "Just a minute or two. I saw the red light, so I waited."

"Oh, that," she said, "that stays on all the time. It hasn't worked right in years. What can I do for you?" She was striking, maybe forty, small-boned and slim, with a boyish Debbie Reynolds haircut. She placed the box on the desk. Her eyebrows rose to say, "Well?"

"Uhm." Where to start? "I want to make a record."

"What kind of record?" she said.

"Two songs. They're both pretty short."

"Just you by yourself."

"Yes ma'am. And my guitar."

"Do you already know about our rates?"

"I called awhile back." Leroy fingered his lip. "I think I'm ready, I—I'm not sure."

She was having a good look at him—the opposite of the Miss Waverly kind of look. "That's quite a haircut," she said.

"Thank you, ma'am," said Leroy. "I usually dress better than this, but I was at work."

"Those sideburns," she said.

"Yes ma'am."

"Please stop calling me ma'am. My name's Claudia Cash. And yours is?"

"Leroy," he said, "Leroy Kirby."

"What kind of songs do you sing, Leroy?"

"I sing all kinds," he said.

"Who do you sound like?"

He thought about a minute. "Well, I don't guess I sound like anybody."

Her smile flickered. "Let's go back and see what we can do. I hope you've rehearsed. Thirty minutes means you've got time for two songs. One take on each song." She slid on a pair of cat-eyed glasses like those worn by sophisticated girls in the movies. Leroy liked her right away.

He followed her into the studio, a tall, narrow room with perforated acoustical tile on the ceiling and walls. Two upright pianos were shoved against the rear wall, under an elevated plate-glass window that stretched the width of the room. Three steps led up to the control room.

Miss Cash pointed out a microphone: a trapezoid of wire mesh hanging from a boom, one of many microphones jumbled in with speakers and chairs and wooden stools and music stands and guitars in open cases. Some band might have just put down these instruments and slipped out the back.

"Do you want me to stand up?" said Leroy.

"Whichever way you're more comfortable." Miss Cash adjusted the mike. "But you have to pick one spot and stand still."

"This is my first time for this," he said. "I'm kind of nervous."

"There's nothing to it. I'll get you to sing a little so I can get a level. Then when you're ready, you tell me, I'll point, and you start. Just open your mouth and sing."

"Will you be there?" He indicated the control room.

She nodded. "I can hear everything you say, but you can't hear me. Got it?"

"Yes ma'am—yeah, okay. I think so." Leroy strummed with his fingers. The Sound Star was as much in tune as it ever would be.

Miss Cash went up behind the glass. Leroy was overcome with wonder at what he was about to do. It was going too fast. He wanted to remember every moment. He stood in a pool of white light. There was no air in the studio, only heat and absolute, close-in dead silence.

He listened. He snapped his fingers. The sound was dead. No echo. Wing-shaped panels of dotted tile dipped down at angles from the ceiling. Maybe that was the Sonocoustic part.

The studio seemed three hundred yards long, the petite Miss Cash floating behind glass at the far other end, fiddling at a control panel that was hidden from where Leroy stood.

He picked out the G chord and settled in to play the first verse of his song. The room swallowed the sound, no reflection at all.

Miss Cash moved her hand in a circle that meant keep playing. He played. She pointed to her mouth. He started in singing: *When your sweetheart tells you she's busy tonight. . . .*

Her hand circled faster, keep singing. Her other hand fiddled on the panel before her. She was all-powerful in the glass room, hovering over everything.

The beginnings of sweat trickled down Leroy's face, but inside he was calm. He was in the right place. All of his life had brought him to this microphone. All he had to do was stand in this spot and sing.

"I think I'm ready," he said.

She held her finger to her lips—shh—then nodded and pointed go.

He played four opening bars, then sang in his smoothest starting-out voice the first part of the line, *When your sweetheart,* and the melody soared way high on sweet*heeeeaaaart, tells you she's busy tonight, we-ell, that's when you know it's over.* . . .

It was a soap opera song, a favorite of Dodger's. It told of two lovers and a best friend. When the best friend gets too friendly with the girl, it all goes to pieces. There was a quiet part in the middle where Leroy spoke the verse aloud; it was a little corny but nice. Simple chords, not too many words, and the melody swooped up and down, allowing Leroy to show off the high and low ends of his voice.

He tried to sound tender. He wanted girls to fall in love with his voice. He wanted them to squeal, the way they did for Frankie Sinatra on the old live recordings.

By the time he reached the last verse, he was hamming it up, holding on to the notes, loading on the emotion.

When all her hellos
Start to sound like good-byes
We-heh-hell, that's when you know it's over

Buhm, buhm, buhm, buhm. Thrinnggg!

Leroy grinned. Victory!

Miss Cash smiled and nodded and flipped switches. No time to think. Time to sing again. Leroy found his spot on the floor. She pointed to him.

This was "My Happiness." He sang this one soft and romantic, acting the part of a failed, heartsick lover. *Evening shadows make me blue.* . . .

In the chorus he glanced up to see Claudia Cash bustling about the control room. He wondered if the machine had messed up, but she didn't make any signal, so he kept on to the end.

She ducked around the door and came to the top of the steps with a delighted smile. "That was very, very nice," she said. "You're good."

Leroy felt himself glowing like the red light on the wall. He *was* good. He knew it. She said it. He couldn't quit grinning. "Well thank you," he spluttered, "could you hear me in there?"

"Loud and clear. You know, you have a good voice for a ballad."

He nearly split open with joy.

"Come on in now and let's hear the playback," she said.

"Wait! You mean—that's all? But. . . . I kind of messed up that second one. I was hoping I could do it over."

"Don't be silly," said Miss Cash. "We get people in here, a lot of people think they can sing. But I really liked you just then. With the right kind of material, I think you might get someone to listen to you."

Leroy unslung the guitar and tiptoed up the steps after her, into a breathtaking wall of cold air. "Air conditioning!" he said. "Y'all have everything."

"It's for the equipment. Shut that door." Miss Cash stepped to the console. She knew just which buttons to press among all the buttons and switches and dials and lights and cords everywhere. She transferred a tape from the reel-to-reel recorder to a large, complicated record-cutting machine and set it to spinning.

The Sound Star made a lonesome twang. The sound came at Leroy from six speakers overhead. His voice sounded nasal and thin, awful country. Almost hillbilly. *When awwwlll her helloos start to sooooound like good-byes. . . .* He winced. "Is that how I sound?"

"Oh go on, you know it's good," she said, pulling the cat glasses to the end of her nose. "You were right. You don't sound like anybody."

Leroy thought he sounded puny and country and ragged, like an underage Hank Williams. At least he would know to sing deeper next time, not so much through his nose. He wished he could do it over.

Claudia Cash tapped her fingers on the console in time to his clumsy guitar. He began to relax. The talking part was nice and dramatic and sad. Once he got over the strange sensation of hearing his voice, he decided it was not all that terrible. He really sang those last verses. He jumped on top of them and rode them right down to the end.

He stared at the floor between songs, a long silence.

The Sound Star started up again, and then the hillbilly boy was back, singing "My Happiness." Leroy sat on the edge of the table. The dread had faded away, and now a thrill was spreading through him, like warm new blood. That was his voice, that was Leroy Kirby singing all by himself on a record, folks! Step right up! Listen! The lady says he has a good voice for a ballad!

"How much singing have you done?" said Miss Cash.

"A lot," he said, "I don't know. Since I was little."

"I mean, have you ever performed?"

Play it cool, now. Don't look too eager. "No, ma'am, not really. School, and stuff. But I'd like to, sometime."

The song ambled on. "I got part of this down on tape," she said. "Maybe I'll play it for Dan when he comes in. Why don't you give me a number in case we want to reach you."

Leroy thought fast. There was no phone at Alabama Street because of an old unpaid bill from Lauderdale Court.

"Our telephone's out of order," he said. "I'll give you our neighbors'. They can find me." He searched the phone book for Hastings on Alabama Street, scratched his address and their number on the index card. His hand was shaking so he could hardly hold the pen.

From the mouth of the record-cutting machine Claudia Cash brought forth a ten-inch circle of black flexible plastic, threaded with grooves like any phonograph record. She slid it into a white envelope.

"Now, don't get too excited," she said. "I don't think Dan has anything for you now. Maybe sometime, if we get the right song. You owe me three ninety-five."

"Oh. Right." Leroy fumbled in his pocket. Four crumpled ones. She gave him a nickel in change. "Miss Cash," he said.

"Yes."

"Just. . . . I guess you tell everybody they're good."

"I meant what I said." She showed him what she had written on the card: LEROY KIRBY—GOOD BALLAD SINGER—HOLD. "This will go right in my file," she said. "Don't worry. We'll call you sometime."

She handed over the envelope. Leroy took it with both hands, stammered more thanks, and walked into the blinding white heat of noon. He carried his record to the truck, baking in the high sun.

He had found magic in that darkened room—the enchanted circle under the microphone, the machine cutting records with its mouth, inscribing his voice as a groove on black acetate. He felt at home in that room. He wanted to spend time there.

He climbed into the truck. The gearshift seared his hand. That felt like real life. He wrapped his shirttail around it, glanced at his watch—one-thirty. Three circuit breakers had been due thirty minutes ago at Mr. Mallory's across town.

He made a wide, screeching U-turn and put down the pedal.

He got there in time, but the delivery took longer than he expected. He came out to find his record melted into an exact impression of the top of his toolbox.

Ray Davies

Ray Davies is, of course, best known as the lead singer and songwriter of the Kinks, probably the most literate of the British Invasion bands of the sixties. In 2000, he published Waterloo Sunset, *a rather uneven collection of short stories, many of which are linked by the character of Les Mulligan, an aging English rock star. Some of Davies's finest songs provide the title and themes for several of the stories, including "Misfits," "Waterloo Sunset," and "Celluloid Heroes." The best of the bunch though is "Rock-and-Roll Fantasy," as Davies gives us the back story of his rock and roll tale of obsession and loneliness. The main character, a sad sack figure named Dan, is an edgier, more pathetic version of Nick Hornby's record store owner Rob Fleming in* High Fidelity *(see page 136). Both characters live and die for rock.*

"Rock-and-Roll Fantasy"

NYC, Spring 1977

THE SEASONS IN NEW YORK were in a state of transition when Les arrived there in March 1977. The apartment was low rent and Les had signed a long lease. He was burnt out by Britain, and the apartment in a slightly run-down building on the Upper West Side of Manhattan offered Les a breath of fresh air. He opened his window and looked at the view but was disappointed to find that all he could see were other high-rise buildings. There was a slight view of Central Park, but it was mostly obscured by other buildings, so Les's eyes were drawn to the street fifteen floors below.

He'd visited New York many times but was always astounded by the sheer immensity of the skyline and the boundless energy of the people on the street. Now, they would provide Les with a new supply of material. It was spring and the whole population seemed to buzz with enthusiasm. The collective consciousness of the New Yorkers seemed to be in accord. It made New York seem like a village, but Les, being a cynical Brit, sneezed and took an allergy pill before venturing out. He walked into a small diner in the building opposite to sample the local tea and cake. He sat in a quiet corner where he was able to observe the clientele without being seen himself. He would sit there for hours on end, like a kind of creative vampire, extracting lines from overhead anecdotes and sound bites from conversations. Slipping into other people's lives as another piece of the Manhattan jigsaw is acted out in the Dakota Diner.

The celebrity photographs hanging on the wall of the Dakota Diner on the Upper West Side were well known to the clientele. The comedian Henny Youngman gazed down fondly at the little old ladies who came into the diner for the two-dollar special. Milton Berle looked down compassionately as the Puerto Rican office boy carried out twenty-four orders of coffee. The Dakota Diner was on the ground floor of a sprawling, run-down old apartment block that once upon a time had jutted above the Manhattan skyline. Now, it lay in the shadow of newer buildings. The Carnegie or Stage delicatessen it wasn't. One look at the menu and you could see through its pretense; it was a Greek diner masquerading as a chic Upper West Side eatery.

Christo, the overweight owner, proudly displayed an autographed photo of Elvis Presley, and he swore the signature was authentic. The story went that in 1973 Elvis's limousine had pulled up outside, and he had walked in and ordered a deluxe cheeseburger and a chocolate milkshake to go. Christo had asked for a signed photograph, and two or three weeks later the picture had arrived: "To Christo. Many thanks. Your old friend, Elvis." Other celebs had come into the diner, but no one as big as Elvis.

On this particular day, Danny, a downcast-looking fellow, carrying a large satchel full of autograph books and rock albums, walked past the diner two or three times before going in. He was one of the regulars, but for some reason he hesitated before coming in. Christo sighed. He knew the reason.

Danny was either short and fat or tall and thin, depending on how life was treating him. Today he was unshaven and had dark rings under his eyes, as if he hadn't slept. Hunched up, in his mind in turmoil.

Danny finally decided to go in, and took a good, hard look at Christo whose days of rock and roll were over. Surely he could never have danced to it. He could just about buy the notion of Milton Berle or Henny Youngman sending Christo an autographed picture, but Danny, a collector himself, remained skeptical about the signature on the photo of the King. Okay, the Dakota Diner was on the fashionable Upper West Side, spitting distance from Central Park West, near the Dakota apartment building where John Lennon lived with Yoko Ono. Sure, Shelley Winters could sometimes be seen walking her poodles along the street. True, you could see Mia Farrow wheeling a baby in a stroller outside the Dakota, and yes, everybody knew that once Paul Simon had sat in the corner having eggs over easy with his attorney, but Elvis Presley walking up to Christo to order a deluxe cheeseburger during a busy lunch hour? Unlikely. Les watched unnoticed from a quiet booth in the back room as the Latino busboy shouted across the café.

"Here comes Danny, the wacko rock-and-roll fan."

Les put his head down and scribbled some notes on his copy of the *New York Post*. "*Hello you, hello me. Hello people, we used to be. Isn't it strange, we never changed. We've been through it al, yet we're still the same. . . .*"

Danny flashed his discolored teeth and looked over at the water boy threateningly. Christo tried to defuse the heat of the moment.

"Let's face it, Danny, you've got to be a wacko to be that passionate about rock music."

Danny gritted his teeth and took a deep breath, then sat in his usual seat at the counter and gave the busboy that I'll-deal-with-you-later look. Danny had been a rock fan ever since he had seen Elvis appear on the Ed Sullivan show. He had moved across the Brooklyn Bridge into Manhattan to work in a small record store six blocks away, just off Broadway and Amsterdam—a big step from the working-class neighborhood he had grown up in. It was a small store that catered mainly to record collectors and specialists.

Danny was an expert's expert. An aficionado of the twelve-inch album and a collector of seven-inch singles, he had an encyclopedic knowledge of every record released, every artist. Scrapbooks full of signatures. Letters from all over the world, from the international network of rock-and-roll fans. Danny had always been a loner, but when he became an adult he became even more isolated when all his friends got steady jobs, married, and forgot about rock music. For Danny, rock music was his life. Everything revolved around music and record magazines. The move from Brooklyn was inevitable once he heard that John Lennon had bought that apartment. All Danny's friends were still in Brooklyn, and whenever he went back to visit he would spin yarns about how well he was doing in Manhattan. The record business was on the upswing. Sales were at an all-time high. But today, Danny looked like he was on a short fuse. He looked like a vagrant. Over the edge. All hope gone. Desperate.

"Paulette isn't coming back."

Christo cleaned the counter and said nothing. The old lady looked up from her two-dollar special. Danny continued, even though nobody really wanted to hear about it.

"She's gonna get married. It was on the radio, for Christ's sake.

She's marrying a rock singer."

Christo felt he had to say something, even though he had heard the saga a hundred times before.

"The guy in the heavy metal band?"

Danny considered this to be a major humiliation.

"That's right. It'll be all over the city. Everyone will know. It'll probably be in the music trades. They were seen coming out of Studio 54. What will I do? What will I say to my friends? My folks?"

Christo slid over a glass of ice water. Danny was still talking.

"To think I asked her to marry me. I told everyone. We were as good as engaged. The humiliation!"

Christo put a menu in front of Danny and tried to commiserate.

"These things happen, you know. Maybe it's a flash in the pan. The rock singer will find somebody else and pretty soon she'll be back. Hey! Do you want the special or what?"

Danny was in no mood to be humored.

"She returned my vintage Vic Damone collection. It's over between us."

Christo shrugged. He knew the score. Paulette was a pretty, if somewhat stupid, nineteen-year-old from New Jersey, who worked in a boutique on Columbus Avenue. She wore thick, bright, rock-and-roll makeup, and her big, black, wirelike hair was piled up on top of her head. Her body was straight off a centerfold. Neat tush, just about covered by a leather miniskirt, and tits like melons. One day she had walked into Danny's store looking for an Aerosmith album, and once they had started talking, and she had looked at him with her big brown eyes, he knew that she was the one for him. To Danny it was all too psychic. They were meant for each other. He'd never thought to ask if she felt the same way. Paulette was a trophy he could take home to Brooklyn and show his friends. He had spent all he had on her. He had taken her to the Copacabana on a date. To a ball game at Shea Stadium, where he'd bored her with stories about when the Beatles had played there. Danny had borrowed money to treat Paulette, and, eventually, people had come to collect. Christo had taken pity on him and had offered him work in the kitchen to earn extra cash. Paulette never moved in with Danny, but he called her "his girl" and treated her like a goddess. After she had endured the relationship for six months, Danny was still looking for new ways to impress her, anything so she would stay with him. He pandered to her every whim. One night, he took her backstage after that fatal heavy metal concert, and she'd run off with the singer. Now that she had gone off with him for good, Danny was devastated, a wreck. He was in love with her. He kept calling her, leaving messages, asking her to come back. Offering any albums she wanted, just as long as she'd return. Talking about her constantly. It had been a month now. Christo tried to snap Danny out of it.

"Listen, Danny. You know you're better off without her. You know when guys looked at her it always put you on edge. Why are you still carrying a torch for this broad?"

Danny wouldn't stop talking about her. She didn't return his calls. He'd gone to her parents' house in Yonkers to find her. They'd thrown him out, and gotten a restraining order. Christo just shook his head and put a bowl of soup in front of Danny.

"It's barley today. Do me a favor, Danny. Get yourself a life. Forget her."

This hit a chord with Danny.

"That's what Paulette's dad said. He told me to get a life. Said rock music wasn't life."

He ate, and went on talking. The landlord at his apartment had served him with an eviction notice. It was only a tiny room, but the Upper West Side was out of Danny's league. Christo tried to cheer him up.

"I don't know why you keep that apartment. You spend all your time here, at work, or hanging around at rock concerts. Sublet it."

Christo wasn't wrong. The few people who had seen Danny's apartment said it was nothing more than a storeroom for all his records and memorabilia. And not a big enough storeroom either. Danny continued to complain.

"It's a real struggle. The music industry may be on the upswing, but in the city, everybody's broke. You have to be a millionaire to live in this city."

Christo was in philosophical mode. He had his own problems. The Dakota Diner had seen better times. Each day he'd try another scam, another cheap combo to entice customers in.

"Tell me about it. I'm not looking for millionaires. Just regular poor folks would be fine, as long as they can pay for a two-dollar special."

He started looking through the albums in Danny's satchel.

"This record collection must be worth something. If you sold it, you'd make a fortune."

Danny got protective and closed the bag.

"Don't worry about me. I'm fine. I'll die before I sell my collection."

Christo knew when to stop. Danny didn't like talking about money. Music was all that mattered. But it made him less than a person. He was a collector, a dealer in trivia. He neglected himself, his own life; his collection, and Paulette, were his only sources of pride. Even the daily ritual of going to the diner at lunchtime was not to feed himself, but to feed his obsession with music and Paulette by talking, talking, talking. Christo looked out at the street.

"This used to be a neighborhood. Working people. Small stores. Now the businessmen are moving in. Boutiques everywhere. Smart restaurants, with fancy decor. Nobody likes plain food anymore. You can't have a conversation with anybody. Nobody has the time."

Danny just nodded his head.

"That's why I have music. Without that, I couldn't hang on." When Danny's eldest brother had gone off to Vietnam and never come back, he had played his old Frank Zappa albums day in, day out. Danny felt there was some of his brother left on those albums.

Christo hadn't known Danny very long, but he was easy to read. Danny was hanging tough right now, but the telltale signs were there. He was heading for a slump, beginning to neglect himself more than usual. Some lunchtimes he hadn't even come in—a sure sign self-pity had set in. He'd disappeared before, and Christo would receive a postcard from Memphis or some such place. Danny had been to visit Graceland, a pilgrimage in his time of despair. Christo was getting used to it. Once he hitchhiked upstate to Rochester because two of the Jimi Hendrix Experience were playing a club date. On the way back, he had been mugged and all of his money had been taken. They had even taken a few albums. He'd hustled a pass into the club, though. Christo wondered what would pick him up this time.

Danny finished his soup and walked out of the diner, but instead of going back to the record store, he walked around the Upper West Side, revisiting all the places he had taken Paulette. He walked past the Ansonia on Broadway. A large, sprawling, apartment building. Paulette had had an exercise class on the second floor, and Danny had waited for her there. Then there was the Genoa, the Italian restaurant opposite the subway station at Seventy-second and Broadway where he had taken her on their first date. He walked around the neighborhood until the restaurants had closed and the chefs piled the wasted food on the street, ready for the garbage collection the following morning. Danny looked at a dog foraging through the garbage and remembered how he and Paulette had laughed at the dogs and their owners leading them around the Upper West Side. They'd wondered how so many large dogs could live in so many small apartments. Then, standing outside Lincoln Center, he decided he had to get her back. The following day he talked to Christo again.

"She always loved breakfast on the West Side. Sunday brunch up the road at Ruskay's, she can't refuse."

Danny was optimistic, Christo a realist.

"There's no way she'll come. It's too late."

Danny wouldn't listen, and started writing the letter. Paulette had loved walking along Columbus Avenue on a Sunday morning. Danny had the *New York Times* under his arm. He never read it, but it made him feel like a real New Yorker. They would stroll up to Ruskay's, stand in line until a table was free. The stares hadn't started getting to him yet. As long as she went home with him, that's all he cared about. If she read the letter and met him one more time at Ruskay's, he could convince her that she was making a big mistake. The dream of a last-ditch reconciliation gave Danny new hope, but Christo knew his Brooklyn friend was grasping at a straw. Danny messengered the letter over, to Paulette's parents' house.

Sunday morning came, and Danny was up at the crack of dawn,

showered and sparkling and ready to meet Paulette. He'd bought a new tie-dyed T-shirt, and checked out his new look with Christo.

"Not bad," said the Greek. "You look too classy for this place. Get out of here."

Danny smiled and swaggered cockily out of the diner. The satchel full of albums over his shoulder made him lurch. Across the street he saw a familiar face. Lester Mulligan was standing outside the building opposite. Lester looked at Danny and smiled as if he knew him, then disappeared back into the building. Danny was of two minds. Paulette wouldn't be at Ruskay's for at least half an hour. Surely there'd be time to get Les Mulligan's autograph. He went over and hassled the doorman for information. "Is Mr. Mulligan moving into the neighborhood? Is he just visiting?"

The doorman tried to say nothing, but eventually gave in to Danny's persistence.

"Yes. Mr. Mulligan is staying in New York for a while to write some songs. Now get lost, will ya?"

Danny bought a coffee and sat in the street until he saw Les Mulligan come out. Then he rushed over and bombarded him with questions, treating him like an old friend, showing his press clippings, talking nonstop.

Danny reeled off his own story as Lester signed autographs. His childhood and growing up in Brooklyn as a rock fan. About his brother dying in Vietnam and how the only sane thing in his life was rock music. He told him about Paulette and his love for her. Lester listened attentively and barely spoke. Danny was spilling his guts on the sidewalk but Lester just stood and listened. Danny's emotional state would have been a cause for concern to a psychoanalyst, but Lester Mulligan just listened quietly as if taking notes. Then Danny asked about Les.

"It's such a trip to think that you and John Lennon are gonna be next-door neighbors. It's too far out."

The singer was not so enthusiastic.

"Yeah, I guess everybody's got to live somewhere."

Danny became overexcited, overinquisitive. Overstepping the boundaries of professional etiquette.

"You must get together a lot with John and Yoko. Do you still fight with your band? I guess John can relate because of the way he quarreled with Paul. You sure must have a lot to talk about." Danny started to drool.

The rock singer smiled and promised to leave a photograph of his band with the doorman. Danny stood and watched Lester Mulligan walk toward Central Park. A limousine pulled up outside the Dakota. Danny couldn't believe his luck as he saw John Lennon walk out and get in. Two of his teen idols in the space of five minutes, and on the same street. It was more than he could have hoped for. It had to be a good omen. He'd get back with Paulette. He hung around the limo as Lennon signed autographs for a couple of giggling girls. Danny was talking again, showing off his insider knowledge.

"I hear that you and the other Beatles are going to get together again to make another album?"

John Lennon looked over.

"Not in the foreseeable future, I shouldn't think. I've got my own project with Yoko. That takes up all of my time."

Danny jumped in with another question.

"Are you aware of the Shea Stadium bootleg album? We had a couple in the store where I work, but when my boss found out they were bootlegs he refused to sell them. Just thought you ought to know that, John."

He'd hit a nerve. John looked hard at Danny, and threw it off by saying that Shea Stadium was a long time ago. He mumbled a few more inaudible sentences before getting into the limousine and driving off down Central Park West.

Danny ran down to the newspaper stand by the subway station at Columbus Avenue holding his *New York Times* as a talisman. He was in Ruskay's in time to claim a decent table where he could sit and watch the street. Hours seemed to pass. Danny flicked through the paper and reluctantly ordered brunch for one: eggs over easy, jelly, cheesecake, coffee. After six refills, it was obvious that Paulette wasn't coming. Maybe she hadn't gotten the letter, maybe she had. Maybe she had arrived early, while Danny was getting John Lennon's autograph? The waiter told Danny they needed the table. Danny left, but walked up and down the street hoping she'd just been delayed. He felt like one of those sad dogs tied up outside, waiting for their owners to come and reclaim them. The streets were getting crowded, the Upper West Side was starting to buzz. So many people. But for Danny, without Paulette, it was the loneliest place on earth.

He found himself back in his apartment, surrounded by rent demands and his memorabilia. He started to write a suicide letter. He blamed his parents, his poor start in Brooklyn. He even lost faith in his music. Paulette had been driven away by his obsession. He blamed anything, any excuse to mask the simple reality that Paulette just didn't love him anymore. Perhaps she never had. Danny put the note in his wallet to carry around with him, just in case he could summon up the courage to end it all.

Time went by. Danny walked around, unwashed, existing in a blurred, meaningless world. He had lost his job at the record store. He had stopped going to the Dakota Diner. Its cold air conditioning had only made him anticipate being in a warm bed with Paulette. People didn't seem to smile. He was alone, and the cold was just an accompaniment to his empty life. He still had the suicide letter in his wallet. Every day he thought of death. He'd left his love records to Paulette. Even in death he could serenade her through the voices of Paul McCartney, Roy Orbison, and Elvis. "Yesterday," "Only the Lonely," and "Are You Lonesome Tonight?" would be the epitaph of his love for Paulette. Maybe he was only now living in the real world. There was no place for him in it.

Christo would look for Danny on the street. He could see only the black panhandler in his usual spot outside the Olcott Hotel. Christo longed for the cold winter when he could move a lot of soup.

At this time Danny would often see Lester Mulligan on the street and on a few occasions the rock singer would ask how Danny was doing, almost as though he was keeping tabs on the soap opera of Danny's failed love life. These encounters with Lester always lifted Danny's morale—"talking to you, Mr. Mulligan, helps me put my life in perspective and I know that no matter how bad things get, rock 'n roll will always pull me through in the end." Lester would watch Danny walk off clutching his satchel full of records, clutching a strand of hope of the time being until the realities of life came back to send him into another depression. Les would go back to his apartment and write more lyrics.

The seasons came and went. Danny took any work he could, washing dishes in restaurants, walking dogs for little old ladies on the West Side. Anything to help take his mind off Paulette and his humiliation. One day he even walked past Lester Mulligan as he jogged through Central Park. He'd shouted out to Danny, but he had been too depressed to answer back, too ashamed to say that he had rejected the music he'd once loved. He had set the time for his death. The day was fixed in his mind, circled on the calendar. On August 16 his alarm clicked on as usual at 7:30 A.M. It was his and Paulette's anniversary. Today he wasn't going to shift himself from his bed. Today was the day when somebody would finally get to read his suicide note. He spent the morning tidying his room so it would be clean when they discovered his body. He flicked around the dial on the radio and settled on WNEW to listen to rock and roll for the last time. Then a reporter cut into a track to give the world news from Memphis, Tennessee.

Elvis Presley had been found dead at his home at Graceland. Listeners were advised to stay tuned for further updates. Danny stayed by the radio to hear the details as they emerged. The sound of the announcer's voice echoed deep inside his head. The King was dead. Rock and roll had crashed into the real world, and Danny's world had been stopped dead in its tracks. His own death would have to be delayed. He spent all day and night tuned into various rock stations for the latest news. He started to wonder how Christo would deal with it. It didn't seem to matter now whether or not the autograph was authentic. That wasn't important. The fact that Christo believed it was what mattered. For once Paulette didn't fill his mind. His problems were miniscule compared to facing a world without Elvis. He wrote her a kiss-off note, a final good-bye. He was going back to Brooklyn to be with real people, people he knew and trusted. Then suddenly, amid the tributes, he heard one of the deejays playing a stereo remix of "It's All

Right, Mama" instead of the original mono mix. He looked through his collection for the original, and his taste for music came back.

That night Danny couldn't sleep. At three in the morning he looked up at the large hotel building where Lester Mulligan had been staying and saw a light in one of the windows. He fantasized that it was Mulligan, still up listening to the radio for news of Elvis.

"Yeah," Danny thought, "he must be a fan too. I guess he can't sleep either." Up in his apartment, Lester Mulligan typed out his own version of Danny's life.

There's a guy in my block, he lives for rock, he plays records
    day and night,
And when he feels down he puts some rock and roll on and it
    makes him feel all right,
And when he feels the world is closing in, he turns the stereo
    way up high,
He just spends his life living in a rock-and-roll fantasy,
He just spends his life living on the edge of reality,
He just spends his life in a rock-and-roll fantasy.

Look at me, look at you, you say we've got nothing left to
    prove,
The King is dead, rock is done, you might be through but I've
    just begun,
I don't know, I feel free but I won't let go,
Before you go there's something you ought to know.

Dan is a fan and lives for our music, it's the only thing
    that gets him by,
He's watched us grow and he's seen all our shows, he's seen us
    low and he's seen us high,
Oh but you and me keep thinking that the world's just passing
    us by,
Don't want to spend my life living in a rock-and-roll fantasy,

Don't want to spend my life living on the edge of reality,
Don't want to waste my life hiding away anymore.
Don't want to spend my life living in a rock-and-roll fantasy.

Don DeLillo

Don DeLillo is the author of Running Dog *(1978);* Libra *(1988), a fictional speculation on the assassination of John F. Kennedy;* The Names *(1982);* Mao II *(1991);* Underworld *(1997); and, most recently,* Cosmopolis *(2003). He has also written two plays,* The Day Room *(1986) and* Valparaiso *(1999). The first selection,* Great Jones Street *(1973), captures a particular place—the East Village—at a particular time—the 1970s—with the rock star as protagonist. Bucky Wunderlick, the novel's reluctant hero, tries to escape the grasp of celebrity by holing up in a dingy East Village apartment but finds fame and all its trappings follows him wherever he goes. There are shades here of Bob Dylan, Jim Morrison, Mick Jagger, and Kurt Cobain. In the second excerpt,* White Noise *(1985), we follow the career of Jack Gladney, a professor of Hitler Studies at a liberal arts college in the Midwest. Many of his colleagues are exiles from New York, including Murray Jay Siskind, an ex-sportswriter but now a visiting lecturer on living icons. It is Siskind who suggests to Gladney that the college should offer a course on Elvis studies. But DeLillo has more on his mind than cultural studies. Before long, a deadly black chemical cloud, unleashed by an industrial accident, engulfs them all.*

From
Great Jones Street

FAME REQUIRES every kind of excess. I mean true fame, a devouring neon, not the somber reknown of waning statesmen or chinless kings. I mean long journeys across gray space. I mean danger, the edge of every void, the circumstance of one man imparting an erotic terror to the dreams of the republic. Understand the man who must inhabit these extreme regions, monstrous and vulval, damp with memories of violation. Even if half-made he is absorbed into the public's total madness; even if fully rational, a bureaucrat in hell, a secret genius of survival, he is sure to be destroyed by the public's contempt for survivors. Fame, this special kind, feeds itself on outrage, on what the counselors of lesser men would consider bad publicity—hysteria in limousines, knife fights in the audience, bizarre litigation, treachery, pandemonium and drugs. Perhaps the only natural law attaching to true fame is that the famous man is compelled, eventually, to commit suicide.

(Is it clear I was a hero of rock 'n' roll?)

Toward the end of the final tour it became apparent that our audience wanted more than music, more even than its own reduplicated noise. It's possible the culture had reached its limit, a point of severe tension. There was less sense of simple visceral abandon at our concerts during these last weeks. Few cases of arson and vandalism. Fewer still of rape. No smoke bombs or threats of worse explosives. Our followers, in their isolation, were not concerned with precedent now. They were free of old saints and martyrs, but fearfully so, left with their own unlabeled flesh. Those without tickets didn't storm the barricades, and during a performance the boys and girls directly below us, scratching at the stage, were less murderous in their love of me, as if realizing finally that my death, to be authentic, must be self-willed—a successful piece of instruction only if it occurred by my own hand, preferably in a foreign city. I began to think their education would not be complete until they outdid me as teacher, until one day they merely pantomimed the kind of massive response the group was used to getting. As we performed they would jump, dance, collapse, clutch each other, wave their arms, all the while making absolutely no sound. We would stand in the incandescent pit of a huge stadium filled with wildly rippling bodies, all totally silent. Our recent music, deprived of people's screams, was next to meaningless, and there would have been no choice but to stop playing. A profound joke it would have been. A lesson in something or other.

In Houston I left the group, saying nothing, and boarded a plane for New York City, that contaminated shrine, place of my birth. I knew Azarian would assume leadership of the band, his body being prettiest. As to the rest, I left them to their respective uproars—news media, promotion people, agents, accountants, various members of the managerial peerage. The public would come closer to understanding my disappearance than anyone else. It was not quite as total as the act they needed and nobody could be sure whether I was gone for good. For my closest followers, all it foreshadowed was a period of waiting. Either I'd return with a new language for them to speak or they'd seek a divine silence attendant to my own.

I took a taxi past the cemeteries toward Manhattan, tides of ash-light breaking across the spires. New York seemed older than the cities of Europe, a sadistic gift of the sixteenth century, ever on the verge of plague. The cab driver was young, however, a freckled kid with a moderate orange Afro. I told him to take the tunnel.

"Is there a tunnel?" he said.

The night before, at the Astrodome, the group had appeared without me. Azarian's stature was vast but nothing on that first night could have broken the crowd's bleak mood. They turned against the structure itself, smashing whatever was smashable, trying to rip up the artificial turf, attacking the very plumbing. The gates were opened and the police entered, blank-looking, hiding the feast in their minds behind metered eyes. They made their patented charges, cracking arms and legs in an effort to protect the concept of regulated temperature. In one of the worst public statements of the year, by anyone, my manager Globke referred to the police operation as an example of mini-genocide.

"The tunnel goes under the river. It's a nice tunnel with white tile walls and men in glass cages counting the cars going by. One two three four. One two three."

I was interested in endings, in how to survive a dead idea. What came next for the wounded of Houston might very well depend on what I was able to learn beyond certain personal limits, in endland, far from the tropics of fame.

I WENT to the room in Great Jones Street, a small crooked room, cold as a penny, looking out on warehouses, trucks, and rubble. There was snow on the window ledge. Some rags and an unloved ruffled shirt of mine had been stuffed into places where the window frame was warped and cold air entered. The refrigerator was unplugged, full of record albums, tapes and old magazines. I went to the sink and turned both taps all the way, drawing an intermittent trickle. Least is best. I tried the radio, picking up AM only at the top of the dial, FM not at all. Later I shaved, cutting myself badly. It was strange watching the long fold of blood appear at my throat, collecting along the length of the gash, then starting to flow in an uneven pattern. Not a bad color. Room could do with a coat. I stuck toilet paper against the cut and tried with no luck to sleep a while. Then I put Opel's coat over my shoulders and went out for food.

It was dark in the street, snowing again, and a man in a long coat stood in the alley between Lafayette and Broadway. I walked around a stack of shipping containers. The industrial loft buildings along Great Jones seemed misproportioned, broad structures half as tall as they should have been, as if deprived of light by the great skyscraper ranges to the north and south. I found a grocery store about three blocks away. One of the customers nudged the woman next to him and nodded in my direction. A familiar dumb hush fell over the store. I picked up the owner's small brown cat and let it curl against my chest. The man who'd spotted me drew gradually closer, pretending to read labels along the way, finally sidling in next to me at the counter, the living effigy of a cost accountant or tax lawyer, radiating his special grotesquerie, that of sane men leading normal lines.

Slowly along Great Jones, signs of commerce became apparent, of shipping and receiving, export packaging, custom tanning. This was an old street. Its materials were in fact its essence and this explains the ugliness of every inch. But it wasn't a final squalor. Some streets in their decline posses a kind of redemptive tenor, the suggestion of new forms about to evolve, and Great Jones was one of these, hovering on the edge of self-revelation. Paper, yarn, leathers, tools, buckles, wire-frame-and-novelty. Somebody unlocked the door of the sandblasting company. Old trucks came rumbling off the cobblestones on Lafayette Street. Each truck in turn mounted the curb, where several would remain throughout the day, listing slightly, circled by heavy-bellied men carrying clipboards, invoices, bills of lading, forever hoisting their trousers over their hips. A black woman emerged from the smear of an abandoned car, talking a scattered song. Wind was biting up from the harbor.

I had the door half-open, on my way out for food, when someone spoke my name from the top of the next landing. It was a man about fifty years old, wearing a hooded sweat shirt. He was sitting on the top step, looking down at me.

"I've been waiting for you," he said. "I'm your upstairs neighbor. Eddie Fenig. Ed Fenig. Maybe you've heard of me. I'm a writer, which gives us something a little bit in common, at least retroactively. I write under my full name. Edward B. Fenig. You're tops in your trade, Bucky, looking at your old lyrics, never having attended a live performance. So when I saw you from my window yesterday when you were crossing the street this way, I was naturally delighted. Sheer delight, no exaggeration. Maybe you've heard of me. I'm a poet. I'm a novelist. I'm a mystery writer. I write science fiction. I write pornography. I write daytime dramatic serials. I write one-act plays. I've been published and/or produced in all these forms. But nobody knows me from shit."

Americans pursue loneliness in various ways. For me, Great Jones Street was a time of prayerful fatigue. I became a half-saint, practiced in visions, informed by a sense of bodily economy, but deficient in true pain. I was preoccupied with conserving myself for some unknown ordeal to come and did not make work by engaging in dialogues, or taking more than the minimum number of steps to get from place to place, or urinating unnecessarily.

From
White Noise

Department heads wear academic robes at the College-on-the-Hill. Not grand sweeping full-length affairs but sleeveless tunics puckered at the shoulders. I like the idea. I like clearing my arm from the folds of the garment to look at my watch. The simple act of checking the time is transformed by this flourish. Decoratively gestures add romance to a life. Idling students may see time itself as a complex embellishment, a romance of human consciousness, as they witness the chairman walking across campus, crook'd arm emerging from his medieval robe, the digital watch blinking in late summer dusk. The robe is black, of course, and goes with almost anything.

There is no Hitler building as such. We are quartered in Centenary Hall, a dark brick structure we share with the popular culture department, known officially as American environments. A curious group. The teaching staff is composed almost solely of New York émigrés, smart, thuggish, movie-mad, trivia-crazed. They are here to decipher the natural landscape of the culture, to make a formal method of the shiny pleasures they'd known in their Europe-shadowed childhoods—an Aristotelianism of bubble gum wrappers and detergent jingles. The department head is Alfonse (Fast Food) Stompanato, a broad-chested glowering man whose collection of pre-war soda pop bottles is on permanent display in an alcove. All his teachers are male, wear rumpled clothes, need haircuts, cough into their armpits. Together they look like teamster officials assembled to identify the body of a mutilated colleague. The impression is one of pervasive bitterness, suspicion and intrigue.

An exception to some of the above is Murray Jay Siskind, an ex-sportswriter who asked me to have lunch with him in the dining room, where the institutional odor of vaguely defined food aroused in me an obscure and gloomy memory. Murray was new to the Hill, a stoop-shouldered man with little round glasses and an Amish beard. He was a visiting lecturer on living icons and seemed embarrassed by what he'd gleaned so far from his colleagues in popular culture.

"I understand the music, I understand the movies, I even see how comic books can tell us things. But there are full professors in this place who read nothing but cereal boxes."

"It's the only avant-garde we've got."

"Not that I'm complaining. I like it here. I'm totally enamored of this place. A small-town setting. I want to be free of cities and sexual entanglements. Heat. This is what cities mean to me. You get off the train and walk out of the station and you are hit with the full blast. The heat of air, traffic and people. The heat of food and sex. The heat of tall buildings. The heat that floats out of the subways and the tunnels. It's always fifteen degrees hotter in the cities. Heat rises from the sidewalks and falls from the poisoned sky. The buses breathe heat. Heat emanates from crowds of shoppers and office workers. The entire infrastructure is based on heat, desperately uses up heat, breeds more heat. The eventual heat death of the universe that scientists love to talk about is already well underway and you can feel it happening all around you in any large or medium-sized city. Heat and wetness."

"Where are you living, Murray?"

"In a rooming house. I'm totally captivated and intrigued. It's a gorgeous old crumbling house near the insane asylum. Seven or eight boarders, more or less permanent except for me. A woman who harbors a terrible secret. A man with a haunted look. A man who never comes out of his room. A woman who stands by the letter box for hours, waiting for something that never seems to arrive. A man with no past. A woman with a past. There is a smell about the place of unhappy lives in the movies that I really respond to."

"Which one are you?" I said.

"I'm the Jew. What else could I be?"

There was something touching about the fact that Murray was dressed almost totally in corduroy. I had the feeling that since the age of eleven in his crowded plot of concrete he'd associated this sturdy fabric with higher learning in some impossibly distant and tree-shaded place.

"I can't help being happy in a town called Blacksmith," he said. "I'm here to avoid situations. Cities are full of situations, sexually cunning people. There are parts of my body I no longer encourage women to handle freely. I was in a situation with a woman in Detroit. She needed my semen in a divorce suit. The irony is that I love women. I fall apart at the sight of long legs, striding, briskly, as a breeze carries up from the river, on a weekday, in the play of morning light. The second irony is that it's not the bodies of women that I ultimately crave but their minds. The mind of a woman. The delicate chambering and massive unidirectional flow, like a physics experiment. What fun it is to talk to an intelligent woman wearing stockings as she crosses her legs. That little staticky sound of rustling nylon can make me happy on several levels. The third and related irony is that it's the most complex and neurotic and difficult women that I am invariably drawn to. I like simple men and complicated women."

Murray's hair was tight and heavy-looking. He had dense brows, wisps of hair curling up the sides of his neck. The small stiff beard, confined to his chin and unaccompanied by a mustache, seemed an optional component, to be stuck on or removed as circumstances warranted.

"What kind of lectures do you plan giving?"

"That's exactly what I want to talk to you about," he said. "You've established a wonderful thing here with Hitler. You created it, you nurtured it, you made it your own. Nobody on the faculty of any college or university in this part of the country can so much as utter the word Hitler without a nod in your direction, literally or metaphorically. This is the center, the unquestioned source. He is now your Hitler, Gladney's Hitler. It must be deeply satisfying for you. The college is internationally known as a result of Hitler studies. It has an identity, a sense of achievement. You've evolved an entire system around this figure, a structure with countless substructures and interrelated fields of study, a history within a history. I marvel at the effort. It was masterful, shrewd and stunningly preemptive. It's what I want to do with Elvis."

I put on my dark glasses, composed my face and walked into the room. There were twenty-five or thirty young men and women, many in fall colors, seated in armchairs and sofas and on the beige broadloom.

Murray walked among them, speaking, his right hand trembling in a stylized way. When he saw me, he smiled sheepishly. I stood against the wall, attempting to loom, my arms folded under the black gown.

Murray was in the midst of a thoughtful monologue.

"Did his mother know that Elvis would die young? She talked about assassins. She talked about the life. The life of a star of this type and magnitude. Isn't the life structured to cut you down early? This is the point, isn't it? There are rules, guidelines. If you don't have the grace and wit to die early, you are forced to vanish, to hide as if in shame and apology. She worried about his sleepwalking. She thought he might go out a window. I have a feeling about mothers. Mothers really do know. The folklore is correct."

"Hitler adored his mother," I said.

A surge of attention, unspoken, identifiable only in a certain convergence of stillness, an inward tensing. Murray kept moving, of course, but a bit more deliberately, picking his way between the chairs, the people seated on the floor. I stood against the wall, arms folded.

"Elvis and Gladys liked to nuzzle and pet," he said. "They slept in the same bed until he began to approach physical maturity. They talked baby talk to each other all the time."

"Hitler was a lazy kid. His report card was full of unsatisfactorys. But Klara loved him, spoiled him, gave him the attention his father failed to give him. She was a quiet woman, modest and religious, and a good cook and housekeeper."

"Gladys walked Elvis to school and back every day. She defended him in little street rumbles, lashed out at any kid who tried to bully him."

"Hitler fantasized. He took piano lessons, made sketches of museums and villas. He sat around the house a lot. Klara tolerated this. He was the first of her children to survive infancy. Three others had died."

"Elvis confided in Gladys. He brought his girlfriends around to meet her."

"Hitler wrote a poem to his mother. His mother and his niece were the women with the greatest hold on his mind."

"When Elvis went into the army, Gladys became ill and depressed.

She sensed something, maybe as much about herself as about him. Her psychic apparatus was flashing all the wrong signals. Foreboding and gloom."

"There's not much doubt that Hitler was what we call a mama's boy."

A note-taking young man murmured absently, *"Muttersöhnchen."* I regarded him warily. Then, on an impulse, I abandoned my stance at the wall and began to pace the room like Murray, occasionally pausing to gesture, to listen, to gaze out a window or up at the ceiling.

"Elvis could hardly bear to let Gladys out of his sight when her condition grew worse. He kept a vigil at the hospital."

"When his mother became severely ill, Hitler put a bed in the kitchen to be closer to her. He cooked and cleaned."

"Elvis fell apart with grief when Gladys died. He fondled and petted her in the casket. He talked baby talk to her until she was in the ground."

"Klara's funeral cost three hundred and seventy kronen. Hitler wept at the grave and fell into a period of depression and self-pity. He felt an intense loneliness. He'd lost not only his beloved mother but also his sense of home and hearth."

"It seems fairly certain that Gladys's death caused a fundamental shift at the center of the King's world view. She'd been his anchor, his sense of security. He began to withdraw from the real world, to enter the state of his own dying."

"For the rest of his life, Hitler could not bear to be anywhere near Christmas decorations because his mother had died near a Christmas tree."

"Elvis made death threats, received death threats. He took mortuary tours and became interested in UFOs. He began to study the *Bardo Thödol*, commonly known as *The Tibetan Book of the Dead*. This is a guide to dying and being reborn."

"Years later, in the grip of self-myth and deep remoteness, Hitler kept a portrait of his mother in his spartan quarters at Obersalzberg. He began to hear a buzzing in his left ear."

Murray and I passed each other near the center of the room, almost colliding. Alfonse Stompanato entered, followed by several students, drawn perhaps by some magnetic wave of excitation, some frenzy in the air. He settled his surly bulk in a chair as Murray and I circled each other and headed off in opposite directions, avoiding an exchange of looks.

"Elvis fulfilled the terms of the contract. Excess, deterioration, self-destructiveness, grotesque behavior, a physical bloating and a series of insults to the brain, self-delivered. His place in legend is secure. He bought off the skeptics by dying early, horribly, unnecessarily. No one could deny him now. His mother probably saw it all, as on a nineteen-inch screen, years before her own death."

Murray, happily deferring to me, went to a corner of the room and sat on the floor, leaving me to pace and gesture alone, secure in my professional aura of power, madness and death.

"Hitler called himself the lonely wanderer out of nothingness. He sucked on lozenges, spoke to people in endless monologues, free-associating, as if the language came from some vastness beyond the world and he was simply the medium of revelation. It's interesting to wonder if he looked back from the *führerbunker*, beneath the burning city, to the early days of his power. Did he think of the small groups of tourists who visited the little settlement where his mother was born and where he'd spent summers with his cousins, riding in ox cars and making kites? They came to honor the site, Klara's birthplace. They entered the farmhouse, poked around tentatively. Adolescent boys climbed on the roof. In time the numbers began to increase. They took pictures, slipped small items into their pockets. Then crowds came, mobs of people overrunning the courtyard and singing patriotic songs, painting swastikas on the walls, on the flanks of farm animals. Crowds came to his mountain villa, so many people he had to stay indoors. They picked up pebbles where he'd walked and took them home as souvenirs. Crowds came to hear him speak, crowds erotically charged, the masses he once called his only bride. He closed his eyes, clenched his fists as he spoke, twisted his sweat-drenched body, remade his voice as a thrilling weapon. 'Sex murders,' someone called these speeches. Crowds came to be hypnotized by the voice, the party anthems, the torchlight parades."

I stared at the carpet and counted silently to seven.

"But wait. How familiar this all seems, how close to ordinary. Crowds come, get worked up, touch and press—people eager to be transported. Isn't this ordinary? We *know* all this. There must have been something different about those crowds. What was it? Let me whisper the terrible word, from the Old English, from the Old German, from the Old Norse. *Death*. Many of those crowds were assembled in the name of death. They were there to attend tributes to the dead. Processions, songs, speeches, dialogues with the dead, recitations of the names of the dead. They were there to see pyres and flaming wheels, thousands of flags dipped in salute, thousands of uniformed mourners. There were ranks and squadrons, elaborate backdrops, blood banners and black dress uniforms. Crowds came to form a shield against their own dying. To become a crowd is to keep out death. To break off from the crowd is to risk death as an individual, to face dying alone. Crowds came for this reason above all others. They were there to be a crowd."

Murray sat across the room. His eyes showed a deep gratitude. I had been generous with the power and madness at my disposal, allowing my subject to be associated with an infinitely lesser figure, a fellow who sat in La-Z-Boy chairs and shot out TVs. It was not a small matter. We all had an aura to maintain, and in sharing mine with a friend I was risking the very things that made me untouchable.

People gathered round, students and staff, and in the mild din of half heard remarks and orbiting voices I realized we were now a crowd. Not that I needed a crowd around me now. Least of all now. Death was strictly a professional matter here. I was comfortable with it, I was on top of it. Murray made his way to my side and escorted me from the room, parting the crowd with his fluttering hand.

Roddy Doyle

Roddy Doyle, a former schoolteacher at a community school in North Dublin, is best known for his so-called Barrytown trilogy, which focuses on the adventures of the Rabbitte clan, a working-class family who live in North Dublin. His novels rely less on narrative than dialogue, and earthy dialogue at that— Doyle has a keen ear for the nuances, often profane, of ordinary Dublin speech. His mastery of slang and colloquialisms can be quite hilarious. His popular novel, The Commitments *(1987), was made into an equally popular film (1991), followed by* The Snapper *(1990) and* The Van *(1991). Subsequent novels,* Paddy Clarke Ha Ha Ha *(1993),* The Woman Who Walked into Doors *(1996), and* A Star Called Henry *(1999), continued to explore working-class Dublin's raw underbelly, with terrific results. In 2002, Doyle told the story of his parents rather uneventful life in* Rory & Ita. *His latest novel,* Oh Play That Thing *(2004), the sequel to* A Star Called Henry, *follows Henry Smart from Ireland to New York to Chicago, where he becomes the unofficial manager of a young Louis Armstrong. In the following excerpt from* The Commitments, *Jimmy Rabbitte, the leader of the Dublin soul band, interviews a potential band member—a God-loving, scooter-driving trumpet player named Joey The Lips Fagan.*

From
The Commitments

Things were motoring.

James Clifford had said yes. Loads of people called looking for J. Rabbitte over the weekend. Jimmy was interested in two of them: a drummer, Billy Mooney from Raheny, and Dean Fay from Coolock who had a saxophone but admitted that he was only learning how to Make It Talk. There were more callers on Monday. Jimmy liked none of them. He took phone numbers and threw them in the bin.

He judged on one question: influences.

—Who're your influences?

—U2.

—Simple Minds.

—Led Zeppelin.

—No one really.

They were the most common answers. They failed.

—Jethro Tull an' Bachman Turner Overdrive.

Jimmy shut the door on that one without bothering to get the phone number. He didn't even open the door to three of them. A look out his parents' bedroom window at them was enough.

—Who're your influences? he'd asked Billy Mooney.

—Your man, Animal from The Muppets.

Dean Fay had said Clarence Clemons and the guy from Madness. He didn't have the sax long. His uncle had given it to him because he couldn't play it any more himself because one of his lungs had collapsed.

Jimmy was up in his room on Tuesday night putting clean socks on when Jimmy Sr., the da, came in.

—Come 'ere, you, said Jimmy Sr.—Are you sellin' drugs or somethin'?

—I AM NOT, said Jimmy.

—Then why are all these cunts knockin' at the door?

—I'm auditionin'.

—You're wha'?

—Aud-ish-un-in. We're formin' a group. —A band.

—You?

—Yeah.

Jimmy Sr. laughed.

—Dickie fuckin' Rock.

He started to leave but turned at the door.

—There's a little fucker on a scooter lookin' for yeh downstairs.

When Jimmy got down to the door he saw that his da had been right. It was a little fucker and he had a scooter, a wreck of a yoke. He was leaning on it.

—Yeah? said Jimmy.

—God bless you, Brother J. Rabbitte. In answer to your Hot Press query, yes, I have got soul.

—Wha'?

—And I'm not a redneck or a southsider.

—You're the same age as me fuckin' da!

—You may speak the truth, Brother Rabbitte, but I'm sixteen years younger than B.B. King. And six years younger than James Brown.

—You've heard o' James Brown—

—I jammed with the man.

—FUCK OFF!

—Leicester Mecca, '72. Brother James called me on for Superbad. I couldn't give it my best though because I had a bit of a head cold.

He patted the scooter.

—I'd ridden from Holyhead in the rain. I didn't have a helmet. I didn't have anything. Just Gina.

—Who's she?

—My trumpet. My mentor always advised me to imagine that the mouthpiece was a woman's nipple. I chose Gina Lollabrigida's. A fine woman.

He stared at Jimmy. There wasn't a trace of a grin on him.

—I'm sure you've noticed already, Brother Rabbitte, it was wild advice because if it had been Gina Lollabrigida's nipple I'd have been sucking it, not blowing into it.

Jimmy didn't know what was going on here. He tried to take control of the interview.

—What's your name, pal?

—Joseph Fagan, said the man.

He was bald too, now that he'd taken his helmet off.

—Joey The Lips Fagan, he said.

—Eh———Come again?

—Joey The Lips Fagan.

—An' I'm Jimmy The Bollix Rabbitte.

—I earned my name for my horn playing, Brother Rabbitte. How did you earn yours?

Jimmy pointed a finger at him.

—Don't get snotty with me, son.

—I get snotty with no man.

—Better bleedin' not. ——An' are YOU tryin' to tell me that yeh played with James Brown?

—Among others, Brother.

—Like?

—Have we all night? ——Screaming Jay Hawkins, Big Joe Turner, Martha Reeves, Sam Cooke, poor Sam, Sinatra. ——Never again. The man is a thug. ——Otis Redding, Lord rest his sweet soul, Joe Tex, The Four Tops, Stevie Wonder, Little Stevie then. He was only eleven. A pup. ——More?

—Yeah.

—Let's see. ——Wilson Pickett, Jackie Wilson, Sam an' Dave, Eddie Floyd, Booker T. and the MGs of course, Joe Tex.

—Yeh said him already.

—Twice. Em ——an unusual one, Jimi Hendrix. Although, to be honest with you, I don't think poor Jimi knew I was there. ——Bobby Bland, Isaac Hayes, Al Green.

—You've been fuckin' busy.

—You speak the truth, Brother Rabbitte. And there's more. Blood, Sweat and Tears. The Tremeloes. I know, I know, I have repented. ——Peter Tosh, George Jones, The Stranglers. Nice enough dudes under the leather. I turned up for The Stones on the wrong day. The day after. They were gone.

—Yeh stupid sap, yeh.

—I know. ——Will that do? ——Oh yeah, and The Beatles.

—The Beatles, said Jimmy.

—Money for jam, said Joey The Lips. —ALL YOU NEED IS LOVE ——DOO DUH DOO DUH DOO.

—Was tha' you?

—Indeed it was me, Brother. Five pounds, three and sixpence. A fair whack in those days. ——I couldn't stand Paul, couldn't take to him. I was up on the roof for Let It Be. But I stayed well back. I'm not a very photogenic Brother. I take a shocking photograph.

By now Jimmy was believing Joey The Lips. A question had to be asked.

—Wha' do yeh want to join US for?

—I'm tired of the road, said Joey The Lips. —I've come home. And my mammy isn't very well.

Jimmy knew he was being stupid, and cheeky, asking the next question but he asked it anyway.

—Who're your influences?

—I admit to no influences but God My Lord, said Joey The Lips. —The Lord blows my trumpet.

—Does he? said Jimmy.

—And the walls come tumbling down.

Joey The Lips explained: —I went on the road nine, no ten maybe eleven years ago with a gospel outfit, The Alabama Angels, featuring Sister Julie Bob Mahony. They brought me to God. I repented, I can tell you that for nothing, Brother Rabbitte. I used to be one mother of a sinner. A terrible man. But The Lord's not a hard man, you know. He doesn't kick up at the odd drink or a swear word now and again. Even a Sister, if you treat her with proper respect.

Jimmy had nothing to say yet. Joey The Lips carried on.

—The Lord told me to come home. Ed Winchell, a Baptist reverend on Lenox Avenue in Harlem, told me. But The Lord told him to tell me. He said he was watching something on TV about the feuding Brothers in Northern Ireland and The Lord told the Reverend Ed that the Irish Brothers had no soul, that they needed some soul. And pretty fucking quick! Ed told me to go back to Ireland and blow some soul into the Irish Brothers. The Brothers wouldn't be shooting the asses off each other if they had soul. So said Ed. I'm not a Baptist myself but I've a lot of time for the Reverend Ed.

Jimmy still had nothing to say.

—Am I in? Joey The Lips asked.

—Fuck, yes, said Jimmy. —Fuckin' sure you're in. —Are yeh on the phone?

—Jesus on the mainline, said Joey The Lips, —tell him what you want. 463221.

Jimmy took it down.

—I'll be in touch with yeh. Definitely. The lads'll have to see—to meet yeh.

Joey The Lips threw the leg over his scooter. His helmet was back on.

—All God's chillun got wings, he said, and he took off out the gate, over the path and down the road.

Jimmy was delighted. He knew now that everything was going to be alright. The Commitments were going to be. They had Joey The Lips Fagan. And that man had enough soul for all of them. He had God too.

Robert Dunn

There's something about the early days of rock and roll that appeals to writers. In Pink Cadillac *(2001), Robert Dunn tells a haunting fable about the writing and recording of a classic song from another musical era, about a lost 45, that seems to represent everything that was good and mysterious about that time. The story takes place in a magical roadhouse outside of Memphis, owned by Thomas "Bearcat" Johnson, a blues entrepreneur who has fallen on hard times, and his common-law wife, blues singer Sonesta Clarke. We also meet Dell Dellaplane, a white saxophone player, and Daisy Holliday, a young white singer who has a voice that stops people in their tracks. Along the way, Daisy encounters a young Elvis Presley. It is he who gives Daisy the pink Cadillac of the title. Almost two decades before Dunn's novel was published, Bruce Springsteen, in 1984, released "Pink Cadillac," a rowdy homage to a car that has come to represent the ultimate in decadence. Robert Dunn is also the author of* Cutting Time: A Novel of the Blues. *He has published short fiction and poems in the* New Yorker, *the* Atlantic, *and other publications. His music group, Thin Wild Mercury, performs often in New York City. For more information, see* **www.coralpress.com**.

From
Pink Cadillac

She loved to play man tricks on men, and they came easy to her. Specially mechanicals. Even before her mother died and everything went to hell there'd been some things her daddy taught her good, what with Daisy not having a brother, even though there were other things she wished she'd never had to learn. But cars? Cars and trucks and tractors, she knew inside out. Hunting. Trapping. Fishing. Gutting a fish. Gutting a pig. . . .

She could tell the shorter man and the bigger man were put out. They stood round the engine, watched her work her magic, and started making *Oh, that looks easy* noises. *That wasn't nothing. We coulda done that.*

But the pretty boy/man with the greasy black hair and the bold sideburns, the splatter of acne and the luscious eyes, just stood back in admiration, asked her name.

"Daisy Holliday. Two *l*'s."

"Elvis Presley," the boy/man said, holding out a delicate white hand. He looked to see if there was recognition, but saw none. "Only one *l*."

"That's a curious name."

"You don't know who he is?" the short man said with a straining upward voice.

"Do you know who *I* am?" Daisy said.

Elvis took a step back, regarded Daisy with direct interest. "So, who are you?"

"I'm a singer."

The small man and the big man started snickering.

"You mean," Elvis said in a drawl, "you're no Formula One auto mechanic, you just do that in your spare time?"

"I'm on my way to Memphis to sing." Dug-in-her-heels determined, Elvis could see that.

"And you're walking?" A lift of his eyebrow. He loved to flirt with girls and was still astonished at how ready they were these days to flirt back.

A smile from this very pretty, if dirty and ragged girl. She wore her miles on her, but they hadn't really worn her down. She kept a fresh-burst energy, like a flower just popped out of the bud.

"Not anymore." She looked from Elvis Presley to the small man, who was Elvis's guitarist, Scotty Moore, and the larger one, who was his bassist, Bill Black, and when Elvis started laughing, she knew she was home free.

When Daisy started singing, she was on top of the rhythm like petals and leaves. Her tone was crystal-bell clear, the words dropping just right.

She started off the first chorus singing *"How long the road to Jesus,"* but it just didn't work, and the next time she sang it—and through the rest of the song—she was without thinking changing the words, and the chorus rang out, *"How long the road to love."*

At that Dell stepped back, a smile on his face. He went low with his sax, under the melody, blowing low, growling notes that just seemed to push Daisy along.

The amazing thing was, you were in that audience and closed your eyes—and almost everyone had their eyes closed by now—you were dead sure that it was a negro lady up there singing. There was that husk and depth, and that pain and all-powerful release, and you were thinking, It's like Bessie, but newer; like Ruth Brown, but saltier; like a young'un you'd heard recently, Etta James, yeah, just an awful lot like her.

But that wasn't just it, because there was a sweet country fizz on top of everything, sunny day, hay wagon—this picture you got was this black, black woman with this white, white hair . . . and a big polka-dot kerchief tied round it to boot. This was your inner eyes playing tricks on you, and so you opened 'em, and this is what you saw: A blonde-ponytail-swaying, slim, plain-cotton-clothes-wearing, rosy-cheeked, obsidian-souled girl, couldn't have been over 20, with a voice that sounded like passed-down ebony, singing so powerful it was like she was pulling it all up from a bottomless well.

Dawn broke over them a few hours later, pink and yellow-blue over the river.

They woke in each other's arms, on a blanket Daisy had found in the Cadillac's trunk, their clothes mussed but fully intact.

"Sweet," was the first word out of Daisy's mouth. She breathed it gentle and cottony, a benediction to the morning.

Dell stretched his arms beside her, then quickly popped onto his side, propped up by his elbow. His determined look startled her.

"What?" she said.

"I want Bearcat to hear our song."

"It's *our* song now?"

"It was always our song."

"Oh, men. Whoever says women got all the soft thinking."

"What's soft about me having written you a song?"

"Oh. You mean?"

"I mean, we got to come up with some lyrics. I was thinking earlier, chorus should go *'I don't care if I never look back / in my Pink Cadillac.'*" He sang the melody softly.

"You mean, like somebody taking off?" Daisy yawned, brought a hand to her mouth. "Sorry," she breathed.

Dell was looking direct at her.

"I mean, like the Cadillac sets you free."

"Is that what you want, freedom?"

"Doesn't everyone?" Dell said.

Daisy yawned again. "Damn," she said, "being up this early, makes me think of the summer I was twelve. I spent it at my Aunt Ruth's slopping pigs." She grimaced.

"So what do you think?"

"You mean—*what?*"

"Lyrics."

Daisy took a deep breath. "How about, *'You can keep the magic in Bearcat's mojo sack, I'd rather have my Pink Cadillac'?*"

Dell frowned. "That doesn't sound like any pop song."

"Just a notion."

"No, no, pink Cadillac, think wheels, moving, getting yourself *along*—" Dell tooted the melody. "That's what the music says."

"I see."

"Come on, help me with a verse. What's the story gonna be?"

"O.K., how about this," Daisy said. "Girl comes to town, girl gets Cadillac, then the girl meets a boy—" Wide, playful eyes up at Dell.

"Then what?" Bright young smile.

"Well, if it's storytellin' like out in Hollywood, after the boy gets the girl, he's got to lose her, then—"

Dell looked suddenly chastened. "I don't know if that's the right story—"

"Why not? You're the one who wants it to go, 'I don't care if I never look back. . . .'"

Dell jumped up and said, "The important thing is that I've got the whole melody. We gotta get Bearcat to hear it. Come on, we'll think up some kind of lyrics on the way." When they were standing, Dell waited for Daisy to pick up the blanket and fold it. Then he went over and climbed into the driver's seat.

Daisy, blanket clenched before her, stood next to the open window.

"Come on," Dell said, "get in."

"Aren't we, um, forgetting something?"

"What?" Dell said, consternation in his tone. "You got hours yet till you got to get to your waitress job. Come on."

"No, silly," Daisy said, standing firm by the driver's side window. "Whose, um, Cadillac is this?"

"You mean, you're gonna *drive?*"

"Hey, somebody's gotta take us where we gotta go. Remember Elvis?"

Dell glowered for a second, then scooted across the wide leather seat. Daisy got in and fired up the car with one turn.

As she pulled away from the river, she punched her foot on the accelerator and the car burned down the road.

"Whoeee!" she cried. "Maybe you are right, we ain't *never* gonna look back."

She was in love, and the power of her love scared her. Well, the object of her love scared her a little, too, but how could she not be absolutely gaga? Except that it wasn't a man, it was a car. Not just any car, of course, but her pink Cadillac.

When she wasn't waitressing or at the roadhouse, she spent far too much time just driving around in it, through the streets of Memphis, down Poplar to Third, then back out Union, all the while tooling slow, loving the way people would stop on the sidewalk and gawk at her; and then out into the countryside, where she could jam the pedal to the floor and feel the beast inside it leap down the road. More than the actual car itself, Daisy loved more and more the *idea* of it—the idea of her, Daisy Holliday from Bent Knee, Kentucky, owning and being known in and talking and dreaming out her life inside her pink Cadillac.

There was something magical about it, no question. Here she was, this backwoods, hick girl, and the car made her so . . . glamorous. No other word for it. Even though she was all unconfidence and nervous newness to Memphis and to singing seriously, in the pink Cadillac not a trace of anxiety was betrayed.

Jeffrey Eugenides

The Virgin Suicides *(1993), the debut novel of Jeffrey Eugenides, is about five sisters—Therese, Mary, Bonnie, Lux, and Cecilia—who live on a tree-lined street in '70s suburbia. All five commit suicide during "the year of the suicides." It is a startling novel with themes that revolve around memory, imagination, and indescribable loss. The story itself is told from the perspective of a group of neighborhood boys who adore the sisters, mostly from afar, and who become obsessed with them. In 1999, the critically acclaimed novel was adapted into an equally effecting film by Sofia Coppola. Eugenides's fiction has appeared in the* New Yorker, *the* Paris Review, *the* Yale Review, *and* Granta, *among others. In this excerpt, we discover that the sisters can only communicate with the outside world through the universal language of music. Quirky and poignant, creepy and chilling, Eugenides creates magic from the most mundane of circumstances.*

From
The Virgin Suicides

In the daytime, the Lisbon house looked vacant. The trash the family put out once a week (also in the middle of the night because no one saw them, not even Uncle Tucker) looked more and more like the refuse of people resigned to a long siege. They were eating canned lima beans. They were flavoring rice with sloppy-joe mix. At night, when the lights signaled, we racked our brains for a way of contacting the girls. Tom Faheem suggested flying a kite with a message alongside the house, but this was voted down on logistical grounds. Little Johnny Buell offered the recourse of tossing the same message on a rock through the girls' windows, but we were afraid the breaking glass would alert Mrs. Lisbon. In the end, the answer was so simple it took a week to come up with.

We called them on the telephone.

In the Larsons' sun-faded phone book, right between Licker and Little, we found the intact listing for Lisbon, Ronald A. It sat halfway down the righthand page, unmarkled by any code or symbol, not even an asterisk referring to an appendix of pain. We stared at it for some time. Then, three index fingers at once, we dialed.

The telephone tolled eleven times before Mr. Lisbon answered. "What's it going to be today?" he said right away in a tired voice. His speech was slurred. We covered the phone and said nothing.

"I'm waiting. Today I'll listen to all your crap."

Another click sounded on the line, like a door opening onto a hollow corridor.

"Look, give us a break, will you?" Mr. Lisbon muttered.

There was a pause. Assorted breathing, mechanically reformulated, met in electronic space. Then Mr. Lisbon spoke in a voice unlike his own, a high screech . . . Mrs. Lisbon had grabbed the receiver.

"Why don't you leave us alone!" she shouted, and slammed down the phone.

We stayed on. For five more seconds her furious breath blew through the receiver, but just as we expected, the line didn't go dead.

On the other end, an obscure presence waited.

We called out a tentative hello. After a moment, a faint, crippled voice returned, "Hi."

We hadn't heard the Lisbon girls speak in a long time, but the voice didn't jog our memories. It sounded—perhaps because the speaker was whispering—irreparably altered, diminished, the voice of a child fallen down a well. We didn't know which girl it was, and didn't know what to say. Still, we hung on together—her, them, us—and at some adjacent recess in the Bell telephone system another line connected. A man began talking underwater to a woman. We could half hear their conversation ("I thought maybe a salad"... "A salad? You're killing me with these salads"), but then another circuit must have freed, because the couple were shunted off suddenly, leaving us in buzzing silence, and the voice, raw but stronger now, said, "Shit. See you later," and the phone was hung up.

We called again next day, at the same time, and were answered on the first ring. We waited a moment for safety's sake, then proceeded with the plan we'd devised the night before. Holding the phone to one of Mr. Larson's speakers, we played the song which most thoroughly communicated our feelings to the Lisbon girls. We can't remember the song's title now, and an extensive search through records of the period has proved unsuccessful. We do, however, recall the essential sentiments, which spoke of hard days, long nights, a man waiting outside a broken telephone booth hoping it would somehow ring, and rain, and rainbows. It was mostly guitars, except for one interlude where a mellow cello hummed. We played it into the phone, and then Chase Buell gave our number and we hung up.

Next day, same time, our phone rang. We answered it immediately, and after some confusion (the phone was dropped), heard a needle bump down on a record, and the voice of Gilbert O'Sullivan singing through scratches. You may recall the song, a ballad which charts the misfortunes of a young man's life (his parents die, his fiancée stands him up at the altar), each verse leaving him more and more alone. It was Mrs. Eugene's favorite, and we knew it well from hearing her singing along over her simmering pots. The song never meant much to us, speaking as it did of an age we hadn't reached, but once we heard it playing tinily through the receiver, coming from the Lisbon girls, the song made an impact. Gilbert O'Sullivan's elfin voice sounded high enough to be a girl's. The lyrics might have been diary entries whispered into our ears. Though it wasn't their voices we heard, the song conjured their images more vividly than ever. We could feel them, on the other end, blowing dust off the needle, holding the telephone over the spinning black disk, playing the volume low so as not to be overheard. When the song stopped, the needle skated through the inner ring, sending out a repeating click (like the same time lived over and over again). Already Joe Larson had our response ready, and after we played it, the Lisbon girls played theirs, and the evening went on like that. Most of the songs we've forgotten, but a portion of that contrapuntal exchange survives, in pencil, on the back of Demo Karafilis's *Tea for the Tillerman*, where he jotted it. We provide it here:

the Lisbon girls	*"Alone Again, Naturally," Gilbert O'Sullivan*
us	*"You've Got a Friend," James Taylor*
the Lisbon girls	*"Where Do the Children Play?," Cat Stevens*
us	*"Dear Prudence," The Beatles*
the Lisbon girls	*"Candle in the Wind," Elton John*
us	*"Wild Horses," The Rolling Stones*
the Lisbon girls	*"At Seventeen," Janis Ian*
us	*"Time in a Bottle," Jim Croce*
the Lisbon girls	*"So Far Away," Carole King*

Actually, we're not sure about the order. Demo Karafilis scribbled the titles haphazardly. The above order, however, does chart the basic progression of our musical conversation. Because Lux had burned her hard rock, the girls' songs were mostly folk music. Stark plaintive voices sought justice and equality. An occasional fiddle evoked the country the country had once been. The singers had bad skin or wore boots. Song after song throbbed with secret pain. We passed the sticky receiver from ear to ear, the drumbeats so regular we might have been pressing our ears to the girls' chests. Occasionally, we thought we heard them singing along, and it was almost like being at a concert with them. Our songs, for the most part, were love songs. Each selection tried to turn the conversation in a more intimate direction. But the Lisbon girls kept to impersonal topics. (We leaned in and commented on their perfume. They said it was probably the magnolias.) After a while, our songs turned sadder and sappier. That was when the girls played "So Far Away." We noted the shift at once (they had let their hand linger on our wrist) and followed with "Bridge over Troubled Water," turning up the volume because the song expressed more than any other how we felt about the girls, how we wanted to help them. When it finished, we waited for their response. After a long pause, their turntable began grinding again, and we heard the song which even now, in the Muzak of malls, makes us stop and stare back into a lost time:

> *Hey, have you ever tried*
> *Really reaching out for the other side*
> *I may be climbing on rainbows,*
> *But, baby, here goes:*
>
> *Dreams, they're for those who sleep*
> *Life, it's for us to keep*
> *And if you're wandering what this song is leading to*
> *I want to make it with you.*

The line went dead. (Without warning, the girls had thrown their arms around us, confessed hotly into our ears, and fled the room.) For some minutes, we stood motionless, listening to the buzz of the telephone line. Then it began to beep angrily, and a recording told us to hang up our phone and hang it up now.

We had never dreamed the girls might love us back. The notion made us dizzy, and we lay down on the Larsons' carpet, which smelled of pet deodorizer and, deeper down, of pet. For a long time no one spoke. But little by little, as we shifted bits of information in our heads, we saw things in a new light. Hadn't the girls invited us to their party last year? Hadn't they known our names and addresses? Rubbing spy holes in grimy windows, hadn't they been looking out to see us? We forgot ourselves and held hands, smiling with closed eyes. On the stereo Garfunkel began hitting his high notes, and we didn't think of Cecilia. We thought only of Mary, Bonnie, Lux, and Therese, stranded in life, unable to speak to us until now, in this inexact, shy fashion. We went over their last months in school, coming up with new recollections. Lux had forgotten her math book one day and had to share with Tom Faheem. In the margin, she had written, "I want to get out of here." How far did that wish extend? Thinking back, we decided the girls had been trying to talk to us all along, to elicit our help, but we'd been too infatuated to listen. Our surveillance had been so focused we missed nothing but a simple returned gaze. Who else did they have to turn to? Not their parents. Nor the neighborhood. Inside their house they were prisoners; outside, lepers. And so they hid from the world, waiting for someone—for us—to save them.

But in the following days we tried to call the girls back without success. The phone rang on hopelessly, forlornly. We pictured the device howling under pillows while the girls reached for it in vain. Unable to get through, we bought *The Best of Bread*, playing "Make It with You" over and over. There was grand talk of tunnels, of starting from the Larsons' basement and going beneath the street. The dirt could be carried out in our pant legs and emptied during strolls like in *The Great Escape*. The drama of this pleased us so much we momentarily forgot that our tunnel had already been built: the storm sewers. We checked the sewers, however, and found them full of water: the lake had risen again this year. It didn't matter. Mr. Buell had an extension ladder we could easily prop against the girls' windows. "Just like eloping," Eugie Kent said, and the words made our minds drift, to a red-faced, small-town justice of the peace, and a sleeper compartment in a train passing through blue wheat fields at night. We imagined all sorts of things, waiting for the girls to signal for us.

None of this—the record-playing, the flashing lights, the Virgin cards—ever got into the papers, of course. We thought of our communication with the Lisbon girls as a sacred confidence, even after such fidelity ceased to make sense. Ms. Perl (who later published a book with a chapter dedicated to the Lisbon girls) described their spirits sinking further and further in an inevitable progression. She shows their pathetic last attempts to make a life—Bonnie's tending the shrine, Mary's wearing bright sweaters—but every stone the girls built shelter with has, for Mrs. Perl, an underside of mud and worms. The candles were a two-way mirror between worlds: they called Cecilia back, but also called her sisters to join her. Mary's pretty sweaters only showed a desperate adolescent urge to be beautiful, while Therese's baggy sweatshirts revealed a "lack of self-esteem."

We knew better. Three nights after the record playing, we saw Bonnie bring a black trunk into her bedroom. She put it on her bed and began filling it with clothes and books. Mary appeared and threw in her climate mirror. They argued about the trunk's contents and, in a huff, Bonnie took out some of the clothes she'd put in, giving Mary more room for her things: a cassette player, a hair dryer, and the object we didn't understand until later, a cast-iron doorstop. We had no idea what the girls were doing, but we noticed the change in their demeanor at once. They moved with a new purpose. Their aimlessness was gone. It was Paul Baldino who interpreted their actions:

"Looks like they're going to make a break for it," he said, putting down the binoculars. He made this conclusion with the confident air of someone who had seen relatives disappear to Sicily or South America, and we believed him at once. "Five dollars gets you ten those girls are out of here by the end of the week."

He was right, though not in the way he intended. The last note, written on the back of a laminated picture of the Virgin, arrived in Chase Buell's mailbox on June 14. It said simply: "Tomorrow. Midnight. Wait for our signal."

Bill Flanagan

Former music journalist and now senior vice president of the TV music chan-
nel VH1, Bill Flanagan has written several books, all nonfiction, including
Written in My Soul: Conversations with Rock's Great Songwriters
(1987), Last of the Moe Haircuts *(1986), and* U2: At the End of the
World *(1995).* A&R *(2001) is his first novel. The book's protagonist is Jim*
Cantone, the A&R man for WorldWide Records. His job is to sign up new
talent for his record label. Cantone, a rather naive young father from Maine,
seems far too nice to survive in the cutthroat world that he finds himself in.
On the other hand, his boss, J. B. Booth, has no qualms about doing whatev-
er needs to be done to turn a profit, while the label's millionaire founder, Wild
Bill DeGaul, is too busy enjoying his decadent lifestyle to really see what's
going on. Meanwhile, Cantone tries to do right by the band he discovered,
Jerusalem. A&R *is a witty and knowing look at the behind-the-scenes*
machinations—the power, the glamour, and the runaway ambition—that
engulf the music world.

From
A&R

Cantone pulled his easygoing subordinate Flute Bjerke into his office and asked him to translate some arcane bookkeeping gobbledygook between A&R and product management. It looked to Jim like doublebilling, and Flute's signature was on a pile of odd documents. Flute kept smiling and repeating that this was just how it always worked, the forms were filled out by the product managers and sent to A&R for signatures before going on to accounts payable. Jim backed up and walked through what was wrong—or at least confusing—about the system as he read it. Jim went through his entire thought process three times, holding up the forms to illustrate each point as he did. Flute smiled and nodded.

Finally Jim gave up and said, "So who would know?"

"Business affairs, I guess," Flute said. Then he smiled inscrutably at Jim and said, "I know where you got that shirt."

"What?"

"That shirt. You had that made at Veston and Arles, didn't you?"

"My shirt? No." He looked at his shoulder. "My wife gave me this for Christmas."

"She got it made at Veston and Arles. Very nice."

Jim let Flute go back to whatever he did all day. He knew his shirt came from the Gap. It was pressed, which set it apart from the combat gear he wore most days. Jim was inclined to khaki T-shirts under loose military jacket shirts. He often wore army pants with multiple pockets or imitations from the secondhand stores on St. Mark's Place. He wore sneakers in the summer and work boots in winter. He had been dressing like this as long as he'd been in New York. It was only a slight variation on how he dressed in college. Bjerke's comment brought to the top of Jim's mind a feeling that had been creeping up on him since his first day at WorldWide.

This was a place where people judged you by what you wore. Flute Bjerke, a bit of a traditionalist, still dressed in the classic middle-period David Geffen ensemble aped by aspiring music honchos since the early eighties: short hair, pressed jeans, loafers without socks, a simple but expensive T-shirt, and a thousand-dollar jacket. Most of the WorldWide brass had moved on with the times to a slick but comfortable post-ICM elegance.

Jim did not want to be shallow or give in to some unspoken corporate dress code. Neither did he want to be one of those sad cases who keeps trying to dress like a kid years after it stops being appropriate.

I hope I'm not turning into one of those lingerers, Jim said to the ghost of his reflection in the window. Oh, those lingerers were sad cases. He had seen them in rock clubs as long as he could remember. Middle-aged men squeezing into tight pants and then walking like cowboys from the pain. Bald men growing long ponytails. Men with expanding melon heads who wrapped desperate goatees around their double chins. Squat gnomes in faded tour T-shirts and black jeans with baggy asses and even—the saddest sight of all—the Levi's label with the waist measurement ripped off.

Jim had long ago promised himself that when the jig was up he'd know it, and he'd make smooth the midlife transition from beauty to dignity. He realized that no man ever thinks that day is here, which is why those poor pony-tailed baggy-assed melon-headed gnomes keep combing their hair forward to fool only themselves.

Is thirty too young for a midlife crisis? Or, Jim wondered, is a midlife crisis what happens when a man keeps doing what he's always done but starts to look ridiculous doing it? A twenty-four-year-old who buys his first motorcycle just came into some money and can finally afford to satisfy a dream. A forty-year-old who buys his first motorcycle is battling menopause.

Jim was thirty. He wasn't sure what that meant these days. It still felt young, but maybe that was self-deluding. When he was nineteen he worked summers with a thirty-year-old guy who thought he was one of the kids. It was pathetic.

Like many of his friends, Jim had extended his teenage years through most of his twenties. His job at Feast had been an extension of adolescent interests. The last three years had been a series of shocks and adjustments: Jane getting pregnant; the decision to have the baby; the baby being twins; getting married; Jane quitting work; leaving Feast and moving into the high tax bracket at WorldWide. This career he had stumbled into out of college without consideration was now a necessity.

Jim had to work out how to become a man. How much of your youth were you meant to keep, and what should a man let go? He wished, in a new way, that his father were alive to talk with. For years after his dad's death Jim had taken comfort in being able to know what his father would say about most big issues that faced him. But now his father had been dead for more of Jim's life than he had been alive, and on these middle-aged matters, he had no idea what the old man would think. This next bit Jim would have to work out for himself.

He picked up hints like an illegal immigrant learning English from the radio. When the other male SVPs were in public they'd make small talk about sports or investments or the opening figures on the latest movie. (Sex was not generally on the agenda, as the wrong word in front of the wrong person could plant a red flag in your personnel file.) But in private groups of no more than two or three, when there was no one around to overhear, they would whisper about hair-dressers, tailors, and personal trainers like second wives at the country club social. Jim learned that if he played along a little, if he asked where one of his buddies got those shoes, or mentioned that he was worried about a strand of gray, he would be invited into a brotherhood of secret enthusiasm and shared passion. All around him, he came to understand, high-powered middle-aged heterosexual men were enhancing their complexions with creams and whitening their teeth, trading diets, comparing strategies to thicken and color their hair, poking in contact lenses, sharing tips on cleansing scrubs and worry-ing about—no other word for it—their figures.

It was as if every boy who dreamed of growing up to be Keith Richards had decided as a man to become Felix Unger.

Jim noticed that among the well-groomed, there was a subtle exclusion of those who remained off-the-rack. On three different occasions Jim heard executives with expensive dental work and beau-tiful skin choose to pass over qualified Oscar Madisons for important assignments or, in one case, a promotion with the same subtle dismissal. "He's a talented guy, but he's not really buttoned-down."

Jim studied himself in the mirrored wall as he rode up the escalator and wondered if those *GQ*-groomed arbiters considered him sufficiently buttoned-down, figuratively and literally.

Had Jim been a wiseass or a finger pointer he might have mocked these conceits and become cocky about his own good looks and athletic health. But he was by nature a joiner, and so he overcame a reluctance born of years of low budgets and went out to buy some new clothes.

He went to Emporio Armani but he couldn't handle the salesman telling him to have a drink at the little Armani bar and "Put it on my tab" while he rang up two hundred dollars' worth of cummerbund.

He went to Barney's and saw a nice brown sport coat and a blue Sunday go-to-meeting suit. He tried them on, got his inseam measured, and felt pretty good about it. But when the clerk said, "Two thousand, eight hundred dollars," Jim could not let go of his credit card. He could afford it, but he could not stand it. He could buy a jacket and suit indistinguishable from these at Sears, and give the three-thousand-dollar difference to PETA.

He went home a failure.

"I don't see any bags," Jane said. "Getting alterations?"

"I bought two pairs of black wingtip lace-up shoes," Jim said. "One with little airholes for summer, like my grandfather used to wear. But it was, like, three grand for a blue suit with a pair of pants. I couldn't do it, Jane."

"Then don't do it. It's only clothes. What do you care about the opinion of anyone who would judge you by what you wear?"

"I feel like some kind of arrested adolescent that I can't get this together. The senior staff at work all dress a certain way. And the people who dress the way I do now are sort of the rank and file. I don't want to look like I'm copping an attitude toward the other executives and I don't want to seem like I'm condescending to the staff."

Jane turned away and started going through the bills. "No one but you is thinking about this. You should forget it."

Jim felt foolish. He went to work the next day in his old army pants, with a starched white shirt and a tie. One of the guys who bought the mail around said, "Court date?"

At lunch he heard the head of business affairs say to the head of human resources, "I like his policies but I can't vote for a man who wears a Timex watch. What will Wall Street think?"

In the restroom Legal advised Marketing, "If you tuck your undershirt in your underpants your shirt won't punch up at the waist."

That afternoon Jim went to Mano 2 Mano, a reasonably priced clothing store on Sixth Avenue, and bought two suits, six blue dress shirts, eight pairs of socks, cuff links, two blazers, and three pairs of dark blue slacks—for a total price considerably less than what the suit and jacket cost at Barney's.

He was so hopped-up from his breakthrough that he even bought some workshirts at Abercrombie & Fitch that were exactly like the ones he usually bought at the Salvation Army except that these cost seventy bucks. Home and triumphant, he wrote a two-thousand-dollar check to People for the Ethical Treatment of Animals and put it in an envelope and stuck on a stamp.

Jane kept her feelings to herself.

On his third day dressed for success, he learned a lesson about cost-cutting. He stooped for a pee on his way to a staff meeting. He flushed, closed up, and the zipper came off in his hand. It did not just snap or break—it lifted right off his pants like the skeleton coming out of a split fish.

He gathered his pants together as well as he could, and closed his jacket to try to disguise his open fly as he walked stiff-legged down the corridor and sunk into a chair and under the table. Al Hamilton, who paid no discernible notice to fashion, came and sat next to him, and in the moments while the others at the table were rustling papers and making small talk, Jim whispered, "Al, whatever you do, don't ask me to stand up in front of the group. The zipper just came off my new pants."

Hamilton glanced down at Jim's suit and said matter-of-factly, "What did you do? Buy from Mano 2 Mano?"

That's how Cantone, a simple boy from Maine, ended up in Prada.

Cantone was in his office going through a pile of tapes. He had put off listening to the A-list demos from unsigned acts bought in by his own department, top lawyers, big managers, and friends of Booth. Now he was trying to make up for lost time, shoveling away at the pile. He sat in a big armchair next to the stereo and rotated DATs, cassettes, CDs, and the dreaded audio-visual demos presented by the representation of artists more photogenic than musical. "To get this one," the code went, "you need to see the whole package."

In his lap he had a schoolboy's ringed binder. He made a list of names down the left side and filled in his comments. He tried to listen to each tape all the way through but sometimes he had to fast-forward.

The longer he listened the shorter his comments got:

"Gangsta rapper with ANTI-gangsta rap. Send to R&B division. *Could be on to something here.*"

"Boy group à la Backstreet/NSync. White? Second song good. Too late."

"Reunion with two of five original members. No one misses them."

"Hippie jam band. Not as good as a lot of acts who don't sell anyway."

"Female rocker. If Bob Seger were a girl. Too 1998."

"NOT Stupid-smart. Stupid-stupid."

"Puffy copy—bad pitch."

"Britney of France? Sounds like Tiffany of Taiwan."

"John Cafferty imitator."

He came to the next tape and stopped. It was from a musician named Paul Slocum whom Cantone had loved as a kid. He had three of Slocum's albums and had played them every day of eleventh grade. He saw him play at college gigs and clubs around New England. Slocum had not had a record deal in five or six years. He had written Cantone a personal note mentioning the name of a mutual friend in Maine.

Cantone put it on. It was good, it reminded him of home—which made him worry that it was dated. He listened more. It was good. But it was probably not as good as Slocum's best work, which no one bought. The third song was great. He rewound and played it again. This one could have been on one of the albums Jim had loved so much as a teenager. But maybe Jim couldn't trust his own reaction, was bringing more sympathy to it than another listener would. Slocum was old now, forty at least. There was no photo included. Jim read the letter again. It struggled to be cordial, but there was a touch of desperation. Slocum was tugging at his sleeve. Thank goodness he doesn't know what a big fan I was, Jim thought. I'm glad he doesn't know I'm the same kid who used to wait by the back door after the show to talk to him. He was nice enough, then, but pretty smug, kind of condescending. Of course, I was seventeen with my mouth hanging open. He was nice enough.

Jim rewound the tape again. He didn't know how to separate his feelings about Slocum's old records from his obligation to evaluate the tape objectively. DeGaul, he was sure, would like it, but DeGaul was not part of this process. If they followed DeGaul's taste WorldWide would sign Bo Diddley. No one knew that better than DeGaul, so he stayed out of it. Jim had learned that was a sign of real power. When asked for a favor the man close to power rushes to prove he can do it. The man with real power smiles and says, "Oh, I would love to but my people don't let me get involved with that sort of thing! They're afraid I'll mess it up!"

Jim put the Slocum tape in his bag to take home. He knew he'd carry it back and forth for a few days and then empty out his bag and add it to a stack of other undecideds where it would be slowly buried. It would be kinder to Paul Slocum to just say no. But Jim was sure that if there was even a tiny chance of a yes down the line, Slocum would rather be in the pile of possibilities.

Jim wondered if the pressure of his job was corrupting his ability to trust his own taste.

His assistant leaned in. "Booth's on the phone."

She was supposed to be holding all his calls, but Jim was grateful for the excuse. He answered and Booth said, "Go home and put on a suit, we're going to a political fund-raiser in the Hamptons."

"Not that I don't appreciate the invitation, J. B., but I wish I'd known earlier."

"You're filling in for DeGaul. Our CEO can't tear himself away from jungleland for a dinner with the next president of the United States. Stay on the line, Leilani will give you the details."

William Gibson

Considered one of the fathers of cyberpunk literature, William Gibson is the author of the seminal science-fiction novels, Neuromancer *(1984) and* Virtual Light *(1994).* Idoru *(1996) is a prophetic, cyberpunk thriller that takes place in twenty-first century Tokyo, after a devastating millennial earthquake has caused geographical and cultural havoc. Rez, the lead singer for the rock band Lo/Rez, is said to be engaged to an "idoru" or "idol singer," an artificial celebrity software creation, which sets in motion two recurring plot lines: a fourteen-year-old teenager, Chia Pet McKenzie, is sent by the Seattle chapter of the band's fan club to Tokyo to discover the truth while Colin Laney, a data specialist for a television network named Slitscan, uncovers a pop-culture scandal. An excerpt from the latter follows.*

From
Idoru

When Laney had worked for Slitscan, his supervisor was named Kathy Torrance. Palest of pale blonds. A pallor bordering on translucence, certain angles of light suggesting not blood but some fluid the shade of summer straw. On her left thigh the absolute indigo imprint of something twisted and multibarbed, an expensively savage pictoglyph. Visible each Friday, when she made it her habit to wear shorts to work.

She complained, always, that the nature of celebrity was much the worse for wear. Strip-mined, Laney gathered, by generations of her colleagues.

She propped her feet on the ledge of a hotdesk. She wore meticulous little reproductions of lineman's boots, buckled across the instep and stoutly laced to the ankle. He looked at her legs, their taut sweep from wooly sock tops to the sandpapered fringe of cut-off jeans. The tattoo looked like something from another planet, a sign or message burned in from the depths of space, left there for mankind to interpret.

He asked her what she meant. She peeled a mint-flavored toothpick from its wrapper. Eyes he suspected were gray regarded him through mint-tinted contacts.

"Nobody's really famous anymore, Laney. Have you noticed that?"

"No."

"I mean *really* famous. There's not much fame left, not in the old sense. Not enough to go around."

"The old sense?"

"We're the media, Laney. We *make* these assholes celebrities. It's a push-me, pull-you routine. They come to us to be created." Vibram cleats kicked concisely off the hotdesk. She tucked her boots in, heels against denim haunches, white knees hiding her mouth. Balanced there on the pedestal of the hotdesk's articulated Swedish chair.

"Well," Laney said, going back to his screen, "that's still fame, isn't it?"

"But is it real?"

He looked back at her.

"We learned to print money off this stuff," she said. "Coin of our realm. Now we've printed too much; even the audience knows. It shows in the ratings."

Laney nodded, wishing she'd leave him to his work.

"Except," she said, parting her knees so he could see her say it, "when we decide to destroy one."

Behind her, past the anodyzed chainlink of the Cage, beyond a framing rectangle of glass that filtered out every tint of pollution, the sky over Burbank was perfectly blank, like a sky-blue paint chip submitted by the contractor of the universe.

The man's left ear was edged with pink tissue, smooth as wax. Laney wondered why there had been no attempt at reconstruction.

"So I'll remember," the man said, reading Laney's eyes.

"Remember what?"

"Not to forget. Sit down."

Laney sat on something only vaguely chairlike, an attenuated construction of black alloy rods and laminated Hexcel. The table was round and approximately the size of a steering wheel. A votive flame licked the air, behind blue grass. The Japanese man with the plaid shirt and metal-framed glasses blinked furiously. Laney watched the large man settle himself, another slender chair-thing lost alarmingly beneath a sumo-sized bulk that appeared to be composed entirely of muscle.

"Done with the jet lag, are we?"

"I took pills." Remembering the SST's silence, its lack of apparent motion.

"Pills," the man said. "Hotel adequate?"

"Yes," Laney said. "Ready for the interview."

"Well then," vigorously rubbing his face with heavily scarred hands. He lowered his hands and stared at Laney, as if seeing him for the first time. Laney, avoiding the gaze of those eyes, took in the man's outfit, some sort of nanopore exercise gear intended to fit loosely on a smaller but still very large man. Of no particular color in the darkness of the Trial. Open from collar to breastbone. Straining against abnormal mass. Exposed flesh tracked and crossed by an atlas of scars, baffling in their variety of shape and texture. "Well, then?"

Laney looked up from the scars. "I'm here for a job interview."

"Are you?"

"Are you the interviewer?"

"Interviewer?" The ambiguous grimace revealing an obvious dental prosthesis.

Laney turned to the Japanese in the round glasses. "Colin Laney."

"Shinya Yamazaki," the man said, extending his hand. They shook. "We spoke on the telephone."

"You're conducting the interview?"

A flurry of blinks. "I'm sorry, no," the man said. And then, "I am a student of existential sociology."

"I don't get it," Laney said. The two opposite said nothing. Shinya Yamazaki looked embarrassed. The one-eared man glowered.

"You're Australian," Laney said to the one-eared man.

"Tazzie," the man corrected. "Sided with the South in the Troubles."

"Let's start over," Laney suggested. "'Paragon-Asia Dataflow.' You them?"

"Persistent bugger."

"Goes with the territory," Laney said. "Professionally, I mean."

"Fair enough." The man raised his eyebrows, one of which was bisected by a twisted pink cable of scar tissue. "Rez, then. What do you think of *him*?"

"You mean the rock star?" Laney asked, after struggling with a basic problem of context.

A nod. The man regarded Laney with utmost gravity.

"From Lo/Rez? The band?" Half Irish, half Chinese. A broken nose, never repaired. Long green eyes.

"What do I *think* of him?"

In Kathy Torrance's system of things, the singer had been reserved a special disdain. She had viewed him as a living fossil, an annoying survival from an earlier, less evolved era. He was at once massively and meaninglessly famous, she maintained, just as he was massively and meaninglessly wealthy. Kathy thought of celebrity as a subtle fluid, a universal element, like the phlogiston of the ancients, something spread evenly at creation through all the universe, but prone now to accrete, under specific conditions, around certain individuals and their careers. Rez, in Kathy's view, had simply lasted too long. Monstrously long. He was affecting the unity of her theory. He was defying the proper order of the food chain. Perhaps there was nothing big enough to eat him, not even Slitscan. And while Lo/Rez, the band, still extruded product on an annoyingly regular basis, in a variety of media, their singer stubbornly refused to destroy himself, murder someone, become active in politics, admit to an interesting substance-abuse problem or an arcane sexual addiction—indeed to do anything at all worthy of an opening segment on Slitscan. He glimmered, dully perhaps, but steadily, just beyond Kathy Torrance's reach. Which was, Laney had always assumed, the real reason for her hating him so.

"Well," Laney said, after some thought, and feeling a peculiar compulsion to attempt a truthful answer, "I remember buying their first album. When it came out."

"Title?" The one-eared man grew graver still.

"Lo Rez Skyline," Laney said, grateful for whatever minute synaptic event had allowed the recall. "But I couldn't tell you how many they've put out since."

"Twenty-six, not counting compilations," said Mr. Yamazaki, straightening his glasses.

Laney felt the pills he'd taken, the ones that were supposed to cushion the jet lag, drop out from under him like some kind of rotten pharmacological scaffolding. The walls of the Trial seemed to grow closer.

"If you aren't going to tell me what this is about," he said to the one-eared man, "I'm going back to the hotel. I'm tired."

"Keith Alan Blackwell," extending his hand. Laney allowed his own to be taken and briefly shaken. The man's palm felt like a piece of athletic equipment. "'Keithy.' We'll have a few drinks and a little chat."

"First you tell me whether or not you're from Paragon-Asia," Laney suggested.

"Firm in question's a couple of lines of code in a machine in a backroom in Lygon Street," Blackwell said. "A dummy, but you could say it's *our* dummy, if that makes you feel better."

"I'm not sure it does," Laney said. "You fly me over to interview for a job, now you're telling me the company I'm supposed to be interviewing for doesn't exist."

"It *exists*," said Keith Alan Blackwell. "It's on the machine in Lygon Street."

A waitress arrived. She wore a shapeless gray cotton boilersuit and cosmetic bruises.

"Big draft. Kirin. Cold one. What's yours, Laney?"

"Iced coffee."

"Coke Lite, please," said the one who'd introduced himself as Yamazaki.

"Fine," said the earless Blackwell, glumly, as the waitress vanished into the gloom.

"I'd appreciate it if you could explain to me what we're doing here," Laney said. He saw that Yamazaki was scribbling frantically on the screen of a small notebook, the lightpen flashing faintly in the dark. "Are you taking this down?" Laney asked.

"Sorry, no. Making note of waitress' costume."

"Why?" Laney asked.

"Sorry," said Yamazaki, saving what he'd written and turning off the notebook. He tucked the pen carefully into a recess on the side. "I am a student of such things. It is my habit to record ephemera of popular culture. Her costume raises the question: does it merely reflect the theme of this club, or does it represent some deeper response to trauma of earthquake and subsequent reconstruction?"

Yamazaki phoned just before noon. The day was dim and overcast. Laney had closed the curtains in order to avoid seeing the nanotech buildings in that light.

He was watching an NHK show about champion top-spinners. The star, he gathered, was a little girl with pigtails and a blue dress with an old-fashioned sailor's collar. She was slightly cross-eyed, perhaps from concentration. The tops were made of wood. Some of them were big, and looked heavy.

"Hello, Mr. Laney," Yamazaki said. "You are feeling better now?"

"Better than last night," Laney said.

"It is being arranged for you to access the data that surrounds . . . our friend. It is a complicated process, as this data has been protected in many different ways. There was no single strategy. The ways in which his privacy has been protected are complexly incremental."

"Does 'our friend' know about this?"

There was a pause. Laney watched the spinning top. He imagined Yamazaki blinking. "No, he does not."

"I still don't know who I'll really be working for. For him? For Blackwell?"

"Your employer is Paragon-Asia Dataflow, Melbourne. They are employing me as well."

"What about Blackwell?"

"Blackwell is employed by a privately held corporation, through which portions of our friend's income pass. In the course of our friend's career, a structure has been erected to optimize that flow, to minimize losses. That structure now constitutes a corporate entity in its own right."

"Management," Laney said. "His management's scared because it looks like he might do something crazy. Is that it?"

The purple-and-yellow top was starting to exhibit the first of the oscillations that would eventually bring it to a halt. "I am still a stranger to this business-culture, Mr. Laney. I find it difficult to assess these things."

"What did Blackwell mean, last night, about Rez wanting to marry a Japanese girl who isn't real?"

"Idoru," Yamazaki said.

"What?"

"'Idol-singer.' She is Rei Toei. She is a personality-construct, a congeries of software agents, the creation of information-designers. She is akin to what I believe they call a 'synthespian,' in Hollywood."

Laney closed his eyes, opened them. "Then how can he marry her?"

"I don't know," Yamazaki said. "But he has very forcefully declared this is to be his intention."

"Can you tell me what it is they've hired *you* to do?"

"Initially, I think, they hoped I would be able to explain the idoru to them: her appeal to her audience, therefore perhaps her appeal to him. Also, I think that, like Blackwell, they remain unconvinced that this is not the result of a conspiracy of some kind. Now they want me to acquaint you with the cultural background of the situation."

"Who are they?"

"I cannot be more specific now."

The top was starting to wobble. Laney saw something like terror in the girl's eyes. "You don't think there's a conspiracy?"

"I will try to answer your questions this evening. In the meantime, while it is being arranged for you to access the data, please study these . . ."

"Hey," Laney protested, as his top-spinning girl was replaced by an unfamiliar logo: a grinning cartoon bulldog with a spiked collar, up to its musical neck in a big bowl of soup.

"Two documentary videos on Lo/Rez," Yamazaki said. "These are on the Dog Soup label, originally a small independent based in East Taipei. They released the band's first recordings. Lo/Rez later purchased Dog Soup and used it to release less commercial material by other artists."

Laney stared glumly at the grinning bulldog, missing the girl with pigtails. "Like documentaries about themselves?"

"The documentaries were not made subject to the band's approval. They are not Lo/Rez corporate documentaries."

"Well, I guess we've got that to be thankful for."

"You are welcome." Yamazaki hung up.

The virtual POV zoomed, rotating in on one of the spikes on the dog's collar: in close-up, it was a shining steel pyramid. Reflected clouds whipped past in time-lapse on the towering triangular face as the Universal Copyright Agreement warning scrolled into view.

Laney watched long enough to see that the video was spliced together from bits and pieces of the band's public relations footage. "Art-warning," he said, and went into the bathroom to decipher the shower controls.

He managed to miss the first six minutes, showering and brushing his teeth. He'd seen things like that before, art videos, but he'd never actually tried to pay attention to one. Putting on the hotel's white terry robe, he told himself he'd better try. Yamazaki seemed capable of quizzing him on it later.

Why did people make things like that? There was no narration, no apparent structure; some of the same fragments kept repeating throughout, at different speeds . . .

In Los Angeles there were whole public-access channels devoted to things like this, and home-made talkshows hosted by naked Encino witches, who sat in front of big paintings of the Goddess they'd done in their garages. Except you could *watch* that. The logic of these cut-ups, he supposed, was that by making one you could somehow push back at the medium. Maybe it was supposed to be something like treading water, a simple repetitive human activity that temporarily provided at least an illusion of parity with the sea. But to Laney, who had spent many of his waking hours down in the deeper realms of data that underlay the worlds of media, it only looked hopeless. And tedious, too, although he supposed that that boredom was somehow meant to be harnessed, here, another way of pushing back.

Why else would anyone have selected and edited all these bits of Lo and Rez, the Chinese guitarist and the half-Irish singer, saying stupid things in dozens of different television spots, most of them probably intended for translation? Greetings seemed to be a theme. "We're happy to be here in Vladivostok. We hear you've got a great new aquarium!" "We congratulate you on your free elections and your successful dengue-abatement campaign!" "We've always loved London!" "New York, you're . . . *pragmatic!*"

Laney explored the remains of his breakfast, finding a half-eaten slice of cold brown toast under a steel plate cover. There was an inch of coffee left in the pot. He didn't want to think about the call from Rydell or what it might mean. He'd thought he was done with Slitscan, done with the lawyers . . .

"Singapore, you're beautiful!" Rez said, Lo chiming in with "Hell-o, Lion City!"

He picked up the remote and hopefully tried the fast-forward. No. Mute? No. Yamazaki was having this stuff piped in for his benefit. He considered unplugging the console, but he was afraid they'd be able to tell.

It was speeding up now, the cuts more frequent, the whole more content-free, a numbing blur. Rez's grin was starting to look sinister, something with an agenda of its own that jumped unchanged from one cut to the next.

Suddenly it all slid away, into handheld shadow, highlights on rococo glit. There was a clatter of glassware. The image had a peculiar flattened quality that he knew from Slitscan: the smallest lapel-cameras did that, the ones disguised as flecks of lint.

A restaurant? Club? Someone seated opposite the camera, beyond a phalanx of green bottles. The darkness and the bandwidth of the tiny camera making the features impossible to read. Then Rez leaned forward, recognizable in the new depth of focus. He gestured toward the camera with a glass of red wine.

"If we could ever once stop talking about the music, and the industry, and all the politics of that, I think I'd probably tell you that it's easier to desire and pursue the attention of tens of millions of total strangers than it is to accept the love and loyalty of the people closest to us."

Someone, a woman, said something in French. Laney guessed that she was the one wearing the camera.

"Ease up, Rozzer. She doesn't understand half you're saying." Laney sat forward. The voice had been Blackwell's.

"Doesn't she?" Rez receded, out of focus. "Because if she did, I think I'd tell her about the loneliness of being misunderstood. Or is it the loneliness of being afraid to allow ourselves to be understood?"

And the frame froze on the singer's blurred face. A date and time-stamp. Two years earlier. The word "Misunderstood" appeared.

The phone rang.

"Yeah?"

"Blackwell says there is a window of opportunity. The schedule has been moved up. You can access now." It was Yamazaki.

"Good," Laney said. "I don't think I'm getting very far with this first video."

"Rez's quest for renewed artistic meaning? Don't worry; we will screen it for you again, later."

"I'm relieved," Laney said. "Is the second one as good?"

"Second documentary is more conventionally structured. In-depth interviews, biographical detail, BBC, three years ago."

"Wonderful."

"Blackwell is on his way to the hotel. Goodbye."

Robert Hemenway

Teacher and editor, Robert Hemenway was awarded first prize in Prize Stories 1970: The O. Henry Awards *for his short story, "The Girl Who Sang with the Beatles," a poignant tale of a young woman who is obsessed with celebrity and pop culture. Cynthia is a lost soul who comes fully alive only when performing to an audience of one.*

"The Girl Who Sang with the Beatles"

Of course their tastes turned out to be different. Cynthia was twenty-eight when they married, and looked younger, in the way small, very pretty women can—so much younger sometimes that bartenders would ask for her I.D. Larry was close to forty and gray, a heavy man who, when he moved, moved slowly. He had been an English instructor once, though now he wrote market-research reports, and there was still something bookish about him. Cynthia, who was working as an interviewer for Larry's company when he met her, had been a vocalist with several dance bands for a while in the fifties before she quit to marry her first husband. She had left high school when she was a junior to take her first singing job. She and Larry were from different generations, practically, and from different cultures, and yet when they were married they both liked the same things. That was what brought them together. Thirties movies. Old bars—not the instant-tradition places but what was left of the old ones, what Cynthia called the bar bars. Double features in the loge of the Orpheum, eating hot dogs and drinking smuggled beer. Gibsons before dinner and Scotch after. Their TV nights, eating delicatessen while they watched "Mr. Lucky" or "Route 66" or "Ben Casey," laughing at the same places, choking up at the same places, howling together when something was just too *much*. And then the eleven-o'clock news and the Late and Late Late Shows, while they drank and necked and sometimes made love. And listening to Cynthia's records—old Sinatras and Judys, and Steve and Eydie, or "The Fantasticks" or "Candide." They even agreed on redecorating Cynthia's apartment, which was full of leftovers from her first marriage. They agreed on all of it—the worn (but genuine) Oriental rugs; the low carved Spanish tables; the dusky colors, grays and mauve and rose; the damask sofa with its down pillows; and, in the bedroom, the twin beds, nearly joined but held separate by an ornate brass bedstead. Cynthia's old double bed had been impractical; Larry was too big, and Cynthia kicked. When they came back from their Nassau honeymoon and saw the apartment for the first time in ten days, Cynthia said, "God, Larry, I *love* it. It's pure *Sunset Boulevard* now."

The place made Larry think of Hyde Park Boulevard in Chicago, where he had grown up in a mock-Tudor house filled with the wrought iron and walnut of an earlier Spanish fad. Entering the apartment was like entering his childhood. "Valencia!" sang in his head. "Valencia! In my dreams it always seems I hear you softly call to me. Valencia!"

They were married in the summer of 1962 and by the spring of 1963 the things they had bought no longer looked quite right. Everyone was buying Spanish now, and there was too much around in the cheap stores. Larry and Cynthia found themselves in a dowdy apartment full of things that looked as if they had been there since the twenties. It was depressing. They began to ask each other what they had done. Not that either of them wanted out, exactly, but what had they done? Why had they married? Why couldn't they have gone on with their affair? Neither had married the other for money, that was certain. Larry had made Cynthia quit work (not that she minded) and now they had only his salary, which was barely enough.

"We still love each other, don't we? I mean, I know I love you." Cynthia was in Larry's bed and Larry was talking. It was three in the morning, and they had come back from their usual Saturday-night tour of the neighborhood bars. "I love you," Larry said.

"You don't like me."

"I *love* you, Cynthia."

"You don't like me." Propped up by pillows, she stared red-eyed at a great paper daisy on the wall.

"I love you, Cindy."

"So? Big deal. Men have been telling me they loved me since I was fourteen. I thought you were different."

Larry lay flat on his back. "Don't be tough. It's not like you," he said.

"I *am* tough. That's what you won't understand. You didn't marry *me*. You married some nutty idea of your own. I was your secret fantasy. You told me so." Cynthia was shivering.

"Lie down," Larry said. "I'll rub your back."

"You won't get around me that way," Cynthia said, lying down. "You tricked me. I thought you liked the things I liked. You won't even watch TV with me anymore."

Larry began to rub the back of Cynthia's neck and play with the soft hairs behind one ear.

"Why don't you ever watch with me?" Cynthia said.

"You know. I get impatient."

"You don't like me." Cynthia was teasing him by now. "If you really liked me, you'd watch," she said. "You'd *like* being bored."

Larry sat up. "That isn't it," he said. "You know what it is? It's the noise. All the things you like make *noise*."

"I read."

"Sure. With the radio or the stereo or the TV on. I can't. I have to do one thing at a time," Larry said. "What if I want to sit home at night and read a book?"

"So read."

"When you have these programs you quote have to watch unquote?"

"Get me headphones. That's what my first husband did when he stopped talking to me. Or go to the bedroom and shut the door. I don't mind."

"We'll do something," Larry said, lying down again. "Now let's make love."

"Oh, it's no use, Larry," Cynthia said. "Not when we're like this. I'll only sweat."

And so it went on many nights, and everything seemed tainted by their disagreements, especially their times in bed. After they had made love, they would slip again into these exchanges, on and on. What Cynthia seemed to resent most was that Larry had not been straightforward with her. Why had he let her think he cared for her world of song and dance? She knew it was trivial. She had never tried to make him think she was deep. Why had he pretended he was something he wasn't?

How was Larry to tell her the truth without making her think he was either a snob or a fool? There was no way. The thing was, he said, that when they met he *did* like what she liked, period. Just because she liked it. What was wrong with that? He wanted to see her enjoying herself, so they did what she wanted to do—went to Radio City to see the new Doris Day, or to Basin Street East to hear Peggy Lee, or to revivals of those fifties musicals Cynthia liked so much. Forget the things he liked if she didn't—foreign movies and chamber music and walks in Central Park, all that. She must have known what he liked, after all. She had been in his apartment often enough before they were married, God knows. She had seen his books and records. She knew his tastes.

"I thought you gave all that up," Cynthia said. "I thought you'd changed."

"I thought you *would* change," Larry said. "I thought you wanted to. I thought if you wanted to marry me you must want to change."

"Be an *intellectual?*" Cynthia asked. "You must be kidding."

No, he was serious. Why didn't she get bored with the stuff she watched and the junk she read? *He* did. When you had seen three Perry Masons, you had seen them all, and that went for Doris Day movies, the eleven-o'clock news, and "What's My Line?"

"I know all that," Cynthia said. She *liked* to be bored. God, you couldn't keep thinking about reality all the time. You'd go out of your mind. She liked stories and actors that she knew, liked movies she had seen a dozen times and books she could read over and over again. Larry took his reading so seriously. As if reading were *life*.

Larry tried to persuade himself that Cynthia was teasing him, but it was no use. She meant what she said. She *liked East of Eden, Marjorie Morningstar, Gone with the Wind*. She liked Elizabeth Taylor movies. She found nourishment in that Styrofoam. He could see it in her childlike face, which sometimes shone as if she were regarding the beatific vision when she was under the spell of the sorriest trash. What repelled him brought her to life. He could feel it in her when they touched and when, after seeing one of her favorite movies, they made love. How odd that he should have married her! And yet he loved her, he thought, and he thought she loved him—needed him, anyway.

Sometimes they talked of having a child, or of Cynthia's going back to work or of attending night classes together at Columbia or the New School, but nothing came of it. They were both drinking too much, perhaps, and getting too little exercise, yet it was easier to let things go on as they were. Larry did set out to read Camus, the first serious reading he had done since their marriage, and in the evenings after dinner he would go into the bedroom, shut the door, turn on WNCN to muffle the sounds from the living room, put Flents in his ears, and read. Although the meaningless noises from the TV set—the not quite comprehensible voices, the sudden surges of music—still reached him, he was reluctant to buy Cynthia the headphones she had suggested. They would be too clear a symbol of their defeat.

Cynthia often stayed up until three or four watching the late movies or playing her records, and Larry, who usually fell asleep around midnight, would sometimes wake after two or three hours and come out of the bedroom shouting "Do you know what *time* it is?" and frighten her. Sometimes, though, he would make a drink for himself and watch her movie, too, necking with her the way they used to do, without saying much. They were still drawn to each other.

Sometimes, very late at night when she was quite drunk, Cynthia would stand before the full-length mirror in their bedroom and admire herself. "I'm beautiful," she would say. "Right now, I'm really beautiful, and who can see me?" Larry would watch her from the bed. Something slack in her would grow taut as she looked in the mirror. She would draw her underpants down low on her hips, then place her hands on her shoulders, her crossed arms covering her bare breasts, and smile at her reflection, a one-sided smile. "I'm a narcissist," she would say, looking at Larry in the mirror. "I'm a sexual narcissist. How can you stand me?" Then she would join Larry in his bed.

Larry couldn't deny Cynthia anything for long. If he insisted on it, she would turn off the set, but then she would sulk until he felt he had imposed upon her, and he would turn the set back on or take her out for a drink. How could he blame her? They had so little money. What else was there for her to do?

One Saturday night after their tour of the bars, Cynthia changed clothes and came out of the bedroom wearing a twenties black dress and black net stockings and pumps. The dress was banded with several rows of fringe and stopped just at the knee. She had to add the last row of fringe, she told Larry. Her first husband had made her, just before they went to a costume party, because the dress showed too much of her thighs. Larry knelt before her and tore off the last row. Cynthia danced for him (a Charleston, a shimmy, a Watusi) and after that she sang. She had sung to him now and then late at night before they were married—just a few bars in a soft, almost inaudible voice. Tonight the voice seemed full and touching to Larry, and with a timbre and sadness different from any voice he had ever heard. "*Like* me. Please like me," the voice seemed to say. "Just like me. That's all I need. I'll be nice then." She might have charm and the need for love, but perhaps the voice was too small and her need too great. She had told him that twice while she was singing with a band in Las Vegas she had been "discovered" by assistant directors and offered a movie audition, and that each time she had been sick in the studio—literally sick to her stomach—and unable to go on. She had been too scared. Yet she still might have a career somehow, Larry thought. He could encourage her to practice. It would be an interest for her—something to do. She was barely past thirty and looked less. There was time.

Larry decided to read Camus in French and to translate some of the untranslated essays, just for practice, into English. One night he came home with the headphones Cynthia wanted, the old-fashioned kind made of black Bakelite, and hooked them up to the TV set through a control box that had an off-on switch for the speaker. Now that he could blank out the commercials, Larry would watch with Cynthia now and then—some of the news specials, and the Wide World of Sports, and the late-night reruns of President Kennedy's press conferences, one of the few things they both enjoyed. They could both acknowledge his power, pulsing in him and out toward them—that sure, quick intelligence and that charm.

Cynthia was happier now, because with the headphones on and the speakers off she could watch as late as she wanted without being afraid of Larry. When the phone rang, she would not hear it. Larry would answer, finally, and if it was for her she would stand in front of the set gesturing until she took the headphones off. She would sit on the sofa for hours, dressed as if for company, her eyes made up to look even larger than they were were, wearing one of the at-home hostessy things from Jax or Robert Leader she had bought before they were married, which hardly anyone but she and Larry had ever seen. Looking so pretty, and with those radio operator's black headphones on her ears.

The sight made Larry melancholy, and he continued to work lying on his bed, propped up with a writing board on his lap. He would hear Cynthia laughing sometimes in the silent living room, and now and then, hearing thin sounds from her headphones, he would come out to find her crying, the phones on her lap and the final credits of a movie on the screen. "I always cry at this one," she would say. With the headphones, Cynthia was spending more time before the set than ever. Larry encouraged her to sing—to take lessons again if she wanted. But she did sing, she said, in the afternoons. She sang with her records, usually. There were a few songs of Eydie's and Peggy's and Judy's she liked. She sang along with those.

In spite of everything, when Larry compared his life now with his first marriage or with the bitter years after that, he could not say that this was worse. Cynthia seemed almost content. She made no demands upon him and left him free to think or read what he pleased. But there were nights when he would put his book aside and lie on his bed, hearing Cynthia laugh now and then or get up to make herself another drink, and ask himself why he was there. Little, in his job or in his life, seemed reasonable or real.

Why had he fallen in love with Cynthia? It was just because she was so *American*, he decided one night. She *liked* canned chili and corned-beef hash, the Academy Awards, cole slaw, barbecued chicken, the Miss America contest, head lettuce with Russian dressing, astrology columns, *Modern Screen*, takeout pizza pies. She liked them and made faces at them at the same time, looking up or over at him and saying, "Oh God, isn't this awful? Isn't this vile?" Everything he had turned his back on in the name of the Bauhaus and the Institute of Design, of Elizabeth David and James Beard, of Lewis Mumford, Paul Goodman, D. H. Lawrence, Henry Miller, Frank Lloyd Wright— here it all was dished up before him in Cynthia. All the things that (to tell the truth) he had never had enough of. He had lost out on them in high school, when he had really wanted them, because he was studious and shy. He had rejected them in college, where it was a matter of political principle among his friends to reject them, before he had the chance to find out what they were like. At thirty-eight, when he met Cynthia, what did he know? Weren't there vast areas of the American experience that he had missed? Why, until Cynthia he had never shacked up in a motel. Nor had he ever been in a barroom fight, or smoked pot, or been ticketed for speeding, or blacked out from booze.

What had he fallen in love with, then, but pop America! One more intellectual seduced by kitsch! He could almost see the humor in it. It was the first solid discovery about himself he had made for years, and he lay back in bed, smiling. How glittering Cynthia's world had seemed, he thought. The sixties—this is what they *were*! Thruways, motels, Point Pleasant on a Saturday night twisting on the juke! That trip to Atlantic City in winter where, at the Club Hialeah, the girls from South Jersey danced on the bar, and in the Hotel Marlborough-Blenheim he and Cynthia wandered through the cold deserted corridors and public rooms like actors in a shabby *Marienbad*. And the music! Miles, Monk, Chico, Mingus, the M.J.Q., Sinatra and Nelson Riddle, Belafonte, Elvis, Ray Charles, Dion, Lena Horne—all new to him. He had stopped listening to music before bop, and with Cynthia he listened to everything. Progressive or pop or rhythm and blues, whatever. Did he like it all—how was it possible to like it *all*?—because Cynthia did, or did he fall in love with Cynthia because she liked it all? What difference did it make? It was all new—a gorgeous blur of enthusiasms. For the first time in his life he had given himself away. How wonderful it had been, at thirty-eight, on the edge of middle age—*in* middle age—to play the fool! This was experience, this was *life*, this was the sixties—*his* generation, with his peers in charge, the

Kennedys and the rest. Wasn't that coming alive, when you were free enough to play the fool and not care? And if there had been enough money, he and Cynthia might have kept it up. . . . They might.

Yet hardly a moment had passed during the first months with Cynthia when he did not know what he was doing. He had got into a discussion of pop culture one night in the Cedar Street Tavern not long after he and Cynthia were married. "You don't know what you're talking about," he had said to the others while Cynthia was on a trip to the head. "You only dip into it. Listen. You don't know. I've *married* it. I've married the whole great American *schmier*."

But how nearly he had been taken in! Cynthia never had. She knew show business from the inside, after all. She dug it, and liked it, and laughed at herself for liking it. She knew how shabby it was. Yet it did something for her—that trumpery, that fake emotion, that sincere corn. Once he found out something was bad, how could he care for it any longer? It was impossible. If he had gone overboard at first for Cynthia's world, wasn't that because it was new to him and he saw fresh energy there? And how spurious that energy had turned out to be—how slick, how manufactured, how dead! And how dull. Yet something in it rubbed off on Cynthia, mesmerized her, and made her glamorous, made her attractive to him still. That was the trouble. He still wanted her. He was as mesmerized as she. Wasn't it the fakery he despised that shone in Cynthia and drew him to her? Then what in their marriage was real? He felt as detached from his life as a dreamer at times feels detached from his dream.

Quiet and sedentary as it had become, Larry's life continued to be charged with a forced excitement. The pop love songs, the photographs of beautiful men and women in the magazines Cynthia read, the romantic movies on TV, Cynthia herself—changing her clothes three or four times a day as if she were the star in a play and Larry the audience—all stimulated him in what he considered an unnatural way. He recognized in himself an extravagant lust that was quickly expended but never spent when he and Cynthia made love, as if she were one of the idealized photographs of which she was so fond and he were returning within her to the fantasies of his adolescence, their intercourse no more than the solitary motions of two bodies accidentally joined.

"We shouldn't have got married," Cynthia said one hot Saturday night in the summer of 1963 as they were lying in their beds trying to fall asleep.

"Maybe not," Larry said.

"Marriage turns me off. Something happens. I told you."

"I didn't believe you," Larry said. "And anyway we're married."

"We sure are."

"I picked a lemon in the garden of love," Larry said. Cynthia laughed and moved into Larry's bed.

Late that night, though, he said something else. "We're like Catholics and their sacrament," he said. "When you're married for the second time, you're practically stuck with each other. You've almost got to work it out."

"You may think you're stuck, but *I'm* not," Cynthia said, and moved back to her own bed. The next Saturday night she brought up what Larry had said about being "stuck." Why had he said it? Didn't he know her at all? Whenever she felt bound she had to break free— right out the door, sooner or later. That was what had always happened. Was he trying to drive her away? He knew how independent she'd been. That's what he liked about her, he'd said once. All that talk about protecting each other's freedom! What a lot of crap. Look at them now. Two birds in a cage, a filthy cage.

Cynthia's anger frightened Larry, and, to his surprise, the thought of her leaving frightened him, too. But nothing changed. There wasn't much chance of her breaking away, after all. They didn't have enough money to separate, and neither of them really wanted to—not *that* routine, not again.

More and more often now Larry would sit in the living room reading while Cynthia watched her programs, headphones on her ears. He would look over at her, knowing that at that moment she was content, and feel some satisfaction, even a sense of domestic peace. At times he would lie with his head on Cynthia's lap while she watched, and she would stroke his hair.

One payday Larry came home with a second pair of headphones, made of green plastic and padded with foam rubber, the sort disc jockeys and astronauts wear, and plugged them into the stereo through a box that permitted turning off the speakers. Now he, like Cynthia, could listen in silence. He stacked some of his records on the turntable—the Mozart horn concertos, a Bach cantata, Gluck. It was eerie, Larry thought, for them both to be so completely absorbed, sitting twenty feet apart in that silent living room, and on the first night he found himself watching Cynthia's picture on the TV screen as the music in his ears seemed to fade away. Finally, he took off his earphones, joined Cynthia on the sofa, and asked her to turn on the sound. After a few nights, however, the sense of eeriness wore off, and Larry was as caught up in his music as Cynthia was in her shows. The stereo sound was so rich and pure; unmixed with other noises, the music carried directly into his brain, surrounding and penetrating him. It was so intense, so mindless. Listening was not a strong enough word for what was happening. The music flowed through him and swallowed him up. He felt endowed with a superior sense, as if he were a god. Yet there was something illicit about their both finding so intense a pleasure in isolation. He was troubled, off and on, by what they were falling into, but their life was tranquil and that was almost enough.

One night when Larry was reading (something he rarely did now) and there was nothing on TV she cared for, Cynthia put some of her records on the turntable and Larry's headphones on her ears and listened to Eydie and Judy and Frank, dancing a few steps now and then and singing the words softly. "Why didn't you tell me!" she said. It was *fantastic*. She could hear all the bass, and the color of the voices, and things in some of the arrangements she had never known were there. More and more often as the summer wore on, Cynthia would listen to her music instead of watching the tube, and Larry, thinking this a step in the right direction—toward her singing, perhaps—turned the stereo over to her several evenings a week and tried to concentrate again on his reading. But music now held him in a way books no

longer could, and after a few weeks he bought a second stereo phonograph and a second set of headphones. By the fall of 1963, he and
Cynthia had begun to listen, each to his own music, together. "This is
really a kick," Cynthia would say. The intensity of it excited them
both.

On the day President Kennedy was assassinated, Larry and
Cynthia were having one of their rare lunches in midtown at an Italian
place near Bloomingdale's, where Cynthia planned to go shopping
afterward. There was a small television set above the restaurant bar,
and people stood there waiting for definite news after the first word of
the shooting. When it was clear that the President was dead, Larry
and Cynthia went back to their apartment. Larry didn't go back to
work. They watched television together that afternoon and evening,
and then they went to bed and began to weep. When Larry stopped,
Cynthia would sob, and then Larry would start again. So it went until
after four in the morning, when they fell asleep. Until the funeral was
over, Cynthia sat before the set most of the day and night. Much of the
time she was crying, and every night when she came to bed the tears
would start. Larry, dry-eyed sooner than she was, was at first sympathetic, then impatient, then annoyed.

"He was such a *good* man," Cynthia would say, or "He was *ours*. He
was all we had," and after the burial she said, half smiling, "He was a
wonderful star." Nothing in her actual life could ever move her so
deeply, Larry thought. How strange, to feel real sorrow and weep real
tears for an unreal loss! But she was suffering, no question of that, and
she could not stop crying. The Christmas season came and went, and
she still wept. She had begun to drink heavily, and often Larry would
put her to bed. On the edge of unconsciousness, she would continue
to cry.

What was she, he thought, but a transmitter of electronic sensa-
tions? First she had conveyed the nation's erotic fantasies to him, and
now it was the national sorrow, and one was as unreal as the other. But
there was more to it than that. John Kennedy had been a figure in her
own erotic fantasies. She had told Larry so. She wept for him as a
woman for her dead lover. She was like a woman betrayed by Death,

Larry thought, when what had betrayed her was the television set she had counted upon to shield her from the real. It had always told her stories of terror and passion that, because they were fictitious, might be endured, and now it had shown her actual death and actual sorrow. There was no way to console her, because her loss was not an actual loss, and Larry began to think her suffering more than he could endure. He began to wonder if she might not have lost her mind.

Cynthia read nothing for weeks after the assassination but articles on it, and so she did not hear of the Beatles until Larry, hoping to distract her, brought home their first album. She thought little of it at first, but after the Beatles appeared on the Ed Sullivan Show in February she became an admirer and then a devotee. Larry brought her the new Beatles 45's as they came out, and he stood in line with teen-age girls at the newsstands on Forty-second Street to buy the Beatles fan magazines. "I guess the period of mourning is over," Cynthia said one Saturday night. She still saved articles about the assassination, though, and photographs of Jacqueline in black.

When Cynthia began to sing as she listened to the Beatles late at night, Larry, listening from the bedroom, was pleased. She would play their records over and over, accompanying them in a voice that seemed flat and unresonant, perhaps because with the headphones on she could not hear the sounds she made. She no longer wept, or Larry was asleep when she did.

One night, Larry woke around three to the tinny noise of "I Want to Hold Your Hand" spilling from Cynthia's phones and found he was hungry. On his way to the kitchen, he stopped in the dark hall to watch Cynthia, who stood in the center of the living room with the astronaut headphones on, singing what sounded like a harmonizing part, a little off-key, holding an imaginary guitar, swaying jerkily, and smiling as if she were before an audience. Her performance, empty as it was, seemed oddly polished and professional. Afraid of startling her, he stood watching until the end of the song before he entered the room.

"How much did you see?" Cynthia said.

"Nothing," Larry said. "I was going to get a glass of milk, that's all." The look on Cynthia's face as she stood before him with those enormous headphones clamped to her ears troubled him, as if he had discovered her in some indecency better forgotten. "After this I'll flick out the lights and warn you," he said.

And he said no more about it, though often now he awoke during the night to the faint sounds from Cynthia's headphones and wondered what she was doing that held her so fast. He was jealous of it in a way. She was rarely in bed before four, and always in bed when he left for work in the morning. In the evening, though, as she watched television, she seemed happy enough, and much as she had been before Kennedy's death.

For some time after the assassination, they gave up their Saturday nights in the bars, but by April they were again making their rounds. Once, when they came home higher and happier than usual, Cynthia danced and sang for Larry as she had before, and for a while Larry danced with her, something he did not do often. They were having such a pleasant time that when Larry put on a Beatles album and Cynthia began her performance for him, she explained. "We're at the Palladium in London, you see," she said. "The place is mobbed . . . . The Beatles are onstage . . . . I'm singing with them, and naturally everybody loves us. I work through the whole show . . . playing second guitar. I back up George." And then she sang, a third or so below the melody. "'She was seventeen if you know what I mean . . . .'"

"I never sing lead," Cynthia said when the number was over. "I play a minor rôle."

"Is this what you do at night?" Larry asked her.

Cynthia was breathing heavily. "Sure," she said. "It sounds silly, but it's not. Besides, it's possible, isn't it? It *could* happen. I can sing." She looked at Larry, her eyes candid and kind. "Don't worry," she said. "I'm not losing my grip."

"It's a nice game," Larry said later when they were in bed.

"Oh, it's more than a game," Cynthia said. "When I'm with them in the Palladium, I'm really *there*. It's more real than here. I know it's a fantasy, though."

"How did you meet the Beatles?" Larry asked her.

"D'you really want to hear?" Cynthia said. She seemed pleased at his interest, Larry thought, but then she was drunk. They both were.

"It's not much of a story," she said. "The details vary, but basically I am standing on Fifth Avenue there near the Plaza in the snow waiting for a cab at three in the afternoon, dressed in my black flared coat and black pants and the black boots you gave me, and I have a guitar. No taxis, or they're whipping right by, and I'm *cold*. You know how cold I can get. And then this Bentley stops with a couple of guys in front and in back is George Harrison all alone, though sometimes it's Paul. He gives me a lift and we talk. He's completely polite and sincere, and I can see he likes me. It seems the Beatles are rehearsing for a television special at Central Plaza and they'll be there the next day, so he asks me to come up and bring my guitar. I go, naturally, and it turns out they are auditioning girls, and I'm the winner. What would be the point if I wasn't? They want a girl for just one number, but when they see how terrific I am, of course they love me, and when they find out I've already worked up all their songs I'm in."

"You join them."

"Sure. They insist. I have to leave you, but you don't mind, not anymore. In one year, we're The Beatles and Cynthia and we're playing the Palladium, and Princess Margaret and Tony are there, and Frank, and Peter O'Toole, and David McCallum, and Steve McQueen, and Bobby Kennedy. And all those men *want* me, I can feel it, and I'm going to meet them afterward at the Savoy in our suite."

" 'Our'?"

"I'm married to a rich diamond merchant who lets me do whatever I want. Played by George Sanders."

"I thought you were married to me," Larry said.

"Oh, no. You divorced me, alleging I was mentally cruel. Maybe I was once, but I'm not anymore, because the Beatles love me. They're my brothers. They're not jealous of me at all."

"Are you putting me on?" Larry said.

"No. Why should I? I made it all up, if that's what you mean, but I *really* made it up."

"Do you believe any of it?" Larry said.

Cynthia smiled at him. "Don't you? You used to say I had a good voice and you used to say I was pretty. Anyway, I don't have fantasies about things that couldn't possibly happen. I could get a job tomorrow if you'd let me."

Cynthia's voice had the lilt Larry remembered from the days before they were married. The whole thing was so convincing and so insane. He began to indulge her in it. "I'm going to Beatle now," Cynthia would say nearly every night after dinner, and Larry would go into the bedroom. Whenever he came out, he would flick the hall lights and she would stop. She was shy and did not let him watch often at first. She seemed embarrassed that she had told him as much as she had—if, indeed, she remembered telling him anything at all.

Larry liked the Beatles more and more as the nights went by, and often he would listen to their records with the speakers on before Cynthia began her performance. "Listen, Cynthia," he said one Saturday night. "The Beatles are filled with the Holy Ghost." He was really quite drunk. "Do you know that? They came to bring us back to life! Out of the old nightmare. Dallas, Oswald, Ruby, all of it, cops, reporters, thruways, lies, crises, missiles, heroes, cameras, fear—all that mishmash, and all of it dead. All of us dead watching the burial of the dead. Look at *you*. They've brought you back to life. I couldn't— not after November. Nothing could."

"You're right," Cynthia said. "I didn't want to tell you. I thought you'd be jealous."

"Jealous? Of the Beatles?"

"They're very real to me, you know."

"I'm not jealous," Larry said.

"Then will you read to me the way you used to? Read me to sleep?"

"Sure."

"Can I get in your bed?"

"Sure."

Before Larry had finished a page, he was asleep, and Cynthia was asleep before him.

For her birthday in September, Larry gave Cynthia an electric guitar. Though she could not really play it and rarely even plugged it in, she used the guitar now in her performances, pretending to pluck the strings. She began to dress more elaborately for her Beatling, too, making up as if for the stage.

She was a little mad, no question of it, Larry thought, but it did no harm. He no longer loved her, nor could he find much to like in her, and yet he cared for her, he felt, and he saw that she was too fragile to be left alone. She was prettier now than he had ever seen her. She *should* have been a performer. She needed applause and admirers and whatever it was she gave herself in her fantasies—something he alone could not provide. Their life together asked little of him at any rate, and cost little. By now he and Cynthia rarely touched or embraced; they were like old friends—fellow-conspirators even, for who knew of Cynthia's Beatle world but him?

Cynthia discussed her performances with Larry now, telling him of the additions to her repertoire and of the new places she and the Beatles played—Kezar Stadium, the Hollywood Bowl, Philharmonic Hall. She began to permit him in the living room with her, and he would lie on the sofa listening to his music while her Beatling went on. He felt sometimes that by sharing her fantasies he might be sharing her madness, but it seemed better for them both to be innocently deranged than to be as separate as they had been before. All of it tired Larry, though. He was past forty. He felt himself growing old, and his tastes changing. Now he listened to the things he had liked in college—the familiar Beethoven and Mozart symphonies, and Schubert, and Brahms, in new stereophonic recordings. Often as he listened he would fall asleep and be awakened by the silence when the last of the records stacked on the turntable had been played. Usually Cynthia's performance would still be going on, and he would rise, take off his headphones and go to bed.

One night Larry fell asleep toward the end of the "Messiah," with the bass singing "The trumpet shall sound . . ." and the trumpet responding, and woke as usual in silence, the headphones still on his ears. This time, he lay on the sofa looking at Cynthia, his eyes barely open. She had changed clothes again, he saw, and was wearing the silver lamé pants suit, left over from her singing days, that she had worn the first night he had come to her apartment. He saw her bow, prettily and lightly in spite of the headphones on her ears, and extend her arms to her imaginary audience. Then he watched her begin a slow, confined dance, moving no more than a step to the side or forward and then back. She seemed to be singing, but with his headphones on Larry could not hear. She raised her arms again, this time in a gesture of invitation, and although she could not know he was awake it seemed to Larry that she was beckoning to him and not to an imaginary partner—that this dance, one he had never seen, was for him, and Cynthia was asking him to join her in that slow and self-contained step.

Larry rose and sat looking at her, his head by now nearly clear. "Come," she beckoned. "Come." He saw her lips form the word. Was it he to whom she spoke or one of her fantasies? What did it matter? She stood waiting for her partner—for him—and Larry got up, unplugged his headphones, and walked across the room to her. The movement seemed to him a movement of love. He plugged his headphones in next to Cynthia's and stood before her, almost smiling. She smiled and then, in silence, not quite touching her in that silent room, with the sound of the Beatles loud in his ears, Larry entered into her dance.

Nick Hornby

Best-selling author of Fever Pitch *(1998),* About a Boy *(1998), and* How to Be Good *(2001), Nick Hornby is someone who seems to spend an inordinate amount of time thinking and writing about rock music, which is all for the better. In* Songbook *(2002), he describes his favorite recordings which range in style and theme from the Beatles' "Rain" to Bruce Springsteen's "Thunder Road." In his hilarious debut novel,* High Fidelity *(1995), he introduces us to Rob Fleming, a thirty-something pop-music junkie, irrepressible list maker, and owner of a struggling record store in a seedy neighborhood of London. Rob's problem is that he refuses to grow up. He meditates instead on music, of course, but also on loneliness, women, heartbreak, and death. Rob is the king of the off-hand remark, the droll insight, the self-deprecating put-down, and Hornby, the father of lad lit, presents him with all of his warts and imperfections intact. In 2000,* High Fidelity *was made into a motion picture starring John Cusack and Jack Black, with its setting changed from London to Chicago.*

From
High Fidelity

My shop is called Championship Vinyl. I sell punk, blues, soul, and R&B, a bit of ska, some indie stuff, some sixties pop—everything for the serious record collector, as the ironically old-fashioned writing in the window says. We're in a quiet street in Holloway, carefully placed to attract the bare minimum of window-shoppers; there's no reason to come here at all, unless you live here, and the people that live here don't seem terribly interested in my Stiff Little Fingers white label (twenty-five quid to you—I paid seventeen for it in 1986) or my mono copy of *Blonde on Blonde*.

I get by because of the people who make a special effort to shop here Saturdays—young men, always young men, with John Lennon specs and leather jackets and armfuls of square carrier bags—and because of the mail order: I advertise in the back of the glossy rock magazines, and get letters from young men, always young men, in Manchester and Glasgow and Ottowa, young men who seem to spend a disproportionate amount of their time looking for deleted Smiths singles and "ORIGINAL NOT RERELEASED" underlined Frank Zappa albums. They're as close to being mad as makes no difference.

I'm late to work, and when I get there Dick is already leaning against the door reading a book. He's thirty-one years old, with long, greasy black hair; he's wearing a Sonic Youth T-shirt, a black leather jacket that is trying manfully to suggest that it has seen better days, even though he only bought it a year ago, and a Walkman with a pair of ludicrously large headphones which obscure not only his ears but half his face. The book is a paperback biography of Lou Reed. The carrier bag by his feet—which really has seen better days—advertises a violently fashionable American independent record label; he went to a great deal of trouble to get hold of it, and he gets very nervous when we go anywhere near it. He uses it to carry tapes around; he has heard most of the music in the shop, and would rather bring new stuff to work—tapes from friends, bootlegs he has ordered through the post—than waste his time listening to anything for a second time. ("Want to come to the pub for lunch, Dick?" Barry or I ask him a couple of times a week. He looks mournfully at his little stack of cassettes and sighs. "I'd love to, but I've got all these to get through.")

"Good morning, Richard."

He fumbles nervously with the giant headphones, gets one side stuck around his ear, and the other side falls over one eye.

"Oh, hi. Hi, Rob."

"Sorry I'm late."

"No, no problem."

"Good weekend?"

I unlock the shop as he scrabbles around for his stuff.

"All right, yeah, OK. I found the first Liquorice Comfits album in Camden. The one on Testament of Youth. It was never released here. Japanese import only."

"Great." I don't know what the fuck he's talking about.

"I'll tape it for you."

"Thanks."

"'Cos you liked their second one, you said. *Pop, girls, etc.* The one with Hattie Jacques on the cover. You didn't see the cover, though. You just had the tape I did for you."

I'm sure he did tape a Liquorice Comfits album for me, and I'm sure I said I liked it, too. My flat is full of tapes Dick has made for me, most of which I've never played.

"How about you, anyway? Your weekend? Any good? No good?"

I cannot imagine what kind of conversation we'd have if I were to tell Dick about my weekend. He'd probably just crumble to dust if I explained that Laura had left. Dick's not big on that sort of thing; in fact, if I were ever to confess anything of a remotely personal nature—that I had a mother and father, say, or that I'd been to school when I was younger—I reckon he'd just blush, and stammer, and ask if I'd heard the new Lemonheads album.

"Somewhere in between. Good bits and bad bits."

He nods. This is obviously the right answer.

Tuesday night I reorganize my record collection; I often do this at periods of emotional stress. There are some people who would find this a pretty dull way to spend an evening, but I'm not one of them. This is my life, and it's nice to be able to wade in it, immerse your arms in it, touch it.

When Laura was here I had the records arranged alphabetically; before that I had them filed in chronological order, beginning with Robert Johnson, and ending with, I don't know, Wham!, or somebody African, or whatever else I was listening to when Laura and I met. Tonight, though, I fancy something different, so I try to remember the order I bought them in: that way I hope to write my own autobiography, without having to do anything like pick up a pen. I pull the records off the shelves, put them in piles all over the sitting room, look for *Revolver*, and go on from there; and when I've finished, I'm flushed with a sense of self, because this, after all, is who I am. I like being able to see how I got from Deep Purple to Howlin' Wolf in twenty-five moves; I am no longer pained by the memory of listening to "Sexual Healing" all the way through a period of enforced celibacy, or embarrassed by the reminder of forming a rock club at school, so that I and my fellow fifth-formers could get together and talk about Ziggy Stardust and *Tommy*.

But what I really like is the feeling of security I get from my new filing system; I have made myself more complicated than I really am. I have a couple of thousand records, and you have to be me—or, at the very least, a doctor of Flemingology—to know how to find any of them. If I want to play, say, *Blue* by Joni Mitchell, I have to remember that I bought it for someone in the autumn of 1983, and thought better of giving it to her, for reasons I don't really want to go into. Well, you don't know any of that, so you're knackered, really, aren't you? You'd have to ask me to dig it out for you, and for some reason I find this enormously comforting.

I want to see them now: Alison Ashworth, who ditched me after three miserable evenings in the park. Penny, who wouldn't let me touch her and who then went straight out and had sex with that bastard Chris Thomson. Jackie, attractive only while she was going out with one of my best friends. Sarah, with whom I formed an alliance against all the dumpers in the world and who then went and dumped me anyway. And Charlie. Especially Charlie, because I have her to thank for everything: my great job, my sexual self-confidence, the works. I want to be a well-rounded human being with none of these knotty lumps of rage and guilt and self-disgust. What do I want to do when I see them? I don't know. Just talk. Ask them how they are and whether they have forgiven me for messing them around, when I have messed them around, and tell them that I have forgiven them for messing me around, when they have messed me around. Wouldn't that be great? If I saw all of them in turn and there were no hard feelings left, just soft, *downy* feelings, Brie rather than old hard Parmesan, I'd feel clean, and calm, and ready to start again.

Bruce Springsteen's always doing it in his songs. Maybe not always, but he's done it. You know that one "Bobby Jean," off *Born in the USA*? Anyway, he phones this girl up but she's left town years before and he's pissed off that he didn't know about it, because he wanted to say good-bye, and tell her that he missed her, and to wish her good luck. And then one of those sax solos comes in, and you get goose pimples, if you like sax solos. And Bruce Springsteen. Well, I'd like my life to be like a Bruce Springsteen song. Just once. I know I'm not born to run, I know that the Seven Sisters' Road is nothing like Thunder Road, but *feelings* can't be so different, can they? I'd like to phone all those people up and say good luck, and good-bye, and then they'd feel good and I'd feel good. We'd all feel good. That would be good. Great, even.

There aren't really any pop songs about death—not good ones, anyway. Maybe that's why I like pop music, and why I find classical music a bit creepy. There was that Elton John instrumental, "Song for Guy," but, you know, it was just a plinky-plonky piano thing that would serve you just as well at the airport as at your funeral.

"OK, guys, best five pop songs about death."

"Magic," says Barry. "A Laura's Dad Tribute List. OK, OK. 'Leader of the Pack.' The bloke dies on his motorbike, doesn't he? And then there's 'Dead Man's Curve' by Jan and Dean, and 'Terry,' by Twinkle.

Ummm . . . that Bobby Goldsboro one, you know, 'And Honey, I Miss You . . .'" He sings it off-key, even more so than he would have done normally, and Dick laughs. "And what about 'Tell Laura I Love Her.' That'd bring the house down." I'm glad that Laura isn't here to see how much amusement her father's death has afforded us.

"I was trying to think of serious songs. You know, something that shows a bit of respect."

"What, you're doing the DJ-ing at the funeral, are you? Ouch. Bad job. Still, the Bobby Goldsboro could be one of the smoochers. You know, when people need a breather. Laura's mum could sing it." He sings the same line, off-key again, but this time in a falsetto voice to show that the singer is a woman.

"Fuck off, Barry."

"I've already worked out what I'm having at mine. 'One Step Beyond,' by Madness. 'You Can't Always Get What You Want.'"

"Just 'cause it's in *The Big Chill*."

"I haven't seen *The Big Chill*, have I?"

"You lying bastard. You saw it in a Lawrence Kasdan double bill with *Body Heat*."

"Oh, yeah. But I'd forgotten about that, honestly. I wasn't just nicking the idea."

"Not much."

And so on.

I try again later.

"'Abraham, Martin, and John,'" says Dick. "That's quite a nice one."

"What was Laura's dad's name?"

"Ken."

"'Abraham, Martin, John, and Ken.' Nah, I can't see it."

"Fuck off."

"Black Sabbath? Nirvana? They're all into death."

Thus is Ken's passing mourned at Championship Vinyl.

BUT
look:
My five dream jobs

1. *New Musical Express*
   journalist, 1976–1979
   Get to meet the Clash,
   Sex Pistols, Chrissie
   Hynde, Danny Baker,
   etc. Get loads of free
   records—good ones, too.
   Go on to host my own
   quiz show or something.
2. Producer, Atlantic
   Records, 1964–1971
   (approx.)
   Get to meet Aretha, Wilson
   Pickett, Solomon Burke, etc.
   Get loads of free records
   (probably)—good ones, too.
   Make piles of money.
3. Any kind of musician (apart
   from classical or rap)
   Speaks for itself. But I'd have
   settled just for being one of
   the Memphis Horns—I'm not
   asking to be Hendrix or
   Jagger or Otis Redding.
4. Film director
   Again, any kind, although
   preferably not German or
   silent.
5. Architect
   A surprise entry at number 5,
   I know, but I used to be quite
   good at technical drawing at
   school.

And that's it. It's not even as though this list is my *top* five, either: there isn't a number six or seven that I had to omit because of the limitations of the exercise. To be honest, I'm not even that bothered about being an architect—I just thought that if I failed to come up with five, it would look a bit feeble.

It was Laura's idea for me to make a list, and I couldn't think of a sensible one, so I made a stupid one. I wasn't going to show her, but something got to me—self-pity, envy, something—and I do anyway.

She doesn't react.

"It's got to be architecture, then, hasn't it?"

"I guess."

"Seven years' training."

I shrug.

"Are you prepared for that?"

"Not really."

"No, I didn't think so."

"I'm not sure I really want to be an architect."

"So you've got a list here of five things you'd do if qualifications and time and history and salary were no object, and one of them you're not bothered about."

"Well, I did put it at number five."

"You'd really rather have been a journalist for the *New Musical Express*, than, say, a sixteenth-century explorer, or king of France?"

"God, yes."

She shakes her head.

"What would you put down, then?"

"Hundreds of things. A playwright. A ballet dancer. A musician, yes, but also a painter or a university don or a novelist or a great chef."

"A chef?"

"Yes. I'd love to have that sort of talent. Wouldn't you?"

"Wouldn't mind. I wouldn't want to work evenings, though." I wouldn't, either.

"Then you might just as well stay at the shop."

"How'd you work that out?"

"Wouldn't you rather do that than be an architect?"

"I suppose."

"Well, there you are then. It comes in at number five in your list of dream jobs, and as the other four are entirely impractical, you're better off where you are."

Pagan Kennedy

Pop-culture critic, Pagan Kennedy is the author of the novel Stripping and Other Stories *(1994),* Platforms: A Microwaved Cultural Chronicle of the 1970s *(1994),* 'Zine: How I Spent Six Years of My Life in the Underground and Finally Found Myself . . . I Think *(1995).* Spinsters *(1995),* Pagan Kennedy's Living: The Handbook for Maturing Hipsters *(1997), and her very witty novel* The Exes *(1998) is about an indie band consisting of four ex-lovers who play punk music at second-rate clubs around Boston but never quite give up their dream to achieve something bigger. The story is told from the viewpoints of each individual band member— Hank, Lilly, Shaz, and Walt—sort of the rock equivalent of Akira Kurosawa's* Rashomon. *Excerpted here is a portion of Lilly's story.*

From
The Exes

In third grade the teacher picked her to be Mary. She stood in front of the manger, and the kids in donkey and sheep suits had to kneel around her. They were supposed to be adoring the Christ child in her arms, but Lilly knew that they kneeled around her because she was the prettiest girl in the class, with blond hair and honey skin. She kept her eyes cast upward so she'd look like the Mary at the front of the church; she'd tried to hold her fingers in that strange curled way, a girl turning into a stone.

That was the last moment of being normal she could remember. You were either normal or you had something wrong with you—foreign, ugly, fat, black, spastic, retardo, smelly. Sometime in third grade, she turned into one of the smelly ones. When her father left, the other kids could smell it on her. "You stink like a turd," they said.

Maybe she started to stink because she and her mom and her brother had to move into one of those apartment complexes where the old ladies in Woolworth dresses sat on the stairs. They stunk, those ladies. Everything stunk, and it didn't get any better until she met Ann-Marie in tenth grade. One day, Lilly heard "I Wanna Be Sedated" on Ann-Marie's Radio Shack stereo, and the most obvious, simple thought occurred to her: so what if everyone hated her? The songs on that record became her own private soundtrack; she whispered the words to herself as she walked down the halls at school.

So she and Ann-Marie invented their own punk scene in Knoxville, Tennessee; they figured out how to dress and act by studying the pictures on the back of record covers: Patti Smith, Lou Reed, Richard Hell, the Ramones, Poly Styrene, Iggy Pop, those kohl-eyed, leopard-skinned, spike-haired people from another planet. Lilly wore ripped T-shirts and black fingernail polish that she made by mixing bottles of red and blue. Ann-Marie pinned a map of New York to her wall, and with their fingers they'd roam the streets, finding where CBGB and Max's Kansas City must be hidden amid the squiggle of subway paths. Lilly always thought she'd end up there, in some tiny apartment with graffiti splattered across the walls.

But then she began writing to the lead singer of the Pricks, this amazing band up in Boston. "I saw that interview with you in *Trouser Press* and I always felt the same way about Evel Knievel. Wouldn't *Snake River* be a great name for an album?" she wrote the first time. They started out talking about motorcycles and drag racing, but after Lilly sent him a picture, they veered off into kinky jokes. "Kinky"— that was a word everyone used when Lilly was in high school, and she liked to say to people, "I've been getting these incredibly kinky letters from the lead singer of the Pricks."

When he invited her to visit, she didn't think twice. By this time, she was a freshman at the University of Tennessee. She took the bus up, and there he was waiting at the station. From the moment he took her bag and threw it in the back of his Dodge Swinger, she knew she belonged here. They went to shows every night and he introduced her to people who looked like they never left the clubs, with mushroom-colored skin and last-night's makeup still fading on their faces.

Even after she broke up with the Pricks guy, she stayed in Boston. She got a scholarship at Mass. Art. Back then a lot of the rockers were going to art school, so it didn't even occur to her that learning to draw and paint wasn't going to help her get into a band.

Anyway, she didn't necessarily have to be a rock star. It would be okay if she became famous for the cartoons she drew, or the clothes she designed, or her paintings—just as long as she became famous for *something*. Of course, it would take a while. She knew she would have to grope along toward fame, the way you fumble through a dark room, running your hands up and down the walls, until you find the light switch. And in that single instant when she finally managed to flip on the light, her life would all fall into place.

What she didn't anticipate was how long she'd have to spend groping. Every time she was about to look for a band or try and get into a gallery, the group house where she lived would break up, and then she'd have to move. And every time she did, she lost things—phone numbers, important pieces of fabric, drawings, notes, journals. Once she dreamed she was in a deserted factory building walking over brittle shards of something that crunched under her feet. All of a sudden, she realized she was trampling those precious things she'd lost over the years. They lay on the ground, glinting like broken glass, dangerous and sharp and impossible to pick up.

Sometime during all of this messed-up-ness, she burned a pink candle and concentrated on getting a guitar for free, and one day, like a miracle, she found a Gibson under a pile of junk in the basement of her group house, left there by some long-ago occupant—a guy who, a housemate said, had promised to come back and get his stuff years ago.

She took it as a sign that her luck would turn. She thought the music would flow out of her fingers as easily as the clothing designs and the drawings did. But playing the guitar was hideous. All those rules to follow, so many things to think about. She felt like Alice in Wonderland, caught in a topsy-turvy mathematical world where strange beings screamed at her. G minor, with its impossible hand position, bullied her around like the Red Queen; and E flat, one pinkie arched upward, was always angry and dull-sounding. Instead of curling into the chords, her hand clenched in painful positions. It made her cry, and she gave up.

And then she met Hank. He had the same sickness she did, the kind that made your stomach ache whenever you heard a song you loved. Because you should have been the one who wrote it. Because it should have been yours. Hank—at least in this one way—was her twin. He too groped through the dark room, feeling for the switch that would turn everything on.

The thing was, though, he wouldn't admit how much he wanted to be famous. "Don't you want to be a rock star?" she asked him once. "Like get interviewed on MTV and have hit CDs and hang out with the Beastie Boys?"

"Are you kidding, Lill?" he said. "What's the point? You'd be forced to do crap, mainstream crap. I just want to make totally fucking impeccable music."

"Uh-huh," she said, hearing the real meaning underneath his words. He needed to be a star as badly as she did; the only difference between them was the texture and taste of the fame they craved. Lilly longed to be shot, all slit-eyed and sexy, by fashion photographers, to become Miss America in combat boots. Hank, on the other hand, longed to be secretly famous. He was obsessed with identifying the exact moment that different bands sold out to the corporate oligarchy. "I saw the Breeders in the basement of the Rat before they even had a name. They were so spontaneous and raw," he would say. "But as soon as they came out with that first CD, they turned to shit. Total la-la girl pop."

Hank wanted to belong to a band so obscure and brilliant that just knowing the name of this band would be like saying a password that got you into the secret brotherhood of the ultracool indie guys. He wanted his music to be played only on obscure college stations by snotty dee-jays who had piled three thousand records in their rent-controlled apartments. He wanted to get hate mail. He wanted to be a genius.

It took Lilly a while to understand all this, and to figure out what, exactly, he considered genius. At first she assumed that when Hank approved a song, he was judging it by some musical quality she would never understand; but, no, Hank didn't care about technical skill. "That's just decoration," he'd say. Instead, he peered deep beneath the riffs and drumbeats and harmonies to discern whether or not the song had a soul.

This turned out to be the light switch Lilly had been groping for. In the glare of his vision, she suddenly understood it didn't matter how well she played; what mattered was this other nameless thing she'd had all along, her stink. It was the stink of hot dogs in a kitchen with yellow Formica counters; the stink of the Mississippi at the end of summer when the cicadas are screaming; the stink of her own body reeking of cigarettes and incense and something sweet.

"Ever since I started practicing guitar," she told Hank, "I hear tunes in my head. Especially when I'm biking. When I'm on my bike going to work I make up entire songs with words that rhyme and everything."

"You do?" he said, excited.

"Yeah, but they're really dumb."

"Sing one for me."

She sang in just the way she did while she was biking—high and breathy, gulping some of the words like a little kid. He began working the tune out on his keyboard and then showed her what to strum on her guitar. Soon it had turned into a real song, a miracle as amazing as the sudden appearance of the guitar itself.

"I wish I could think up stuff like that," Hank said, his voice cracking. She realized that this was a confession of his most secret shame, what he kept hidden from everyone else—his lack of soul.

"You can do it," she said. "It's easy."

"Not for me," he said.

Hank had a way of wimping out like that; he'd decide something was impossible and then he wouldn't even try. That's why she had to break up with him. "I want my boyfriend to worship me. Or if he doesn't worship me, he should at least be able to pretend he worships me," she told him once.

"I'm not going to pretend, Lilly," he said, which she thought was a very boring answer. Basically, Hank was just too self-obsessed. She needed a man who would wrap her up in fantasy like the finest mink; a man who would indulge her in all things. And then one day she was walking in the park and saw this guy lounging on a park bench with a red velvet notebook. She settled next to him and said, "I'm going to read your palm."

His love line ran in a collection of creases around the side of his hand. His mound of Mercury was pronounced and his fingers tapered elegantly, signs of a creative mind. Right from the beginning, this man—Dieter—humored her. He let her tell his fortune; he bought her a tart covered in kiwis and strawberries; he listened without interrupting. Dieter, descended in an unbroken line of blood from the Hapsburgs, spent his days brooding in his dusty apartment. He lived on a tidbit of a trust fund, occasionally taking jobs as a dog-sitter or a proofreader. That first night, she bossed him into bed with her; they made love languidly, often stopping to discuss some important point or other.

"I sometimes suddenly feel like I've slipped into another time period," Dieter said. "I'll turn a corner and from the way the leaves look, I'll know that I'm in the seventeen hundreds, say. Does that happen to you?"

"Yes," Lilly said, wiggling closer to him. "I was just realizing that we'd become people in the nineteen twenties."

"That's what I was thinking, too," he said. "We're in Berlin between the wars."

After only a few months she moved into Dieter's apartment, and it seemed like everything had ended happily ever after. She stopped losing stuff, because it all accumulated in Dieter's living room: the dressmaker's dummy, the piles of fabric, the effects boxes and patch cords. She littered his queen-sized bed with notebooks and crayons; his kitchen table became her drawing studio. Dieter didn't mind her taking over his apartment; he didn't even mind when she informed him that she was starting a band with her ex-boyfriend.

She'd come up with the concept one morning in the spring while she was drinking coffee, and had immediately called Hank. "We should name our band the Exes," she'd said breathlessly. "Because then we could have the coolest poster for our show. You know that sixties movie about wife-swapping? *Bob & Carol & Ted & Alice?* There's that picture of them all in the same bed together. We could start a band that's two guys and two girls who've all slept together, and we would use that picture."

"What?" Hank had said. "What do you mean we could use the picture?"

"For our posters, I mean. When we make posters to advertise our shows. The posters would make it look like we all sleep in the same bed together." She'd had a vision of it all: the posters, the T-shirts, the band logos. Annoyingly, Hank hadn't been interested in any of the tie-in products she envisioned; instead, he kept questioning her about the Exes concept—who would have slept with whom, and what instruments would they play? But of course that's how Hank managed to get things done.

About nine months later, in the dead of winter, he booked their first gig.

"Remember that poster you thought of a while ago?" he said to her, when they took a breath for a smoke one night during practice.

"What?" she said, watching how the neon of a liquor-store sign made his face look as soft and pink as a fetus's.

"You know, the Bob *&* Carol *&* Ted *&* Alice poster."

"Oh, right."

"Well, you can make it now, for our gig," he said. "We need some posters."

"Okay," she said. She took the picture of Bob & Carol & Ted & Alice and pasted X's over their heads. When she finished, she had just the image she wanted: four people—each one of them with an X instead of a face—crammed into the same bed. As she walked out of the copy shop with a stack of the posters still warm from the machine, a strange sense of wonder washed over her. She'd invented the idea of this particular band with this particular poster, and it had all turned real. Though she was already twenty-nine and not famous yet, she had the sense that everything else she wanted would eventually happen, too. The thought of this scared her—spooked her, really, in the way that made the hairs on the back of her neck prickle.

During that first gig, she kept thinking, "Is this really me up here?" When she plugged in her effects boxes and tuned her guitar, she was aware of how many times she'd fantasized about exactly this moment. It weirded her out—the way she'd walked into one of her own daydreams.

The club began to fill with people holding glossy bottles of beer; most of them were here to see the headlining band, but it didn't matter. Soon they would watch her—and just this, the fact that they would be her audience, made them fascinating to her and she peered down from the stage, trying to size up each one of them.

"You guys ready?" the sound man said, The place was half full, most people clustered around the bar.

"Yeah, we're ready," Hank called over to him.

Lilly swallowed. Her spit felt like acid going down. That's how terrified she was. She glanced at the play list taped near her feet. The first song was "Splatter Movie." As if she didn't know. Hank had made them run through the set over and over.

The song started with Lilly picking her guitar, in a fast surf riff. Her stomach ached. She wasn't sure she could do it without messing up. But then Hank said, "Okay, let's go," and Walt clapped his drumsticks together, and Lilly launched into her solo. Suddenly they were in the middle of the song, and she was singing, "We'll use grapes for the eyeballs/and some ketchup for blood./'Cause I love when your skin crawls/and your cut-off head goes thud." She was too busy singing to check out the audience, but she could sense them gathering close, their eyes like silvery beads on a black dress, their minds playing multiple movies where she was always the star.

The Exes attacked song after song with hardly a beat in between. That's how Hank wanted it. "We won't give them time to blink," he'd said. "We'll knock them on their asses." They ripped through their set in about a half an hour. To Lilly, it felt like a few seconds had gone by, a furious burst of activity and then suddenly she was shielding her eyes from the light, damp with sweat, breathless. Out there, in the dark, they were clapping and screaming.

The sound man jumped onto the stage. "What are you guys doing now? You want an encore?" Lilly realized that all of them had just been standing there, dazed.

"We don't have an encore," Hank said.

"You don't?" the guy said. "Okay, okay, let's break down." And he unplugged a cord and began winding it around his arm.

Lilly woke from her trance and lifted her guitar over her head. The audience had drifted away from the stage. She jumped down and went outside to the van. Walt and Shaz were loading the drums.

"I feel like I'm on drugs," Lilly said.

Walt glanced at her over his shoulder. "Could you hand me that stuff over there?"

Lilly lifted a pile of metal drum do-hickies and carried it over to him. Her hands felt numb. It felt like the time she smoked opium and her body turned into a giant pillow.

"I just feel really, really weird," she said.

"It's the adrenaline," Walt said. "It hangs around in your bloodstream for a while, even after you stop being scared."

Shaz backed out of the van and stood up. "I feel weird, too. Were we any good?"

"Yeah, I think so," Walt said. "Except that feedback."

"There was feedback?" Lilly asked.

"There were other fuckups, too. Like I messed up at the end," Walt said.

They kept going over what had happened, trying to piece together the reality of it from what each of them remembered. Even after they finished loading the van and had gone back inside the club, they couldn't stop analyzing their set from every angle. The next band—the headlining act—was playing, so they had to shout into each other's ears. "At least we all ended on the same beat," someone would say, or "Did they have us turned up this loud?" They all had this compulsion to know exactly what the others had been thinking on stage, as if you could add up the four streams of consciousness—the way you mixed together different instruments on a four-track—and come up with a single song of memory, a studio-produced and cleaned-up version of the truth.

This was the routine, Lilly learned after a few shows. You loaded up the van, and then you huddled together to figure out how the set had gone. After that, Lilly would drift away from the rest of the band to lean against the wall and drink free beer. People would tap her on the shoulder and yell into her ear, "That was great." It was as if they could tell how much she needed to be reassured.

That first night they performed, though, Lilly hadn't expected the postshow flurry of attention. Her friends ran up and hugged her, or kissed her on the cheek. Cool-looking strangers glanced her way. For the first time in her life, she felt like a celebrity. Late that night, some guy grabbed her elbow and ushered her over to the bar. "I need to talk to you," he said, and then he proceeded to rant about the independent film he might shoot someday and how he wanted her to play the lead.

"Would I have to memorize a lot of lines?" Lilly wanted to know.

"Oh, well, the script isn't written yet," he said, clutching his beer. "But I've got the whole thing figured out." And he proceeded to reel off the plot.

After a few months of playing out in clubs, Lilly grew used to these guys with their never-to-be-shot movies and their never-to-be-organized benefit concerts. They wanted to lay claim to you, if only in some imaginary way. For they had seen something magical glinting out of you when you were up there on stage, and they wanted credit for having such good taste. It was as if you were a rare LP on extrathick vinyl that they'd found at a yard sale for five cents—they wanted to show it to all their friends and say, "I noticed this. I noticed this when everyone else walked right by it."

On a good night, lots of people wanted you in that way. They wanted to put you in imaginary movies, plays, and bands; or they stared at you, eager to seduce you; or they tried to edge their way into the cluster of people around you. On a night like that, you felt like the coolest person in the club, but the next morning you woke up as Cinderella with a stale mouth and buzzing ears. Then you had to hustle over to the café and mop up slime from around the refrigerator and kiss-ass the customers, just like always.

P. F. Kluge

Back in the fifties, Eddie and the Parkway Cruisers were considered the hottest rock and roll band along the Jersey Shore. Eddie Wilson, the leader, though is long gone and the only person who remembers those glory days is the band's lyricist, Frank Ridgeway, now a married schoolteacher with a family. When an English rock band turns the Cruiser's classic songs into runaway hits, everyone sits up and takes notice. Such is the premise of Eddie and the Cruisers *(1980), the now classic rock and roll novel by P. F. Kluge.* Eddie and the Cruisers *is available in a reprinted edition with an afterword by the author from the Kenyon College Bookstore in Gambier, Ohio. E-mail Susan Dailey (dailey@kenyon.edu) or phone 740-427-5151. Author-signed copies are available. Kluge is also the author of* Biggest Elvis *(1999), about three Elvis impersonators set in the Philippines near a U.S. naval base and* Final Exam, *a novel involving serial murders on a small college campus, to be published by XOXOX Press of Gambier, Ohio, in 2006.*

From
Eddie and the Cruisers

It began on a Sunday morning.

Not in church. It was at the Safeway supermarket.

We do all our food-shopping on Sundays, before the churches let out, and it's become something of a ritual in itself. Bringing home the bacon, bringing in the sheaves.

Do you remember an old daytime TV show called *Supermarket Sweep*? A half-dozen contestants line up at the checkout counter of one of those huge suburban stores where the aisles go on for miles; the cookies alone take up a hundred yards. At the buzzer, the competitors rush out the starting gate and race up and down the aisles, heaving one item after another into their shopping carts. They have five minutes to rampage through the store, and the winner is the one who makes it back to the cash registers with the most expensive load.

That's my family.

While they cruise the aisles, I sit near the door, atop a pile of twenty-five-pound dog-food bags. Sometimes I flip through *People* magazine, or chat with my students' parents, or smile and wave at my family: buy this not that, get the big size not the little.

On other Sundays, bad-mood Sundays, I just think. This was one of those. I watched my wife and two daughters moving around on the other side of the cash registers. I felt like an outsider, a spectator. They weren't mine, they had nothing to do with me. As I watched them proceed from meats to vegetables, I realized for the first time that more than laziness or mere habit kept me from joining them: something inside me was keeping a distance. Something always had.

What would I have made of this, on my own? Probably nothing. I had grown used to being the man I was and had no idea how to go about changing. I'm sure my perching exile atop the dog-food bags would have become just another habit, like my scary little trick of driving with the headlights off on moonlit nights.

That's when it all began.

I heard a radio playing music, rather loud. A group of checkout clerks and bag-boys were standing around somebody's portable radio, listening to music and moving to the beat. They must have liked it. They turned it up again, and this time it was way too loud. The manager popped up behind his glass-walled cubbyhole, cast me an apologetic glance, and shouted for them to turn that damn thing down or they'd have to turn it off. The kids looked over at the manager. They'd heard him, but there was an irritating ten seconds of noncompliance while they waited for the music to end. By the time the manager was ready for a second warning, the song was over.

Doris and the girls reached the cash register just then, so there was nothing I could do right off. But the kid who helped carry our bags to the car—actually, all he did was push the cart through the parking lot and lift the bags into the trunk—had been in the group around the radio. I knew him from school. He was one of my students, a soon-to-be high school graduate who wasn't college material and wasn't worrying about it.

"How are you, Anthony?" I asked.

"Fine, Mr. Ridgeway. Could you call me Tony?" He asked politely, but in a way that told me he knew my control over him was ending. He was going to be a high school graduate. Named Tony.

"Sure, Tony. Hey, I wanted to ask you about that song."

"What song?"

"On the radio at the checkout counter. A bunch of you were listening. The manager broke it up."

"Oh yeah . . . that song."

"Yes."

"Well . . . what about it?"

"Is it a new hit?"

"I guess so."

"What's it called?"

"I don't know."

"Who's it by?"

"Got me. Some group. Sounded like a bunch of guys."

"You like that sound?"

"Well . . ." He backed off a little, abashed by the older generation's curiosity. A little annoyed. He'd already spent so many mornings scrambling for answers to my questions, and they were always wrong.

"That music up your alley, Anthony?"

"Yeah," he replied. "Yeah. Suits me fine."

I tipped him fifty cents, slammed the trunk, and watched Tony walk away. No doubt he wondered why his high school teacher couldn't mind his own business. Was I trying to get "with it"? That would be a joke!

But the joke was on you, Anthony. And it was my business. And I was "with it."

I wrote that song.

And I was one of the guys you heard singing.

Long time ago.

I sat in the lobby of the Holiday Inn, just outside the lounge, waiting for the lights to dim so I could enter unobtrusively. Posted on the wall was a glossy picture of the Cruisers: Sally and four white kids who didn't look like anybody.

"Trying to spot which one is you?"

Elliott Mannheim, equipped with tape recorder and girlfriend, was preparing to catch the show. He seemed glad to see me. And his girlfriend seemed impressed. Susan Foley wasn't the Mannheim type. He was intense, urban, Jewish. She was the sort of tall, full blonde who might be from Wisconsin, California-bound.

"You were an original Cruiser?" she asked.

"From beginning to end—right, Mr. Ridgeway?"

"I'm not so sure," I answered, pointing to the lounge. "I guess it hasn't ended. I was a Cruiser for one year. There's a man in there who's been one for nearly twenty."

"What brings you out?" Mannheim asked.

"Same as you. Curiosity."

"We're sitting ringside," Mannheim said. He peeked inside. "Not hard to arrange. But we'd love to have you join us. It would add a dimension."

"Please come," the girl said.

"Not now," I answered, with a twinge of regret. It had been a while since a young woman had found me interesting. But she probably wanted to talk about the Cruisers, about what Eddie was like or, God forbid, the details of the crash.

"Sally doesn't know I'm here," I told them. "If he spots me it could be disconcerting for both of us. And he's just crazy enough to call me up onstage. So I think I'll just sit at the bar."

"You're not going to leave without saying hello, are you?"

"No . . . I guess not."

"Then we'll see you in Mr. Amato's room, after the show. It's two-oh-three, in back. I'll be taping an interview. Be great if you could join in, have a dialogue with him. A Cruiser reunion after twenty years!"

"I don't know about that."

"Well, drop by anyway. I'll tell him you're coming."

"No, please. Don't."

"Okay," Mannheim conceded. "It'll be a surprise."

"But you will drop in," the girl insisted. Oh hell, I thought, for sure she's writing an Ohio State thesis on music of the 1950's.

"Sure," I relented. "I'll be there. See you later."

I waited a moment more after they left. The lounge was darker now, and some guitars were being tuned. The microphone growled and squeaked like a metal pig being forced down a slaughterhouse chute.

"Ladies and gentlemen, Holiday Inn is proud to present a group that's been bringing us hits for twenty years. A big hand, please, for some Jersey boys who made good. Eddie Wilson's Original Parkway Cruisers!"

I stepped aside and headed straight for the bar, like a salesman who badly needed a drink. Oh? Live music tonight? I really hadn't noticed. What's on draft? I had a beer in one hand and a bunch of peanuts in the other before I faced the music.

Sally was sitting behind the piano on a stage that was left maybe a foot above a tiny dance floor. To his left, a drummer. To his right, two guitarists. He was heavier, for sure, and his hair looked like it had been combed to cover thin spots, Bill Haley-style, but he was still Sally. Steady work, food that struck between the ribs, and no fuckin' around.

The Cruisers were dressed in the kind of dark, formal suits that would be Sally's idea of class. Sal had an added touch: a white linen scarf around his neck.

I didn't recognize the first tune: a busy little warmup instrumental that musicians use when they've come onstage. It was the kind of tune you just break even on. The audience applauded politely, neither disappointed nor especially pleased. The next was different.

"Shadows are longer now
Where I go
Sun is falling
Down bloody and low . . ."

It wasn't Sally's voice. It was Eddie's. It came from the drummer, a gawky, nondescript kid who gave me a tingly thrilling sensation I hadn't known for years. Close my eyes and it could have been Eddie, singing "On the Dark Side."

"Step to the dark side . . .
Who needs light?
Gonna *feel* my way, baby
And it's gonna feel right . . ."

Eddie Wilson didn't have a great voice. He used to kid about it—"Well, I'm no Frankie Laine." And then he'd do a marvelous thing: a slow, smoky version of "Moonlight Gambler." He treated it the way Ray Charles would have, turning a slap-happy anthem into—what?—a menacing invitation. When Eddie sang it, you knew that bad things could happen in the moonlight. No, you wouldn't mix him up with Frankie Laine, but he had a voice that was his own. And like many such voices, once you heard it, you could imitate it. We all did passable Eddie imitations. But this kid had Eddie down cold.

The audience loved him. There was a sprinkling of kids, but most looked old enough to have caught Eddie the first time around. That didn't make them old, but they weren't young either. Their bodies hinted of children at home.

"Gonna feel for the dark side
Don't care what I find
My love's gonna guide me,
Gonna help me go blind . . ."

They cheered wildly for the kid, who bowed awkwardly when he was done, cast a guilty look at Sally, and ducked back behind the drums. Sally had the kid under tight controls, I saw, an Eddie puppet he dangled in front of the audience.

"That's the memory-lane voice of Eddie Wilson," Sally said from behind the piano. He didn't introduce the kid. "The original sound of the Parkway Cruisers."

The very name brought some cheers. They were ready to sing along, clap hands, dance, turn back the clock.

"We were a bunch of kids from the Jersey shore. Any Jersey people here tonight?" (Hurray.) "You remember the feeling of the fifties? Sand in your shoes, ants in your pants, and a secret weapon in your wallet? Am I right? You made the babies, we made the hits. We're gonna play 'em all for you."

More cheers. Requests. "Far-Away Woman." "Down on My Knees."

"You'll get 'em all," Sally promised. "But you know, we're Cruisers. And Cruisers don't stand still. Gotta keep movin' down that road, knocking off the miles."

He held up an album.

"*The Cruisers Now!* Our latest. We're still moving. At your record stores. In the lobby. Under your windshield wipers. You don't buy it, we'll cop your hubcaps. Like to do a few cuts for you. This next one I wrote myself, 'Disco Boardwalk.' Like to see some dancers in front of me."

Nobody danced. Nobody moved. Hardly anybody applauded. Not for "Disco Boardwalk," or for Sally's soon-to-be-released novelty tune about joggers, or for his impressions of Little Richard, Fats Domino, and Chuck Berry. Sally's act didn't fall into the toilet: it dove in and stayed there and pretended it was an Olympic-size swimming pool. It laughed and splashed and shouted, "Come on in, the water's fine."

You could see the audience turn old and sour and disappointed. One moment they were young again; the next minute they were worried about their babysitters. "Uh . . . this was a mistake . . . not what we thought." "Honey . . . it's late . . . the kids."

I was into my fourth beer. There were moments when going back to check out the Cruisers seemed absolutely right. It wasn't the tapes. It was the idea of getting in touch with a time when I'd been part of something good.

Now, once again, the pendulum had swung to the other side. I saw an aging audience out for cheap thrills and a pathetically out-of-step musician who refused to provide them. I felt terrible just then. It was too bad for everybody: for dead Eddie and misfit Sally, for the ripped-off audience and the cuckold English teacher at the bar.

I checked out Mannheim's table, wondering about how to break my promise to show up in Sally's room. I ran straight into a stare and a sad smile from the girl. Susan Foley understands, I thought. I shrugged and waved good-bye. She shook her head. No, don't leave yet. I know it's awful, of course, but don't go. So I stayed.

Sally was in the middle of more "new material" when the audience got out of hand. I think he was doing something inspired by *Star Wars*, with lots of flashing lights and weird notes and clanging sounds. It reminded me of a Spike Jones routine, it was that bad.

"Just play the hits," a man shouted. "Fuck the kid stuff!"

"Oldies but goodies," cried a woman, and before long they took up the chant, stomping their feet and clapping their hands in unison. "Oldies but goodies! Oldies but goodies!"

Sally tried finishing the space number, but it was hopeless. He motioned for the others to stop playing. Then he turned on his piano stool and faced the still-chanting audience, waiting for them to quiet down.

"You been a great audience," he said, and I hoped I was the only one who knew him well enough to spot the hate in his eyes.

"Okay music lovers. Get on with the music! Time to rock and roll! Eddie Wilson time! Wendell Newton, Kenny Hopkins, Frank

Ridgeway, and yours truly, keeping faith on the piano. Are you ready?"

The audience loved him now, knowing they'd won.

The Cruisers broke into a fast, angry version of "Down on My Knees," with Sally singing lead.

"Saying to you baby, baby please,
What else you want
When I'm down on my knees?"

There were a dozen cuts on our one and only l.p., and Sally went through all of them. In order. On the demanding tunes like "Leavin' Town" and "It'll Happen Tonight," he called on the drummer, but otherwise he took the lead himself, pounding out the songs with an angry competence that the audience mistook for conviction. How many times has Little Richard keened "Long Tall Sally"? Or Jerry Lee Lewis slugged his way through "Whole Lotta Shakin' Goin' On"? That many times and more, Sally had worked his way through Eddie's dozen songs. And, to judge from his new material, the future held nothing but more of the same. Twenty years from now, he'd be held over in Sun City and St. Pete. They'd need a doctor in attendance.

At last the customers were getting what they paid for, drinking hard, crowding the dance floor. The whole room felt like a high school reunion, with everyone out to demonstrate that they were still young.

"Hold on, everybody," Sally shouted when he'd almost worked his way through the album. "Time to light a candle."

Some dancers stayed on the floor, leaning against each other. Some retreated to their tables, holding hands. The Cruisers began playing "Those Oldies But Goodies Remind Me of You," very slow and melancholy.

"I wanna say a word about the past," Sally intoned. "The past isn't gone." (Cheers for the past.) "The past's not dead!" ("You bet your ass it ain't!" someone shouted.) "Not as long as we carry the music in our hearts. Not as long as we remember the good things. I wanna tell you about one of the good things that happened to me."

A hush fell over the Holiday Inn. A few gasps. A reaching for handkerchiefs. They knew they were being set up. And they loved it.

"You'd think it'd be hard to remember someone who's been gone for twenty years," Sally said. "Well, I got news. Not Eddie Wilson. He's part of yesterday, sure. But he's part of today, too, you'd better believe. And tomorrow . . . never doubt it."

Now the Cruisers were singing "Those Oldies but Goodies . . ." and Sally's monologue sounded like one of those spoken passages that turn up in the middle of country-and-western records.

"He was a kid, like any other kid. Like you and me used to be . . . He was one of us, always, and that's how come he wrote songs that reached out and touched us, touched us where we live…

"People ask me, how come this group is still called Eddie Wilson's Original Parkway Cruisers. Is it for the money? Publicity? Let 'em think what they want, because down deep I've settled that one for myself. Because Eddie Wilson is as much a part of this group as I am. We're still together, him and me. Never a day passes, I don't think he's around somewhere. Down the road a ways. Around a corner. In the neighborhood. Not far away at all . . ."

You can guess what happened next: a sudden silence, a dimming of the lights, and the sound of Wendell Newton's sax leading into "Far-Away Woman."

No point in calling for an encore. "Far-Away Woman" ended the show like an anthem or a hymn. There was nothing left for Sally to play and nothing for the audience to do but head home.

I took time finishing my beer. I needed time to calm down. Granted, there was an integral sleaziness in Sally's act. It reminded me of a show we'd seen at Disney World, where they have moving, talking, life-sized replicas of U.S. presidents onstage, and Abe Lincoln delivers a snatch of the Gettysburg oldie-but-goodie. That's the kind of act that Sally had. I didn't envy him. He shared the stage with robots, a ventriloquist upstaged by his dummies. He invoked Eddie's ghost and made a living out of it, but he was that ghost's dependent. The least stir of independence and his audience was gone.

And yet, how could you account for the overwhelming magic of those songs? The singer was dead, and the songs were two decades old. But look at what had happened tonight! The songs were part of people's lives, milestones and measuring sticks. They turned people into dancers, brought tears, evoked memories, made them young again. Where books and movies didn't reach, Eddie's songs arrived so effortlessly, riveted in time and place and yet . . . transcendent. I could see him now, lifting his hands, an amazed look on his face, just like after I'd dug out a poem he liked: "Holee shit!"

Eddie never figured he was writing classics. His songs were the offspring of moods: a knockout girl in Cape May, a hangover in Absecon. He tossed them off and they met their fates in the most transient of trades, a Number Eight or a Number Eighty. An upward curve and an inevitable downward fall on the *Billboard* list. And that was it. Nobody listened to "golden oldies" back then. We didn't get nostalgic about dead singers and disbanded groups. Russ Colombo? Glenn Miller? We looked ahead, to tonight, this weekend, next summer. Now, everybody was looking back. Even the kids. That was the difference between then and now. Something had changed in the land, and Eddie's music was part of the change.

"You're coming, aren't you?"

Mannheim had sent Susan Foley to fetch me.

"Yeah, I'll be there."

"How'd you like the show?" she asked.

"Mixed emotions."

"I could see them on your face."

"What about you?"

"I was glad I saw it," she said. "But I wouldn't come back."

"Do you think I could buy you a drink before we go?"

I was ready to step over to a table, but she hopped right up on a bar stool and seemed perfectly at home.

"What are you doing here?" I asked. "I mean, I was a Cruiser. A historic Parkway Cruiser. That's my excuse."

"I need an excuse?"

"Excuse me. But I'm still curious. Is it Mannheim? Or the music?"

"School's out."

"I wasn't sure of that. I pegged you as a graduate student in . . . I don't know . . . sociology or American studies. 'A Typical Musical Group of the Nineteen-Fifties.' Another writer, like your boyfriend."

"I'm not a writer."

"And?"

"He's not my boyfriend. We went to college together, back East. I'm a graduate student now. And my thesis has nothing to do with the Cruisers. Unless you sang about martial law in the Philippines."

"Political science."

"Law."

"I'm sorry. I ask a lot of awkward questions. That is, I ask them awkwardly."

I'm not sure my apology was needed. Susan Foley seemed more amused than offended. My clumsiness amused her.

"What were they doing when you left?" I asked.

"Elliott had started taping. Your name popped up, by the way."

"Mannheim didn't tell Sally?"

"No. He didn't say you were coming. He asked him to appraise the musical talent of the original Cruisers. He mentioned you first, like you were the easiest to dispose of. 'Well, there was that Ridgeway kid on guitar. A José Feliciano, he wasn't. He could make a guitar sound like a ukulele!'"

I laughed at that, and she did too.

"Maybe we better head over there," I said, "and save my reputation."

We walked out of the lounge together. She was good-looking enough to turn some heads, I saw, and nice enough to take my arm.

"That's not all Sal said," she told me as we passed the deserted swimming pool.

"Oh no. Let's hear it. Count on Sally to get in with the low blows."

"This wasn't. He said you were quote some kind of genius with words, a regular whiz kid, close quote. He said you helped Eddie Wilson write a lot of the songs. Like 'Far-Away Woman' and 'On the Dark Side.' Is that true?"

"I helped. Eddie had the ideas and some of the words. But they took a lot of organizing and smoothing out. That was my job."

"It sounded like a lot more than that. And those are great songs. I'm no nostalgia buff, but I know when a song gets under my skin. Those are great. Did you ever follow up?"

"Follow up?"

"After Eddie Wilson died. Didn't you write any more songs?"

"No."

"Or poems or books?"

"No."

"What did you get into?"

"Teachers' college."

"That's not what I meant."

"I'm sorry." I paused, sensing that she was waiting for an explanation, but there wasn't much I could add. "That part of my life stopped dead when Eddie died."

"So then—pardon me—but why are *you* here?" I guessed she had me there: a solitary thirty-seven-year-old man who drove six hundred miles to catch a lounge act at a motel in Ohio. For what?

She persisted. "You said that part of your life had stopped dead. So what's *your* excuse?"

"I wanted to see how things turned out for some old friends of mine," I said.

"That's all?"

"No. . . ." The next part came hard. It was the first time I'd put it into words. "I wanted to see how things . . . how things might have turned out for me."

Rick Moody

Rick Moody's first novel, The Garden State *(1992), about a New Jersey rock band trying to get by. His second novel,* The Ice Storm *(1994), a disturbing tale about a dysfunctional family in New Canaan, Connecticut, was made into a movie directed by Ang Lee and received much critical acclaim. Moody is also the author of* The Ring of Brightest Angels Around Heaven: A Novella and Stories *(1995), which includes "The James Dean Garage Band," a terrific short story in which the iconic actor survives the car crash that killed him in real life and walks away unscathed from the scene of the accident only to be recruited by a group of feckless teenagers as a guitarist in their band;* Purple America *(1997); and* The Black Veil: A Memoir with Digressions *(2002), about his battle with depression. With Darcey Steinke, he co-edited* Joyful Noise: The New Testament Revisited *(1997). "Wilkie Fahnstock, The Boxed Set," written in the form of liner notes, is from* Demonology *(2001), a collection of short stories.*

Wilkie Fahnstock,
The Boxed Set

The ground-breaking, innovative collection you have before you represents a new milestone in the history of Bankruptcy Records, a profound effort to bring to the public one of the representative lives of the last century. Bankruptcy here endeavors to depict Wilkie Ridgeway Fahnstock in a format he personally favored during his lifetime, that of the old-time magnetic tape cassette—in this instance a ten-volume anthology of such cassettes, one for each of the important periods of Fahnstock's life, including the Greenwich Years, the years in Kingston, Rhode Island, etc. (See our Website for more information about other exciting Bankruptcy releases, including collections like the home videos of the McGill family of Poughkeepsie, NY ("Shannon's fifth birthday party" "Summer Theater Production of OUR TOWN, 6/21/76!"), and the laser-disk-only release of *STAR TREK* EPISODES I REALLY LIKE by Rochester, NY, soft-

Cassette One
(A)
"There was a lot of space in the living room to dance. My sister had a hula hoop and she used to put on Neil Diamond's early work, like 'Mother Love's Traveling Salvation Show.' Now she's a social worker in Sandusky, Ohio, with two kids named Jenny and Mike."
1. Peter Ilyich Tchaikovsky (1840 –93), 1812 Overture, Op. 49, *edit.*
2. The Beatles, "I Saw Her Standing There" (1965).
3. The Beach Boys, "I Get Around" (1965).
4. Byrds, "Turn, Turn, Turn" (1967).
5. Bob Dylan, "Tambourine Man" (1966).
6. Otis Redding, "(Sitting on) The Dock of the Bay" (1968).
7. Tommy James & the Shondells, "Mony, Mony" (1969).
8. Jimi Hendrix, "The Star Spangled Banner" (1969).
9. Simon and Garfunkel, "Bridge Over Troubled Water" (1970).

(B)
"The most important place to learn about music was on the AM-only radio dial of my mom's station wagon. Cousin Brucie, Wolfman Jack, Imus in the morning, and Harry Harrison."
10. Bobby Sherman, "Julie, Do You Love Me?" (1971).
11. Three Dog Night, "Mama Told Me Not to Come" (1971).
12. Smokey Robinson and the

ware designer Greg Tanizaki.)

The earthquake-like cannon blasts of Tchaikovsky's *1812 Overture* serve here as an éclat for Wilkie Fahnstock's 1964 birth, without complications, at the Mercy Hospital of Greenwich, CT. His mother, Elise Fahnstock (née Roosevelt) was and is a classical music fanatic, and Tchaikovsky and other classical greats such as Beethoven and Mozart were often spinning on the playroom hi-fi near Wilkie's crib, especially in renditions by Arthur Fieldler's Boston Pops. Later, when Wilkie briefly tried to learn the violin, he surreptitiously played records of the Bach Cello suites (the Pablo Casals recording) in an effort to fool his mom into believing he was practicing.

Tragedy struck in 1970, when Elise Fahnstock's marriage to Stannard Buchanan Fahnstock ended in acrimonious divorce—to the sounds of Simon and Garfunkel's *Bridge Over Troubled Water*. Wilkie's dad took to an apartment in New York City in order to date a succession of chain-smoking,

Miracles, "Tears of a Clown" (1970).

13. Jackson Five, "I Want You Back" (1971).

14. Edwin Starr, "War" (1972).

15. Dobie Gray, "Fade Away" (1972).

16. Ohio Players, "Fire" (1972).

17. The Allman Brothers Band, "Ramblin' Man" (1972).

18. James Taylor, "Fire and Rain" (1971).

19. Looking Glass, "Brandy (You're a Fine Girl)" (1972).

20. The Brady Bunch Kids, "Candy" (1972).

Cassette Two

(A)

"Danny Berry's dad accidentally killed someone mountain climbing—roped snapped and the guy sailed into a gorge. Danny liked really dark stuff. He turned me on to Pink Floyd. I remember reading the lyrics to 'Brain Damage' and thinking it was really scary."

1. Gary Glitter, "Rock 'n Roll" (1972).

2. Deep Purple, "Smoke on the Water" (1971).

3. Led Zeppelin, "Black Dog" (1971).

4. Focus, "Hocus Pocus" (1972).

5. Traffic, "John Barleycorn Must Die" (1973).

6. Yes, "Roundabout" (1972).

7. Edgar Winter Group, "Frankenstein" (1973).

8. Elton John, "Philadelphia Freedom" (1973).

9. Alice Cooper, "School's Out" (1972).

high-fashion models. Poor Wilkie! Poor little sister Samantha! Suddenly the tender pop classics of the middle and late sixties—the sunny harmonies of the Beach Boys, the raucous fun of Tommy James and the Shondells, the prepubescent funk of the Jackson Five—gave way to the darker moods of early seventies "progressive rock" stylings. Wilkie, alone in his room (in a succession of split-level Tudor homes throughout the County of Westchester), was contemplating the multiples of Rusty Staub baseball cards while the ominous chords of Mike Oldfield and Pink Floyd floated through his depressive consciousness on a monophonic Zenith brand "record player." Of course, the surge of *national drug experimentation* was also a part of Wilkie Fahnstock's adolescence, as with so many of his peers, and on cassette two (actually dubbed from a moldering Memorex ninety-minute tape found in an old summer camp foot locker), we see for the first time the "heavy" music of such acknowledged "drug" bands as Led Zeppelin,

(B)

10. Jethro Tull, "Skating Away on the Thin Ice of a New Day" (1974).
11. Emerson, Lake and Palmer, "Hoedown" (1973).
12. Pink Floyd, "Money" (1972).
13. Hot Butter, "Popcorn" (1973).
14. Genesis, "I Know What I Like (In Your Wardrobe)" (1973).
15. Mike Oldfield, "Tubular Bells" (1973).
16. The Who, "Baba O'Riley" (1971).
17. Electric Light Orchestra, "Roll Over Beethoven" (1972).
18. Moody Blues, "Legend of a Mind" (1968).

Cassette Three
(A)
"Had to hide my Kiss albums from my roommate in freshman year. But now I'm proud of them. These days, Kiss records sound really cool."
1. The Tubes, "White Punks on Dope" (1975).
2. Kiss, "Rock 'n Roll All Nite" (1974).
3. Lou Reed, "Sweet Jane" (1973).
4. Roxy Music, "Re-Make, Re-Model" (1972).
5. David Bowie, "Rebel, Rebel" (1973).
6. Queen, "We Will Rock You" and "We Are the Champions" (1976).
7. Ian Hunter, "Once Bitten, Twice Shy" (1976).
8. Sweet, "Fox on the Run" (1976).
9. The Who, "Squeeze Box" (1976).

(B)
"When I got older I started to learn to play Frisbee and hackey sack."

Alice Cooper, and the Moody Blues, especially as these portentous sounds vied for Wilkie's attentions with the simple easy confections of Elton John.

Now, as Fahnstock's parents shipped him off to the Phillips Academy at Andover, as Elise Fahnstock—newly betrothed to Fred Bolger, the reinforced-carton magnate—undertook a demanding career as Metropolitan Museum docent, as Stannard Fahnstock relocated his consulting business to Marblehead, Mass., the collection succumbs to a brief infatuation with the dazzling surfaces of "glam" rock, characterized by the abundant makeup of bands like Kiss and David Bowie. (Fahnstock tried, at this point, to get a few other prep school chums interested in forming a band featuring fire-breathing and spitting up blood, but given his own character—bad hair combined with high grades, unflattering eyeglasses and a poor sense of rhythm—this plan was doomed from the start.) On the B side of cassette three, however, there's a precipitous-turning toward the introspec-

10. Bruce Springsteen, "Rosalita" (1973).
11. Grateful Dead, "Truckin'" (1972).
12. Bob Dylan, "Tangled Up in Blue" (1975).
13. Neil Young, "Cortez the Killer" (1975).
14. Joni Mitchell, "For Free" (1972).
15. Fleetwood Mac, "Go Your Own Way" (1975).
16. KC and the Sunshine Band, "Get Down Tonight" (1975).
17. Daryl Hall and John Oates, "She's Gone" (1977).
18. The Eagles, "Hotel California" (1976).

Cassette Four
(A)
"I knew this guy, Mike Frew—he went on to become a big lawyer for Greenpeace—used to wear dog collars and listen to the Stranglers. He broke in punk rock big for my school. Single-handedly. He had these dances featuring the Bee Gees and the Pistols albums."
1. Peter Gabriel, "Solsbury Hill" (1976).
2. Iggy Pop, "Passenger" (1977).
3. Elvis Costello, "Radio, Radio" (1978).
4. Sex Pistols, "Anarchy in the U.K." (1977).
5. Devo, "Satisfaction" (1978).
6. Stranglers, "Hanging Around" (1977).
7. Blondie, "Hanging on the Telephone" (1977).
8. The Police, "Walking on the Moon" (1979).

tive, Californian singer-song-writer stylings of the seventies. Probably it was peer pressure. Probably it was the influence of his boarding school contemporaries. In any case, it's as if Fahnstock comes home across the big Atlantic puddle. Take it easy, dude! Skip trigonometry! Smoke a reefer!

Just as this easy-listening nationalism took root, however, there was *the shot heard round the world*. The punk rock explosion! The revolution! Wow! Safety pins! In the space of a few short months, Wilkie Fahnstock turned away from the soft-rock conventions of the mid-seventies entirely and embraced instead the anarchic celebrations flowing out of London's King's Row.

Meanwhile, after years of loneliness and romantic starvation in high school, and with only the simple addiction of a diet of beer, speed, and filched prescription medication, Wilkie Fahnstock suddenly achieved campus celebrity as an oddball, *the guy with the Devo albums*— just as he was being expelled *from* Andover for curfew viola-

9. The Clash, "Safe European Home" (1978).
10. Sid Vicious, "My Way" (1979).
11. The Dickies, "Tra La La (The Banana Splits Theme Song)" (1979).
12. The Vapors, "Turning Japanese" (1980).
13. Plastique Bertrand, "Ca Plane Pour Moi" (1979).

(B)
14. Patti Smith, "Horses" (1976).
15. The Dead Boys, "Sonic Reducer" (1977).
16. Bee Gees, "Stayin' Alive" (1976).
17. Television, "Marquee Moon" (1977).
18. Richard Hell and the Voidoids, "Blank Generation" (1978).
19. Talking Heads, "Warning Sign" (1978).
20. B-52's "52 Girls" (1980).
21. Ramones, "Rock and Roll Radio" (1979).
22. Sex Pistols, "God Save the Queen" (1978).

Cassette Five
(A)
1. Orchestral Manoeuvres in the Dark, "Enola Gay" (1979).
2. Peter Gabriel, "Games Without Frontiers" (1979).
3. The Cure, "Boys Don't Cry" (1980).
4. Patti Smith, "Rock and Roll Nigger" (1979).
5. Modern Lovers, "Road Runner" (1972).
6. M, "Pop Music" (1979).
7. Human Sexual Response,

tions. So it was back to Mamaroneck High to complete the twelfth grade without a letter *in any sport*. (I can report here that Fahnstock did, however, finally manage to "cop a feel," as he put it, from Pauline Vanderbilt of Park Ave., NYC, a fellow Andover casualty, while in the next room her close-and-play mangled a copy of Blondie's "Heart of Glass." Oaths of eternal fealty followed.)

At home in Westchester, Fahnstock managed to parlay acceptable board scores and indifferent recommendations into an acceptance at the University of Rhode Island, a school which (according to atlases available to the compiler of these notes) was a mere road trip from the recherché and enigmatic Moonstone Beach of the Rhode Island coast. A known nudist bathing location! Fahnstock, with his beer-related paunch and excessive chest hair, was often a sight at Moonstone playing, with various nursing students, volleyball *en deshabillé!* The best music for nudism, at least in those days, was *funk*, and thus it blasted from the sound

"What Does Sex Mean to Me?" (1980).
8. Klark Kent, "On My Own" (1980).
9. Pretenders, "2000 Miles" (1983).
10. dB'S "I Thought You Wanted to Know" (1979).
11. Rockpile, "Teacher, Teacher" (1982).

(B)
"I spent most of college drinking beer at the campus bar and buying clothes from that nice girl at the used clothing store in Newport."
12. Funkadelic, "Hardcore Jollies" (1978).
13. Talking Heads, "Once in a Lifetime" (1980).
14. Brian Eno, "Kurt's Rejoinder" (1976).
15. Gang of Four, "Outside the Trains Don't Run on Time" (1981).
16. Public Image Limited, "Poptones" (1981).
17. Pere Ubu, "Dub Housing" (1979).
18. Blondie, "Rapture" (1982).
19. The English Beat, "Ranking Full Stop" (1979).
20. ABC, "The Look of Love" (1982).
21. R.E.M., "Sitting Still" (1983).

Cassette Six
(A)
1. The Replacements, "Unsatisfied" (1984).
2. Hüsker Dü, "Celebrated Summer" (1984).
3. Minutemen, "History of the World, Part II" and "This Ain't No Picnic" (1985).

system of Fahnstock's car. We located, in the glove box of his 1982 Volkswagen Rabbit, a battered compendium of funk and "new wave" classics to support the selections from this period.

In 1984, Fahnstock, turning aside the advice of his more liberal friends, and notwithstanding his countercultural personal habits, nonetheless voted in his first presidential election *for former California governor Ronald Reagan.* Proving that the G.O.P. can indeed be a big tent, he did not however endorse the conservative "hair" bands of the period—Poison, Ratt, Whitesnake, Loverboy. He concentrated instead on the nascent pop form known as "hardcore": the sound of the empty landscapes of the American plains, without Dolby noise reduction or compression. Dairy farms in foreclosure. Permafrost. Songs a minute long, played at four hundred beats per.

A period of retrenchment followed, featuring a flirtation with the local, NYC-related phenomenon called Rap or Hip Hop. Fahnstock learned of it at after-hours clubs, where he

4. Cocteau Twins, "Lorelei" (1985).
5. Dead Kennedys, "California Über Alles" (1980).
6. Violent Femmes, "Good Feeling" (1984).
7. Black Flag, "Slip It In" (1984).
8. James "Blood" Ulmer, "Are You Happy in America?" (1982).
9. Laurie Anderson, "O Superman" (1982).
10. The Smiths, "What Difference Does It Make?"(1984).

(B)
11. The Beastie Boys, "Cookie Puss" (1982).
12. Run-DMC, "Rock Box" (1983).
13. New Order, "Bizarre Love Triangle" (1984).
14. Echo and the Bunnymen, "Never Stop" (1984).
15. Van Halen, "Panama" (1984).
16. Velvet Underground, "Jesus" (1970).
17. Bruce Springsteen, "Born in the U.S.A." (1983).
18. Michael Jackson, "Beat It" (1983)
19. The Feelies, "The Boy with the Perpetual Nervousness" (1979) and "On the Roof" (1986).

Cassette Seven
(A)
"Don't ask me about the mid-eighties."
1. Van Morrison, "Sweet Thing" (1969).
2. Bob Dylan, "Most of the Time" (1986).
3. Big Star, "September Gurls" (1972).
4. Yo La Tengo, "Five Years" (1984).

spent far too many nights during these summers in college. Rap gave way almost immediately to various *artists from the past*, the Velvet Underground, Bruce Springsteen, Bob Dylan. And this organic past sustained him overland to rehab in Minnesota, where, *admitting complete defeat* (in Hazelden parlance) less than a month after graduation, he dogged female cocaine addicts and disdained a belief in God until transferred summarily to a halfway house in Queens. He then turned up briefly at confirmation classes at Greenwich Village's Grace Church.

A succession of bad day jobs gave way to a bad streak of *sobriety jobs*, as they are called in the *demimonde* of recovering types, at a succession of New York fashion magazines—in copy-editing, and then fact-checking departments. At *Self*, for example, Fahnstock worked closely with beauty columnist Denise D'Onofrio, whose office beat box listed toward Janet Jackson and Paula Abdul, and whose gin and tonic he accidentally sipped at an Xmas party, scaring him-

5. Chris Stamey, "Cara Lee" (1985).
6. They Might Be Giants, "Dead" (1984).
7. Victoria Williams, "The Holy Spirit" (1987).
8. Robin Holcomb, "Going, Going, Gone" (1988).
9. The Proclaimers, "I'm Going to Be (500 Miles)" (1988).
10. A.C./D.C., "Back in Black" (1978).
11. Hall & Oates, "You Make My Dreams Come True" (1984).

(B)
12. R.E.M., "It's the End of the World As We Know It (And I Feel Fine)" (1987).
13. Elvis Costello, "I Want You" (1987).
14. Prince, "Sign O' the Times" (1986).
15. Captain Beefheart, "Low Yo Yo" (1973).
16. Metallica, "Enter Sandman" (1990).
17. The Cucumbers, "My Town" (1987).
18. Pogues, "Fairytale in New York" (1988).
19. Tom Waits, selections from RAIN DOGS (1986).
20. The Silos, "Let's Go Get Some Drugs and Drive Around" (1990).
21. The Feelies, "Sooner or Later" (1991).

Cassette Eight
(A)
1. Sonic Youth, "Teenage Riot" (1988).
2. Ciccone Youth, untitled

self witless, such that he fled home on the PATH train to his sixth-floor walkup in downtown Jersey City, and didn't come out again for a week. When he did, it was to relapse.

Have we spoken already of the Garden State and its influence on Wilkie Fahnstock? Of its flat, Netherlandish aspect? Of the local bands of Hoboken? How in the cauldron of that old waterfront town he went through a sort of flowering of compassion for fellow man, however short-lived, as evidenced by his sudden, precipitous decision to take in rehab acquaintance Kristina Ruiz, fleeing at the time a pugilistic husband, so that the two of them might share that tiny space, Wilkie's apartment, *chastely, platonically*, until a furious row, after which Wilkie slunk home again to Westchester.

It was *back under the roof* of his stepfamily, two years sober, ashamed, unemployable, that Wilkie Fahnstock first saw the MTV video (measuring worthlessness by the amount of daily consumption of that channel)

instrumental from *The Whitey Album* (1988).
3. The Pixies, "Here Comes Your Man" (1990).
4. Jane's Addiction, "Stop" (1991).
5. Sugar, "That's a Good Idea" (1992).
6. Pavement, "Summer Babe (Winter Version)" (1992).
7. Syd Barrett, "Golden Hair" (1972).
8. Sebadoh, "Brand New Love" (1992).
9. Television, "Rhyme" (1992).
10. Slint, "Nosferatu Man" (1988).

(B)
"In 1991, I was living in the basement at home. I'd take out the trash for my mom. I had an idea for a screenplay. I was going to get a broker's license."
11. Nirvana, "Smells Like Teen Spirit" (1991).
12. My Bloody Valentine, "Glider" (1991).
13. Pearl Jam, "Jeremy" (1991).
14. The Pixies, "U.Mass" (1992).
15. P. J. Harvey, "Rub Till It Bleeds" (1992).
16. Liz Phair, "Fuck and Run" (1993).
17. Sebadoh, "Spoiled" (1993).
18. Morphine, "In Spite of Me" (1993).
19. Vic Chestnutt, "West of Rome" (1994).
20. Dog Bowl, "Love Bomb" (1992).
21. Nine Inch Nails, "Head Like a Hole" (1992).

Cassette Nine
(A)
1. Nirvana, "Heart-Shaped Box" (1993).

for a song entitled "Smells Like Teen Spirit." Another relapse ensued. However, his sheer delight in the movement of rock and roll fashion—in the direction of the so-called *grunge* music—revivified Wilkie Fahnstock enough to apply to law school, financed mainly by his reinforced-carton magnate stepfather. This plan lasted about one year (1994), as did Wilkie's marriage, contemporaneously, to law classmate Arlene Levy of Scarsdale. On the occasion of their first anniversary, Arlene informed her own parents that Wilkie's refusal to study, his concentration on such disagreeable racket as The Shaggs, and his crack binges were unacceptable. Thus, Wilkie took an apartment by himself in Park Slope, Brooklyn, and began to write his roman à clef (untitled), of which, after six months, he completed thirteen pages. Applications to the writing and film programs of city institutions were to no avail.

Bringing us to the present. The tale, then, of a confused, contemporary young person, a young man overlooked by the

2. Hole, "Doll Parts" (1994).
3. The Breeders, "Cannonball" (1993).
4. Offspring, "Genocide" (1994).
5. Half Japanese, "Roman Candle" (1989).
6. G. Love and Special Sauce, "Blues Music" (1995).
7. Beck, "Loser" (1995).
8. Guided by Voices, "Goldheart Mountaintop Queen Directory" and "Hot Freaks" (1994).
9. The Shaggs, "Philosophy of the World" (1972).
10. Fly Ashtray, "Barry's Time Machine" (1995).
11. Smashing Pumpkins, "Today" (1995).
12. Stereolab, "Lock Groove Lullaby" (1994).

(B)
13. Soul Coughing, "Screenwriter's Blues" (1994).
14. Bad Religion, "Television" (1995).
15. Rancid, "Roots, Rockers, Radicals" (1995).
16. The Sixths, "San Diego Zoo" (1995).
17. Boss Hog, "Nothing to Lose" (1995).
18. The Innocence Mission, "Happy. The End" (1995).
19. Neil Young, "The Ocean" (1995).
20. Guided By Voices, "Atom Eyes" (1996).
21. Steve Earle, "Ellis Unit One" (1996).
22. Rage Against the Machine, "Bulls on Parade" (1996).
23. White Zombie, "More

public, a person of meager accomplishment, a person of bad temperament, *but a guy who nonetheless has a very large collection of compact discs!* For this reason, Bankruptcy Records presents to you the music of Wilkie Fahnstock in his thirty-third year. The last WASP (one of them anyway), the last of this nation's culturally homogenous offspring deluded enough to believe in the uniqueness of this cultural designation, a young man whose *beloved rock and roll* has finally apparently become a thing of the past, a quaint, charming racket from another eon. We present to you, ladies and gentlemen, the life and music of an undistinguished American!

Human Than Human" (1994).

Cassette Ten
(A)
1. John Cage, "In a Landscape" (1984).
2. Frédéric Chopin, "Nocturne #1" (1839).
3. U. Srinivas, "Saranambhava Karuna" (1994).
4. Frank Zappa, "Get Whitey" (1995).
5. David Lang, "Face So Pale" (1993).
6. Thurston Moore, from the soundtrack to HEAVY (1996).

(B)
7. Brian Eno, "Ikebura" (1993).
8. J. S. Bach, "Contrapunctus XIV," from DIE KUNST DER FUGUE (1750).
9. John Coltrane, "Stellar Regions" (1965).
10. Carl Stone, "Banteay Srey" (1992).
11. Aphex Twin, "1" (1994).

Production, Remastering, and Sequencing at Bankruptcy studios by Mike Hubbard.
A&R by Jules Hathaway.
Liner Notes by Rick Moody.
Special thanks to Wilkie Fahnstock, and the Fahnstocks of Mamaroneck, NY, and Marblehead, MA.
http://www.chapter11.com

Brian Morton

With The Dylanist *(1991), Brian Morton creates a memorable character in Sally Burke, the daughter of former Communists, who grows up, a post-'60s child, to be an emotional drifter, detached from life, committed fully to no place, no cause, and no one. She is, as Ben McMahon, the labor organizer she meets and ultimately falls in love with, a "Dylanist," someone who believes only in feelings and then only fleetingly at that. Burke never does quite fit in;* The Dylanist, *told in a quietly episodic style, is the story of her journey and ongoing struggle to find some sort of meaning in her life. It's significant that Morton summons the name of Bob Dylan, that most enigmatic of contemporary singer-songwriters. This isn't the only work of fiction of course where Dylan's name and persona are evoked. His spirit haunts the music-obsessed characters of Ann Beattie's* Chilly Scenes of Winter *(1976) and he appears in one form or another in Salman Rushdie's* The Ground Beneath Her Feet, *Don DeLillo's* Great Jones Street, *and especially Scott Spencer's* The Rich Man's Table *(excerpts of DeLillo and Spencer appear in this volume). Morton is also the author of* Starting Out in the Evening *(1998) and* A Window Across the River *(2004).*

From
The Dylanist

She was a romantic about love, a cynic about everything else. Sally Burke, seven years old, consented to go to the World's Fair for only one reason: she thought she might meet her future husband there.

Both of her parents had attended the last New York World's Fair, in 1939, although they hadn't met until ten years later. She sat in the back seat, next to her brother, trying to imagine a world in which her parents had not yet met.

At the 1939 World's Fair, had they noticed each other? She imagined it as a scene from a movie: her mother, no more than a girl, catches a glimpse of a handsome young man in the crowd. Suddenly, it's as if the two of them are alone, and everything is utterly silent.

And then the crowd swallows him up and the noises return. And the girl, her mother, shakes her head, wondering whether she'd only imagined it all.

Or maybe it was nothing like that. Maybe they saw each other and felt nothing. Could that be?

Sally vowed to be on the alert. If she saw her future husband, she'd know.

Marijuana. OPEC. Bob Dylan. These were the instruments of her downfall.

From her window she could see all the way down the hill. Brightly dressed students were heading to the cafeteria for lunch.

It was noon on a Saturday. She'd just gotten out of bed.

She'd smoked pot the night before, for the first time in months. She still felt a little high. She wondered if she should go back to sleep.

Pot. In her last year of high school she'd smoked almost every weekend; at Oberlin, almost every night. At first, pot had seemed an educational resource: when she and Beth took their endless walks, their endless drives, mapping out the universe with their conversations, marijuana had seemed an indispensable part of it all.

That didn't last. By her second year of college, when she found herself missing more classes than she was showing up for, she had come to the conclusion that the "amotivational syndrome" was not a myth. She decided to kick the habit, and she was surprised by how easy it was: she smoked every few months now, when the spirit moved her, and the rest of the time she didn't think about it much. But on days like today, as she sat in her bathrobe at noon, feeling much more tired than it was reasonable to feel, she wondered if those years had drained her of her energy.

But sometimes she thought this tiredness wasn't hers alone: the world itself seemed tired. When she was a kid, and Daniel would come home from college talking about demonstrations and teach-ins, she couldn't wait to grow up and be a rebel herself. But everything had changed. She still felt like a rebel, but she didn't know quite what to rebel against. Politics had disappeared. In the sixties, during the war, some witty senator had proposed that the United States should declare victory and come home. Instead, the peace movement had declared victory and gone home. The war had come to an end three years ago—in 1975; but the peace movement had faded away long before that. The whole "counterculture," if there ever was such a thing, had vanished. Everybody just got tired.

Life no longer seemed limitless. One night about a year ago, she and Beth, home for Christmas break, had borrowed her parents' car, intending to have one of their traditional late-night driving and talking sessions . . . and they'd run out of gas. They had to call AAA and get themselves towed. They'd fallen into a time warp—they'd thought they were back in the early days of high school, before the oil crisis, when you could put two dollars in the tank and drive all night. You couldn't do that anymore. As the newspapers were always saying, they were living in a new era of limits.

The presiding spirit over all this, somehow, was Bob Dylan. The Dylan she'd fallen in love with, in high school, was full of anger, wildness, hope. She still bought all his records; she was in love with him still. But somewhere along the line he'd been chastened. Now he wrote songs of vague renunciation, vague spiritual yearning. Even Dylan was tired.

In the spring of her junior year she'd seen Scorsese's movie *The*

Last Waltz, about the final concert of the Band. At the end of the concert, all the evening's guest performers came back onstage—Dylan, Van Morrison, Joni Mitchell, Clapton, Neil Young—and joined the Band in a version of Dylan's "I Shall Be Released." It was as if they were singing an anthem.

It was one of Sally's favorite songs; sitting in the movie theater, she'd cried. Later, though, she'd wondered what it said about her time. Years before, these people might have taken "We Shall Overcome" for their anthem. Now they sang "I Shall Be Released." Released from what?

She fell into conversation with the first fat man she saw.

"What do you do?" he said, fitting two potato chips inside his mouth.

I go to parties and only talk to the fat guys, she thought.

Owen was home writing. She thought of it as an act of fidelity to talk only to the unattractive guys.

She started to tell him about her jobs. She was talking on automatic pilot, hardly listening to what she was saying—instead, she was listening to Dylan. Going through the host's record collection, she'd found a bootleg album that included "I'm Not There," a legendary, never-released, never-completed song from the Basement Tapes sessions—a song that she'd heard just once, the summer after high school, and that she'd been searching for ever since. It came on as she was talking; it was even more haunting than she'd remembered.

She touched the fat guy's wrist. "This," she said, "may be the greatest song ever written."

He laughed. He had nice brown eyes, when you really looked at him. Intelligent eyes.

"Anyway," she said, "I like reading to these old people—it's more interesting than it sounds. Like, this Frenchwoman, she's a great lady. She's an old Socialist—she was in the Resistance when Hitler conquered France."

"That does sound interesting," he said. "Are you an old Socialist?"

"Me?" She took a half-step backward.

"Of course not. How foolish of me. You're a Dylanist."

"Meaning . . . ?"

"You don't believe in causes. You only believe in feelings. Am I right?"

Sally was grinning with pleasure. She didn't know quite why she was so pleased. The fat guy—she still didn't know his name—was leaning forward flirtatiously. Maybe he wasn't so unattractive after all.

"I deserve this. I come all the way up to Boston for a party when I have work to do, and I run into another Dylanist."

That sounded like he had a girlfriend. Why was she jealous? "You have a Dylanist back home?"

"About a thousand. I work for a union. I go around talking about solidarity and other corny ideas, to people who are just too hip to believe in anything but their own feelings."

A union guy.

The union guy touched her shoulder. "I'm sorry. It's just that I've got some headaches in New York. I shouldn't assume I know you. You're interested in that Socialist lady—that's unusual. How'd you get to be unusual?"

She found herself blushing. And she knew why she'd quickly felt something for this fat guy, on the basis of a two-sentence conversation. He asked questions.

In a classic episode of "Star Trek," Kirk and the crew come down to a deserted planet where they find this huge weird glowing arch, and when Kirk wonders what it's there for, the arch intones: "A question. Since before your earth was born . . . I have waited . . . for a question."

"Since before your earth was born," she said, "I have waited . . . for a question."

"I was about to ask if you needed a drink, but it doesn't appear that you do."

"But I do need a drink. I very much need a drink."

So the fat guy got her a drink. He really wasn't that fat, if looked at with a sympathetic eye. Let's think of him as husky, Sally thought.

She was about to ask him if he knew her father, but she decided not to. She preferred to remain a little anonymous. "How'd you get into union work?" she said.

"I read about the Wobblies at an impressionable age. So I thought

I'd become a Wobbly myself. The only thing I didn't realize is there aren't any Wobblies anymore."

He pushed his glasses up to the top of his head and rubbed his eyes. He did have a large roll around his stomach, but he had a strong face. She guessed that he was about five or six years older than she was. He seemed . . . he seemed like a man.

"So what does a union guy do if he can't be a Wobbly?"

"He just talks union. There's probably no hope for the labor movement. People don't want to know from solidarity . . . which is just a fancy word for helping each other out. But if there's no hope for that, there's no hope for anything. So you just keep plugging away. You pretend you have a chance, even if you don't really believe it. What the hell. You might end up being surprised."

He put his glasses back down over his eyes. "It's nice of you to be interested in all this. Usually when I tell people I work for a union, they look at me like I said I was a chariot mender—like I belong in a museum." He held out his drink and examined it. "I'm talking too much. I don't know if it's you or this . . . I can't remember the last time I went off the tape."

"The tape."

"Sometimes I feel like everything I ever say is stored on tape. And if somebody asks me something I just play back the right part of the tape. But I didn't mean to tell you that stuff about pretending. That wasn't on the tape."

Sally didn't say a word, just looked at him, smiling. Thinking that maybe it would be nice to be single.

She left the museum and walked into Central Park. On a bench near the Great Lawn she sat and watched the runners, with their muscular legs. Everyone in New York had muscular legs. They all looked splendid; determined and fierce; their bodies were taut, tight, intimidating; each of them, man and woman, ran alone. Each of them dedicated to the perfection of the body, in proud singleness. With a regard for their own bodies so extreme it seemed doubtful they could ever really love anyone else. And for the first time in her life, she found herself in a situation in which she didn't think herself the most isolated person there, the most alone. Each of the runners was dedicated to an idea of self-creation, of solitary perfection, that she couldn't believe in any longer. Most of them were older than she was; but as she watched them she felt as if she were watching children at play. Their dream of self-creation seemed the naivest delusion in the world. She felt old; she felt tethered by a thousand commitments. She had never in her life entered into a commitment without trying to make sure it had an escape clause, but nevertheless she'd been committed. She was committed to her own past. Committed to her people, the living and the dead. She carried them inside her. She lived with them.

She wondered if she was still what Ben would call a Dylanist. She probably was, and she'd probably always be one: restless; not really political, yet edgily intent against selling out; putting her feelings first. Dylan himself, with his restless honesty, would probably always mean a lot to her. But lately, when she'd looked at his records, she could never find anything she wanted to hear. His concerns weren't her concerns. His work contained nothing about loss; nothing about aging—his own, or that of the people he loved; nothing about being a father, or being a son. Nothing about the complexities of relationships that last.

Tom Perrotta

When we first meet Dave Raymond, he is a thirty-one-year-old guitarist with the Wishbones, a New Jersey wedding bar band. He still lives at home with his parents, and to make ends meet and add a few bucks to his coffers, he also works as a courier. When not playing music, Dave spends a great deal of his time downing beers and talking music. Everything is going along smoothly, until he ruins it all by proposing to his girlfriend. Then, things get . . . complicated. Such is the premise of Tom Perrotta's very funny and charming novel The Wishbones *(1997). Perrotta is also the author of* Bad Haircut: Stories of the Seventies *(1997),* Election *(1998),* Joe College *(2001), and, most recently,* Little Children *(2004). As with many of his characters, the always likeable Dave Raymond is at the crossroads between childhood and adulthood, torn between freedom and responsibility, and hoping to prolong his adolescence as long as possible. In many ways, Dave is the American equivalent of Rob Fleming, the music-obsessed Londoner in Nick Hornby's* High Fidelity *(see page 136 of this volume). For both characters, music forms the crux of their existence.*

From
The Wishbones

One of the things Dave liked best about the wedding band was its efficiency. They could set up in twenty minutes and break down even faster than that. Some of the rock bands he'd played in had been weighed down by so much equipment that he'd felt more like a roadie than a musician. Löckjaw was the worst offender. He remembered an outdoor Battle of the Bands where they'd taken four hours to set up for a forty-five-minute performance marred by such earsplitting shrieks of feedback that even the die-hard headbangers in the audience were squeezing their ears, begging for mercy. (Löckjaw came in fifth out of five bands and dissolved a few months later.)

The Wishbones made music on a more human scale. Dave had joined the band with a number of reservations—the uniforms, the cheesy tunes, Artie's reputation as a ballbuster—but he quickly came to realize that the rewards went far beyond the two hundred dollars he got for playing a four-hour gig.

It turned out, amazingly enough, to be a blast. People drank at weddings. They danced like maniacs. They clapped and hooted and made requests. Every now and then, when the chemistry was right, things got raucous. And when that happened, the Wishbones knew how to crank up the volume and rock, with no apologies to anyone.

Dave had friends who were still chasing their dreams, playing in dingy clubs to audiences of twelve bored drunks, splitting thirty-nine dollars among four guys at the end of the night, then dragging themselves home at three o'clock in the morning. He saw the best of them growing exhausted and bitter, endlessly chewing over the thankless question of why the world still didn't give a shit.

Dave himself still hadn't completely surrendered his dream of the Big Time, but he had moved it to the back burner. Someday, maybe, the perfect band would come along, a band so good that no one would be able to say no to them. Until then, though, Dave was a Wishbone, and it was a helluvu lot better than nothing.

Dave couldn't remember the last time they'd spent an afternoon like this—a picnic on a blanket in the shade by a lake, Julie stretched out beside him, eyes closed, maybe sleeping, maybe not, nothing unpleasant hanging over their heads, no fights or disappointments or lurking grievances. It almost seemed to him that they'd managed to return to an earlier time in their relationship, as if they themselves had been rejuvenated.

He sat up on the blanket and looked around. Over in the parking area, shirtless teenage boys were waxing muscle cars while girls in tight jeans looked on, smoking with the squinty-eyed concentration of beginners. In a grassy clearing nearby, three teenage boys with flannel shirts tied around their waists were showing off with a Frisbee, catching it between their legs and behind their backs, popping it in the air over and over again with one finger. On a picnic table to their right, a couple of high-school kids were making out as though their faces had been stuck together with Krazy Glue, and they were trying every trick they could think of to pull them apart. In the lake, a black lab with a blue bandana collar swam regally toward shore, a fat stick jutting from its mouth. Somewhere across the water, "Sugar Magnolia" was blaring from a radio.

It could really have been 1979, he thought, except that he and Julie would have been the teenagers with adhesive faces rather than the adults who had just spent more than they could afford on an engagement ring. There were days when a realization like that would have struck him with sadness, days when he ached to be sixteen again, but today wasn't one of them. Today he felt richer for possessing a past, maybe even a little wiser. They had had their moment; they hadn't let it pass. That was the most anyone could say.

He looked down at her, the halo of dark outspread hair fanned out around her peaceful face. She wasn't seventeen anymore, but she was still beautiful. He thought about Phil Hart and his wife, the fact that they'd managed to stick it out for more than a half century. Did he look at her on the morning of his death and think, *Well, she's not sixty-five anymore, but she's still beautiful?* Was that a way it could happen?

"Heads up, dude!"

Dave turned toward the voice, just in time to see an orange Frisbee slicing toward his face. Reacting with the grace born of self-preservation, he ducked out of the way while simultaneously reaching up with his right hand to snag the errant disc. In a surprisingly fluid motion, he rose to his feet and zipped the Frisbee back to the long-haired Chinese kid who had yelled out the warning, not with the cumbersome cross-body discus hurl of the neophyte, but with the precise, economical flick of the wrist he had perfected during countless lazy spring days like this when he was flunking out of college.

Acknowledging Dave's membership in the elite, wrist-flicking fraternity, the kid jumped up and caught the Frisbee between his outscissored legs, then fired it off to one of his friends before his feet even touched the ground.

"Thanks, dude."

"No problem," said Dave. He felt deeply pleased, as though he'd just proven something important to himself and the world.

Julie was stirring when he sat back down. She yawned and opened her eyes, blinking a few times to readjust to the brightness of the day. Then she rolled easily onto her side and smiled at him.

"Hey," she said.

"Hey."

She poked a finger into his thigh. "You know what I want to do?"

"What?"

She pushed herself up from the ground into sitting position and glanced around to make sure no one was within listening range.

"I want to go to a motel."

"Right now?"

She nodded slowly, biting her bottom lip, her face flushed with color.

"This very minute," she said.

Dave's blood began to celebrate; a giddy torrent of ideas flooded his brain. Aside from a few hurried, mostly clothed interludes on the rec room couch, they hadn't really made love in well over a month, not since her parents' ill-fated jaunt to Atlantic City. He wanted to watch her undress slowly, one article of clothing at a time. He wanted to reacquaint himself with her body.

"It's quarter to three," he said, glancing quickly at his watch. "That gives us almost an hour and a half."

Her expression changed. Her teeth let go of her lip.

"Shit," she said.

"What?"

"You have a wedding." She made it sound like an awful thing—a disease, something to be ashamed of.

"I'm sure I told you."

"I forgot. We were having such a nice day, I guessed I pushed it out of my mind."

"An hour and a half is enough. We've done it before in a lot less time than that."

"I'm sick of hurrying." To illustrate this point, she reached up with both hands and gathered her loose hair into a ponytail with exquisite, painstaking care. "I just want to have a nice quiet Saturday alone with you for once."

"Sorry. I'm not the one who schedules the gigs."

She grabbed her shoes from the corner of the blanket and slipped them on her feet. Just like that, he realized, their picnic had been canceled. She pulled the laces tight and stared at him.

"How much longer do you plan on doing this?"

"Doing what?"

"The Wishbones."

Dave felt shell-shocked. On the blanket, a black ant was struggling with an enormous bread crumb, bigger than its own head. The ant kept lifting it, staggering forward, dropping it, then lifting it again.

"Are you asking me to quit the band?"

Her voice softened. "Haven't you thought about it?"

"It never even occurred to me."

"Well, I don't feel like spending the rest of my life alone on Saturday night while my husband's out having a good time."

"It's not a good time," he said, still reeling from the suddenness of her attack. "It's a job. A good one. I wouldn't be making a living without it."

"You're not planning on being a courier for the rest of your life, are you?"

"No," he said. "But it's not like I've got lots of other prospects at the moment."

"You should start thinking about it. I'd like to start a family in the next couple of years."

"Me, too. What does that have to do with the band?"

She stood up and grabbed two corners of the blanket. "Come on. Help me fold this."

Obediently, Dave rose to his feet, still trying to figure out how they'd moved from talking about checking into a motel to talking about him quitting the band.

"Heads up!"

This time Dave was ready. He turned and poised himself for the catch, waiting with his hands up as the Frisbee drifted toward him at a dreamy velocity, a vibrating curve of neon. At the very last second, though, it took a freak hop, jumping right over his hands and striking him smack in the middle of his forehead, much harder than he'd expected, more like a dinner plate than a flimsy piece of molded plastic. Fireworks of pain exploded on the inside of his eyelids.

"Sorry, dude," the kid called out.

"No problem."

Smiling through his discomfort, Dave bent down and picked up the Frisbee. He flicked his wrist to return it, but something slipped. It wobbled feebly through the air and died like a duck at the kid's feet. He turned sheepishly to Julie, rubbing at the sore spot between his eyebrows.

"I guess I'm a bit rusty."

She ignored the comment, frowning pointedly at the limp blanket. Dave grabbed the two corners on his end and they pulled it taut between them, flapping it up and down to clean it off. He thought about the ant with the bread crumb, all that hard work gone to waste.

"I just want a normal life," she said, almost pleading with him. "Is that too much to ask?"

"She what?" Buzzy slurped at the foam erupting like lava from the top of his can. "What did you tell her?"

"Nothing. I was in a state of shock."

"I can imagine."

"I mean, we're just sitting there, having this great afternoon, and Bam!"

Dave was indignant. She had no right to ask him to quit the band. Playing music wasn't just some stupid sideline; it was what he did with his life. If he'd been a doctor, she wouldn't have asked him to quit performing surgery. She wouldn't have asked a cop to turn in his badge. It signified a lack of respect, not only for his chosen profession, but for him—her future husband—as an individual.

"What was her reasoning?" Buzzy had his head thrown back like Popeye, mouth wide open to receive the last drops of Meister Bräu dribbling out of his upended can. He could drain a beer faster than anyone Dave had ever known.

"Saturday night. She doesn't want to be stuck home alone while I'm out playing a gig."

"It's a problem," said Buzzy. "Just ask Stan."

"What am I supposed to do? People don't get married on Tuesday."

Buzzy dropped his can on the floor and produced a full one from the side pocket of his tuxedo jacket. He popped the top and vacuumed off the foam with fishily puckered lips.

"You wanna know the solution?"

"What?"

"Kids."

"Please," said Dave. "Just getting married is scary enough. Don't start tossing kids into the mix."

"I'm serious," Buzzy insisted. "Once you got kids, having fun on Saturday night isn't even an option. The whole argument is moot."

"Kids are a long ways off," Dave assured him. "A vague rumor from a distant galaxy."

Buzzy shrugged. "It worked for us. Before JoAnn got pregnant, she was into that whole death metal thing—the spike bracelets, the white makeup, the whole nine yards. Her idea of a balanced meal was a Diet Coke to wash down her speed. Now she's the only mother in the PTA who can name all the guys in Anthrax."

Dave had only met JoAnn once, but she'd made an impression. She was a skinny, tired-looking woman with stringy, dishwater blond hair and pants so tight—they were some sort of spandex/denim blend that zipped up in the back—you had to worry about her circulation. No matter what anyone said, her expression remained fixed somewhere between boredom and indifference. Dave didn't think she was in danger of being elected president of the PTA anytime soon.

"Did she ever bug you about quitting the band?" he asked.

Buzzy shook his head. "Only thing like that, she made me sell my bike."

"Bicycle bike? Or motorcycle?"

"Motor," Buzzy replied, pausing mid-chug to see if Dave was putting him on. "I had me a beautiful Harley."

"I didn't know that."

"Oh yeah. Jo loved to ride it too. We had matching helmets and everything. Used to ride all over the place with this club I was in, stoned out of our minds. Amazing I'm even here to tell about it."

"So what happened?"

"This guy we knew wiped out in a rainstorm one night. Billy Farell. He was in a coma for three months."

"He came out?"

"Yeah. Seems okay too. He was a little off to begin with, so you can't really tell the difference. After that, though, Jo said she'd leave me if I didn't get rid of the bike."

"You miss it?"

Buzzy polished off the second beer and deposited the empty on the floor, which Dave used as a storage area for cassettes and their boxes, separate entities he kept meaning to reunite. He wanted to ask Buzzy to stop treating his car like a garbage can, but didn't want to come across as one of those neat freaks who act like their vehicle is some sort of sacred space, not to be defiled by evidence of human habitation, burger wrappers or the odd plastic fork.

"I dream about it," Buzzy said. "Every night. Before I fall asleep."

Dave's car was stopped at a red light. Buzzy grabbed a pair of imaginary handlebars and pulled back on the throttle. Except for the tuxedo, he looked a little like Dennis Hopper. The expression on his face was pure ecstasy, sexual transport.

"Every night," he repeated, as Dave shifted into first and eased up on the clutch of his Metro. "Nothing else even comes close."

Tom Piazza

The twelve stories that comprise Blues and Trouble *(1996), Tom Piazza's intoxicating short story debut for which he won a James Michener Award, takes place in locales scattered throughout the country, from Memphis to New Orleans, from Florida to New York. It is a quintessentially American collection where music—the blues, jazz, early rock and rock, country—echo prominently in the lives of the characters. Piazza's other books include* The Guide to Classic Recorded Jazz *(1995),* Blues Up and Down: Jazz in Our Time *(1997),* True Adventures with the King of Bluegrass *(1999), and* My Cold War *(2003). Piazza's essay on the history and nature of the blues in the five CD boxed set* Martin Scorsese Presents the Blues: A Musical Journey *won a 2004 Grammy Award for Best Album Notes. "Burn Me Up" is the story of Billy Sundown, a washed-up Jerry Lee Lewis-style singer and his encounter with a former classmate.*

"Burn Me Up"

"Fuck you. Fuck you. Stay the fuck out of my dressing room. I'm not the fucking janitor here, and I don't want you the fuck in my dressing room." Billy Sundown stopped hollering at the club owner for a moment as he opened the door to his dressing room and saw his younger sister, a middle-aged woman in a pink blazer that was too tight on her, sitting in a folding chair. "Hey, Georgia," Billy said. "How you doin'? You need anything?"

"Hi, Billy," she said.

"No, man," Billy started up again, turning to find the club owner still there, "I'm not foolin' with you, son. I'm not too old to cut you a new asshole. And why wasn't the piano tuned, as is *stipulated*"—he paused on the word, for effect—"in my contract?"

The club owner, whose father had been in grade school with Billy, stood there, looking at Billy's Adam's apple, unsure what to say. Billy watched him for a second and shook his head pitingly. "Come in here, son," Billy said suddenly. "You look like you need a drink. You look like you're gonna pass out. Come on in. Give us your tired, your weary . . ."

He held the door open and the club owner, a pale, nervous man of thirty-four with a receding hairline and a half-hearted mustache, walked into the small, cramped room, nodded to Billy's sister, and sat down next to some stacked-up beer cases, wiping his forehead with a handkerchief. It was springtime in Memphis, but inside the Alamo Show Bar it was always some indeterminate season of extremes, with hot, torpid air smelling of beer and sweat suddenly giving way to blasts of freezing air from the overworked air-conditioning system.

"Now, what do you need to talk to me about, son?" Billy said, pouring bourbon into a small, pleated paper cup. "Why don't you put some goddamn glasses in the dressing rooms, too. This Wild Turkey'll burn a hole right through these things. How was that first set, Jo-jo?" He began stripping off his bright green shirt; perspiration had soaked through the tuxedo-shirt ruffles that ran down the front.

His sister smiled at the pet nickname and said, "Great. Ron wanted to know if you'd play 'Burn Me Up' in the next set."

"Anything any husband of any sister of mine wants he gets, as long as it's not a loan. I been broke too goddamn long." He looked at the club owner again, as if he had just appeared out of nowhere. "What the fuck do you want? I thought I told you to get out of here."

"We should probably talk about it in private," the club owner said, wincing as he watched Billy down the bourbon.

"Anything you got to say to me you can say in front of my own flesh and blood." Billy peeled off his undershirt, picked a towel off the top of the stack of beer cases, and began toweling himself off.

"So be it," the young man said. "Several of the customers complained about the language you used onstage, and the man you threw the wet napkin at is a city councilman."

Billy looked at him in stunned amazement. "A city councilman? You mean Lucas?"

"Yes, I mean Mr. Lucas."

"Look, son. I went to junior high school with that pencil dick. I remember when he used to try and keep his girlfriends away from me. Fuck him." He looked over at his sister and began to laugh. She raised her eyebrows noncommittally and opened her purse, looking in it for something. "Well, what do you want me to do, get his suit dry-cleaned for him?"

"I want you to apologize. You embarrassed the man in front of his wife and two guests that he brought to hear you play."

"Hear me play? Am I doing that peckerwood some kinda favor by playing here? He used to keep away from me like you'd keep away from a goddamn copperhead. Now he wants to show his friends he's a pal of Billy Sundown's, then they talk through the middle of when I'm playing—"

"You don't understand—"

"Don't tell me I don't understand shit. Since when did city councilmen come to see rock and roll? I remember when they tried to run me out for playin' it. Now I'm rediscovered and it's a big gravy train for everybody. What do you need, Jo-jo? You're making me nervous."

"I was just looking for my lipstick."

"Son, why don't you be a good boy and go back to the sound booth and tell them to bring the mike up a little more on the bass, and leave me alone."

"Look, Billy, everybody loves to hear you perform—"

"I know it."

"—and I do, too."

"Fine. Your daddy used to help me set up equipment."

"I know that." The younger man looked at the floor between his feet for a moment; he was suddenly very tired. "Would you please do me a favor and just go out and apologize to Mr. Lucas? It would help me out, believe me."

Billy scratched his head; the red hair so prominent in the history-of-rock books and retrospective television specials was dyed now to cover the gray. "What is your poppa doing now, anyway?" he asked the young man.

"He still owns the dealership out on North Parkway."

"That's good," Billy said, thoughtfully. "All right, let me visit with my sister a little bit here."

"Please," the young man said, "go out to see Mr. Lucas before your next—"

"Goddamn it anyway, son," Billy said. "I told you I would, now quite crawling up my asshole."

"Okay," the younger man said. He couldn't remember Billy agreeing to do it, but he decided not to make an issue of it. "I'm sorry. Fine. Thanks." He left the room, closing the door soundlessly behind him.

"That fella just ain't in the right business," Billy said, shaking his head.

"You talked pretty rough to him."

"I know it," he said, pulling on a fresh shirt. "Me and his daddy used to be friends. Maybe I'll go out and say something to Lucas in a bit. Maybe I won't. City councilman . . . Christ on a Harley. You sure you don't want something to drink? They put some Cokes in the little fridge."

"I'm fine," she said, looking up at her brother through her bifocals and smiling.

This was the second time Billy had played at the Alamo Show Bar since the resurgence of interest in 1950s rock and roll that had led to his rediscovery. The Alamo was a roadhouse just northeast of down-town Memphis, a giant, barnlike room with pool tables and pinball machines at the far end and a parquet dance floor around which tables were arranged, the kind of place that featured small acts on their way to the top and big acts on their way to the bottom. And sometimes it featured someone like Billy, a big act that had hit bottom and bounced back up to the middle.

In the late 1950s, he had been one of the original Wild Men of Rock and Roll. Film footage from that time shows him standing on the piano, throwing his head back, playing bare-chested. One columnist called him the "Redneck Rachmaninoff." Big package tours, lots of money, leopard-print Cadillacs. Then, while Billy was on tour in Ohio, an enterprising reporter discovered that Billy's female traveling companion of the moment was only sixteen years old, and a resident of Kentucky to boot. That Billy had transported a minor across state lines made all the newspapers; he narrowly escaped imprisonment for violating the Mann Act, his first wife divorced him, and by that time—1960—his brand of rock and roll was being eclipsed in favor of milder teen idols like Pat Boone and Frankie Avalon. Billy's career went into a long slide.

For most of the ensuing three decades, he ground out a living playing in dismal bars and lounges, living on hamburgers and Dexedrine, driving alone to Holiday Inns in Biloxi, Mississippi, or Carbondale, Illinois, playing on a portable electric piano with a local drummer. A small sign in the lobby, maybe—TONIGHT ONLY—BILLY SUNDOWN—with one or two of his hit song titles listed under it to jog people's memories. Drunken salesmen would sing along with him as he did perfunctory versions of his own hits and stan-dard rock and roll covers like "Blue Suede Shoes" and "Great Balls of Fire." About midway through any given evening, the bourbon and speed that he liked to mix would kick in, and Billy would abandon his set pattern and begin playing boogie woogie versions of obscure tunes he remembered from childhood, like "Shadow in the Pines" and "The Girl with the Blue Velvet Band." He was famous for getting into fights, and his reputation was not good.

In the mid-1970s, he underwent a supposed religious conversion. He had his own evangelical television show for a while in Los Angeles, on which he played piano and sang songs like "I'll Fly Away" and "Walk and Talk with Jesus" with a beat that some felt was not conducive to a prayerful attitude. Every month he sent home as much as he could to his mother, sometimes as little as thirty dollars after dry-cleaning bills and alimony payments to his first and second wives. Eventually he got into a mess over the wife of one of the television station executives, and he went back to the rounds of Holiday Inn lounges.

After about twenty-five years, nostalgic pieces about early rock and roll began to appear in magazines. Several television specials were produced; it was far enough behind, safe enough, to have become a period piece. Billy Sundown, certainly one of the best-known figures of the time, a real outlaw, was prominent in all of them. Promoters hunted him up, helped him put together a band; he played a series of big arenas, often in package shows teaming him with other legends like Chuck Berry and Fats Domino. He headlined large, hip rock clubs in major cities. His old recordings were packaged into new boxed sets with attractive graphics.

Billy Sundown didn't seem to have changed at all, except for a slight paunch and the obviously dyed hair. He would still do anything to get to a sluggish crowd—bang the piano cover against the piano's body, throw things, stand on the keys. The promoters made money off of him, but he was trouble. Billy felt not so much grateful for as vindicated by the revival of his career. He acted as if the fans and the promoters were the ones who had been missing in action for thirty years.

Archie Lucas and his party sat at a table just outside the circle of fuchsia and yellow lights from the bandstand and dance floor, amid all the din of the Alamo. Walter Phillips, a partner from Archie's old siding business, sat next to Archie, yelling in his ear.

"Let's get the hell out of here," Walter Phillips said, sharply, into Archie Lucas's ear. "I know you like his singing and all, but he's a freak. If we don't leave, *I'm* gonna punch him out."

"No, you're not, Walter," Phillips's wife said, from across the table.

"Look, man," Archie said, "I been wanting to hear him play live for years, and I'm not going to leave now. Besides, I want to see his expression when I tell him who I am. That's it, Walter. If you don't want to wait around, that's fine."

"Look," Walter Phillips said, "I got you into this by talking, all right? Whyn't you let me go talk to the manager myself?"

"Whyn't you have another drink?" Archie took his glasses off and rubbed his eyes. He pushed inward on the bridge of his nose with both thumbs and wished that he had come to see Billy Sundown alone.

With his eyes still closed he thought back to an April day in 1948. He was in seventh grade, the first entry class to attend Albert H. Fletcher Junior High School, which had just opened out east of the city, where they were starting to build the neighborhoods for the servicemen who had made it back from the war. The new school pulled in kids from the nearby neighborhoods, as well as some from farther away; children from solid middle-class families like Archie's sat in scrubbed new classrooms next to the ragged children of factory hands and truck drivers and cotton exchange strongbacks. Archie's father owned a liquor store downtown; his older brother had been killed in the Pacific, two months before V-J Day. He and his parents had moved to a new house in a subdivision that winter, in the middle of the school year, a gray, dislocating time. The houses there were small and identical, and they sat on small, treeless plots on tracts of land that had been farmland before the war.

Spring came; the sun bore down on the shadowless sidewalks and fledgling lawns. The days were getting longer. Every week Archie went with his parents to the outdoor concerts in Overton Park, and sat under the sky with its early moon and listened to light opera, or whatever they were offering. Some essential tension that had been in the air for as long as he could remember had dissipated. Archie would always mark that spring as the beginning of a new feeling in himself that he couldn't quite identify, a sense of longing and possibility mixed with a strange directionless. The war had given his entire early childhood a direction, a valence. Things were important; letters arrived from far away. Now there was just an odd sense of reality spreading out around him, getting thinner and thinner, like a drop of oil on water.

One day, after school had let out for the afternoon, the new feeling came over Archie suddenly, and especially powerfully. Everything around him seemed new, yet timeless and static at the same time. The warm air, the patches of weeds here and there, the sunlight on the beige bricks of the school building, all seemed oddly palpable, full of meaning. He decided to walk the mile back to his house. He began walking across the school grounds, past the blacktop playground, and started across what would someday be a broad lawn but what was at the time only a field of dirt with a few tufts of weed sticking up. The top of his head felt hot from the sun.

Suddenly someone appeared in front of him, a skinny kid he had seen in school, one of the older kids, with red hair and a big nose and what looked like a perpetual sneer. White trash, basically, Archie remembered thinking, the kind whose parents lived in the low-income projects along Poplar Avenue. The kid wore a red-and-white striped T-shirt and pants that were a couple of inches too short. He had just appeared, like a vision in the desert. Archie was startled.

"What about you?" the red-haired kid said. His voice had a high, nasal twang to it.

Archie didn't understand the question. "What do you mean 'what about me?'"

The redhead stared at him for a second. "You got any money?"

"No," Archie said. He could hear the drone of an airplane above them in the blue ether, still an unusual sound, but he didn't look up to see it. He kept his eye on the red-haired kid as if he were a snake that had just appeared in his path.

"Lookit this," the redhead said. He held out the palm of his hand and Archie looked at it. On it sat a light pink, translucent rubber ring, like a miniature trampoline, about an inch and a half across.

"You know what that is?"

"No," Archie said.

"You put that on your John Henry when you do it to a girl."

Across the field in front of the school, Archie saw others walking off toward their homes, in small groups. A circle of sweat had plastered his polo shirt to his belly.

"Cost you a dollar."

"I don't have a dollar for that," Archie said.

"What do you got a dollar for, then?" the redhead said. "You got a dollar to keep me from kicking the shit out of you?"

Archie just sat looking at the redhead. He didn't say anything. The redhead was watching him.

"You like it here?" the redhead said.

"Where?"

The redhead shook his head, looked across the playground. He bent over and picked up a rock from the scrubby ground. "You dress like you got money," he said. "I mean don't you want to get out of here?"

"Out of school?" Archie said.

The redhead squinted at him. Archie looked at his big ears; a big dimple sat right in the middle of his narrow chin. "I'm-a buy a whore." After a moment he said, "What's your name?"

"Archie Lucas."

"You're stupider than a rock," the redhead said. He threw the stone he had in his hand off across the hazy playground. "I'm gonna go to California." He walked away.

Archie would always remember the flavor of that encounter, a sense that the red-haired boy couldn't decide whether he wanted to beat him up or be friends with him. He ran into the redhead, who's name was Billy Sindine, several times over the next few years, the last time at a high school dance, while Archie was spooning out some punch for his date. Suddenly Billy appeared next to him, took the ladle when Archie was finished and spooned himself some punch. For a moment they stood side by side, watching the band; Archie's only thought was that Billy might say something to embarrass him in front of his date. Finally, without looking at Archie, Billy said, "That bassist ought to be bagging up groceries down at the Piggly Wiggly." Then

Billy was gone, and Archie never heard of him again until 1956; Archie was attending Memphis State and Billy's voice was suddenly coming out of jukeboxes and car radios.

Here was the strange thing: in that piercing, sometimes mocking, sometimes defiant voice, Archie heard something that cut through to the feeling he had the spring he met Billy in the schoolyard. That voice, tremulous and arch one moment, high and nasal and lonesome the next, along with his boogie woogie piano, all run through a heavy echo chamber, somehow expressed both the loneliness and the sense of possibility that he had felt eight years earlier. As Archie ground his way through college and the stages of providing for his family, Billy became a private hero to Archie. He had gotten out of Memphis, seen the world, taken his lumps and stuck by his guns, and Archie admired him for it. For years he had wanted the chance to tell him that, and he had decided that he wasn't leaving tonight before he'd done it.

Billy and Georgia sat nearly knee-to-knee in the tiny dressing room. "How's Mama?" Billy asked his sister. "When'd you start smoking?"

"I been off and on," his sister said, shaking out a match. "She's good. You oughta go out and see her."

"I'm-a get out there tomorrow and visit with her. I'm stayin' up to the Radisson. They got an all-white baby grand piano in the lobby. How's Ron treatin' you?"

"He's fine. He's still out with Federal Express, doing routing. He took me down to Pascagoula for my birthday."

"When was that? How old were you?"

"Month ago. I turned forty-nine. I tell everybody down to the bank I'm thirty-nine, though, just like Jack Benny."

"Jesus ground hog," Billy said. "I got a sister forty-nine years old. You don't look a day over forty-five."

Georgia laughed, exhaling a plume of smoke and stubbing out her cigarette in a plate.

"Luther and Leon are always asking about you," she said.

"Where the hell are my nephews, anyway?"

"They both had to work tonight. Luther's playing in a band."

"In a band?" Billy said. "He's playing that guitar?"

Georgia nodded. "They call the band Alcohol, Tobacco, and Firearms."

"Alcohol, Tobacco, and goddamn Firearms," Billy said, laughing and slamming a beer case with the flat of his hand. "That's what I should call my autobiography."

Georgia laughed, opened her mouth as if to say something, then closed it again without speaking. They were quiet for a moment.

"You know, Billy," she said, picking at a loose thread on her jacket sleeve, "I feel like I'm getting old and I never get to see you anymore. All I catch is a glimpse of you once every year or two."

"More than that and you'd get sick of me quicker'n you could believe."

"Do you still have the place out in California?"

"I pay taxes on it," Billy said, "so I guess I got it." He ran the backs of his fingers under his chin, meditatively, feeling for stubble. "The IRS has got a ring through my nose the size of a Hula Hoop."

"You ever think about getting a home back here, Billy?" she said.

Absently, as if he hadn't heard her, Billy said, "I wish Luther'd stay the hell out of this business."

"You'd be around family," Georgia continued, looking at her brother through her bifocals. "We miss you."

Billy looked up at her now with an appraising look. He could almost, he thought, see the love coming off of her in waves, like heat off a radiator. "You know, Jo," he said, "sooner or later you manage to get around to the same old thing, don't you? I must have told you half a hundred times what I feel about it, but I still hear this. All I ever wanted was to get the hell out of here. Why in the name of Jesus Christ would I want to move back?"

"Billy, please don't get mad."

"This town is a goddamn minimum-security prison. All the gates are wide open, but there's no place to go for a million miles in any direction. These shit heels around here never gave me the time of day. Everybody wanted to kneel on my goddamn nuts. I remember very single one of them dildos. Who the hell ever stayed in Memphis had anyplace better to go?"

Billy looked at his sister, then up at the ceiling. He ran the palm of his hand over his face.

"Look, Jo," he said, "I don't mean it against you. I couldn't be happy anyplace. I got the devil inside me—"

"Billy, I wish you wouldn't say that."

"Well, shit, it's true, ain't it? When have I ever been satisfied with what God gave me? What the fuck did I ever do for anybody?"

"Watch your language around me sometimes, Billy," Georgia said. "You are so . . . prideful. You talk like the Lord has singled you out to suffer."

"I'm not sayin' that—"

"It's a way of setting yourself above others. The Lord gives every-one his own portion, Billy. Everybody has a load to bear."

Billy looked at the floor while she said this. After she finished, he looked up at her, then back down again. He ran his hand through his hair. After a moment he said, "It's hotter'n eight hells in here, isn't it?"

"Billy," his sister began.

"Listen, Jo," he said, "I should get myself together here a little."

"Billy, why don't you come by on Sunday. I'll fix up a dinner."

"That'd be nice," Billy said, standing up. "Tell Ron to get his Ping-Pong table fixed. He still got that thing sitting down in the basement?"

"I think we threw that out a couple of years ago."

"Yeah," Billy said. "Well . . . we can play flip the spoon or some-thing. Give me a kiss. I'll see you on Sunday not too early."

Georgia gave her brother a kiss and a hug. As she left the dressing room he was fitting cufflinks into his shirt cuffs.

After the door closed, Billy reached into a small briefcase on his dress-ing table. He hummed softly, "She got a man . . . on her man . . . and a kid man on her kid . . ." He pulled out a tiny plastic bag and opened it.

"Everybody wants to go to heaven," he said to himself, "but nobody wants to die."

From the small bag he pulled out two tiny translucent crystals that looked like rock candy and popped them into his mouth under his tongue. He zipped the bag closed again and stuck it back into the briefcase, which he closed and put on the floor. The crystals dissolved quickly in his mouth, as he buttoned up his shirt. "Sweet to papa," he said, his heart already beating harder.

He tucked his shirt in, breathed deeply. *Love*, he thought, was a word that everybody used, himself included, without knowing what it meant. Some people said God was love. But God was also judgment. They were two sides of the same coin. You get love, but then you have to be worthy of it.

His talent was God-given. But talent can be a judgment on you, too, he thought, just like somebody's love, a gift you didn't ask for. His talent had never seemed like something he owned; it was more like having a brother, a separate part of himself that was better than he was; people loved it and stupidly mistook it for the real him. If they knew what he was really like, they would run away screaming.

He felt the need of some cool water on his face, and he unbuttoned the shirt again and took it off. Jesus loves me, he thought. This I know. Why? 'Cause the Bible tells me so. But I can't sit still for His love. God is love, but love means you have to disappear. If you aren't willing to sacrifice yourself, you can't love. They had been trying to make him disappear without his consent for as long as he could remember. But he wouldn't. Man, he thought, if he wasn't going to hell grits weren't groceries and Mona Lisa was a man.

"I can't sit still . . . ," he sang, now, splashing water on his face, making up a song, "for your love, baby." The water refreshed him, pulled him a little bit into focus. He toweled off his face. "I'm doing the multiplication tables of love. Love times five is thirty-five. Love times six is thirty-six . . ." For a second he rested his face in the towel. "Love times seven," he went on, "puts you in heaven. Love times eight turns into hate."

He felt bad about yelling at Georgia. He'd make it up by swallowing his pride in front of Lucas. Just don't let him try and get a piece of me, he thought. Just let me say my piece and get away. How, he wondered, did somebody like Lucas do it? Stay in one place, probably married, kids, a house, friends, cookouts, bowling league, sun comes up, sun goes down, out to dinner once a week when they could get the baby-sitter. Yeah, well, if Lucas has kids, they're probably all grown now. Wonder if he has a daughter . . .

A knock came on the door, and Billy yelled out, "Talk to me."

His bassist, Buzz Clement, opened the door and stuck his head in. "Billy, you want in on a coupla hands of tonk before we got to hit again?"

"Son, I can't take your money like that and get to sleep at night. Besides, I got to go talk to a man out here about something."

Archie Lucas and his party still sat at their table; an embarrassed quiet clung to the group now. Archie tapped a matchbook against the table-top, rotating it a quarter of a turn for each tap, hitting each edge in turn. His wife, Rose, sat across from him, watching him with a sad look on her face. Walter Phillips and his wife, Rena, were quiet, too. Walter sat to Archie's right, trying to bounce quarters off the table into an empty highball glass.

"Five," Walter Phillips said. "That's five for me. Archie, it's your turn."

"Archie," Rose said. "Why don't we just head out. There's no point—"

"Listen," Archie said, "I want to give it a few minutes, all right? You want to head home, take the car and I'll call a taxi when I'm ready. Please." Archie took his glasses off and began wiping them with a cocktail napkin. The glasses lent his face definition; without them, it was a little unfocused, lined but still boyish, although he was only a year younger than Billy Sundown, and his gray-streaked hair was care-fully combed to cover a large bald spot.

"Well, look," Walter Phillips said, pushing his chair back from the table, "we're gonna head home. You sure you're gonna wait around?"

Archie put his glasses back on. "Yeah, I am, in fact."

"Well, I hope you get what you're after," Phillips said, as they walked away.

"Safe home," Archie said.

As his friends walked off through the intermission crowd, Archie tried to formulate in his mind what he would say to Billy when he came out. He could give him an ironic look and say something like,

"See if you can guess where we know each other from." Then he could sit there while Billy raked through his mind for the answer. When Billy finally gave up, Archie would remind him of that day on the playground and see if he remembered. Then Archie would tell Billy that he'd been following his career all these years, and how Billy's recording of "That Lucky Old Sun" had seen him through some tough times. "You made it out of here," he imagined himself saying. "You stuck to your guns." "So did you," he imagined Billy saying. Archie's heart beat harder and he felt a funny tightening in his throat.

As Archie was thinking these thoughts, Billy Sundown emerged from his dressing room and began making his way through the noisy room. He wore a bright purple shirt with tuxedo ruffles down the front, and white pants with white shoes and a yellow belt. As he made his way between the crowded tables he responded to greetings, shook hands, waved, all the while grinding his teeth from the Methedrine he had taken. He made his way straight over to the table where Archie Lucas sat with his wife.

"Howdy, neighbors," Billy said, approaching their table. "Howdy, Mr. Lucas . . . ma'am," nodding to Rose.

Archie felt an adrenaline rush, and an odd, dislocated feeling, too—how had Billy remembered his name after all those years?

"Listen," Billy said, "I wanted to apologize for that incident earlier. Sometimes I get a little jacked up and I forget myself. My apologies to you, too, ma'am."

Archie looked up at Billy Sundown in wonder; the red hair that he remembered from childhood was no longer unkempt, but waved and pomaded into an emblem of controlled wildness. Billy's face looked hollow-cheeked and puffy at the same time. Set into it were a pair of sharp eyes—weird, razorlike eyes like those of old men he'd seen as a boy in trips to visit relatives out in the country, seemingly backlit by a flame compounded of pure backwoods fanaticism and a strong and uncultivated intelligence. He realized he needed to say something, to acknowledge Billy's apology.

"Well, we shouldn't have been talking while you were playing," Archie said.

"It happens all the time," Billy said, distractedly, his hands in his back pockets. He felt the love waves coming up at him again, just as they did off of Georgia, making him squirm, making him angry. Where, he thought, were all these parasites when he was playing lounges for thirty years? They all wanted something off of him; they wanted him to stamp their ticket, tell them it was all right. He looked around the room to clear his head, grinding his teeth some more and sweating. "Well, I'll tell you . . ." he began, as if getting ready to go.

"Would you like to sit down?" Archie said. "Let me buy you a drink."

"Well . . ." Billy began, shifting uncomfortably on his feet, telling himself to just breathe, and that it would be over in a second. "I really ought to get over here and see my sister. I don't get home too often, and when I do, I like to visit as much as possible."

The encounter was not going according to the scenario Archie had envisioned. Still, he had to ask the question on his mind, out of pure curiosity. "Billy," Archie said, "can I ask you, how did you remember my name?"

Billy didn't fully understand the question; to him it seemed as if the man facing him was trying to make a point about his age. "Partner," Billy began, "I'm not as senile as I might look. Don't push me, now. I'm sorry I acted up, but I gotta go see my sister."

Archie sensed that if he was going to say what he had wanted to say, he would have to say it quickly. "Billy," he began, "I just wanted to tell you—"

"*Jesus goddamn it,*" Billy said, leaning across the table toward his old schoolmate, his forehead dripping sweat and his eyes burning. "Don't say it. Stop right there. You love me, right?"

Archie was so taken aback by this outburst that he blurted out the word "Yes," hardly even knowing he was saying it.

But before Archie had formed the word Billy had already pushed himself away from the table, turned around and walked away, barely able to rein in his contempt for all those fools who wanted some kind of salvation from someone like him.

Lewis Shiner

Like fellow novelist William Gibson, Lewis Shiner's work is often classified as cyberpunk, which is vastly unfair since his fiction is far more complex than that and not easily classified. Shiner's novel, Glimpses *(1993), tells the story of Ray Shackleford, a guy who repairs stereos for a living. One day he begins to hear music in his head but this is no ordinary music but rather recording sessions of famous albums that never took place and that he then is able to recreate on his tape deck. Eventually, he feels that he is having real encounters with such artists as the Beatles, Jim Morrison, Jimi Hendrix, and Brian Wilson.* Glimpses, *ostensibly a story about middle-aged angst and lost dreams, sparkles. Its essence can be condensed into one thought: how music, in whatever form it takes, can change your life. Shiner has written about music before, including* Say Goodbye: The Laurie Moss Story *(1999), a bittersweet novel that chronicles the rise and fall of a female rocker; and in two short stories, "Mystery Train," about a pill-popping Elvis (1983) and "Jeff Beck" (1986) about a morose sheet metal worker with an obsession for the music of the seminal English blues-rock guitarist. The latter is a haunting morality tale of magic realism about the consequences of getting what you asked for. Both stories appear in* Love in Vain *(2001).*

From
Glimpses

Once upon a time there was going to be a Beatles album called *Get Back*. They tried to record it in January of 1969, first at Twickenham Film Studios, then in the basement of Apple Corps at 3 Savile Row. Their own overpriced twenty-four-track dream studio wasn't finished and they had to bring in a mobile unit. So there they were, under bright lights, using rented gear, with cameras filming every move they made.

Paul had this idea he could turn things around. He wanted to get back to the kind of material the band did in '61 and '62, at the Kaiserkeller in Hamburg and the Cavern Club in Liverpool. It must have seemed like another century to them, looking back. They tried to warm up with Chuck Berry standards and "One After 909," something of John's from when he was seventeen. But it was winter and snowy and cold. The soundstage echoed and the basement was cramped. It just wasn't happening.

That summer they would try again, and this time it would work, and they would come away with *Abbey Road*. The tapes from the other sessions would end up with Phil Spector, who would overproduce the living Jesus out of them to make them sound alive and finally they would come out as *Let It Be*.

The new title pretty much says it all. Between winter and summer everything changed. Paul married Linda, John married Yoko, and Allen Klien took over Apple. By then it was too late to get back, ever again.

My father died not quite two weeks ago. I can say the words but they don't seem to mean anything or even matter much. My mind goes blank. So I think about other things. I put *Let It Be* on the stereo and wonder what it would sound like if things had been different.

Music is easy. It isn't even that important what the words say. The real meaning is in the guitars and drums, the way a record *sounds*. It's a feeling that's bigger than words could ever be. A named Paul Williams said that, or something close to it, and I believe it's true.

I've been in Dallas with my mother, straightening out the VA insurance, helping her write a form letter to use instead of a Christmas card, answering the phone, getting Dad's name off the bank account, a million little things that can bleed you dry. Now I'm home again in Austin trying to make sense of it.

It's November of 1988. The old man died the week before Thanksgiving, a hell of a thing. He was scuba diving in Cozumel, which he was too old for, with my mother along for the ride. He used to teach anthropology at SMU but since he retired all he wanted to do was dive. My wife and I flew up to Dallas to meet my mother's plane as she came back alone, looking about a hundred years old. She'd had him burned down there in Mexico, brought a handful of ashes with her in a Ziploc bag. Elizabeth came home that weekend and I stayed up there ten days, all I could stand. Then I drove back here in his white GMC pickup truck, my inheritance. The inside still smells like him, sweat and polyester and old Fritos.

Anyway, it's 1988 and it was just last year that they finally released all the Beatles' albums on CD, making a big deal out of how it was the twentieth anniversary of *Sgt. Pepper*. It was like everybody had forgotten about the sixties until we had this nationwide fit of nostalgia. Suddenly every station on the radio has gone to some kind of oldies format, and they play the same stuff over and over again that you haven't heard in twenty years, and now you're sick to death of "Spirit in the Sky" and "The Year 2525" all over again. Tie-dyed shirts are back and bands that should never have been together in the first place have reunion tours and everybody shakes their heads over how dumb and idealistic they used to be.

I run a stereo repair business out of the house. Most of the upstairs is my shop. The north wall is my workbench, covered with tools, an oscilloscope and a digital multimeter, a couple of my clients' boxes with their insides spread out. The wall above it is cork and there are a million pieces of junk pinned to it: circuit diagrams, pictures of me and Elizabeth and the cat, phone messages, business cards from my parts people, a big black-and-white poster of Jimi Hendrix that I've had since college. The west wall is windows, partly covered by corn plants, palms, and dieffenbachia that Elizabeth fixed me up with, all rugged stuff that even I haven't been able to kill. The south side is shelves, over and under a countertop. That's where I keep the boxes I'm not currently working on, as well as my own system. Harmon Kardon amp, Nakamichi Dragon cassette deck, four Boston Acoustics A70 speakers, linear tracking turntable, CD player, graphic equalizer, monster cables all around. There's something almost spiritual about it, all that matte black, with graphs and numbers glowing cool yellow and white and green, like a quiet voice that tells you everything is going the way it should. It's just hardware, metal and silicon and plastic, but at the same time it has the power to turn empty air into music. That never ceases to amaze me.

I only have *Let It Be* on vinyl. The second side was playing, halfway in, and "The Long and Winding Road" came on, full of crackles and pops. I was running on automatic, my hair tied back, house shoes on, resoldering a couple of cold joints. The song is just Paul on the piano, a McCartney solo track really, with a huge orchestra and chorus that Phil Spector dubbed on afterward. A decent tune, though, even John admitted that.

I don't remember the first time I heard it, but I remember the one that stuck. It takes me back to Nashville, early June of 1970. I remember it was a Sunday. I heard this announcement on the radio that my band, the Duotones, was supposed to play that afternoon in Centennial Park. It was news to me. I showed up and sure enough, there they were, sounding a little hollow and tinny inside the big concrete band shell, and there in the middle was their new drummer. Scott, the lead player, came out in the audience during the break and said, "We were going to tell you. That promoter we hooked up with, he had his own drummer."

I remember being able to see the individual pebbles in the pinkish concrete under the bench. The bench, I think, was green. There wasn't a lot for me to say. My bridges were burned. I'd spent the last month flunking out of Vanderbilt, too busy with band practice or protests over the shootings at Kent and Jackson State to go to class. I hadn't managed to stop the war, and now I didn't have a band either.

I hung around until they closed my dorm and then I hit the road.

I'd already told my parents I wasn't coming home for the summer, so I just drove on through Dallas, headed for Austin, where Alex was. She wasn't my girlfriend anymore. We'd broken up the fall before. But then we'd broken up a million times and if I was there, staying at her house, maybe she would change her mind.

All I had was AM radio in my car and it seemed like they only played two songs that whole trip. One was Joe Cocker's cover of "The Letter," with Leon Russell's piano sharp as an ice pick, making me push the gas to the floor and feel the hot wind through the open windows. The other was "The Long and Winding Road." It had been a pretty long road for me and Alex. I'd known her since sophomore year in high school, since we were all in drama club together. I'd seen her long hair go from red to brown to black, listened to her rave about everything from astrology to Bob Dylan to BMW motorcycles. I'd spent the last half of my senior year and the summer after helplessly in love with her. It was my first real love affair, full of jealousy and tears, the unendurable pain of an unanswered phone, long drives back from her mother's apartment at two in the morning, dozing off at the wheel. But mostly it was making love: in the car, on the floor of her mother's den, at friends' houses, in my bed with my parents watching TV in the next room.

The Beatles didn't get it together for *Get Back* and Alex and I didn't get it together in the summer of 1970. I moved off her couch after a week or so and rented a room up on Castle Hill. Before I left I got this letter, care of her, from my father. It was always my mother who wrote me, I guess that's true in most families. This time it was him, on a sheet of yellow legal paper, printed in block capitals, "GO AHEAD AND PLAY IN THE TRAFFIC," it said. Then, at the bottom, "ONE THING YOU FORGOT: LOVE." I can't remember him ever using the word before. It looked like a lie. He signed it "DAD." I didn't tear it up, bad as I wanted to. Maybe I just wanted to keep hating him the way I did right that minute.

During those long summer days in Austin I looked for work. Everything turned out to be door-to-door sales. At night I tried to put a band together with a guy who'd just learned to play guitar and an organist who'd done nothing but classical. One day the bass player disappeared in his ice-cream truck en route to Houston, and that was the last straw. I ended up back in Dallas in spite of myself, getting a degree in electrical engineering from DeVry Institute. That got me my first decent job, printed circuit design for the late lamented Warrex Computer Corporation.

There's magic, see, and there's science. Science is what I learned at DeVry and it bought me this nice two-story house off 290 in East Austin. Magic says if maybe the Beatles could have hacked it, then maybe Alex and me could have hacked it.

If the Beatles had hacked it, "The Long and Winding Road" would have sounded a lot different. Paul always hated what Spector did to it, wanted it to be a simple piano ballad. John might have written a new middle eight for it, something with an edge to cut the syrupy romanticism. George could have played some of the string parts on the guitar, and Ringo could have punched the thing up, given it more of a push.

It could have happened. Say Paul had realized the movie was a stupid idea. Say they'd given up on recording at Apple and gone back to Abbey Road where they belonged, let George Martin actually produce instead of sitting around listening to them bicker. I'd seen enough pictures of the studio. I could see it in my head.

Here's George Martin, tall, craggy-looking, big forehead, easy smile. Light brown hair slicked back tight. He's got on his usual white dress shirt and tie, sitting near the window of the control room which looks down on Studio 2. Studio 2 is the size of a warehouse, thirty-foot ceiling, quilted moving blankets thrown over everything, microphones of every shape and size from the slim German condensers to the old-fashioned oblong ribbon types, miles of cable, music stands like small metal trees. Here's John, his beard just starting to come in, hair down to here, Yoko growing out of his armpit. Paul's beard is already there, George Harrison and Ringo have mustaches. Paul is in a long-sleeved shirt and sleeveless sweater, John and Yoko are in matching black turtlenecks, George has a bandanna tied cowboy-style around his neck. The tape is on a quarter-inch reel, not the inch-wide stuff they use now. It's been less than twenty years, after all, since the studio stopped recording directly onto wax disks. Everything about the mixers and faders is oversized, big ceramic handles, big needles on the VU meters, everything painted battleship gray. The air smells of hair oil and cigarette smoke. Everyone bums Everest cigarettes off of Geoff Emerick, who is in a white lab coat like all the other EMI engineers.

They're listening to the playback. Here's Ringo's deadened toms, four quick chord changes on John's sunburst Strat at the end of each line . . .

And there it was. Coming out of the speakers in my workshop. For half a minute it didn't even seem weird. I put down my soldering gun and listened, feeling all the emotion that had been buried under the strings rise to the surface.

Then it hit me, really hit me, what I was listening to. As soon as it did the music slowed and went back to the way it always has been.

I was waiting for Elizabeth when she got home. She stopped in her tracks when she saw me. "What's wrong?"

I said, "I want you to come upstairs and listen to something."

"Right now?"

"I think so, yeah."

She dumped her purse and her books and sighed theatrically as she climbed the stairs. She sat on the couch and listened to the tape all the way through. "The Beatles, right?"

"Did you notice anything different about it?"

"I guess. It sounded faster maybe."

"It's a totally different version."

"One of those bootlegs or something?"

"Uh-uh. It's not like that at all." I got up and went over to the deck and shut it down. "I made it," I said.

"I don't understand."

"I don't either." I turned around and faced her, leaning back against the countertop. "I know this sounds completely crazy. I was trying to imagine the song, I mean the Beatles playing it this way, and it started to come out of the speakers. So I, like, did it again, with the recorder on, and I got a tape of it."

Elizabeth sat there for a long time, looking at me. The sun behind her made it hard to read her expression. She was perched on the very edge of the sofa, like she didn't mean to stay. A half smile on her face came and went, like a rheostat dimming and raising the lights. Finally she said, "This is some kind of joke, right?"

"It's not a joke."

"I don't understand. What is it you want me to say?"

"You heard the tape. It *is* something different."

"I can't authenticate a Beatles record for you. I mean, come on. I can tell you that yes, you sound pretty crazy."

"I can do it again."

"Ray, listen to yourself. Do you really expect me to believe this is some kind of, I don't know, psychic phenomenon? I'm worried about you. I know this business with your father has been hard. You're not sleeping, you're having all these nightmares. Maybe you ought to get some help."

"I can do it again. I'll show you." I was dead tired, and it was hard to concentrate with her in the room. But I did, and a few seconds of music came out of the speakers.

Elizabeth stood up. "It's not funny, Ray. If you want me to tell me what's really going on, fine, I'll be downstairs. I can't handle this right now. I need a hot shower and a little peace and quiet."

She went downstairs. I lay down on the couch in a band of warm sunlight and went to sleep.

"Jeff Beck"

FELIX WAS thirty-four. He worked four ten-hour days a week at Allied Sheet Metal, running an Amada CNC turret punch press. At night he made cassettes with his twin TEAC dbx machines. He'd recorded over a thousand of them so far, over 160 miles of tape, and he'd carefully hand lettered the labels for each one.

He'd taped everything Jeff Beck had ever done, from the Yardbirds' *For Your Love* through all the Jeff Beck Groups and the solo albums; he'd had the English singles of "Hi Ho Silver Lining" and "Tally Man"; he had all the session work, from Donovan to Stevie Wonder to Tina Turner.

In the shop he wore a Walkman and listened to his tapes. Nothing seemed to cut the sound of tortured metal like the diamond-edged perfection of Beck's guitar. It kept him light on his feet, dancing in place at the machine, and sometimes the sheer beauty of it made tears come up in his eyes.

On Fridays he dropped Karen at her job at *Pipeline Digest* and drove around to thrift shops and used book stores looking for records. After he'd cleaned them up and put them on tape he didn't care about them anymore; he sold them back to collectors and made enough profit to keep himself in blank XLIIs.

Occasionally he would stop at a pawn shop or music store and look at the guitars. Lightning Music on 183 had a Charvel/Jackson soloist, exactly like the one Beck played on *Flash*, except for the hideous lilac-purple finish. He had an old Sears Silvertone at home and two or three times a year he took it out and tried to play it, but he could never manage to get it properly in tune.

Sometimes Felix spent his Friday afternoons in a dingy bar down the street from *Pipeline Digest*, alone in a back booth with a pitcher of Budweiser and an anonymous brown sack of records. On those afternoons Karen would find him in the office parking lot, already asleep in the passenger seat, and she would drive home. She worried a little, but it never happened more than once or twice a month. The rest of the time he hardly drank at all, and he never hit or chased other women. Whatever it was that ate at him was so deeply buried it seemed easier to leave well enough alone.

ONE THURSDAY afternoon a friend at work took him aside.

"Listen," Manuel said, "are you feeling okay? I mean you seem real down lately."

"I don't know," Felix told him. "I don't know what it is."

"Everything okay with Karen?"

"Yeah, it's fine. Work is okay. I'm happy and everything. I just...I don't know. Feel like something's missing."

Manuel took something out of his pocket. "A guy gave me this. You know I don't do this kind of shit no more, but the guy said it was killer stuff."

It looked like a Contac capsule, complete with the little foil blister pack. But when Felix looked closer the tiny colored spheres inside the gelatin seemed to sparkle in rainbow colors.

"What is it?"

"I don't know. He wouldn't say exactly. When I asked him what it did all he said was, 'Anything you want.'"

He dropped Karen at work the next morning and drove aimlessly down Lamar for a while. Even though he hadn't hit Half Price Books in a couple of months, his heart wasn't in it. He drove home and got the capsule off the top of his dresser where he'd left it.

Felix hadn't done acid in years, hadn't taken anything other than beer and an occasional joint in longer than he could remember. Maybe it was time for a change.

He swallowed the capsule, put Jeff Beck's *Wired* on the stereo, and switched the speakers into the den. He stretched out on the couch and looked at his watch. It was ten o'clock.

He closed his eyes and thought about what Manuel had said. It would do anything he wanted. So what did he want?

This was a drug for Karen, Felix thought. She talked all the time about what she would do if she could have any one thing in the world. She called it the Magic Wish game, though it wasn't really a game and nobody ever won.

What the guy meant, Felix told himself, was it would make me see anything I wanted to. Like mild hit of psilocybin. A light show and a bit of rush.

But he couldn't get away from the idea. What would he wish for if he could have anything? He had an answer ready; he supposed everybody did. He framed the words very carefully in his mind.

I want to play guitar like Jeff Beck, he thought.

HE SAT UP. He had the feeling that he'd dropped off to sleep and lost a couple of hours, but when he looked at his watch it was only five after ten. The tape was still playing "Come Dancing." His head was clear and he couldn't feel any effects from the drug.

But then he'd only taken it five minutes ago. It wouldn't have had a chance to do anything yet.

He felt different though, sort of sideways, and something was wrong with his hands. They ached and tingled at the same time, and felt like they could crush rocks.

And the music. Somehow he was hearing the notes differently than he'd ever heard them before, hearing them with a certain knowledge of how they'd been made, the way he could look at a piece of sheet metal and see how it had been sheared and ground and polished into shape.

Anything you want, Manuel had said.

His newly powerful hands began to shake.

He went into his studio, a converted storeroom off the den. One wall was lined with tapes; across from it were shelves for the stereo, a few albums, and a window with heavy black drapes. The ceiling and the end walls were covered with gray paper egg cartons, making it nearly soundproof.

He took out the old Silvertone and it felt different in his hands, smaller, lighter, infinitely malleable. He switched off the Beck tape, patched the guitar into the stereo and tried tuning it up.

He couldn't understand why it had been so difficult before. When he hit harmonics he could hear the notes beat against each other with perfect clarity. He kept his left hand on the neck and reached across it with his right to turn the machines, a clean, precise gesture he'd never made before.

For an instant he felt a breathless wonder come over him. The drug had worked, had changed him. He tried to hang on to the strangeness but it slipped away. He was tuning a guitar. It was something he knew how to do.

He played "Freeway Jam," one of Max Middleton's tunes from *Blow By Blow*. Again, for just a few seconds, he felt weightless, ecstatic. Then the guitar brought him back down. He'd never noticed what a pig the Silvertone was, how the strings sat over the fretboard, how the frets buzzed and the machines slipped. When he couldn't remember the exact notes on the record he tried to jam around them, but the guitar fought him at every step.

It was no good. He had to have a guitar. He could hear the music in his head but there was no way he could wring it out of the Silvertone.

His heart began to hammer and his throat closed up tight. He knew what he needed, what he would have to do to get it. He and Karen had over $1300 in a savings account. It would be enough.

HE WAS HOME again by three o'clock with the purple Jackson soloist and a Fender Princeton amp. The purple finish wasn't nearly as ugly as he remembered it and the guitar fit into his hands like an old lover. He set up in the living room and shut all the windows and played, eyes closed, swaying a little from side to side, bringing his right hand all the way up over his head on the long trills.

Just like Jeff Beck.

He had no idea how long he'd been at it when he heard the phone. He lunged for it, the phone cord bouncing noisily off the strings.

It was Karen. "Is something wrong?" she asked.

"Uh, no," Felix said. "What time is it?"

"Five thirty." She sounded close to tears.

"Oh shit. I'll be right there."

He hid the guitar and amp in his studio. She would understand, he told himself. He just wasn't ready to break it to her quite yet.

In the car she seemed afraid to talk to him, even to ask why he'd been late. Felix could only think about the purple Jackson waiting for him at home.

He sat through a dinner of Chef Boyardee Pizza, using three beers to wash it down, and after he'd done the dishes he shut himself in his studio.

For four hours he played everything that came into his head, from blues to free jazz to "Over Under Sideways Down" to things he'd never heard before, things so alien and illogical that he couldn't translate the sounds he heard. When he finally stopped Karen had gone to bed. He undressed and crawled in beside her, his brain reeling.

HE WOKE UP to the sound of the vacuum cleaner. He remembered everything, but in the bright morning light it all seemed like a weirdly vivid hallucination, especially the part where he'd emptied the savings account.

Saturday was his morning for yard work, but first he had to deal with the drug business, to prove to himself that he'd only imagined it. He went into the studio and lifted the lid of the guitar case and then sat down across from it in his battered blue-green lounge chair.

As he stared at it he felt his love and terror of the guitar swell in his chest like cancer.

He picked it up and played the solo from "Got the Feelin'" and then looked up. Karen was standing in the open door.

"Oh my god," she said. "Oh my god. What have you done?"

Felix hugged the guitar to his chest. He couldn't think of anything to say to her.

"How long have you had this? Oh. You bought it yesterday, didn't you? That's why you couldn't even remember to pick me up." She slumped against the door frame. "I don't believe it. I don't *even* believe it."

Felix looked at the floor.

"The bedroom air conditioner is broken," Karen said. Her voice sounded like she was squeezing it with both hands; if she let it go it would turn into hysteria. "The car's running on four bald tires. The

TV looks like shit. I can't remember the last time we went out to dinner or a movie." She pushed both hands into the sides of her face, twisting it into a mask of anguish.

"How much did it cost?" When Felix didn't answer she said, "It cost everything, didn't it? *Everything.* Oh god, I just can't believe it."

She closed the door on him and he started playing again, frantic scraps and tatters, a few bars from "Situation," a chorus of "You Shook Me," anything to drown out the memory of Karen's voice.

It took him an hour to wind down, and at the end of it he had nothing left to play. He put the guitar down and got in the car and drove around to the music stores.

On the bulletin board at Ray Hennig's he found an ad for a guitarist and called the number from a pay phone in the strip center outside. He talked to somebody named Sid and set up an audition for the next afternoon.

When he got home Karen was waiting in the living room. "You want anything from Safeway?" she asked. Felix shook his head and she walked out. He heard the car door slam and the engine shriek to life.

He spent the rest of the afternoon in the studio with the door shut, just looking at the guitar. He didn't need to practice; his hands already knew what to do.

The guitar was almost unearthly in its beauty and perfection. It was the single most expensive thing he'd ever bought for his own pleasure, but he couldn't look at it without being twisted up inside by guilt. And yet at the same time he lusted for it passionately, wanting to run his hands endlessly over the hard, slick finish, bury his head in the plush case and inhale the musky aroma of guitar polish, feel the strings pulse under the tips of his fingers.

Looking back he couldn't see anything he could have done differently. Why wasn't he happy?

When he came out the living room was dark. He could see a strip of light under the bedroom door, hear the snarling hiss of the TV. He felt like he was watching it all from the deck of a passing ship; he could stretch out his arms but it would still drift out of his reach.

He realized he hadn't eaten since breakfast. He made himself a sandwich and drank an iced tea glass full of whiskey and fell asleep on the couch.

A LITTLE AFTER noon on Sunday he staggered into the bathroom. His back ached and his fingers throbbed and his mouth tasted like a kitchen drain. He showered and brushed his teeth and put on a clean T-shirt and jeans. Through the bedroom window he could see Karen lying out on the lawn chair with the Sunday paper. The pages were pulled so tight that her fingers made ridges across them. She was try-ing not to look back at the house.

He made some toast and instant coffee and went to browse through his tapes. He felt like he ought to try to learn some songs, but nothing seemed worth the trouble. Finally he played a Mozart sym-phony that he'd taped for Karen, jealous of the sound of the orches-tra, wanting to be able to make it with his hands.

The band practiced in a run-down neighborhood off Rundberg and IH35. All the houses had large dogs behind chain link fences and plastic Big Wheels in the driveways. Sid met him at the door and took him back to a garage hung with army blankets and littered with empty beer cans.

Sid was tall and thin and wore a black Def Leppard T-shirt. He had acne and blond hair in a shag to his shoulders. The drummer and bass player had already set up; none of them looked older than 22 or 23. Felix wanted to leave but he had no place to go.

"Want a brew?" Sid asked, and Felix nodded. He took the Jackson out of its case and Sid, coming back with the beer, stopped in his tracks. "Wow," he said. "Is that your ax?" Felix nodded again. "Righteous," Sid said.

"You know any Van Halen?" the drummer asked. Felix couldn't see anything but a zebra striped headband and a patch of black hair behind the two bass drums and the double row of toms.

"Sure," Felix lied. "Just run over the chords for me, it's been a while." Sid walked him through the progression for "Dance the Night Away" on his ¾ sized Melody Maker and the drummer counted it off. Sid and the bass player both had Marshall amps and Felix's little

Princeton, even on ten, got lost in the wash of noise.

In less than a minute Felix got tired of the droning power chords and started toying with them, adding a ninth, playing a modal run against them. Finally Sid stopped and said, "No, man, it's like this," and patiently went through the chords again, A, B, E, with a C# minor on the chorus.

"Yeah, okay," Felix said and drank some more beer.

They played "Beer Drinkers and Hell Raisers" by ZZ Top and "Rock and Roll" by Led Zeppelin. Felix tried to stay interested, but every time he played something different from the record Sid would stop and correct him.

"Man, you're a hell of a guitar player, but I can't believe you're as good as you are and you don't know any of these solos."

"You guys do any Jeff Beck?" Felix asked.

Sid looked at the others. "I guess we could do 'Shapes of Things,' right? Like on that Gary Moore album?"

"I can fake it, I guess," the drummer said.

"And could you maybe turn down a little?" Felix said.

"Uh, yeah, sure," Sid said, and adjusted the knob on his guitar a quarter turn.

Felix leaned into the opening chords, pounding the Jackson, thinking about nothing but the music, putting a depth of rage and frustration into it he never knew he had. But he couldn't sustain it; the drummer was pounding out 2 and 4, oblivious to what Felix was play-ing, and Sid had cranked up again and was whaling away on his Gibson with the flat of his hand.

Felix jerked his strap loose and set the guitar back in its case.

"What's the matter?" Sid asked, the band grinding to a halt behind him.

"I just haven't got it today," Felix said. He wanted to break that puissant little toy Gibson across Sid's nose, and the strength of his hatred scared him. "I'm sorry," he said, clenching his teeth. "Maybe some other time."

"Sure," Sid said. "Listen, you're really good, but you need to learn some solos, you know?"

Felix burned rubber as he pulled away, skidding through a U-turn at the end of the street. He couldn't slow down. The car fishtailed when he rocketed out onto Rundberg and he nearly went into a light pole. Pounding the wheel with his fists, hot tears running down his face, he pushed the accelerator to the floor.

KAREN WAS GONE when Felix got home. He found a note on the refrigerator: "Sherry picked me up. Will call in a couple of days. Have a lot to think about. K."

He set up the Princeton and tried to play what he was feeling and it came out bullshit, a jerkoff reflex blues progression that didn't mean a thing. He leaned the guitar against the wall and went into his studio, shoving one tape after another into the decks, and every one of them sounded the same, another tired, simpleminded rehash of the obvious.

"I didn't ask for this!" he shouted at the empty house. "You hear me? This isn't what I asked for!"

But it was, and as soon as the words were out he knew he was lying to himself. Faster hands and a better ear weren't enough to make him play like Beck. He had to change inside to play that way, and he wasn't strong enough to handle it, to have every piece of music he'd ever loved turn sour, to need perfection so badly that it was easier to give it up than learn to live with the flaws.

He sat on the couch for a long time and then, finally, he picked up the guitar again. He found a clean rag and polished the body and neck and wiped each individual string. Then, when he had wiped all his fingerprints away, he put it back into the case, still holding it with the rag. He closed the latches and set it next to the amp, by the front door.

For the first time in two days he felt like he could breathe again. He turned out all the lights and opened the windows and sat down on the couch with his eyes closed. Gradually his hands became still and he could hear, very faintly, the fading music of the traffic and the crickets and the wind.

Scott Spencer

It's rare that a rock star, never mind a famous one, is successfully transformed into the lead character of a major novel. Scott Spencer in The Rich Man's Table *(1998) does just that. In the novel, Spencer gives Dylan the name of Luke Fairchild, a self-absorbed and not always likeable American icon—the most idolized singer of his generation—who is seen through the eyes of his illegitimate son, Billy Rothschild. Billy also happens to be the narrator of this finely wrought tale of a son trying desperately to connect with his elusive father. Spencer is also the author of* Endless Love *(1979),* Waking the Dead *(1986),* Men in Black *(1997), and* A Ship Made of Paper *(2003).*

From

The Rich Man's Table

I have been trying to tell this story for more than twenty years. Often, I thought of stopping everything and doing a kind of Huck Finn and taking off for the territory of my father. There was always something to stop me. The hurdle jump of my daily life. Exhaustion. Fear. Lack of money. An illusion that it was no longer necessary and that I could do very well without a father, especially a father who had abandoned my mother. I did not have a particularly good life and I was not a particularly good man, but, as we say in our ambivalent culture, *on the other hand*, I wasn't leading a bad life and I wasn't a *bad* man, so there were always reasons—persistent if not persuasive—to leave well enough alone.

I don't know that there was a vivid, defining moment that launched me in pursuit of Luke. I had always kept an eye on him. I read the adoring biographies, bought the albums, followed the gossip, and made it my business to attend whatever concerts I could—staring now at his spotlight figure on the stage and now at the enraptured faces of the fans in the rows around me. Over the years, I was not exactly secret about Luke being my father. I mentioned it whenever it suited my purposes—it was obviously a great sexual aid, a kind of celebrity-mad Spanish fly. And then, about three years ago, using my job as a substitute teacher to finance my research, I began to devote myself to the study of my father in earnest, thinking and dreaming of little else, writing letters, having long phone conversations, and criss-crossing the country to gather the testimony of anyone who knew him.

There were things I wanted to know: how did a shapeless Jewish kid from the Midwest become so famous, so beloved, so despised, so lonely, so pious, so drug-addicted, so vicious, so misunderstood, so overanalyzed? How did he break so many hearts, crash so many cars, how did all that money rush in and out like water through the gills of a fish? The history of my father, it's been said, is the history of the second half of twentieth-century America. I mention this not only to impress (you), but to excuse (me)—for pursuing him, even though I am past the age when it can be considered in any way seemly.

I think I look like him (high forehead; less-than-granite chin; graceful, girlish hands). And my mother, upon repeated questionings, made it clear there is no possibility, logical or biological, that any other man could have planted the seed in her in the winter of 1964. Nevertheless, Luke has never admitted I was his son. By the time she told me that Luke was my father, my mother had given up trying to get him to accept his responsibility. She had made her peace with the situation and with him—though there was a slightly nauseating implication of payoff when he gave her shared composing credit in three songs off his fifth album. But that wasn't much of a bribe, it was just uncharacteristically decent behavior on Luke's part, since my mother in fact did help write "Early to Bed," "Sweet Freedom," and "Lorca in New York," the publishing rights to which largely financed my private-school education and which, even as they sputtered into antiquity—they were not exactly Luke's Greatest Hits—still shed enough capital for Mother to buy an antique little house near the Hudson River in Leyden, New York.

It was there that I saw her on what turned out to be my last field trip in search of new bits of Lukology. I'd taken a couple of days off from work; there were some people I couldn't get to on weekends. It was the last week in May, and I was primarily concentrating on the priest who had been so central to Dad's Christian conversion, Father Richard Parker, who had been oddly neglected in all of the many, many books about Luke. I spent all day Monday and the beginning of Tuesday with my Aiwa, filling those dollhouse tapes with testimony.

On my way back to New York from Father Parker in Albany, and a couple of other upstate stops while I was at it (Gig Kurowsky, Luke's old bassist, and Terrence St. James, Dad's driver and drug courier in the early seventies), I stopped to see my mother. I came to her isolated cabin (steep snow-resistant roof, red shutters) on Snake Mountain Road in Leyden, which is exactly one hundred miles, to the last click of the odometer, from my apartment on West 105th Street.

As I drove toward her house, the spring sky was streaked with sunset colors—light charcoal clouds strewn like rubble in a field of flame red—

but around her house the night had already settled in. I smelted the flowering trees—the crab apples, the peach—but I couldn't see them.

There wasn't another house within a mile of Mother's. The sound of my car's engine brought her onto the porch, and as my headlights turned this way and that on her winding driveway, illuminating here a flowering mountain laurel, and there a copper-eyed cat perched on a capped well, Esther shielded her eyes against the glare of my brights. She wore a long flowered dress, a crocheted shawl, Chinese slippers. Her long dark hair was well past her shoulders and showed a fair amount of gray.

I parked next to her maroon van and stretched the monotonous thruway miles out of my aching back—these bottom-of-the-line rental cars are murder on the spine. As glad as she was to see me, Esther stayed on the porch, waiting for me to approach her. The most beautiful girl in Greenwich Village doesn't run toward anyone, not even her own son. She waited for me, the golden light of the windows behind her, giant moths orbiting frantically around her yellow porch light.

"Billy," she said, holding her hands out to me.

We embraced, kissed, embraced again. She smelled faintly of camphor; she was forever storing and unpacking her clothes. She had of late become careful about material things, even a little compulsive. She wanted to extend the life of every possession. Her house was paid for, but she worried about the property taxes. That sort of thing. Her share of the royalties from the songs she wrote with Luke couldn't keep up with inflation. To stretch her funds, Mother had gotten into the stock market and was, in fact, weirdly successful with her investments, which she chose on wild but somehow useful hunches, bringing in astrology and her own personal assessment of the company's products.

"You look tired," she said, breaking our embrace, stepping back to look at me more closely.

"Can I spend the night? I can't drive another inch."

"Since when do you have to ask?" She narrowed her eyes. "Your color's not good."

"I have to be at school by eight-fifteen. That means getting up by five."

"Fine by me. I'm up before dawn anyhow. I'll go out and get fresh bagels."

It was code, her way of telling me she wasn't drinking.

When there was alcohol in her life, she woke at noon, sometimes slept straight through until dinner, with the curtains drawn, the phone unplugged.

She linked her arm through mine, pulled me indoors.

Her house was neat, but it showed evidence of someone living alone with her own thoughts. There were tidy little piles of things in the corners and on the tables, books to be read, books to be loaned or returned, clothes she planned to repair or restyle. There were flats of geraniums in the windows and a half-completed jigsaw puzzle (nuns, balloons) on the threadbare Persian rug. The fireplace was sweat clean of its long winter of silvery ash and was filled now with dried flowers— pale purple, rust orange, and white. Mother had no TV, nor did she own a radio. Like a one-woman jury in a trial without end, she lived sequestered from the media.

I stood with her in the kitchen while she took our dinner out of the oven—lasagna. I found a couple of clean plates and she served it up.

"So what's going on with you and Joan?" she asked me. "I was hoping you'd have her with you."

Joan Odiack. My girlfriend. A well-packaged bundle of nerves. Raised in Detroit by elderly Slav immigrants, she'd been on her own since running away from their not terribly tender mercies at the age of fifteen. Self-taught and self-justifying, she had chopped fish in canneries, slept in parks, stolen. I'd met her at a bookstore reading by Grace Paley, bit deeply into the hook of her pathologically passionate nature, and had been either with her or waiting for her to come back to me for nearly two years. Now, just past her quarter-century mark, she was finally getting tired of being poor; and the fact that I was Luke's son, which had impressed her far less than most of my girlfriends, had now begun to gall her. Where was the money?

"Get a more luxurious house and she'll visit. Maybe something with an indoor swimming pool. She could do laps while we talked."

"You are with her, aren't you?"

"She moved back in with me. I guess her great romantic adventure fell flat. She expected me to take her back." I shrugged. I thought that was going to sound rather more jaunty than it had.

"You took her back because you missed her."

"She was with someone from Louisiana. A businessman, fat as a pig. And she's brought his little habits home with her. She's got me drinking all this New Orleans coffee and eating Cajun food and listening to Professor Longhair."

"You shouldn't be drinking coffee. And I'm not so sure about that Cajun food, either. Anyhow, you must be glad to have her back."

"If I was well, I probably wouldn't even know her. We went to bed three hours after we met. Things like that never work out."

"You said she loved you. You were sitting in this very room and you said that."

"I was deluded. She wasn't into Luke—I mistook that for love. I don't seem to know the difference."

"She's very beautiful, in that wild way. A runaway horse."

"She sees ghosts and she's in a bad mood at least forty hours a week. She's got a mood that ought to be paying her a salary."

We ate in the kitchen; the night and its tiny flying things ticked against the windows, hungry for the pale orange candlelight. Esther's sink was full of pots and pans, but in the candlelight it wasn't very noticeable. We talked about the job Esther had taken, a two-day-a-week gig reading Thackeray to a rich old woman who lived in a spooky old Leyden estate on a bluff overlooking the Hudson.

"She wants me to read as slowly as possible," my mother said. "She's convinced she'll die when it's over."

"Maybe she'll leave you all her money," I say.

"Yes. I'm sure she will. Like in a fairy tale."

She breathed deeply and exhaled slowly. I had a sudden, frightening sense of her, a body running down, slowly but surely. Time was catching up with her, its bony hands plucking at her skirt as she tried to outdistance it. And there was something else, a more specific heaviness on her spirit: she could not abide my continuing to look for clues about my father. Each time she thought I'd finally come to the end of it, I disappointed her by beginning the search again. I was not and could not be cured of it, and she watched at the bedside of my life as the fever took me again and again.

"Why don't you just say it," I said.

"Say what?"

"Whatever's bothering you. I know what it is anyhow."

"Do you now."

"Yes. I do."

"Then there's no real reason to converse, is there?"

"Just say it, Mom. You don't like it when I rummage through the past, taking to people who knew Dad."

"Dad," she says, shaking her head. "Dad. Daddy Da-da."

"Well, he is my father. Whatever else he may or may not be."

"Do you really think you're going to get the goods on him?" she said, resting her fork a little too carefully against the edge of her plate. She folded her hands, moved her face closer to mine. "And then what? Write a book about it? Do you think you're going to blow him out of the water with a torpedo made of words?"

"Sounds good to me."

"But is that what you want?"

"I don't know. It might be. I won't know until . . . until I know."

I closed my eyes but I felt the room move a little and I quickly opened them again.

"Then what, Billy? Are you trying to settle a score?"

"That can never be done. Not after what he's done to us."

"Us? Speak for yourself, Billy. Please don't delude yourself into thinking you're doing this for me. I don't want it. And all you're going to succeed in doing is racking up a ton of bad karma."

"Spare me. Bad karma. There's too many goddamned Buddhist retreats up here. Where's your anger?"

"Gone. What do I need with it? I have my son, my house, my friends, my plants."

"Your *plants*?"

"Stop it, Billy. I don't appreciate that kind of rough kidding. What I'm trying to tell you is, I feel no anger toward him. Luke and I had a relationship and then we broke up. That's not exactly a capital offense. I should be grateful."

"Grateful."

"Yes. For the time I had with him. The places he goes, in his mind, with his music, the things he understands, the things he feels—a normal person can hang on for just so long."

"You can't believe this. You're just trying too—"

"Even when he was wrong, or mean, or too stoned to make sense, there was always something there. Even when he blew out his voice, or couldn't hold a tune—he's a genius, Billy. A real live genius. And he was mine, for a while. He loved me, deeply. Why shouldn't I be grateful?"

"He wrote songs about you. He invaded your privacy. He wrote songs about your vagina, for Christ's sake."

"We have no idea whose vagina that song was about. And why do you dwell on that one, anyhow? He wrote so many songs. His songs got people out of jail—"

"Yeah, and some of them were murderers, like Sergei Karpanov."

She drew back a little. We did not speak lightly of Sergei; we barely spoke of him at all. Was what Luke did for Sergei worse than what he didn't do for us? Perhaps; perhaps not. But since Esther seemed willing now to forget, or at least minimize, the wrongs Luke committed against her and her son, Sergei seemed to stand in for everything that might be rotted at the core of her old lover.

"Luke made people brave," said Esther, recovered, and even stronger than she was the moment before. "When some of us thought we could change the world, it was partly because of him. He wrote our songs. Genius is its own defense, Billy. I don't need to protect him. But I certainly don't need to take pot shots at him, and neither do you."

"He betrayed you. He left you with a child."

"I loved being your mother. I was fine."

"But what about me?"

"I hate that phrase."

"I know you do. But I wanted a father. Even now, when I see kids, little kids with their father, it makes me ache. I see them holding hands. I see them kissing. Little boys and their fathers in the sunshine, kissing on the lips. Not handshakes, or hugs, or little pecks on the cheek. Lips! The whole world is like one big Father's Day picnic." I tepeed my fingers and tapped the tips together.

"That's new. You wouldn't have had that, anyhow. Look at you. My goodness."

"Exactly. Look at me. I'm stuck. I'm spinning my wheels. I want to know him. I don't even know why anymore. Maybe just to blow past him, and get my life started."

"I meant the way you're holding your fingers—it's just like Luke used to."

"So you've said. Look, Mom, he won't even return my calls. He won't say he's related to me, or that he even knows me."

"Feel sorry for him, then, for what he's missed."

"I can't. And I don't even want to. I want him to tell me he's my father and then I want to tell him to go fuck himself."

"He was the love of my life, Billy. The kind of love that only happens once."

Her eyes misted over. Lately, she had been drifting into sentimentality. Age. She seemed to enjoy it. Poignant memories, a good cry, it all appealed to her. The previous winter, staying at her house, I discovered her sitting in the living room at the window, watching the day break. The red glow of the rising sun moved across the frozen landscape like blood through icy veins. When she heard my footsteps, she turned. And I saw her face streaked with tears. Mom? I said, frightened for a moment. What's wrong? And she shook her head, smiled. It's all so beautiful, is what she said. Our little planet. All alone in space. And what I thought was: Oh my God, she's losing her mind. Yet I envied her the voluptuousness of her feelings. A few months before that she had visited me in New York and when we walked through the Village—MacDougal Street, West Third Street, her old haunts—she was so overcome by feelings that she was breathless, we had to stop a dozen times and finally fled in a taxi. Yet even as we rattled up Sixth Avenue, I thought: There are no streets that mean as much to me as these streets mean to her; I have no memories to match hers. What am I doing with my life? I remember clutching at my heart.

Further Reading

An anthology of this scope and length can only include so many selections. The following then is an annotated guide to additional novels and short stories— some considered classics, others less so—that are influenced by rock music, have rock and/or popular music as their main theme, or are written by musicians. I have also included a brief biography of rock lit anthologies. Like this volume itself, I hope that this annotated list encourages readers to listen to the music and the artists who have inspired much of what appears between these pages.

Literary Rock

Rock music is the music of choice of several notable writers, none more so perhaps than **T. Coraghessan Boyle**. (A rock sensibility also imbues the street-smart writing of his contemporary **Richard Ford**, poets with a rock and roll heart such as **Jim Carroll** as well as **Jonathan Lethem** and others represented in this volume, including **Tom Perrotta** and **Nick Hornby**). Boyle's *Drop City* (Viking, 2003), about hippies who move from a commune in Northern California to Alaska, is laced with music ("the dull hum of rock and roll leaking out the kitchen windows," as Boyle describes it). But Boyle has also used Elvis, or at least an Elvis impersonator, as the subject of one of his short stories (which appears in this volume) while the funky characters that populate Bruce Springsteen's "Spirit in the Night" come to literary life in another great Boyle short story, "Greasy Lake."

As the title indicates, *One Pill Makes You Smaller* (Farrar, Straus & Giroux, 2004) by **Lisa Dierbeck** is inspired by *Alice's Adventures in Wonderland* although one imagines that Grace Slick cannot be too far behind—sort of Lewis Carroll in Haight Ashbury during the height of psychedelia. Indeed, the story takes place in the counterculture seventies and features as its protagonist, an eleven-year-old named Alice Duncan, who looks and acts older than her years, as a punk rock singer and a world—and a supremely surreal world it is—turned morally upside down.

The protagonist of **Jessica Hagedorn's** second novel, *The Gangster of Love* (Houghton Mifflin, 1996), is Raquel (Rocky) Rivera. The story begins in Manila, before moving to San Francisco. It's the seventies and Rocky's hero, Jimi Hendrix, has just died. In San Francisco, she meets a guitarist named Elvis Chang. They form a rock band called Gangster of Love, with Elvis on guitar and Rocky on vocals. Themes of alienation, assimilation, and Asian-American identity permeate the novel. And always in the background is the pervasive sound of rock.

The stories and novels of **Stephen King** are riddled with pop music references, from Bruce Springsteen ("No Surrender," "Glory Days," and "Born in the USA" in *It* alone; "Cadillac Ranch," "Racing in the Street," "Ramrod," and "Wreck on the Highway" in *Christine*) to Blue Oyster Cult ("Don't Fear the Reaper" in *The Stand*) to Creedence Clearwater Revival ("Bad Moon Rising" in *The Shining*), and too many others to cite. In between writing best-sellers, King—along with other literary notables, including at various points, Amy Tan, Dave Barry, Michael Dorris, Roy Blount Jr., Greil Marcus, Matt Groening, Barbara Kingsolver, and Dave Marsh—plays rhythm guitar and vocals with the Rock Bottom Remainders.

In *The Fortress of Solitude* (Doubleday, 2003), **Jonathan Lethem** creates two sharply etched characters with first names that recall musical American icons: one black, Mingus, and one white, Dylan. It's about many things—loyalty and betrayal, racial politics and gentrification—as it follows the motherless boys through seventies Brooklyn. The soundtrack to the novel is the music of the era, not only punk rock but also soul and rap.

The hero of **Thomas McGuane's** *Panama* (Farrar, Straus & Giroux, 1978) is a washed-up rock star trying to recuperate in Key West, but the music is not particularly important to the story itself.

The larger-than-life persona of Bruce Springsteen and the release of his blockbuster *Born in the U.S.A.* during the summer of 1984 features prominently in **Bobbie Ann Mason's** tender *In Country* (Harper Collins, 1985), about the tenuous relationship between a Vietnam War veteran and his young female cousin.

Rock music also features prominently in **Rick Moody**'s novels and short stories. *Garden State* (Pushcart Press, 1992), a bleak novel about poverty, sex, nihilism, drugs, and suicide in New Jersey, involves the members of a dissolute rock band, while *The Ring of Brightest Angels Around Heaven: A Novella and Stories* (Little, Brown & Company, 1995) includes "The James Dean Garage Band," a wonderful story that imagines what life would have been like if James Dean survived his famous car crash and joined a rock band. In Moody's somber world, people are often adrift, lost with no moorings. Moments of fleeting humor (dark, of course) only occasionally assuage the sad desperation of their plight.

Salman Rushdie's novels are admired for their flights of fancy, their flirtation with magic realism, and their comic allegory. Rushdie possesses one of the most inventive minds of all contemporary novelists as *The Ground Beneath Her Feet* (Henry Holt, 1999) avidly proves. It is a robust mixture of mythology and science fiction, written in Rushdie's distinctively exuberant style. Essentially it is a take on the Orpheus and Eurydice myth but set in the rock world. Rushdie creates a sort of alternative universe, where things are not quite as they seem: where, for example, Jesse Aron Parker wrote "Heartbreak Hotel" and Carly Simon and Guinevere Garfunkel sang "Bridge Over Troubled Water" and where the ground may collapse at any moment (the novel begins with the lead character perishing in an earthquake, a setting that Rushdie returns to later). Also here are Bono, Lou Reed, David Bowie, and Brian Eno, or at least variations of them. *The Ground Beneath Her Feet* tells the story of the fateful love between Ormus Cana, a Bombay-born musician and songwriter, and Vina Apsara, the daughter of a Greek-American woman and an Indian father, who discover rock and roll and form a group that becomes the most popular rock band in the world. The music they create is music that crosses "all frontiers, belonging everywhere and nowhere, and its rhythm is the rhythm of life." Their music and their story have become, in other words, immortal.

But wait. Rock is supposed to be all about the pleasure principle, right? So why not rock lit? *Tom, Dick, and Debbie Harry* (Thomas Dunne Books, 2002) by **Jessica Adams** is a fun read about relationships, the meaning of life, and a Debbie Harry–tribute band.

The premise behind *The Carpet Frogs: Music after Tomorrow* (Booklocker, 2000) by **Alan Arlt** is a chilling one. Protagonist Symon Smith dreams of making a great rock album, but when his dreams come true, his nightmares pretty much begin. This small book with a big cult following also pays musical homage (of sorts) to the Beatles.

Another cult classic, *Fuel-Injected Dreams* (Thunder's Mouth Press, 2003) by **James Robert Baker**, was inspired by legendary rock producer Phil Spector and involves all manner of musical and sexual intrigue. Long out of print, it has recently been reissued in paperback.

Absolute Beginners (Allison & Busby, 1959) by **Colin MacInnes** is set in late fifties London when the early stirrings of the worldwide youth culture just were being felt and the Mod lifestyle—a bohemian mindset where rebellion and pleasure were irrevocably linked—made its irrepressible first stand.

Truth and fiction come together as music historian and Beatles biographer **Philip Norman** sets *Everyone's Gone to the Moon* (Random House, 1995) in swinging sixties London as we follow the entertaining adventures of a talented young reporter covering some of the most important moments in rock history: the recording sessions of *Sgt. Pepper's Lonely Hearts Club Band*, the Rolling Stones' notorious drug bust, and Brian Epstein's suicide. An often funny send-up of tabloid journalism, Mod-style.

On the other hand, *The Rotters' Club* (Knopf, 2002) by **Jonathan Coe** is a trenchant coming-of-age story set in the blighted industrial heartland of England during the seventies. The birth of punk rock (and the bands' often Tolkien-inspired names) and various social issues such as labor struggles, racism, class warfare, and IRA terrorism all form a major part of Coe's politically-charged, tragicomedic tale.

Bill Fitzhugh writes darkly comic novels laced with acid-tongued social commentary. *Radio Activity* (Morrow, 2004) manages to lampoon the FM rock radio format and the mystery novel genre at the same time while working as many song titles into the text as humanly possible.

Liner Notes (Downtown Press, 2003) by NPR *Car Talk* contributor **Emily Franklin** is part road-trip novel, part mother-and-daughter confessional that is punctuated throughout by a mix tape selection of chart toppers, cult hits, and novelty songs from the seventies and eighties.

The Last Rock Star Book or: Liz Phair, a Rant (Verse Chorus Press, 1998) by **Camden Joy** is a fictionalized autobiographical take on celebrity and obsession written by a morally bankrupt slacker, also named Camden Joy, who is hired by a publisher to write an instant biography of Chicago feminist rocker Liz Phair.

Unplugged: A Novel (Daniel & Daniel, 2002) by writer **Paul McComus**, who also is the founder of Rock Against Depression, tells the story of a bisexual rock musician tormented by depression, who, at the height of her career, shucks it all in for the quietness of the Badlands of South Dakota. Of course, this sudden escape from the tumultuous rock scene only fuels record sales.

Popular Music from Vittula (Seven Stories Press, 2004) by **Mikael Niemi** is a gloriously eccentric coming-of-age novel set in northern Sweden in the early and mid sixties as our hero, Matti, discovers rock (the Beatles), alcohol, girls, and even—what else?—a rock band.

Although the music is hardly rock—the lead character of **Andrew O'Hagan**'s poignant *Personality* (Harcourt, 2003), thirteen-year-old Maria Tambini, daughter of Italian immigrants who have emigrated to the Isle of Bute in Scotland, is said to have a voice like Barbra Streisand and the character herself is loosely based on the life of seventies Scots sensation Lena Zavaroni—the themes are quite in keeping with the rock and roll lifestyle: the dark side of fame, obsessive fans, self-destructive behavior.

Like **Kevin Major**'s similarly thoughtful *Dear Bruce Springsteen* (Dell Publishing, 1988), which looks at how teens look up to rock stars as role models, *Tribute to Another Dead Rock Star* (Sunburst, 2003) by **Randy Powell** offers an introspective portrait of teenage life and the role music plays in it. Here, the narrator is fifteen-year-old Grady Grennan, the son of Debbie Grennan, a world-famous and larger-than-life Janis Joplinesque rock star who died of a drug overdose.

Powder (Jonathan Cape, 2000) by ex–rock manager **Kevin Sampson** chronicles the rise and fall of a Liverpudlian alternative-rock band and the often sordid and sad machinations behind the glamour.

Say Goodbye: The Laurie Moss Story (St. Martin's Griffin, 1999) by **Lewis Shiner** is a powerful novel—dare I say a fine piece of literature?—that chronicles the turbulent life of a Joplinesque rocker, from her small-town Texas roots to her first recording contract, to her final tour. An unsentimental view, it's full of real people and real emotions set in the cutthroat world of the music industry and rock journalism.

In *Sound on Sound* (Dalkey Archive Press, 1995), ostensibly about a struggling rock band playing a gig on the night of Ronald Reagan's first inauguration, first-time author **Christopher Sorrentino** uses the multitrack device to view the story from various angles and, in turn, to comment on eighties America and its obsession with pop culture and flirtation with violence.

And then there's **Neal Pollack**. Cruel. Devastatingly funny. Unfailingly merciless. But what do you expect from the author of *The Neal Pollack Anthology of American Literature* (McSweeney's Books, 2000), and one of America's shrewdest satirists? In *Never Mind the Pollacks: A Rock and Roll Novel* (HarperCollins, 2003), Pollack serves rock—and the journalists who place rock stars on pedestals—on a skewer. Pollack takes no prisoners. No one, absolutely no one, is spared. If you can't take a joke…well, you know the rest.

Rockers turned Writers

Not satisfied with being mere lyricists, a few of the more literary rockers have turned to fiction—with mixed results.

Where Is Joe Merchant? A Novel (Harcourt, 1992), **Jimmy Buffett**'s debut novel, is, in keeping with the singer's own laid-back style, an easygoing tale about the search for a missing rock star. Buffett is also the author of the best-selling *Tales from Margaritaville*, a collection of short stories, published in the early nineties, that is full of typically offbeat characters and situations: dreamers, wanderers, and assorted lost souls.

Whereas the debut novel by the Australian rocker and lead singer of the Bad Seeds, **Nick Cave**, *And the Ass Saw the Angel*

(HarperCollins, 1990), is a bizarre, twisted, and oftentimes disturbing tale of religious fanaticism set in the American South.

Sometimes referred to as the Canadian *Catcher in the Rye*, *The Favorite Game* (Vintage, 2003) by Canadian singer-songwriter **Leonard Cohen** follows the youth and early manhood of the only son of an established Jewish family in Montreal. Cohen's second novel, *Beautiful Losers* (Random House, 1987), an experimental novel and cult hit, focuses on both gay relationships and native Canadians. Like his individualistic songwriting, Cohen's fiction is highly lyrical, perhaps a tad self-conscious, with frequent use of allusion and metaphor.

Steve Earle is well known in music circles as an outspoken, highly opinionated writer of well-crafted songs. Indeed, he is one of only a handful of songwriters on the contemporary scene—others include Bruce Springsteen and John Mellencamp—who compose socially conscious lyrics: he is a ferocious opponent of the death penalty, for example, and has written about it, most prominently, in "Over Yonder" (Jonathan's Song) on *Transcendental Blues* (Artemis Records, 2000), in a play, *Karla*, his meditation on the life and death of convicted murderer Karla Faye Tucker, the first woman executed in Texas since the Civil War, and "The Witness" in his short story collection *Doghouse Roses* (Houghton Mifflin, 2001). Taking a page from his own songbook, *Doghouse Roses* contains tales of various outcasts, drifters, drug addicts, and struggling musicians and songwriters. One of the best pieces is "Billy the Kid," a tough-talking yarn about lost innocence as well as a biting commentary on the music industry in Nashville.

In fiction such as *Blast from the Past* (Ballantine, 1999), **Kinky Friedman**, the wacky country-western singer and self-proclaimed Jewish cowboy turned equally wacky author, has written a series of quirky novels about a former New York City musician turned amateur sleuth. Friedman also takes on Elvis impersonators in *Elvis, Jesus & Coca-Cola* (Bantam, 1996).

A dated and politically incorrect novel, but still with flashes of insight, is **Richard Fariña's** *Been Down So Long It Looks like Up to Me* (Random House, 1966), a druggy coming-of-age tale set at Cornell University on the edge of the sixties. The anti-hero of the story is a notorious womanizer with the unlikely name of Gnossos Pappadopoulis. The book was published two days after Fariña died in a motorcycle crash in 1966. *Long Time Coming and a Long Time Gone* (Random House, 1968), a collection of his unpublished short stories, essays, and poetry, was posthumously released two years after his death. Fariña, who along with wife Mimi Baez (Joan's sister), formed a folk music duo, is probably best known for the infectious folk-rock standard "Pack Up Your Sorrows."

In his debut novel, *Go Now* (Scribner, 1996), **Richard Hell** tells the story of a punk rocker drug addict named Billy Mudd, who is commissioned along with his French photographer girlfriend to drive across country in an ill-fated search for America. Hell can write but in the appropriately named Mudd he has created a vile, despicable, and thoroughly unlikable character.

Ex-rocker **Greg Kihn** has written several books—mostly fun pulp fiction-type books with roots either in the rock or movie industry, such as *Big Rock Beat* (Forge, 1998).

Liverpool Fantasy (Thunder's Mouth Press, 2003), an uneven debut novel by Black 47 leader **Larry Kirwan**, offers an alternative look at musical history: What if the Beatles had broken up and then came back together some twenty-five years later?

John Lennon penned two thin but highly acclaimed volumes: *A Spaniard in the Works* (1965) and *In His Own Write* (1967), both inventively silly and gloriously irreverent books admired as much for their punster humor as their dark underpinnings. In *Blackbird Singing: Poems and Lyrics, 1965–1999* (Norton, 2001) bandmate **Paul McCartney** assembles his finest poems and lyrics from both the Beatles and post-Beatles era.

We will never know how **Jim Morrison**'s literary career would have played out had he had not succumbed to an early death in 1971. The man had talent, and as his writing makes abundantly clear, Morrison was attracted to the dark side—drugs, anonymous sex, the cult of celebrity, death, and what not—and yet there was, under the rock and roll bravado, an underlying sadness and muted vulnerability. In addition to his songs with the Doors, he left behind poems, diary entries, drawings, and photographs in such books as *The Lords, and the New Creatures: Poems* (Fireside Books, 1970), *Wilderness: The Lost Writings of Jim Morrison* (Random House, 1988), and *American Night: The Writings of Jim Morrison, Volume II* (Vintage 1991).

As the prickly lead singer of the Rumour (*Squeezing Out Sparks* is one of the great albums of the rock era), alternative rocker **Graham Parker** has always played by his own rules—perhaps that's why commercial success has proved so elusive. He has written two novels, *The Great Trouser Mystery* (Stiff Records Books, 1980) and *The Other Life of Brian* (Thunder's Mouth Press, 2003), the latter about the adventures of a rock band, the Soulbilly Shakers, while on tour of the world's nether regions. He has also penned *Carp Fishing on Valium and Other Tales of the Stranger Road Traveled: Stories* (St. Martin's Press, 2000), a collection of often absurd short stories, including the hilarious "Me and the Stones."

Literature and music find other ways of sharing common ground. The godfather of punk, **Lou Reed**, has found a kindred spirit in Edgar Allan Poe. In his CD *The Raven* (Warner Brothers, 2003), Reed mixes Poe's darkly evocative poems and stories with his own words. The text of the CD was released in book form by Grove Press in 2004.

Like fellow rockers Davies and Parker, much of **Pete Townshend**'s *Horse's Neck* (Houghton Mifflin, 1985), a collection that contains both poetry and prose, is autobiographical in content. "Each story," he writes in the preface, "deals with one aspect of my struggle to discover what beauty really is."

As we go to press, **Elvis Costello** is penning a collection of short stories for Simon & Schuster, said to be inspired by his own songs. In 2004, **Billy Corgan**, founder of the Smashing Pumpkins, released *Blinking with Fists* (Faber and Faber), his debut poetry collection and was, at press time, working on his first novel while singer-songwriter **Marshall Chapman** uses twelve of her own songs as a way to tell stories from her life in *Goodbye, Little Rock and Roller* (Griffin, 2004).

Elvis

More than any figure in rock history, Elvis Presley has appeared as a character in numerous novels and short stories. Ethnomusicologist and music historian **Samuel Barclay Charters**, best known for his writing on blues and jazz, offers a sweetly naive Elvis in *Elvis Presley Calls His Mother After the Ed Sullivan Show* (Coffee House Press, 1992).

Elvis mysteries are a genre unto themselves. In the political satire, *Elvis in Aspic* (Blue Heron, 1999) by **Gordon Demarco**, a tabloid reporter follows a lead that the CIA murdered Elvis. While in *Blue Suede Clues: A Murder Mystery Featuring Elvis Presley* (St. Martin's, 2002) by **Daniel M. Klein**, Elvis turns sleuth in this follow-up to Klein's *Kill Me Tender* (Minotaur Books, 2000). Klein also wrote another Elvis murder mystery, *Viva Las Vengeance* (St. Martin's Minotaur, 2003).

In *That's All Right, Mama: A Novel* (Baskerville Publishers, 1995) by **Gerald Duff**, Elvis' dead twin, Jesse, lives on. He fills in for the King when necessary, and when Elvis himself dies, Jesse becomes, irony of all ironies, an Elvis impersonator.

Graced Land (Blue Heron Publishing, 1992) by **Laura Kalpakian**, about a welfare mother named Joyce Jackson who has transformed her modest home into a shrine dedicated to the memory of the King, is a moving character study of an inveterate outsider who refuses to succumb to societal norms.

Biggest Elvis (Viking Press, 1999) by **P. F. Kluge** is set at a U.S. naval base in the Philippines in the early nineties. Three Elvis impersonators work in Olongapo, the nearest town to the base: One portrays a young and fit Elvis, the other the cynical movie star Elvis, and the third the bloated Elvis of later years and, in turn, functions as a acerbic commentary on American imperialism and power. As it turns out, the locals come to favor the "biggest" Elvis as their personal favorite.

Inspired by the real-life meeting between Elvis and President Richard Nixon on December 21, 1970, **Jonathan Lowy,** in *Elvis and Nixon: A Novel* (Crown, 2001), brings together the excesses of both the Nixon White House and Presley himself in this rather bizarre but undeniably entertaining debut novel.

Network and *Simone* meet the King in *Elvis Live at Five: A Novel* (Thomas Dunne Books, 2002) by **John Paxson** when a Texas television station tries to boost ratings by using a computer-generated Elvis to host a late-night talk show.

Elvis as God. Sci-fi and a darkly, strangely unappealing Elvis figure come together in *Elvissey* (Grove Press, 1997) by **Jack Womack**, a novel that combines elements of the fiction of Anthony Burgess and William Gibson as a couple from the future (2054 to be exact) return to mid-fifties America to retrieve Elvis Presley as a savior for the human race.

Countless nonfiction books have looked at Elvis, the most iconic figure in American popular culture, and the Elvis phenomenon with a critical eye. Among the most notable, see *Elvis Culture: Fans, Faith, and Image* (University Press of Kansas, 1999), an insightful cultural analysis by scholar **Erika Doss** and *Dead Elvis: A Chronicle of a Cultural Obsession* (Doubleday & Company, 1991) by **Greil Marcus**, in which the noted critic muses on all things Elvis.

Dylan

Bob Dylan arguably is the most literary of rock artists (although Springsteen is not too far behind), the one who more than anyone was expected to write the Great American Rock Novel. So far, that hasn't happened. What he did write, however, was the thoroughly enigmatic *Tarantula* (Macmillan, 1966), an episodic collection of short prose-poetry, which of sort of a Dylanesque take on Joyce's *Finnegans Wake*. In October 2004, Simon & Schuster published the first volume of Dylan's memoirs, *Chronicles*, in which the singer himself writes about his early days in Greenwich Village and his retreat from the celebrity culture that threatened to consume him.

In **Ann Beattie**'s *Chilly Scenes of Winter* (Bantam, 1976), the chatty, introspective characters are waiting for the imminent release of a new Dylan album, in this case *Blood on the Tracks*. It is not so much about music as infused with music, and Dylan's enigmatic persona permeates the characters' lives.

Hard-Boiled Wonderland and The End of the World (Kodansha, 1991) by **Haruki Murakami** (translated by Alfred Birnbaum) is set in Tokyo in a bizarre future of parallel worlds, coded messages, and the search for self. Throughout his work, and this book is no exception, Murakami includes many references to American pop-culture, especially rock music. Among the pop-culture icons mentioned are Lauren Bacall in *Key Largo*, the records of Charlie Parker, the opening riff of Peter and Gordon's "I Go to Pieces," and Bob Dylan, whose voice is described as "like a kid standing at the window watching the rain."

Dylan, of course, has been the subject of countless interpretations. Among the best is the mammoth *Dylan's Visions of Sin* (New York: Ecco/HarperCollins, 2004) by **Christopher Ricks**, a professor of humanities at Boston University. Ricks focuses on the seven deadly sins (pride, anger, lust, envy, sloth, greed, covetousness), the four virtues (justice, temperance, fortitude, prudence), and three graces (faith, hope, love) and how they are expressed in Dylan's songs.

Anthologies

The following rock lit anthologies feature fiction and poetry.

All Shook Up: Collected Poems about Elvis, edited by Will Clemens (University of Arkansas Press, 2001). Features the poems of Charles Bukowski, Joyce Carol Oates, and Thom Gunn.

Carved in Rock: Short Stories by Musicians edited by Greg Kihn (Thunder's Mouth Press, 2003). Features Pete Townshend, Robyn Hitchcock, Ray Manzarek, Pamela Des Barres, Exene Cervenka, David Byrne, Tom Verlaine, and other musical luminaries.

Elvis Rising: Stories on the King, edited by Kay Sloan and Constance Pierce (Avon, 1993).

The Hunger Bone: Rock & Roll Stories, edited by Debra Marquart (New Rivers Press, 2001). Hardscrabble tales about rock musicians on the road.

It's Only Rock and Roll: An Anthology of Rock and Roll Short Stories, edited by Janice Eidus and John Kastan (David R. Godine, 1998).

The King Is Dead: Tales of Elvis Postmortem, edited by Paul Sammon (Delta, 1994). A collection of thirty two fiction and nonfiction selections. The fiction pieces include Joe R. Lansdale's "Bubba Ho-tep" and Nancy Holder's "Love Me Tenderized or You Ain't Nothin' but a Hot Dog."

Lit Riffs: Writers "Cover" Songs They Love, edited by Matthew Miele (Pocket Books, 2004). Among the highlights include "Dirty Mouth" by Tom Perrotta, inspired by "I Won't Back Down" by Tom Petty; "Why Go" by Lisa Tucker, inspired by "Why Go" by Pearl Jam; "She Once Had Me" by Anthony DeCurtis, inspired by "Norwegian Wood (This Bird Has Flown)" by the Beatles; "Bouncing" by Jennifer Belle, inspired by "Graceland" by Paul Simon; and "The Bodies of Boys" by Julianna Baggott, inspired by "Spirit in the Night" by Bruce Springsteen. Other writers include Jonathan Lethem, Neal Pollack, Heidi Julavits, and Nelson George.

Mondo Elvis: A Collection of Stories and Poems about Elvis, edited by Lucinda Ebersole and Richard Peabody (St. Martin's Press, 1994). Includes the work of Alice Walker, Greil Marcus, Nick Cave, Mark Childress, Diane Wakoski, and Pagan Kennedy.

Sweet Nothings: An Anthology of Rock and Roll in American Poetry, edited by Jim Elledge (Indiana University Press, 1994).

—JSS

Rock on Film

The following list is by no means complete, but it does provide a brief sampling of how rock has been represented in the cinema.

Absolute Beginners **(1986)**
Directed by Julien Temple
Patsy Kensit, Eddie O'Connell, David Bowie, James Fox, Ray Davies

Almost Famous **(2000)**
Directed by Cameron Crowe
Kate Hudson, Patrick Fugit, Francis McDormand, Billy Crudup, Phillip Seymour Hoffman (as legendary rock critic Lester Bangs)

American Graffiti **(1973)**
Directed by George Lucas
Ron Howard, Richard Dreyfuss, Cindy Williams, Charles Martin Smith, Candy Clark, Paul LeMat, Harrison Ford, Mackenzie Phillips, Wolfman Jack

American Hot Wax **(1978)**
Directed by Floyd Mutrux
Tim McIntire, Alan Freed, Fran Drescher, Jay Leno, Laraine Newman

The Beach Boys: An American Band **(1985)**
Directed by Malcolm Leo
Brian Wilson, Dennis Wilson, Carl Wilson, Mike Love, Al Jardine, Bruce Johnston

Blackboard Jungle **(1955)**
Directed by Richard Brooks
Glenn Ford, Anne Francis, Sidney Poitier, Vic Morrow, Paul Mazursky

Bubba Ho-tep (2002)
Directed by Don Coscarelli (based on cult writer Joe R. Lansdale's short story)
Bruce Campbell, Ossie Davis

The Buddy Holly Story (1978)
Directed by Steve Rash
Gary Busey, Don Stroud, Charles Martin Smith

The Commitments (1991)
Directed by Alan Parker
Robert Arkins, Michael Aherne, Angeline Ball, Maria Doyle Kennedy, Andrew Strong, Colm Meaney

Dazed and Confused (1993)
Directed by Richard Linklater
Jason London, Matthew McConaughey, Ben Affleck

The Decline of Western Civilization (1981)
Directed by Penelope Spheeris
Exene Cervenka, John Doe

The Decline of Western Civilization Part II: The Metal Years (1988)
Directed by Penelope Spheeris
Steven Tyler, Joe Perry, Alice Cooper, Gene Simmons, Paul Stanley, Ozzy Osbourne

Don't Look Back (1967)
Directed by D. A. Pennebaker
Bob Dylan, Albert Grossman, Joan Baez, Alan Price, Donovan

The Doors (1991)
Directed by Oliver Stone
Val Kilmer, Kathleen Quinlan, Michael Madsen, Billy Idol, Kyle MacLachlan, Meg Ryan

Easy Rider (1969)
Directed by Dennis Hopper
Peter Fonda, Dennis Hopper, Jack Nicholson

Eddie and the Cruisers (1983)
Directed by Martin Davidson
Tom Berenger, Michael Paré, Ellen Barkin

8 Mile (2002)
Directed by Curtis Hanson
Eminem, Kim Basinger, Mekhi Phifer

End of the Century: The Story of the Ramones (2004)
Directed and produced by Michael Gramaglia and Jim Fields
Joey Ramone, Johnny Ramone, Dee Dee Ramone, Joe Strummer, Eddie Vedder

Gimme Shelter (1970)
Directed by Albert and David Maysles
Mick Jagger, Keith Richards, Mick Taylor, Charlie Watts, Bill Wyman, Jerry Garcia, Grace Slick, Ike and Tina Turner

The Girl Can't Help It (1956)
Directed by Frank Tashlin
Edmund O'Brien, Jayne Mansfield, The Platters, Little Richard, Gene Vincent, Fats Domino

Give My Regards to Broad Street (1984)
Directed by Peter Webb
Paul McCartney, Bryan Brown, Ringo Starr, Linda McCartney, Tracey Ullman

Godspell (1973)
Directed by David Greene
Victor Garber, Katie Hanley, David Haskell

Grease **(1978)**
Directed by Randal Kleiser
John Travolta, Olivia Newton-John, Stockard Channing

Great Balls of Fire! **(1989)**
Directed by Jim McBride
Dennis Quaid, Winona Ryder, Alec Baldwin

Chuck Berry *Hail! Hail! Rock 'n' Roll* **(1987)**
Directed by Taylor Hackford
Chuck Berry, Eric Clapton, Robert Cray, Don Everly, Phil Everly,
Etta James, John Lennon, Jerry Lee Lewis, Roy Orbison, Little
Richard, Keith Richards, Linda Ronstadt

Hairspray **(1988)**
Directed by John Waters
Sonny Bono, Divine, Deborah Harry, Ric Ocasek

A Hard Day's Night **(1964)**
Directed by Richard Lester
John Lennon, Paul McCartney, George Harrison, Ringo Starr

The Harder They Come **(1973)**
Directed by Perry Henzell
Jimmy Cliff

Hedwig and the Angry Inch **(2001)**
Directed by John Cameron Mitchell
John Cameron Mitchell, Michael Pitt

Help! **(1965)**
Directed by Richard Lester
John Lennon, Paul McCartney, George Harrison, Ringo Starr

High Fidelity (2000)
Directed by Stephen Frears
John Cusack, Jack Black, Catherine Zeta-Jones, Tim Robbins

I Wanna Hold Your Hand (1978)
Directed by Robert Zemeckis
Nancy Allen, Bobby Di Cicco

Jailhouse Rock (1957)
Directed by Richard Thorpe
Elvis Presley, Judy Tyler

Jesus Christ Superstar (1973)
Directed by Norman Jewison
Ted Neeley, Carl Anderson, Yvonne Elliman

La Bamba (1987)
Directed by Luis Valdez
Lou Diamond Phillips, Esai Morales, Elizabeth Peña, Joe
Pantoliano, Marshall Crenshaw, Brian Setzer

The Last Waltz (1978)
Directed by Martin Scorsese
The Band, Van Morrison, Eric Clapton, Neil Diamond, Emmylou
Harris, Joni Mitchell, Neil Young

Let's Spend the Night Together (1982)
Directed by Hal Ashby
Mick Jagger, Keith Richards, Charlie Watts, Bill Wyman, Ron
Wood, Ian Stewart, Ian McLagan

Light of Day (1987)
Directed by Paul Schrader
Michael J. Fox, Joan Jett, Gena Rowlands

Mad Dogs & Englishmen **(1971)**
Directed by Robert Abel and Pierre Adidge
Joe Cocker, Rita Coolidge, Leon Russell

Madonna: Truth or Dare **(1991)**
Directed by Alek Keshishian
Madonna, Warren Beatty, Sandra Bernhard

Metallica: Some Kind of Monster **(2004)**
Directed by Bruce Sinofsky and Joe Berlinger
James Hetfield, Lars Ulrich, Kirk Hammett, Robert Trujillo

Monterey Pop **(1968)**
Directed by D. A. Pennebaker
Scott McKenzie, John Phillips, "Mama" Cass Eliot, Michelle
Phillips, Paul Simon, Art Garfunkel, Grace Slick

One Trick Pony **(1980)**
Directed by Robert M. Young
Paul Simon, Blair Brown, Lou Reed

Performance **(1970)**
Directed by Donald Cammell and Nicholas Roeg
Mick Jagger, James Fox

Prey for Rock & Roll **(2003)**
Directed by Alex Steyermark
Gina Gershon, Drea de Matteo

Purple Rain **(1984)**
Directed by Albert Magnoli
Prince, Morris Day

Rock Around the Clock **(1956)**
Directed by Fred F. Sears
Bill Haley, Alan Freed

Rock and Roll High School (1979)
Directed by Allan Arkush
P. J. Soles, Vincent Van Patten, Clint Howard, the Ramones

The Rocky Horror Picture Show (1975)
Directed by Jim Sharman
Tim Curry, Susan Sarandon

The Rose (1979)
Directed by Mark Rydell
Bette Midler, Alan Bates

Saturday Night Fever (1977)
Directed by John Badham
John Travolta

The School of Rock (2003)
Directed by Richard Linklater
Jack Black, Mike White, Joan Cusack

Sid and Nancy (1986)
Directed by Alex Cox
Gary Oldman, Chloe Webb, Courtney Love

Sign 'o' the Times (1987)
Directed by Prince
Prince, Sheena Easton

The T. A. M. I. Show (1964)
Directed by Steve Binder
Florence Ballard, Beach Boys, Chuck Berry, James Brown, Marvin Gaye, Mick Jagger, Diana Ross, Phil Spector

That'll Be the Day (1973)
Directed by Claude Whatham
David Essex, Ringo Starr, Keith Moon

This Is Spinal Tap (1984)
Directed by Rob Reiner
Rob Reiner, Michael McKean, Christopher Guest, Harry Shearer

Tommy (1975)
Directed by Ken Russell
Oliver Reed, Ann-Margret, Roger Daltrey, Elton John, Eric
Clapton, John Entwistle, Keith Moon, Jack Nicholson, Pete
Townshend, Tina Turner

U2: Rattle and Hum (1988)
Directed by Phil Joanou
Bono, The Edge, Adam Clayton, Larry Mullen Jr. , B. B. King

Velvet Goldmine (1998)
Directed by Todd Haynes
Christian Bale, Ewan McGregor, Toni Collette, Eddie Izzard

Woodstock (1970)
Directed by Michael Wadleigh
Richie Havens, Joan Baez, The Who, Joe Cocker, Arlo Guthrie,
Crosby, Stills, & Nash, Sly Stone, Jimi Hendrix

Yellow Submarine (1968)
Directed by George Dunning
John Lennon, Paul McCartney, George Harrison, Ringo Starr

—*JSS*

PERMISSIONS

"Death Cube K," "Character Recognition," from *Idoru* by William Gibson. Copyright © 1996 by William Gibson. Used by permission of G. P. Putnam's Sons, a division of Penguin Group (USA) Inc.

"The Girl Who Sang with the Beatles" by Robert Hemenway. Reprinted by permission of Harold Ober Associates Incorporated. Copyright © 1969 by Robert Hemenway. First published in *The New Yorker*, January 11, 1969.

From *High Fidelity* by Nick Hornby, copyright © 1995 by Nick Hornby. Used by permission of Riverhead Books, an imprint of Penguin Group (USA) Inc.

From "Lily." Reprinted with permission of Simon & Schuster Adult Publishing Group from *The Exes* by Pagan Kennedy. Copyright © 1998 by Pagan Kennedy.

From *Eddie and the Cruisers* by P. F. Kluge. Reprinted by permission of the author.

"Wilkie Fahnstock: *The Boxed Set*" from *Demonology* by Rick Moody. Copyright © 2000 by Rick Moody. By permission of Little, Brown and Company, Inc.

Pages 1, 94–96, 140–42, 309 from *The Dylanist* by Brian Morton. Copyright © 1990 by Brian Morton. Reprinted by permission of HarperCollins Publishers Inc.

From *The Wishbones* by Tom Perrotta, copyright © 1997 by Tom Perrotta. Used by permission of Berkley Publishing Group, a division of Penguin Group (USA) Inc.

"Burn Me Up" by Tom Piazza from *Blues and Trouble*. Used by permission of the author.

Glimpses © 1993 by Lewis Shiner. Reprinted by permission of the author. "Jeff Beck" © 1986 by Davis Publications, Inc. Reprinted by permission of the author.

From *The Rich Man's Table* by Scott Spencer. Copyright © 1998 by Scott Spencer. Used by permission of Alfred A. Knopf, a division of Random House, Inc.